FIVE & TEN

BROADWAY EDITION

FIVE AND TEN

by
FANNIE HURST

P. F. COLLIER & SON COMPANY
Publishers   New York

TO

NEW YORK
CITY OF CITIES

. . . Whited sepulchres, which indeed appear beautiful outward, but are within full of dead men's bones.

MATTHEW, XXIII, 27.

Those who want fewest things are nearest to the gods.

SOCRATES.

FIVE & TEN

IN THE long reaches of what had become chronic insomnia John G. Rarick found himself mentally mouthing to himself phrases such as this: I am a rich man. I am a very rich man. Me, John G., rich!

It was his way of striving to grind into his overtaxed realizations the fact that, as he lay there, wheels of industry, turning by now of their own momentum, were pouring more and more gold into Rarick coffers.

Even in a land where such annals of achievement as textbooks and success magazines were crowded with the names of those who had vaulted from petty beginnings into high places, there was something about the rapid phantasmagoria from obscurity to rapid success that never failed to tax Rarick's credulities.

Now, Jenny Rarick, lying there beside him in the elaborate marquetry bed, the first piece of signed furniture, by the way, which they had acquired, had less imagination to startle with the fecundity of events. She had a capacity to take for granted many of the phenomena of the world in which she lived.

A sunset was something to admire, but not to wonder about.

She had once remarked to a poet of no small repute, that she regretted she had never found time to become a writer.

Yet it was obviously a nervous woman lying there asleep beside Rarick. The face, always too angular for beauty, was constantly ridden across with expressions, as if, while the body slept, the mind kept open shop.

Above the fine coverlet, her shoulders, narrow white ones, with firm breasts that had not sagged from child-bearing, rose and fell to irregular breathing. Here was someone asleep with much on her mind.

With Rarick, the difference lay in his not being able to sleep at all. As a boy, back on his stepaunt's farm, twenty miles out of Keokuk, he had known the torments of insomnia, coming in, time after time, from a long back-splitting day in the fields, to lie sleepless for hours after he had sought his bed.

His room then had been an unfurnished attic with a window set into a slanting roof. Stars had gleamed into his insomnia through that window.

Stars gleamed into his insomnia now. They were gilt, hand-wrought ones, against a ceiling of billow, cherub, and streamer, done after the manner of Tiepolo's Labia Palace painting of "Antony and Cleopatra."

Whimsically Rarick lay on the marquetry bed, rumin-ating on the divergence of causes that had contributed to the years of his insomnia. Everything, from a sick calf; the haunting lilt of "The Ancient Mariner"; a harsh word from his stepaunt's farmer husband; fear of losing his clerkship in a hardware store, to one million dish-pans; Avery's croup; a seven-hundred-and-fifty-thousand-dollar bank-loan; a rare and exclusive obsidian mirror with native textile string which he coveted for his Aztec collection, was fodder to his sleeplessness.

No subject was too casual to tempt his insomnia. He built empires and warehouses by night. He dreamed into flooding darkness of achieving his nine-hundred-and-sixty-first store, of possessing the Gutenberg Bible, of tin tacks, of beholding with his own eyes, in his own conservatories, the opening of a passion-flower. Into that darkness he designed window displays, calculated floor space, inau-gurated Eskimo pie for his soda-fountains, and coveted a tode-stone ring from Clusium, the ancient capital of the Etruscans.

Across his relentless insomnia there stalked contemplations of new sites for new Five and Tens. Insolent sites within shadow of Hellenic marble libraries and along boulevarded frontage; more and more Rarick temples to tin tacks, paper napkins, hooks and eyes, sink-swabbers, and paste jewelry mounted on pasteboard and sold in bins.

His way of sleeping over a matter was to lie sleepless over it. A chain of six hundred and forty-two stores might virtually be said to have crocheted itself out of these hours of enforced contemplations. Problems of population of a given town, types and habits of the people, study of main industries, bank deposits and clearings, number of different industries, proportion of workers to clerks, of women employees to men, prevailing local rental conditions, had been pondered to their minutiæ from the flat of his back.

The problems of Jenny, now, or of his small son Avery, or his daughter Jennifer, were another matter. They made him restless and unable to concentrate. The fact that approximately eight per cent of all candy sales in America are made to men was a reasonable hypothesis on which to work out a system of extensive candy departments in those stores which drew their business from the wholesale districts.

The fact, however, that Jenny's nervous dissatisfactions with the gratifications of today, in order that she might yearn for those of tomorrow, seemed to increase in just such proportion as her creature-cares decreased, was an unreasonable hypothesis upon which to base nothing.

How dissatisfiedly she slept, two perpendicular lines flashing in and out between her eyes. Her strong hooked

nose flashed slightly, too, at the nostrils, and in the pale
light from a transom, the triangular planes of her cheeks,
far too thin, rippled now and then. There was something
of a frail, pale Dante about the sleeping face of Jenny.
A face that walked in a hell.

Prop himself on an elbow, and gaze as he would across
the mound of delicate coverings between them, the pale
splotch of the face of Jenny had a habit of seeming to
recede through the darkness.

What was it she wanted? Strange angular woman
whom he called wife, lying there sharing his bed, what
is there that will ease your hunger, slake your thirst,
gratify your indomitable appetites. Appetites for what?
God knows! Love? Bah! she was as empty as a meal-
sack of it for him, yet she was not the woman to seek
it elsewhere. Up to now, hers had been the easy morality
of the frigid.

Lying there beside him, in a house that already contained a sister portrait to an "El Greco" that hung in
the Prado; a pear-shaped pearl said to have been given
by Jérôme Bonaparte to Queen Hortense; and the largest
private collection of Stücks in the world, what was the
secret of the anguish that rippled beneath her cheeks?

Rarick owned, in his already considerable collection of
precious stones of religious uses, a small steatite cup said
to have been found in a Japanese grave of the Iron Age.
There was a pinhead hole through the bottom of the
precious thing. It seemed to Rarick that Jenny's cup
of happiness must be something like that. The contents
ran out of the wrong end when she tilted it to her thirsty
lips.

And what thirsty lips! She was thirsty now in her
sleep. And, as always, that sense of her desire for what
lay just beyond her present transmitted itself to him.

What did she want? She had her children, as much as one seemed to have one's children nowadays.

What did she want? She had the security that goes with a fifteen-year-old marriage that has borne the fruit of offspring and material success. Indeed, a material success that taxed the credulities. As to the underlying gratifications of the passions, romance, oneness of purpose, sympathy, companionship, love—well, well, what proportion of human beings *can* hope to sustain those?

Rarick had once hoped. But the young clerk who had come to St. Louis from Keokuk and had married, rather considerably above his station, a Miss Jenny Avery, had cast off many a dead skin since then. It seemed to him terribly certain that Jenny had. Where was that somewhat caustic, but intellectual-faced girl of those eager, wooing days, who had sat opposite him in a canoe that cut through the Meramac River with the same lean swiftness of their dreams? Where was that girl, a high-school graduate, from whom he could learn; who had talked to him of life in terms of the grave, simple, beautiful things that had somehow started so consistently to elude them, once they seemed to be in a position to make some of those early yearnings come true?

Where was that eager, narrow, intelligent-faced Jenny? Why, he had almost lost sight of her the first year of their marriage, when there had been so little time for the old talks of those days when the mind of each to the other had seemed an oyster-shell crammed with pearls!

Their marriage had routinized so quickly. Perhaps because of the circumstance that it had been Jenny's total capital of twenty-five hundred dollars which had embarked him on the enterprise of the Nick Nack Store on Olive Street.

After that, her face had immediately taken on some of the pinch and strain from which it was never to re-

cover. Jenny's money had started him. Had that had
something to do with the immediate reversal of what
had been their pre-nuptial relationship of idealization of
life and love? Undoubtedly. Jenny had begun to fear
terribly for her investment. Naturally. The money
represented the careful total of the tiny estate that had
been held in trust for her in the five years between the
death of her parents and her coming of age. And the
first few years after, the investment had been unbeliev-
ably precarious. Rarick never held it against her judgment that she had resisted, with all her vehemence, his
determination to try and reëstablish the almost defunct
business which her money had launched, on the new basis
of the five-and-ten-cent Nick Nack Store.

As a matter of fact, it had been a maneuver of desper-
ation rather than of logic. No more than Jenny had
he even remotely anticipated the enormity of that
move. . . .

And now . . . perhaps he had been the one to change.
The desire for passionate love with the Jenny Avery who
had dreamed with him of walking-trips through the Pyrenees, was by now nothing more than a sense of frustration lying back in the dim reaches of his mind.

That walking-trip through the Pyrenees! She had
been so bright! A high-school girl, educated by rote,
rather than by the desultory reading of such books as
his older sister Hildegarde in Keokuk had sometimes sent
him by mail. Jenny, at his very first mention, had known
at once of the Pyrenees, and their highest peak, the
Maladetta. She had leaned so sympathetically into the
yearnings of his untutored mind and spirit . . . and
now. . . . Something of that same frustration, mutual
to them both, must be what kept her face flickering so in
her sleep.

Well? Then what? How many times, leaning on his

elbow, gazing at her through the pale darkness, had that question of his dropped down into the cistern of a silence from which there was no answer.

Presently the gilt stars, among the foliated stars, the festoons, and the adumbrated cherubs on the ceiling, would begin to fade; and dawn, a pale horse, would ride through the Corinthian archway that inclosed the exclusive residential Westmoreland Place where the Raricks occupied the most pretentious house of all the pretentious row.

It was about this time that John Rarick was due to drop off into brief but resuscitative sleep.

It was about this same time that Jenny, an early waker against her will, was due to open her eyes almost with a click, as it were, and start to a sitting posture at once, as if she had been called. Called she had been, by the pressure of the procession of her thoughts, which were marching so closely beneath the surface of her sleep.

Ficke house! Cretonne covers for the sedan. Box for the San Carlo Opera. Mermord and Jaccard's about the twenty-ninth pearl for Jennifer's necklace. Wednesday Club. Wire Long Island Kennels to ship Russian wolfhound to pose in the portrait Shandig was doing. Pour tea at St. Louis Water-Colorists Exhibit. Toy electric motor-boat for Avery. Meeting advisory board Garrison Avenue Home for Wayward Girls. Bridge-tea St. Louis Club. Garden Swing. Sit for Shandig. Oh yes! Mermord and Jaccard's, too, about the gold bouillon-spoons. They could also be used for grapefruit. Avery must be forced, if necessary, to attend dancing-school. Avery's riding-lesson. Rarick must telegraph bid on the Ficke house.

All this on the instant of awakening. Jenny's mind might have been a memorandum-book, the leaves turning.

. . . Oh yes, and remind Rarick to indicate which plants in the conservatory were to be sent to the Chrysanthemum Show, and then, the Ficke house. FICKE HOUSE.

How he slept! Across the mound of the sheets that sprayed lace and sometimes made him flick as if at a fly, she too had to raise herself on an elbow, in order to find his face, which slept in the position of staring upright through closed eyes.

A little man. In the beginning, his shortness of stature had been merely something to regret and then adjust oneself to, with the immemorial processes of a woman compromising between the Lothario of her dreams and the stocky reality of her husband.

Subsequently, she had come almost to hate him for that shortness. A stunted man. Curious, that to her he had always given the effect of a hunchback. Not so much because his head, on a short neck, was so deeply set into the valley of high shoulders, but because, even in the days when he had wooed and fascinated her, the little hardware clerk from Keokuk, who had first been brought to see Jenny by a poor relation who boarded in the same house with him, had somehow had the face of a hunchback. A bony, up-thrust, hurt face. Short sinews of rear neck, rather than the slightest indication of an actual hunch, kept it thrust upward. Rarick's face was always cocked to a world slightly taller than he. It was already upturned to his fourteen-year-old daughter Jennifer. Fervently Jenny found herself hoping, as her son's slight frame and threat of short stature began to prove worrisome, that some day it would be necessary for Rarick to look up to his son.

All this talk that men of brief stature had ruled the world—poppycock! What about Alexander the Great, Charlemagne, Bismarck, Lincoln? Jenny was not sure about the heroic proportions of most of them. Lincoln, of course, and Alexander, the vast-minded Macedonian, and Charlemagne, must surely have matched up to the heroic proportions of their names. On the other hand, Rarick, Jenny felt certain, had steeped himself in the sugared legend of the magnificence of the small.

His collection of Napoleonana already included a desk from Versailles, an inkstand flanked by onyx horses, and an enameled snuff-box worn down by the Corsican's own thumb. The entire north end of his library, fourteen shelves of it behind copper grating, either pertained or appertained to the small Emperor.

How much of his success, Jenny asked herself, leaning on her elbow and gazing at him who slept there with his hunchback's face washed in dawn, was due to luck or power? Without the incalculable boon of her patrimony of twenty-five hundred dollars which had first set him up in the Nick Nack Store, might he not still be clerking in the Schwebbe hardware establishment from which he had taken a day off for his marriage to her?

How much of this man's success was due to an initial stroke of luck, her patrimony, and her distaste for his petty rôle of selling wire nails over Schwebbe's hardware counter? Little as it seemed to matter, this speculation was one of tireless interest to Jenny.

How much foresight had Rarick ever manifested in his business moves? Precious little. Credited already in the industrial world with vision, acumen, and imagination, was it not rather that every move he had made had been a lucky gesture in the dark? The result of an imminent need to jump this way or that; and Rarick had happened to jump right. How well she could recall the move that had precipitated the change in the policy of the Nick

Nack Store to the five-and-ten-cent idea. It had been nothing more or less than a clutch at a straw to avoid going under. Mingling even with her sense of pride, as she had sat beside him one day at a Chamber of Commerce luncheon and heard him referred to by a speaker as "that far-sighted industrial peer right in our very own midst— John Rarick (applause)," had been her merciless appraisal of him. Without the incalculable boon of her patrimony . . . where would he be?

The chain-store idea, originating long before his time, had never really entered Rarick's head as a scheme of scope, insistent as his biographers were to credit him with a canny and pioneer eye that had anticipated the dawn of mass-production and quantity-buying.

It had all just happened. Of this much she felt powerfully certain. Rarick had not foreseen his magnificent business maneuvers. They were born out of circumstance and stress. She did not want the world to know what she knew, but she wanted Rarick to know that she knew!

Without the initial patrimony that had been scrimped for her by deceased parents, where would Rarick be now? She was so fairly sure that she knew. Clerking at Schwebbe's or possibly following up an old dream of his to acquire a Missouri farm and a sufficient formal education to divide his time between working it and teaching in some rural school.

It had taken courage to hand over that sum to a young clerk with such lofty ideals as this and who was constantly chafing under penny-wise business methods of the old German firm that employed him. And moreover, in the very first year of their marriage, when she was already carrying Jennifer and the fear of childbirth was upon her! He had rowed her on the Meramac those days, on Sundays and holidays, or taken her across the river to Cahokia to see the Indian mounds; and they had talked, not of big business, but of a dream which was to be only

deferred by this rather unanticipated coming of the child
—that walking-trip through the Pyrenees. The trip
through the Pyrenees had come true, twice over, in fact,
in a Hispano-Suiza car; and some of the most important
of the excavations at Cahokia had subsequently been
made at Rarick's expense. But what was the use pretending? A wife, peering into the sleeping face of her
husband as he lay beside her, need play no rôle before
her own soul. . . .

In Jenny's mind, Rarick had not even succeeded in
being educated to greatness. He was like a man who, at
fifty, still spends most of his time reliving his college days.
He had not gone on in spirit. The handsome house that
contained him inclosed him as loosely as a gigantic pod
holds an ordinary-sized pea. He rattled about inside his
setting. And talk about penny-wise! He was still dreaming dreams the stature of that walking-trip through the
Pyrenees and the farm that was to be worked as a side-
line to teaching the young that Hannibal crossed the
Alps.

The pea had not grown with its pod. Jenny had,
mark you that! Breeding will tell. Her maternal fore-
bears had been Piexottos who had settled in St. Louis
as early as Pierre Laclede. You could not come of that
kind of colonizing stock and not know how to meet
success with the same kind of indomitability with which
they had met adversity. Jenny spoke frequently of her
colonizing ancestors. One grew to the demands of circumstance. In other words, Jenny Avery was being educated to greatness. After all, not even the Corsican
upon whom Rarick doted, had remained the Corsican.

What was it that this man, her husband, lay there
wanting, even in his sleep? What were the citadels
behind those closed lids of his, upon which shone some
secret inner sun of his private own? Was he inscrutable
or just inadequate? The smallish young man who had

fascinated her, way back there, with his inchoate desires that had never entered the heads of the sons of the St. Louis business men who had milled about the wealthy-in-her-own-name Miss Avery, had remained a sophomore on the campus of that youth.

One outgrew being a sophomore about life. One ceased desiring what one had achieved ten times over. In many ways, Rarick was like a man whose garages are filled with high-power motor-cars, but who, by the force of fondness for old dreams, continues to tour on his velocipede. The comparison was Jenny's.

He had what he wanted ten times, forty times, over, but in the forty times, had missed the once.

But was it desire behind those closed lids, or just a gnawing frustration? As a matter of fact, their marriage had borne the fruits of love, four times over. Two children between Jennifer and Avery had died in infancy. She had submitted to Rarick's bed with the same unequivocal acceptance of marriage that she expected and received from him.

She had seen the glance of this allegedly great little man, her husband, follow many a time the living, flowing line of a beautiful woman's body, but with much the appraisement with which he was fond of observing, in its glass case, a fine example of a wooden statuette of the Virgin of San Domingo in his North American collection, one of whose breasts was studded with a turquoise-incrusted marine clam-shell.

There was no telling . . .

Little man, you, I think I hate you. He must telegraph bid on the Ficke house. He must! He must! He must! Cretonne covers for sedan. Box for the San Carlo Opera. Mermord and Jaccard's about the twenty-ninth pearl for Jennifer's necklace. Wednesday Club. Sealed bid on the Ficke house. . . .

IF ANYONE had told Rarick on the morning of the day he wired the sealed bid on the Ficke house that before his sun set on another afternoon he would be owner of two million five hundred thousand dollars' worth of mortar-stone lace and Italian Renaissance façade, flanked by two famous Grecian urns which guarded a pair of doors, superb copies of the Campanile doors in Florence, he would have listened to it with that polite third ear of his which enabled him to appear attentive to the discourse of another while thinking of something entirely removed. A quality, by the way, which was to win and sustain him the reputation of being a canny and silent listener.

A maid entered on the seven-thirty chime of a hall clock, drew back curtains and lowered spacious windows that looked out upon the elaborately boulevarded, landscaped, and very private precincts of Westmoreland Place, before he lifted back his eyelids from the deep kind of sleep that invariably capped his insomnia.

From the depths of her pillow, where for an hour her open eyes had lain upturned to the gilt stars, it was as if Jenny had heard the flicker of his lids.

It was characteristic of her that she should resume conversation, upon his awaking, at precisely the point where they had left off the night before.

"Sooner or later, Rarick, the move is inevitable! Wire your bid today!" The phrase beat against his brain as if it had been there all night, and yet with his conscious mind he had forgotten it. That room in which he slept was always beating with repetitious little phrases that were Jenny's. Do this. Do that.

Wire what bid? Of course, that had been her last phrase before dropping off to sleep. Ding. Dong. Here it was again. "Sooner or later the move is inevitable. It is Providence that the Ficke house should be on the market just at this time."

"Not necessarily inevitable, Jenny. The roots of our lives are down here."

"Nonsense! The roots of life are where one chooses they should be. You wouldn't have a Guatemala orchid in your conservatory if that were not partially true."

"Well, then, I choose that our roots should be here."

"You choose. You choose. You choose. As usual, that closes the controversy?"

His eyes, as he lifted them into quizzical peaks, made him look Asiatic in a way she detested. Oh yes, that closes the controversy, he was saying to himself. Oh yes. Oh yes. Rather, it kept it running in great sluices of talk through all-too-brief silences which he craved.

"No, Jenny, but it is scarcely necessary to argue that my greatest interests are here."

"At the moment, yes. But your main office is practically now in the East. You are on trains half your time."

That was true. But the prospect of reiterating, as if it had never been said before, this two-year-old argument between them, made him long to close his eyes and sink back, at least on to the rim of the slumber which had visited him so reluctantly.

"We have outgrown St. Louis, Rarick. Anyone can remain a big frog in a small pond."

"My home is here."

"You have the opportunity to live in one of the most

beautiful homes in America. Do you realize that you are rich enough to buy the home of the man who endowed the Metropolitan Gallery with the Ficke Collection? I have been prophesying for the six months, ever since the death of Emanie Ficke, that the house would come on the market. Don't be all kinds of a fool, Rarick. Wire your bid."

"And what then?"

And what then? She sat up in bed at that, her nightgown, plain but impeccably sheer, falling down off one shoulder, her brick-colored, eccentric hair, which she wore brushed up perpendicularly off her ears as if to accentuate the narrowness of her face, falling in thin spray along her shoulders. A sort of tremor, faint as a blue flame, seemed to burn along the pale wick of her lips, making them flicker.

And then what! The most beautiful house in the world, Rarick, built out of damned little ugly things.

Things. Things. Things and things. It was as if, so that he put his hands over his eyes to squeeze back their pressure, there came marching out of his insomnia the nightly procession of the million dishpans, bins of hair-pins, carloads of coin-purses, glass beads, curtain rods, rubber gloves, cotton stockings, eye-shades, flower-seed, pink soaps, tooth-brushes, darning-cottons, water-tumblers, salted peanuts, baby-dolls, lead-pencils, paper flowers, gimcrack vases, and chewing-gums.

"Things."

"Exactly, Rarick. Titians out of stewpans. Conservatories out of cotton stockings. Pipe-organs out of gas tubing. Libraries out of tooth-paste. Polo ponies out of Eskimo pies. Rarick, where is your imagination!"

She was not the one to cajole with any grace. Her thin face, in a way that was no longer lovely to him, propped on its elbow, was all covered over with an expression that, starting with her lips, had burst like paper into flame. She desired with an intensity that was embarrassing. It grated Rarick horribly to see her wanting anything. It stretched her face so, drawing the tight skin back further still from the bony outline, nakedly, like a person biting down pain.

Wherever his imagination was, it left him lying there with his tired hand pressed against his eyes, and his lips lifted back slightly from his teeth, as her voice grated:

"Do you realize that you're a richer man than Cyrus Breckenridge, Rarick?"

Trust Jenny to have heard, almost before the proposition had been put into writing, this newest offer of the Breckenridge group of Southwestern stores to buy in the Rarick chain. His reply to it had been to add six new links to his own. Youngstown, Altoona, Akron, Fall River, Lowell, and New Bedford. Her entire being was like a hateful little antenna. Sensing. He wanted her not to be hateful to him, and the knowledge that she was, kept him in a state of constant mental retribution toward her. Through the lattice of his fingers he regarded her, his lids half down to blur the eager, tight-skinned thrust of her face.

"I suppose I am a richer man than Breckenridge."

"Hellman figures you out about the thirteenth richest man in the world, Rarick. Know that?"

As a matter of fact, he did. His confidential secretary, Harry Hellman, an exceedingly stout young Jew, with excellent qualifications for his position, had called his attention to that new fact only that week. He had thought about it subsequently and with the sustained sort of incredulity that had caused him to clutch toward reality by repeating to himself such phrases as: I am a rich man.

I am a very rich man. Me, John Rarick, born Fancy
Prairie, Iowa, October 7th, 1870, son of Anna Masey
Rarick and John Geoffrey Rarick. m. Jenny Avery, St.
Louis, 1898. President Rarick Chain, Inc. Vice-presi-
dent Dime Savings Bank. Vice-president Ajoy Soap Com-
pany. Board directors Dime Savings Bank. Board
directors Corn Belt Traction Company. Vice-president
Empire State Trust Company. Vice-president Croton
Mills. Trustee Guaranty Trust Association. Director
St. Louis Art Center; Municipal Opera Company; Amer-
icana Association; Lapidarian Club Society; Hispano
Association; Society for Preservation of Indian Culture;
Missouri Historical Association; Member of . . . Me,
John G. . . . all those . . . me, John!

It was like Jenny to take this dazzling fact, rather in-
discreetly handed her by Hellman, for granted, and without wasting either analysis or wonderment upon it, begin
to cut her cloth accordingly. One became the thirteenth
richest man in the world and then set immediately about
adjusting one's life to the requirements of being the thirteenth richest man in the land. Hers not to reason why.

He was being constantly ashamed of the way she
could grate on him. Coming from Jenny, the selfsame
statement that had caused him a rise of goose-flesh when
Hellman had called his attention to this new notch on
his hickory stick, filled him with a dull resentment.

What new desires and cravings and ambitions for herself, and, worst of all, crazy plots for her children, were
there left to set in motion?

What was it that being the wife of the thirteenth
richest man in the world could give her that she had not
enjoyed as the wife of the thirteenth hundredth richest
man in the world?

It did not seem so long ago to Rarick when their first
car, a Buick sedan, had stood new and shiny one Sunday

morning at the curbstone of their seven-room house on Kensington Avenue, and Jenny, with his overcoat thrown on over her kimono, had rushed out to try its upholstery. There had been a small tag on the steering-wheel:

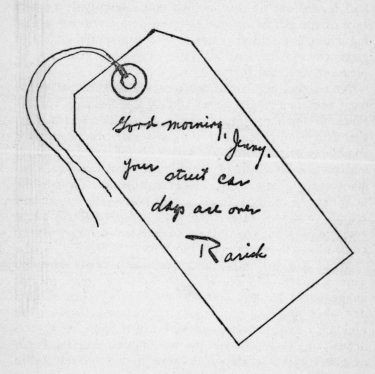

That was about as demonstrative as Rarick could bring himself to be, even back in the days before their fairy tale had begun to happen.

"Good morning, Jenny. Your street car days are over," he had written during the fifth year of their marriage. During the first year he had sent her a modest little traveling-case for a birthday present, but the card had read: "Pack my love and some of our dear dreams in this, for our walking-trip through the Pyrenees."

That had been before the acquisitive, tight-skinned look had spread itself over the face of Jenny: before the fox had leaned out of the nervous and intelligently homely face of the girl he had been proud of himself for choosing from a world that seemed to him populated with girls with no faces at all, only a vacuous geometry of pleasantly related features.

No one but God and Rarick knew that the dowry that went with Jenny had played no part in his choice. Sometimes, as the something flowed out of their relationship that had been precious to him, it seemed there must be some way to tear open the secret chambers of his heart and reveal this truth to Jenny, on to whose lips, not so many years after marriage, had crept occasional innuendo.

What she did not or would not remember was that it actually was well after their engagement that Rarick, a young man from the outside of her circle, had come to know about the twenty-five hundred dollars.

What she did and would remember, as if her mind were a magnifying-glass under which a small mental image could become Gargantuan, was the hot August day when they had taken the street car together for the Union Trust Company, and withdrawn from her safety-deposit box there, the twenty-five hundred dollars' worth of government bonds which were to be converted into capital investment in the Nick Nack Store.

That fact, in these years when Jenny was already buying an eighty-five-hundred-dollar bauble far more casually than she had once bought an eighty-dollar one, never lost its luminosity in the dark places of her mind. It was a piece of phosphorescent memory. A cold, flameless light that tinged every aisle of her mind where he was concerned, and which she kept dancing before the eyes of her husband like a signalman on a bridge at night swinging his lantern.

Behind her reminder to him that he was the thirteenth richest man in the world there trailed the unspoken tagline, "thanks to the start I gave you by intrusting you with my inheritance," a string of words which, spoken or unspoken, traveled through him in a groove that innuendo had worn down, his live nerves the trolley of transmission. Rebuttal would have meant the fatal act of admission to her implied word. Rarick had learned various kinds of silences.

"I haven't minded the years of your stubborn refusal to pretty nearly everything I've asked for myself, Rarick. It is Jennifer now. I want the child to see the light of her fifteenth birthday in the Ficke house. That's not asking much of a man many times a millionaire. The pity is that it has to be coaxed out of you."

"The pity of it" clung in a burr-like phrase to his brain.

The pity of it. The pity somehow of everything, including this flavorless beginning of another day. Pretty Jennifer, who had everything, and now, at barely fifteen, was so cruelly fretted, aided and abetted by a doting mother, with wanting more than everything. After all, if you had two motor-cars, there was only left for you to want three, if the goal of your acquisitiveness was things. And things. And things. It was an entirely different kind of wanting from the desire to own a Buick sedan when you owned no car at all. The difference between desiring a Buick sedan when you owned no car, or desiring a third car when you already owned two, was all the difference in the world. The pity of it. Jennifer at fifteen, who had a good mind, was a good pupil, and was a phantom of delight to her father, already too busy wanting more than everything.

That kind of thinking made him heavy and pedantic and old-as-the-hills, as a father.

The little girl who wanted more than everything.

Damn her mother.

The phrase shot through his mind like a burst of flame, startling him horribly.

Under cover of Jenny's steady runnel of accusative and importuning talk, he began to reason with himself, to calm himself, to rid his mind of the taste of the phrase that had shot through his mind in sacrilege to this woman who shared his bed.

As mothers went, Jenny would have stood impeccable before any jury. She wanted passionately for her young. She was forever baring herself to his scorn by asking in their name. She was a doting, gloating mother, fierce for her offspring, yet, withal, sweet with them and to them. Many a night through she had sat unnecessarily, but tirelessly, beside the bed of Avery, whose first years had been precarious ones. The death of two infants had gone hard with her. Jennifer was her doting, her waking, and her sleeping thought.

Rarick, whose manner was not fortunate with his children because he was seldom at ease with them, could not have formulated into words, except in vague fashion to the effect that she spoiled them, the stubborn wall of opposition which he erected between himself and Jenny's plans and dreams for her children.

"It is as if you were jealous of them," she had barked at him once, hysterically, when he was opposing an indoor roller-skating rink across the top of the house.

No. No. No.

Without his knowing how to reach out a hand to stay them, except in vague fumings and consistent conservatisms, the entire kingdom of his household was drifting like a bit of land disassociating itself from the mainland to become island, out into some high tide beyond his reach. Jenny and Jennifer and his boy Avery were on that island. He was back helplessly on the mainland; and Jenny, mark you, mind you, no otherwise to it, was to blame! The bitterness of that tore at him constantly, like a flame pulling itself off the candle.

Jennifer, for a time, while she had been a little pupil at Mary Institute, had been something of an eager student, with a hint of her mother's old air of desire to know, about her. Rarick had said little, but her school reports had been a source of deep private pleasure to him; and once he had carried about in his pocket an essay of hers, written on ruled paper, called "WHY WE LOVE RUSKIN." He had filched it off her desk and returned it there a few evenings later when he observed the child scrambling among her possessions for what might have been the essay.

Rarick had not, up to that time, known who Ruskin was, and it elated him no little that the enlightenment should have come by way of his daughter. "In mastery of prose language he has never been surpassed," the thirteen-year-old daughter of Rarick, undismayed by discursive eagerness and floriated mannerism, had written in her roundly vertical chirography. It was this phrase out of the mouth of his babe that must have lain engraved upon Rarick's memory when, years later, he acquired, at what was said to be an astonishingly high price, a page of the original manuscript of Ruskin's *Præterita*.

Suddenly that brownish, rather studious Jennifer of those days back in the solid square house on MacPherson Avenue had slipped from her little-girlhood into a high-strung, mature-faced disciple of her mother's ambitions

for her. The home in Westmoreland Place. Finishing
school in Tarrytown.

Now here was family history repeating itself. It had
been the same way when Jenny began to "feel her oats,"
as Rarick was in the habit of putting it, in the Mac-
Pherson Avenue house, and was casting an eye toward
Westmoreland Place. Jennifer's graduation reception
must be held in the new home, and not in the twelve-
room yellow-brick one on MacPherson. The neighbor-
hood was running down so. Stores. Flats. Even the
G. H. Francises were talking of selling.

The little brown jug of a Jennifer of the MacPherson
Avenue house was now the slip of a young miss, straight
as a paper-cutter, with the sophisticated eyes that for the
life of him her father could never catch and hold in a
glance.

And now that brown child back there, whitened because her freckles seemed to have come off, this Jennifer
whom he was casting about, in his futile way, to save,
what was left of her, for himself, must have her fifteenth
birthday in a house on Fifth Avenue that almost faced the
Metropolitan Museum.

To think that he, John Rarick, who had once dreamed
dreams no bigger than that walking-trip through the
Pyrenees, should be in a position to give her such a
house. Was Jenny, after all, the natural and doting
parent, and was he to Jennifer the grudging, silent father?
Was he too finished with youth to know his own children?

Could his dreams for Avery, the boy, slip between his
fingers, too, as this mother of his began to demand his
rights for him? Would Avery grow up alien to a father
who seemed to have no shred of youth left that would
enable him the better to understand the youth in his
children?

From what was it he was struggling to save them?

His own innate sense of rightness could be no deeper than his wisdom, and who was he to be cocksure of his wisdom? After all, what was the meaning of this success, which sometimes threatened to seem chimeric to him, if it was not to enable him to do just such things as give Jennifer her fifteenth birthday in one of the most beautiful and expensive houses in the world?

Success had done its share to teach Rarick himself new and complex appetites. He was a philatelist of elaborate and expensive tastes. There was in one of the pockets of his waistcoat, which was hanging over the foot of the bed, a famous Gnostic gem, heliotrope, engraved with the sacred name "Abrasax." A museum in Boston had been bidder against him for that gem. There were in that same pocket, result of those same tastes acquired through his growing wealth, an ominous and luminous opal, a tiny agate ring with a runic inscription of the late-Saxon period, and a transparent aquamarine cut *en cabochon* with the figure of a hump-bull. In his library, at this period, were celebrated "firsts" upon the shelves; a Tintoretto, a Greuze, and a triptych of the Cimabue period upon his walls.

What Jenny was demanding for herself and her children were the equivalents of the runic gems, the celebrated firsts, and the misty Greuzes.

No wonder, as she lay there beside him, silent for the moment, the lines about her thin lips were tight with the distaste of their state of constant asking, and the stretched look across her face was the look that had been written there by the constant and almost automatic opposition he had been erecting for years against the nature of her desires for herself and her children.

His children, even the small boy Avery, approached him only through the mother. The mother herself approached him as a diplomat goes to the conference table, her points carefully tabulated in the portfolio of her mind.

A man, if he loved them, could hold out only so long against his children. . . .

He swung himself to a sitting posture on the side of the bed, and reached for a robe to slip on over his night-shirt. He was short, somber, gnome-like, and a little ridiculous in his nightshirt; and he never forgot it.

"I'll buy you the Ficke house, Jenny."

DURING the last six months of the six years the Raricks had occupied the Ficke mansion, a man by the name of Dr. Felix Gerkes had lived on the top floor of the house. He occupied two rooms and a green bathroom with a frieze of mermaids over the tub. His meals for the most part were brought to him and served on a card table beside a window that overlooked Central Park, which separated him in a diagonal from the Museum, where he had spent twenty-one years in the archæological department. He was also an Indianologist of first-rank repute, a man who had been frequently endowed with honorary degrees in the realms of scholarship and science.

He was the author of numerous brochures and pamphlets, a text-book on geology that was in general use throughout American colleges, had written three books on amulets, precious stones, and meteorites, and was regarded as a foremost living authority on religious uses of stones among primitive peoples.

He was a lean, shabby fellow, with a walrus-like mustache and a conspicuously prominent forehead with thin stringlets of hair brushed sidewise across what threatened to become a bald horseshoe. His clothing, so loosely it hung, seemed to have no points of contact with his body.

The women of the household, even though weeks might pass without their so much as encountering him, and then only in a hallway or on the rare occasions when he dined with the family, thought him repulsive, and considered it disgusting of Rarick to insist upon having him there.

A curious bond existed between these two men. They had first met when Rarick had been directed to him for advice concerning a contemplated purchase, for his collection, of a necklace of banded and variegated agates, onyx, carnelians, and sards, attributed to the first century, A.D.

In the course of a long and enlightening conversation with this wise, strange man, who wore a hexagon-shaped Chinese skull-cap with a crystal button on its peak, Gerkes had quoted from the *Pantagruel* of Rabelais, reciting almost word for word that part of the book which describes the oracle of the Dive Bouteilly and its seven columns of sapphire, jacinth, dyamont, ruby, emerald, *"more brilliant and glistening than those which were set in place of eyes in the marble lion stretched before the tomb of King Hermias. The sixth column of agate, the seventh of transparent syenite with a splendor like that of Hymettian honey, and within appeared the moon in form and motion such as she is in the heavens, full and new, waxing and waning."* In the further course of that casual hour's conversation, Gerkes had discoursed upon the seven heavens of the Mohammedans, white lapis-lazuli, the sack of Constantinople by the Sassanian Persian king, Khusrau II, Navajo silversmiths, Figdor collection in Vienna, use of black and white enamel on bezel, cramp-rings, Edward the Confessor, native Indian mountaineers of California, Liberian silver, Catherine von Bora and her marriage to Martin Luther, Cleveland Museum of Art, Antiochus IV, aluminum kitchenware, alleged curative effects of violet-blue, John Ruskin on crystals, balas-rubies, Flinders Petrie, Field Museum of Natural History, and the snake story in *Gesta Romanorum*.

Rarick, who had just returned from Atlanta, where he had contracted for the annual run-of-the-mill output of two million cotton handkerchiefs of the largest three

concerns in the South, sat in the musty little office of
Gerkes, which was laid out at the moment with stone
arrow-heads of a Navajo collection, and let the wisdom
of this slow man flow against ear-drums that were still
throbbing with the barter for the delivery of the two
million cotton squares that were to be sold in eleven
hundred and eight stores at five cents apiece.

There were lying undercurrent in Rarick's mind at
the time of this talk, an impending conference of the
Mountain region and Eastern store-managers, with an
eye to further standardization of window display; a contemplated monopoly of the output of a paper-napkin
factory near Brattleboro, Vermont, and a trip to Spring-
field, with one of his buyers, a German, for the purpose
of demonstrating to an American toy-manufacturer how
to produce a celluloid doll, the equivalent of the German
product, which could retail for ten cents. There was
further at work under the surface of Rarick's consciousness, a major plan for the formation of a policy, not yet
revealed to his company, for the establishment of a
Rarick store in every city of seven thousand or over, in
the entire country.

Years of nights of lying awake over that immense
project were about to fructify into action.

The thirteenth richest man in the world sat in that
musty pocket of an office with Gerkes until museum at-
tendants began to turn off the lights and rattle keys.
Then Gerkes, who loved talk, and who, deep in the midst
of a discourse on amber deposits in the Stone Age, had
found a listener, clapped on his shapeless hat and walked
home with Rarick across the twilit park, depositing him
at his door, without so much as a glance up at the pale
splendor of the façade of the Ficke house, which John
Rarick had purchased by sealed bid at sensational auction

seven years before. That meeting was the beginning of an impeccable friendship between these two.

A week later, Rarick invited Gerkes to lunch at a downtown business men's club. Gerkes did not belong to the world of men to whom lunch is a social or business ritual. He either took his off a lunch-stand in the vicinity of the Museum or cut slivers with a pocket knife off the small loaf of American cheese he kept in a desk drawer along with a box of Swedish biscuit.

His imperviousness to surroundings was colossal. He had once lunched with the King of England over a matter pertaining to the Jubilee jewels, and was unable later to describe the occasion in anything except the contents of the discussion.

He ate sparingly of Rarick's carefully ordered luncheon, giving little if any heed to it, and once more, apropos of the first-century string of agates and sards, let his discourse flow from the crammed stock-room of his mind.

Here was a man who, in casual discussion of a mediæval and practically obsolete gem, could quote from the *Divina Commedia* the lines in which Dante uses these stones as a symbol of joy divine:

> "L'altra letizia, che m'era gia nota
> Preclara cosa, me si fece in vista
> Qual fin balascio in che lo sol percota,"

and then, with a mental handspring and a Rabelaisian twist of the old rascal in him, which was absurdly out of keeping with his odor of chalk dust and blackboard, would lean his walrus mustache into Rarick's ear with a foul bit of anecdote about a youth with a ruby studded into his flesh, who fancied the chryselephantine statue of Athena by Phidias.

After the boiling turmoil of a morning that held a

conference on the feasibility of installing soda-water foun-
tains in the west of the Mississippi areas, a complicated
discussion with three architects on the standard fronts of
Rarick stores, a long-distance-telephone conversation with
the Chattanooga real-estate office on a ninety-nine-year
lease for a second store, and the consummation of an
order for one hundred thousand bathing-hats, to walk
with Gerkes through the sarcophagus of his mind was
like emerging from noisy sunlight into the green twilight
of the Italian cypresses Rarick was fond of transplanting,
in long aisles, from Sicilian hillsides to his own.

Here was a man who had a decayed-looking green
circle on the front of his neck, from a brass collar-
button, which he was never to discard, even after Rarick
had sent him precious ones, but to whom, on the other
hand, a blemish on the crystal flesh of an art-object was
something to cause his own flesh to crawl upward.

Some five years after these meetings between the two,
Gerkes fell ill of a flaying neuritis, and, tracing him to the
lair of his dwelling, Rarick found him in a small room
in the high-up rear of a Twenty-third Street rooming-
house, books stacked from floor to ceiling, and exactly
three personal objects in evidence. A wooden-backed
hair-brush, a pocket comb, and a tooth-brush, sharing
the dresser-top with an assortment of Aztec arrow-heads,
proof-sheets of an article on scarabs for the *Encyclo-
pedia Britannica,* a copy of Plato's *Phædon,* William
Langland's *Piers Plowman,* and a *World Almanac.*

If Rarick had expected protest when he suggested the
move from these quarters to the suite at the top of his
home, nothing of the sort happened. With his imperviousness to environment or even to the sense of personal
obligation, Gerkes took up residence under his friend's
roof. One had to live somewhere. Money was something you shared if you had it, or you accepted if you

had not. Within a week the walls which Jenny had recently had done in yellow brocatelle, were plastered with maps, and the furniture itself littered, as the lodging-house room had been, with the story of the dawn of the human race as told by flint-head, ax, and spear, littering up the decorator's idea of a perfect example of a suite done in the manner of the Second Empire.

Jenny's kind of opposition to the invasion of Gerkes had been tinctured with the wisdom of a certain restraint. Here was one of the times it was not good to oppose Rarick. When his head seemed to jam down tightly between his shoulders, and his lower lip shot out, and his eyes, which so seldom met hers any more, slid up under their lids, leaving a horrid effect of just white ball, Jenny had the intuition to know that here was not the time to put up active opposition.

She had missed this scent a few times, once in particular over an apparently trivial matter that had to do with Avery and a week-end stag party of eleven school companions which she planned for him on board a motor-yacht which she was maneuvering for his father to give him on his fifteenth birthday.

The idea of Avery on his own private yacht, lording it as host over eleven youngsters to whom a yacht was that day's toy, was roiling to Rarick. There had been a similar scene, not two months before, over a cigar-shaped roadster for Avery; but then there had been high, bitter, even more terrible words and Rarick's foot had come down with an emphasis that Jenny somehow knew better than to further oppose, and Avery had not even been allowed to come home from school at Newberry over the occasion of his birthday.

There had been a matter that had to do with Jennifer, who had played high stakes beside her mother at the baccarat tables of Nice and won sums large enough for the papers to carry the story in headlines that had been the occasion of peremptory cablegrams for their return to America and had virtually shut off subsequent trips abroad.

There had been the affair, too, of the young Argentinian, son of a castor-bean magnate, driving his Hispano-Suiza into the swimming-pool at the Roslyn, Long Island, estate. Jenny had been as outraged as Rarick, except that he went to the extreme of keeping the house closed for two subsequent seasons.

There were certain well-defined limits to opposing Rarick, which were none the less tricky limits, because there seemed to be no way, except the intuitive one, to anticipate them. He would give in on many a grand issue, such, for instance, as the Ficke house, Jennifer's fabulous string of matched pearls, or Jenny's whim for five thousand acres of French-Canadian tract north of Quebec, upon which they had built an artificial lake, a forty-room châlet, "The Cataract," and which had been opened exactly twenty days in five years. On the other hand, a trifle like Avery's roadster, or this matter of Dr. Gerkes, would set his head rigidly into the valley of his shoulders and square him for fight.

The coming of Dr. Gerkes was one of those occasions. This time Jenny knew it even before she raised the first faint dust of issue; but she could not forego that first faint dust. The coming of Gerkes angered her. It went against the grain. Not that, offhand, it would seem to cause much of a ripple in a household where thirty-one servants reported to the housekeeper every morning; but it did matter more than was discernible at the first glance.

From the first, Jenny had found the Ficke house deceptive. A Gothic library, two stories high, which ran across the entire Fifth Avenue frontage, a drawing-room of enormous proportions, a Roman dining-room into which you ascended by Pompeian-marble steps, and a glassed-in conservatory for which a breakfast-room had been sacrificed as Rarick's passion for difficult and exotic transplantation began to grow, left embarrassingly few bedroom suites.

An additional story would have marred the Hellenic grace of the building, and the owner of the adjoining pile of magnificence felt affronted, rather than tempted, by the Rarick offer to buy.

The yellow suite assigned to Dr. Gerkes subtracted one from the five small suites of guest-chambers that Jenny had so elaborately planned and redone. It is true that the comings and goings of Gerkes, who preferred to use what was known as the service-entrance and the small rear staircase that led quite privately up to his rooms, made practically no dent in that household. He dined in his rooms, except on those rare occasions when the family was home alone and Rarick wanted him at table. He was seldom, if ever, seen in the wide, beautifully vaulted corridors of the house; and yet to Jenny there was something repulsive about his being there at all. The shabby black figure somehow recalled the musty memory and figure of an old music-teacher back in her St. Louis girlhood, whose face, close beside hers at the piano, and his audible breathing had been repellent to her. A lady's-maid had gossiped to Jennifer, who gossiped to Jenny, that he used only three towels a week, and no bed-linen, because he slept on the floor, wrapped in one of the beautiful canary-yellow camel's-hair blankets. A secret survey of his rooms, one day during his absence, revealed to Jenny's horrified eyes the yellow-brocade hangings and bed-coverings removed and crammed into a corner, the tops of her lovely curving period-furniture covered with a layout of lean-looking hair-brush, a whisk broom, and primitive stone implements, her paneled yellow walls hung with pin-studded maps, and, on the mantelpiece, beside the meticulously right ormolu clock, a box of Swedish biscuit, a cube of American cheese, and a huge pocket knife, open.

That evening, before they went down to dinner, Jenny's anger overflowed her discretion.

"There's a time and a place for everything, Rarick," she said to him, as he stood tugging at his collar in the enormous mirrored bathroom which gave off their bedroom. "That man is no more comfortable here than we are in having him."

Standing in a foundation slip of coral-colored silk, over which she was presently to slip a coral-colored evening dress of all front and no back, her carrot-colored hair caught upward in the tight perpendicular line which accentuated the narrowness of her head, she could see Rarick's neck, through the wall of mirror, drop into the slit of his shoulders, and that peculiar look of the hunchback which she dreaded, and of which she was wary, come cunningly into his face.

"What man?"

"Gerson, or whatever it was you said his name is."

He turned, in his black trousers, stiff white shirt, black suspenders, still tinkering with his tie, so that, as he faced her, she could see his eyes ride up under his lids.

"I said his name is Felix Gerkes," he pronounced, slowly and meticulously, as you might mouth a lesson to a child. "Dr. Felix Gerkes has condescended to come and make his home here."

"Isn't it usual, Rarick," she said, her rising anger crowding closer on her discretion, "for even so great a patron saint of indigent college professors as yourself to consult the members of his family before introducing a worthy outsider into the household?"

"There are few demands I make here. This is one of them."

"You have a young-lady daughter to consider."

"That is precisely what I did, when I introduced into this madhouse a human being out of the world of ideas."

"I see. You feel that Jennifer's scientific education has been neglected and that no young woman is equipped for life without a Ph.D. knowledge of the glacial age," she said, and glittered as she stood there with her bronze-colored eyes and the points of light off the tapping toe of her slipper. She could have plunged her long jeweled fingers into the valleys of his shoulders and shaken him, as a smothering sense of futility began to crowd her in.

"Not at all, Jenny. Our daughter's education is all one could ask. She knows a Hispano-Suiza from a Rolls-Royce. She knows a Cartier setting, Theodore at the Ritz, her finishing-school 'R's,' and how to stack her artichoke leaves. I notice our son, too, already has quite a way with his artichokes."

The speech was not like him, but rather in mimicry of what she might have said under similar circumstances.

"What a devil you are, Rarick!"

"A poor devil, Jenny," he said, his face as pulled-looking as tarpaulin.

"You are a poor father." She was going to add, "and a poor husband," but she let the words lodge in her eyes.

"I am that," he said, replying to the spoken and unspoken indictment.

"What is it you want of us?" she cried. "Must you oppose your children on every occasion, just as you have always opposed me? Is merely the fact that we want something, sufficient itself to dispose you against it?

Why must you always be the stern parent to them, with me the buffer between? What do you want?"

She did not know it, but she was voicing the cry within his heart.

What did he want? He wanted some of the intimacy from that boy of his that was Jenny's. He wanted some of that intimacy from Jennifer. He wanted. . . . What did he want? . . .

"Do you want your children to skip their youth, so that they may follow in the footsteps of some doddering college professor who spends his life fiddling among arrow-heads?"

"I want Felix Gerkes in my house," he said, climbing back from what was sure to be a discussion of defeat by reason of what he considered her colossal lack of logic, "because he knows things that we don't know. That we cannot buy for them. He has not mere learning. He has wisdom."

"I see. Why Eskimo Indians like blubber."

There was absolutely no way to capture a focal point of discussion when you found yourself in argument with such a woman. She invariably answered you in terms of something irrelevant, making you wild with futility. Damn her! Damn her! In the years since that thought first lightened into his brain, it had flashed there with recurring frequency.

"Yes, Jenny," he said again, driven to the extremity of employing her same skidding method, "and why your son, a second-year boy at Newberry, maintains two roadsters, a motor-boat, a trotting horse, and fails in his mid-year examinations."

"No man ever understood a high-strung boy less than you understand yours!"

The dart struck sure, and sent his head retreating down into his shoulders. True. True. Too, too true.

"Nor a gay and beautiful daughter, one with brains, let me tell you that, although you prefer to treat her as if she were a moron. She's a match for your professors. Jennifer's got brains!"

"Exactly, damn it all! And for what? Waste. Waste."

In a world of superficial interests, filled with the need to be clever and sophisticated, you could be clever with the sharp edge of your brain, if you had one, and sophisticated on a shoestring of intelligence and no heart.

"Your merely clever person is only a first-rate second rather."

"Try being one."

"I can't; it's not in me."

"Lots of things are not in you, Rarick. The ability to meet your world is not in you."

"I wish to God it were not so deeply in you."

"Gerkes's world, I suppose. . . ."

"I don't know his world. He knows the secret of things and of not being smothered by them. Like you. Like me. Like your children."

"Obviously, from the look of his hair-brush."

You couldn't argue with a woman like that. You couldn't. You couldn't. The crazing sense of futility . . .

She was in her gown by now, a sort of henna-colored affair, as if the threads had been picked from her hair—a gown that wrapped her eccentrically thin body on a diagonal, rushing to a high ruff about her neck in front, cut daringly, almost to her waist line, behind. Between the bang of her hair and a stiff, enormously brilliant dog-collar of diamonds, her eyes were red and level and full of the impudence of her remark.

"Doctor Gerkes remains, Jenny."

She shrugged her shoulders and walked out.

Damn her! Damn her! Damn her!

A STORY about Jennifer Rarick went the rounds that winter, creating hilarity at many a cocktail and dinner party.

It seemed that the Rarick house, shiningly conditioned, was now being shouted out by sight-seeing-omnibus megaphones as the billion-dollar Ficke-Rarick mansion purchased with Rarick dimes.

One morning, just as Jennifer, in riding-habit, was emerging from the house to enter a large fawn-colored roadster which she was accustomed to drive herself across the Park to the academy where she kept her mounts, one of these omnibuses slowed while the megaphone roared of Rarick dimes and billion-dollar mansions.

Throughout this canned oration, the daughter of John Rarick, one hand against her slim hip, the other thumbing her nose at the omnibus, held posture, precipitating the picture by a dash into her roadster at its conclusion, and leaving a gasping and bucolic sight-seeing omnibus load not quite sure that it had happened.

Whether it did happen or not, the gesture might be said to be somewhat typical of Jennifer. I am. You are. Take me. Leave me.

Usually you took her. Even at her worst, when she was cocksure and tiresomely sophisticated and pseudo and pretentious, there was about her a hearty self-loathing, concerning which she was robustly frank.

"I despise myself," she was constantly saying to people on club verandas and in grand stands at polo matches, where patter predominated. "I am a swine. I'm N. G. I'm stealing a ride through life. I'm a panhandler."

After a fashion she meant it. After the fashion of one who attempts to appease a dissatisfaction by throwing to it slops of words.

People were always saying of her, "She has brains," in the key of saying, "Too bad, the girl has brains."

"So's my old man," was Jennifer's usual retort, in the slang with which she hung her speech. She meant this. She admired her father from the distance that lay between them. She wanted his respect and, strangely enough, gave him precious little of hers.

The evening following his scene with Jenny regarding the coming of Gerkes, Rarick sent for his daughter.

In a house filled with the confusions, the comings, the goings, the ringing of telephones, and the hurrying of servants, that the two women, mother and daughter, managed to create about themselves, the occasions of family conference were seldom enough.

When the summons came for Jennifer to go to her father, in the library, she was in the act of slapping about her rooms, with her own confused English maid and her mother's Breton maid hurrying at her heels, in the effort to help her toward a dinner engagement for which she was already thirty minutes late.

The fact of the matter was, she had remained shockingly overtime at a bridge game at the Mayfair, vainly trying to retrieve a several-hundred-dollar loss.

Jennifer was of that species of tormentor who, abusive of her servants, was none the less beloved by them, because, quickly contrite, she wooed them back by anointing their wounds with tips and gifts.

It was her maid Mariana's boast that these tantrums kept her supplied with furs, French gowns, and even jewels.

The last time Jennifer had been summoned in this fashion by her father was about two years before. She had bought on a dare, at the auction of a famous Long Island estate, a cigar-shaped roadster with an Italian engine of very special make, for eleven thousand dollars. The estate was being sold because the owner had been killed in this very car. Jennifer had stood on a table in the garage and led the spirited bidding.

Rarick, after a high and ugly scene with her in the library, had paid the eleven thousand dollars, and the day following, in her enraged and humiliated presence, had sold it to a dealer for twenty-five hundred.

"The meanest man in the world," Jennifer had ground through clenched teeth into her mirror after the episode, the tears of her humiliation splashing down a face which, although molded after her father's, had a lightning beauty that darted into it and played around her eyes and her lips. A straight brown slab of a girl, with a brilliant sort of Jeanne d'Arc directness to her eyes, which were surrounded by a mediæval-looking curtain of straight brown bob.

There had been, too, the highly unpleasant occasion when, like a small girl, Jennifer at twenty had been obliged to endure the unendurable indignity of standing beside her much younger brother for a dressing-down from Rarick that had to do with Avery's presence—to say nothing of her own—at a swimming-pool party at Greenwich that had found its way into insinuating print.

As a matter of fact, both Jennifer's and Avery's presence had been the result of a flat tire in front of the estate of the friends who had detained them. But somehow, facing her father, as she stood beside her slim brother, there on the mysterious beauty of a sixteenth-century Kuba hunting-rug, the truth of the story seemed too flimsy to bear the telling, or something grim and hating in these children kept them silent. Rarick was always to believe, not from what they said, but from what they did not say, that their presence on this notorious occasion had been deliberate.

In any event, a summons to her father in the library was grimly associated with the scratching memory of scenes like those.

Then there had been the excruciating occasion when Jennifer and her mother, returning from a season at Deauville and Le Touquet, had successfully passed customs officials without declaring three important and perfectly matched pearls, which they had sewn on to a beaded gown. There had been an outrageous scene in the library when these facts became known to Rarick; in fact, rage and terror had caused Jenny to swoon—cutting her forehead as she went down—at her husband's reiterated threats to reveal the whole untidy business.

There was rankling, in some terror at the moment, in Jennifer's mind, a dread that an extremely private dramatic evening, entitled "Casanova, Be Careful," which had been staged with great lavishness in the garden-amphitheater of a Connecticut estate, was through some mysterious leak about to find its way into notorious publicity.

Hang it all! she had been lured into the thing chiefly because it had given her an opportunity to try her hand at what she secretly suspected in herself to be a talent for lyrical writing.

Hang it all! the way to avoid such jams as this was to ditch the home condition. Marry forty-million-dollar Charley Kempner and spawn him square-faced little Kempner heirs with Kempner casts in their Kempner eyes. Or not marry Lew Bissinger and live in embroidered sin with an already married man. Or pursue Berry Rhodes, who was simply unassailable with social position, and who fascinated her. Or just ditch it. Open a tea-room. Write a scandalous book. Hang it all! No parent can hope to get away with *moyenâge,* maiden-in-a-tower stuff. Yes, she had written the "Casanova, Be Careful" lyrics and danced in the last of seven veils. Damned talented job, if she did say it. "Well, Father," she improvised to her mirror, "it's come to this between you and me; has been coming to this between you and me since you popped me into a world I didn't ask to be popped into. I'm no nincompoop. You'd see to it that a daughter of yours wasn't. But I'm tired being treated like one. I'm finished. If you want to throw me a million or two to save me from being somebody's expensive hussy, I'm not too proud to accept it. If you don't, and since I'm not made of the stuff you seem to think your daughter should be made of, I'm through, anyway. I'll go off and write a dirty play and show up the whole wretched business of life as it is lived behind the tessellated walls of the million-dollar Rarick mansion that is built out of dimes. If the walls aren't tessellated, they ought to be. I'll give them a megaphonefull that they'll remember. I'll tell the story of how somebody took a couple of hair-pins and bent them into a couple of frowns and stuck them into sour dough and made a little man who lived in tall marble halls that kept him looking like a dwarf, and who would have thought he was Napoleon, if he had quite had the nerve, but who only got as far as owning everything in the world he could lay his hands on that had belonged to Napoleon or was about Napoleon. I'll tell the world about this little man who got so rich on needles and pins that he hated himself—and his family. I'll tell the world, damn it! I'll tell . . ." cried Jennifer to herself, as she ran down the hall toward the library; but not without pausing to snatch up a spangled scarf to throw across the back of her dinner gown, which was cut to one inch above the waist line, where a topaz buckle bit softly into the flesh.

WHAT Rarick wanted with his daughter was to have her meet Gerkes.

He was standing waiting for her, on the hearthstone of a vaulted fireplace that had been lifted out of the palace of a Milanese Sforza, a small man who was forever to be dwarfed by the Gothic grandeur through which he moved, and yet to whom the Druid twilight of such splendor was to become a fetish.

Three enormous chandeliers, designed after the crowns of Merovingian kings, poured cunningly diffused pools of light on to this scene of mediæval resurrection. The very modern young Jennifer, who wore her docked head like Jeanne d'Arc, and whose metallic frock clicked, slouched in on slim, inelegant legs.

Her smartness, even back in the St. Louis days when she had first begun to drift from him, had always been a source of her father's deep admiration. Not her indubitable smartness in the worldly sense, but the brand of it that was indicated in the intelligent bright dark eyes, set into a head that stood so erect and right between its slim shoulders. She could have been anything, Jennifer could have been, except the thing she was. And the thing she was, without his being able to define the exact why, was anathema to her father.

It was not that she carried her cocktails vulgarly, or said gross things with what passed for the new frankness. She was no more and no less than any girl of her upbringing. Or her mother's upbringing. If anything, a little more. She drank rather less, smoked not at all, and, in her own phraseology, had remained a virgin chiefly because she had never let her curiosity get the better of her.

When she said a thing like that, Rarick ground his fingers into his palms to keep from boxing the ears of the consciously modern young Jennifer. She was so cocksure of what a sophisticated, unillusioned, amusing thing it was to be Jennifer. She was tiresome and a swine, yes, she was willing to admit, but only in the sense that her rattling-good brain was going to waste in cocksure and debonair fashion. You couldn't live in her swinish set and take the world seriously enough to concentrate. Hang it all! why try to write plays, even if you felt a talent for it, when, to be true to the life she knew, they would have to be dirty plays? Or why do charity or social work, when the world hadn't time for the dirty-nosed little darlings even after you'd gone to all the trouble to save them for it. Part of the amusing thing it was to be Jennifer was to be brutal and frank and unsentimental and greedy and a little foul-mouthed.

To Rarick, this young woman of his flesh, his board, his keep, who stood there on the hearth-rug before him, glittering in her gown of fake armor, was as strange as if she had just stepped full grown from the life-size silver-and-chalcedony Zeus that stood on a *credenza* against the wall. Everything he felt about this illuminated edition of himself was imbedded in disapproval. Had been, since the Mary Institute days back in St. Louis, when she had stopped bounding the state of Missouri for him in an unaffected little voice that was appealing, and had first started going to football games in the white-kid gloves her mother provided for her, with boys in their first long trousers, who came calling for her in their family automobiles. He despised what she had become, chiefly in terms of what she might have been.

"You sent for me, Father?" she said, the glance she

guarded from ever meeting his sliding to the spot where his graying hair hung in the Napoleonic forelock down his brow, and simulating unconcern by feeling very concernedly along the rear edges of her shining curtain of coiffure.

"Dr. Felix Gerkes, of the National Museum and a scholar of considerable consequence, is going to make his home with us. I suppose you know that, Jennifer?"

Jennifer did. In fact, she was the one who had passed along to her mother the first information concerning the thin-bristled hair-brush and the square of American cheese, as they had sat, in pajamas, in Jennifer's bedroom over coffee one morning. Pretty snide, to stick a fossil in the yellow suite, with the blessed old Gothic mausoleum as cramped as a Harlem flat, when it came down to actual living-quarters.

But nevertheless a sense of relief ran through Jennifer. Thank Heaven, he had not got wind of the whole silly business of "Casanova, Be Careful." They were damned clever lyrics, if she did say so, but fat chance to get anything but a dressing-down for them from her father.

"I'm like the fellow, Father, when it comes to science, who kept 'Stones of Venice' on the geology shelf of his library."

"Dr. Gerkes's scientific achievement is by no means all there is to him, Jennifer. I want you to cultivate him."

His ability to antagonize his children was infallible.

She drew back from his command, with the kind of rearing of the neck that he had beheld countless times in his boy Avery. A dull sense of his impotence, where these youngsters were concerned, was a chronic rage within him.

"I want you to have dinner with Dr. Gerkes and me tonight."

"That's impossible. I'm late as it is for early dinner with the Delaney Stuarts. Shibby sails tomorrow."

The name "Shibby Stuart" was no more anathema to him than a dozen others which were constantly on the lips of his wife and daughter. In fact, there were important reasons of diplomacy why there should be an *entente cordiale* with Delaney Stuart, president of an Eastern Federal Reserve Bank with which the Rarick Chain, Inc., had enormous transactions. But the picture of Shibby Stuart as he had once seen her lying sick-drunk on a couch in his house, during one of Jennifer's dinner dances, rose crazily before him.

"You will remain at home for dinner tonight. It may help you to remember you have a home."

"Don't be absurd, Father," said Jennifer, and began pulling at the net edge of her handkerchief. Her rage, which she felt hitting in hot points against her eyeballs, was out of all proportion to the dilemma of being obliged to cancel her dinner with Shibby Stuart. As a matter of fact, even as she had been sliding into the armor gown that clicked, the thought of evasion had flashed through her brain. What with her back stiff and sore from riding a new mount that afternoon, and a more recent invitation to go off to a speak-easy for dinner and dancing with Berry Rhodes, here was an opportunity to pass up the Stuart farewell dinner and incidentally repay Shibby for a last-minute non-appearance of hers that she had recently staged at one of Jennifer's bridge luncheons.

"It isn't often I make demands, Jennifer. I let weeks go by without so much as seeing you at the dinner table. This is one of the times I want you here."

It seemed to her at the moment that nothing mattered quite so much as dinner at the Stuarts'.

"You should have given me warning."

"You should have had sufficient judgment to know

there comes a time when a halt must be called, if you won't call it yourself. You haven't sat down to dinner in this house for three weeks or more."

"Why should I? Everything I do gets on your nerves. If I'm so much as called to the telephone, you humiliate me before a butler by refusing to let me answer it."

"I have known you to spend twenty minutes of a dinner hour at the telephone."

"If I say the moon is made of green cheese, then I've said something off-color. Hell! why should I want to stay at home, Father?"

He reached out and hit a gong with a bâton of lapis-lazuli, padded in velvet.

"Miss Jennifer will join us at dinner," he said to an immediate butler.

She waited until the door had closed again, and then, with her face clenched and her hands clenched and her gown making jangling little sounds as the quivers of her wrath shot through her, she lowered her face until it almost touched her father's.

"I just hate you sometimes," she said, and began to cry the invariable tears of anger and humiliation to which these scenes could reduce her. "I wish I had the guts to go out and scrub floors for a prostitute, rather than put up with being treated like one here."

A fit of trembling that went through him like a tree-shake caught him at the words which came off her lips, which were so close to his face that it was as if he could feel their shape.

"You will have dinner at home tonight, Jennifer, even if your temper does turn you into a barmaid."

"It must be a splendid feeling to have to force the members of your family to your side."

"It is, Jennifer," he said, and looked at her with what, for a moment, threatening to disarm her, seemed like a film across his eyes. She sat down, still pulling at the net edge of her handkerchief and every so often scraping it angrily along her wet cheeks.

"Well, now you've got me, what is it you want with me? I suppose it isn't asking too much to be allowed leave-of-absence to get a message off to the Stuarts. God knows what I am to say."

He beat the gong again. "Telephone Mrs. Delaney Stuart that, owing to an unavoidable change in her plans, Miss Jennifer will be unable to come to dinner tonight."

She held her face, during this, averted from the butler's view of it, a little squeal of rage rising to her throat.

"Now what? I suppose I am to spend a jolly evening at home talking isinglass, or blue grottos, or dinosaurs' eggs, or whatever it is one talks to fossil-finders." Her rage ended on a spurt of laughter and for the life of him, he could not see her face break into amusement, her eyes crinkling, and keep his own face straight.

"I want you to meet a great and simple person, Jennifer. A man who has not grown simply great in his work, but great simply."

"He sounds as if he ought to be done in stained glass."

"He is witty enough to think that poor wit."

"Thank you, Father. Any more lilies today?"

"Cultivate Dr. Gerkes, Jennifer. Cultivate Gerkes. You want to learn."

He knew he was being roiling and didactic and tiresome again but to his surprise, she flashed a tear-stained face at him that was lit with a sudden sweetness, a clear-eyed curiosity to it that was reminiscent of the small brown jug of a girl who had bounded Missouri.

"I do, Father! I know I'm all of a total loss. I'm on to myself, don't you forget it. I want to sit at the feet of somebody and learn. God knows I don't know anybody with a pair of feet like that. Trot out this wise guy, Father. I'll chuck everything and stay home at the indoor sport of improving my so-called mind. Do you think he'd like to collaborate with me on a book I've long had in mind, called 'Sex O'Clock'? Really, Father, I *am* in favor of more and better brains."

Jenny came in then, wearing a yellow satin gown that had been dry-cleaned to the color of an old tooth, and so shrunken that it spanned. She had long since discarded it from her more formal wardrobe, but, with a survival of an old instinct for economy, went through the mean and futile performance of reserving it for just such occasions as this, when they dined alone and *en famille*.

"You look like the devil, darling," said Jennifer, and kissed her.

"I feel like him and his bride," said Jenny, stooping to draw at a thread that was raveling at her hem. "I thought you were having dinner at Shibby's."

"I'm dining at home with the Department of Arts and Sciences," said Jennifer, and dropped a large slow wink to her mother.

Across the island of the hunting-rug, Jenny regarded her husband with eyes that had no gleam.

"I didn't mind canceling the Dentons at the last moment and leaving a vacancy in her opera box, but I don't relish the idea of also being on Shibby Stuart's black list, any more than you should, Rarick, considering your banking connections with them."

"You leave my banking connections to me."

"Gladly."

"Never mind, Mother. Father and I have evolved a new philosophy of life. Less philosophy and more life."

"The philosophy, I suppose, that the rich are all mean and frivolous and vicious, and the poor holy and right-eous."

He regarded her with the masked look to his face that could cause her to say over and over to herself: "Little man. Little man, you. Little fake Napoleon, you."

"Holy righteousness, my dear Jenny, cannot reside exclusively among the poor while you are you."

"Attaboy, Father!" said Jennifer, and jammed a pillow into the cave between the small of her back and the couch. "I can forgive a dirty dig if it's well dug. Can't you, Mother?"

Her mother glanced at her wrist watch, a singular and precious one, set into the plane surface of a square diamond.

"It's a wise house guest who is on time for his meals."

"At that rate, Jenny, our average run of them must be morons."

"Life among the Raricks," sang out Jennifer and hurling out the pillow, jumped to her feet and to some inner syncopated rhythm, began teetering on her slim toes down the great length of room that led to an organ at its far end.

Carved down the pipes of the towering instrument was the legend of the St. Gregorian Mass, the meeting of Abraham and Melchisedec, and the Last Supper. A chime, somewhere in the complicated heart of the organ, which was rigged with all sorts of mechanical attachments, gave out the half-hours. To Jennifer's hilarity, it played the grand operas, stained-window versions of the action springing into light above the keyboards. "Father's folly," she called it.

"Jennifer, if you turn that on, I'll scream!"

"Keep your well-known equilibrium, Jenny. I just wanted to see the fat Brünnehilde, in purple cheeks and corsets, heave in stained glass."

How small they made him, these women of his. That organ, built in at tremendous expense and effort by tear-

ing out one entire end of the house, was as dear as someone beloved could have been. The storied operas, stalking in stained glass to the pressure of a button, peopled
his solitude, plunged, in the glory of melody, through
his evenings, saturating his thirsting spirit. Chromoesque tinned music, perhaps, but full of solaces. . . .

"Jennifer!"

"I'm not! I'm not turning it on. Surely, if Father
can stand his 'Faust' served up to him like Campbell's
soup, you should be able to endure a magenta and majestic
trickle of 'Tannhäuser.' "

"Do you think Gerkes understood the dinner-hour,
Rarick?"

"Why, Jenny, what *is* the matter? The man is not
even due for five minutes. I've known you to hold dinner
three-quarters of an hour without a whimper when the
guests happen to be yours, as they almost invariably
are."

"She's a cave-in from dieting, Father."

That was doubtless true. It offended him to the point
of disgust to see this angular woman responding to a
herd instinct that apparently deprived her of logic, trying
to reduce herself still closer to her skeleton by nibbling
at meal-time on a special faddistic diet of chop and pine-
apple slices.

"I'm a cave-in, all right," said Jenny, and stretched
her thin body outright on a divan and pressed her fingers
into her eyes and bared her teeth in an on-edge fashion.

"Nerves. Underfed," said Rarick, eyeing her from
the opposite side of the hearth.

"Nerves, all right. Reason, all wrong."

There descended a silence characteristic of their times
together. Taking up an object here and there, as she
wandered aimlessly about the museum-like room, Jennifer
began to whistle in short, breathy snatches.

"For Heaven's sake, Jennifer, stop it!"

"Sorry, Mother."

Silence.

"Say, Dad, what do you call this?"

"That's a Tau-crossed pastoral staff. French, about the eleventh century. . . ."

"No, I mean the gold panel above it!"

"Oh, that's a reredos of St. Peregrine. It's part of an old altar-table. I bought it at the Donetti auction at the same time I got the ivory panel of the Virgin Mary with the pearl crown there, over the doorway."

"I think it's a waste of those lovely seed pearls, Rarick. You might have them done into something wearable for Jennifer or me."

He did not answer.

"I was going to say, Father, I saw what might be a sister panel to that reredos today, at Duveen's. I was there with Mary Dakin. She got caught in a tumbling market and was trying to unload two Romneys that came with her share of her grandmother's estate. By the way, wouldn't be interested, would you, Father, in buying a pair of Romneys? Mangy-looking, but frightfully *bona-fide*. Girl with a lamb. And Boy with a Goat. Or maybe his was a lamb, too. Well, anyway, Mary's asking fifteen thousand for the pair, and Duveen's sent a man to appraise."

"Not interested."

"What did they stick you for the pearl-incrusted reredos, Dad?"

"Hellman bid for me . . . something like twenty-five thousand, if I remember. . . ."

"Good God!" said Jenny from her reclining position, blowing smoke and holding her cigarette at bare arm's length upward from her.

"Good God, what?" barked Rarick, ready to be on edge.

"Good God, she's hungry!" said Jennifer, and resumed her aimless tour.

Silence.

"A Baby Gar speed-boat for your son would have cost half that much. Why is it so much easier to understand your own desire to own a sixteen-thousand-dollar piece of ivory slab than it is for you to understand a boy's desire for the things that mean youth and sport to him?"

"Because it is not his desire. I am convinced that all these notions to add more and more dangerous and expensive toys to the jumble of things with which you are cluttering his school life and educating both your children to demand, come from you."

"In which Jennifer is drawn dirtily into the picture."

"Keep quiet, Jennifer."

"Sorry, Mother."

"Your boy demands precious little."

"I realize that, Jenny. In fact, it is just my point."

"Fortunately, Rarick, I am of sufficiently tough fiber to nag in his behalf for some of the things he is too sensitive to nag for himself."

"What are some of those things, Jenny?"

"The things to which, as a rich man's son, he is entitled."

"Meaning . . ."

"O Lord! Rarick, I haven't it left in me to go over it all again."

"I'll go over it for you. Meaning things. Things to keep him moving instead of thinking. Devices for speed. For motion. Things to distract him from books, *things* to distract him from thinking."

"Good Lord, Dad, where do you get off? Things? You've spent half your life shoveling snide things into the shopping-bags of snide people who need snide things like safety-pins and stewpans. You've glorified the American dime by making it stand for *things*. You're the Thing King!"

How astute she was! Clever, slim Jennifer, with her sophisticated Egyptian-looking eyes, merciless in her ability to lay him open to himself.

"A major reason why I want to spare my own from the tyranny of things," he yapped back at them, trying to express, with the chronic sense of futility, some of the malaria of his spirit which managed to keep his family at this kind of antagonized arm's length.

"You don't seem particularly inclined to spare yourself the tyranny of those fifteenth-century tapestries or that enameled Pietà up there that cost a king's ransom, or unpronounceable and unwearable gems with which your pockets are crammed."

"There is at least something of the story of mankind to be found in historical objects."

"There's beauty in that motor-boat Avery isn't going to get," sang Jennifer, cupping the tall heel of her slipper in her hand and teetering. "Slim, speedy beauty, let me tell you that. And as for that story-of-mankind stuff, if you ask me, it is pretty much the low-down same, whether you read it off the hieroglyphics of an amulet from Hindustan or study our gigolo civilization through a magnifying-glass shaped like a monocle. And, Father, speaking of gigolos, I'm in love! He's a window-dresser for a haberdasher by day, and dances at Florentine's by night. Abbey Chadwick engaged him for her dinner dance, and I'm going to have him for mine next week. He tangos like a patent-leather-haired god, and his name is Nemo."

"Darling, that's the name of a rubber corset or a comic strip or something."

"No, Mother. He wears one and is the other; but, oh, my beating heart!"

"Bicarbonate of soda, darling!"

Why must he stand there with disgust printed on to his features, instead of meeting her vulgarity as Jenny did, by snapping her fingers. Was Jenny, after all, clever and even subtle with her children, giving them their heads, to prevent them from running away? Her children adored her. They were easy and indolent and insolent in her presence. Sometimes he even felt himself hankering for some of that insolence. Avery had once said to his mother in Rarick's presence, "Shut up, old darling," and he had rebuked him for it. At that there had flashed between Avery and his mother a look of amused understanding at his lack of understanding. Letters from Avery to his mother were constantly lying about the gold-stoppered bottles and knickknacks of her dressing-tables. He never read them, even surreptitiously, but he knew they were chatty letters that preyed upon the easy indulgences of his mother; and, meticulous as he was not to read, constantly his glance was being snagged by such salutatory exuberance as "Dearest Brick of a Mother" or "Dearest Mother-on-the-Spot."

That was precisely what Jennifer was saying to her now. "Mother-on-the-Spot, you're beautiful, but dumb."

Dr. Gerkes entered then, after the inconsequential manner he had of appearing on a scene without the slightest preamble. His dinner clothes, which he called his "overalls," because he wore them when he lectured, hung from the rounded part of his back like a suit that had been suspended from a nail. His shuffling footsteps skidded the small rugs from under them like so much silent gravel.

There was a graciousness to Gerkes. A man of almost unlimited intellectual contacts, he could be loquacious enough on subjects where he felt informed, and an indulgent listener to those who, in his opinion, wanted to talk more than he. Stupidity he regarded as a cardinal vice. It made him snappy. His principal income was derived from lecturing, but he could be thoroughly rude to the interrogators who crowded and chirped around him at women's clubs; and even at the meetings of such learned organizations as scientific and historical societies he was capable of rebuking a colleague for the inattention to his lecture that his question had implied.

On the other hand, there was an amusing mixture of the Socratic and Rabelaisian about Gerkes. He loved the private and impolite jokes that had to be told behind the barrier of a hand, and the curbstone and the platform were alike his rostrums. He had never married, due principally to chronic lack of income and what he regarded as the popular fallacy that two could live as cheaply as one. His eye for a pretty woman was a quick, discerning one. It lit on Jennifer, who was standing in one of the pools of light, glittering in her armor, her dress a blaze of winking metallic disks, and her eyes as if they had come off the gown.

Rarick's pride in his friend was pretentious and clumsy.

"Gerkes, I wish you'd tell my daughter that story about the Taoist priest who once found himself, when a meteor fell, in Lahore, India. There's a mighty fine moral there." Or, "Gerkes, I'd like for my wife to hear your opinion of our own Arizona summers and how they compare with say a country like Switzerland. I cannot get my family to realize that they don't have to cross the Atlantic for beauty of scene or variety of climate."

"Three chamber-of-commerce cheers," said Jennifer, and held her cocktail-glass up against the light.

"See America first," said Jenny, and gulped hers down.

It was the kind of patter for which Gerkes had little retort. Persiflage, the smiting word at any price, chic sophistication for the average truism, tea-table and round-table caliber of profundities, disarmed and bewildered him. He was at his worst. The descent to the dining-room through aisles of tapestries was made goose-step. Gerkes, who was never ill at ease, only silent where it seemed the better part of wisdom, plowed solemnly through the high-napped rugs.

Not even port wine or champagne-cup, made by Jenny at table in a frosted-silver pitcher over a *mélange* of fresh, whole, cling-stone peaches and black cherries, could succeed in drawing him out of the slough of amiable silence into which the occasion had thus far submerged him.

"I hope you are finding your quarters comfortable, Doctor Gerkes," said Jenny from the head of her table, where they sat sparsely grouped, because it could have accommodated four times their number. The secret of the icy grace with which Jenny presided at her table, Jennifer was fond of declaring, was that her mother never permitted her head to touch the back of her tall chair, or her hand to lie along its arms.

"Very comfortable, thank you," said Gerkes, who was interested in his portion of slim frizzled smelts. "It's a pleasant room."

"Room?" repeated Jenny, and swung her high, curved glance to her husband.

"You've a couple of them, Gerkes, or is it three? Don't guess you've had time to check up."

"Well now, Rarick, I haven't," said Gerkes without embarrassment. "There's another room leads off, I take it."

"No, old dear, you don't take it," said Jennifer, popping an almond into her mouth and grinning; "you apparently leave it."

"I'm pretty much of an Eskimo," he said. "They live in bare rooms and keep stacked such furniture as they need, outside their houses, until a piece is called in for use. Simplifies."

"Dr. Gerkes has lived up there a lot among them, Jenny. He also spent two years in Lapland, studying."

"You don't say so," said Jenny, regarding him over a smelt poised on the end of her fork. "Wasn't it somebody or other said of the French that no race which eats little *escargots,* suffocated in their shells, can ever achieve civilization? Well, that's the way I feel about Eskimos and blubber. Fancy being the kind of person that can drink it!"

"One must fancy it; because they don't."

"Don't what?"

"Drink blubber."

"But I always thought. . . ."

"No, my dear lady, you never thought, or you wouldn't be of the opinion that Eskimos drink blubber."

"Why don't they?"

"Why can't you drink this wine-tumbler full of olive-oil?"

"Why—er—obviously—I can't."

"Well, for that same obvious anatomical reason, the Eskimo, who, strange as it may seem, is constructed just as you are, could not drink quantities of oil, either, and keep it down. Sorry to have to seem to be concrete."

"You *are* smart, aren't you?" said Jennifer, and propped her elbows on the table and her chin in her palm, and regarded his lusterless figure across the table. "Now tell me how they put ships in bottles, and who wrote 'Titus Andronicus.'"

"The best way to make a ship in a bottle is to begin

working from the inside of the bottle, outward. Glycon is the reputed inventor of a kind of logaœdic verse. Bivalves have snouts. Biology, around the time of the Council of Trent, insisted that the vein of the fourth finger of a *fiancée's* hand led to the heart. Does that square me scholastically with your daughter, Rarick?" said Gerkes, irritated or stimulated to a point of loquacity that took his breath away.

"I think it must be wonderful," said Jennifer, widening her eyes at him, "to be wise enough to play dumb. I'm always trying to be not too dumb to play wise. It can't be got away with."

"Nothing of the sort," championed her mother. "You've a good brain. Jennifer is a graduate of Miss Pratt's, Doctor Gerkes."

"Yes, and I would have gone to college, Doctor, but I would have been sure to fall in love with all my professors under forty, and it would have been so complicated."

Gerkes told a none-too-chaste tale then from the *Cent Nouvelles,* about a lady and a certain three lovers.

"He's a nasty old *roué,*" said Jenny to herself, although she had rocked with laughter through far more pointless tales when her table blazed with friends of her own choosing.

"By the way, Rarick, there's an idea behind the story I just told that ought to interest you. Louis Sixteenth, to whom the authorship is attributed, goes on to relate that this lady, while bathing, lost her diamond ring. While diamonds were undoubtedly not common at this time, it proves, however, that the stone which Henley picked up for you at Bruges, could easily date back to at least 1460."

"By Jove! So it could! It also proves that they faceted their stones back in those days, too, now doesn't it? That's a mighty interesting point. That's what I mean, Jennifer, by the historical value of inanimate things."

It was Rarick's way of attempting to justify to his daughter the telling of the *risqué* story. "Even at his worst, the talk of Gerkes mattered, which was more than he could say of the endless sluices of it that roared through the Rarick functions," was what he was desperately and in his clumsy, antagonizing way, trying to convey to Jennifer.

And strangely enough, Jennifer's reaction to one whom she might just as readily have regarded as a vile old bore, was as rare to herself as it was to Rarick.

After coffee, when the candles softened down closer to their reflection in the long fine pool of table, and Jenny, maneuvering to extricate her daughter from the vise of a dull evening, suggested that she accompany her to the last act of "Louise," for which a pair of tickets were going begging, there was hesitation from Jennifer. She knew that after the opera they were sure to join up with the Chadwicks and the Edgertons for dancing at Florentine's. Except for the seductive fact that Berry Rhodes might also be in the party, and Berry could tango like the Argentine Republic, Jennifer for the moment, wanted to remain around the pool of quiet talk and quiet candlelight and the slow syrupy flow of liqueurs and the intellectual luster of this dim old fogey, Gerkes.

Except there was that seductive possibility that Berry might drop in at Florentine's . . .

"I'm glad you're going to stick around," she told Gerkes, when she gave him her hand in good-night.

"Doctor Gerkes has promised to make this his home indefinitely."

"Let me come up, will you, and get on to some books to read and some things to think about?"

"Come up and I'll show you a manuscript of the ninth century, which I am translating for a library in Cologne. It will make the hottest sex-novel in your library look like a juvenile book."

"I think you're immense. You keep your feet nice and pedicured, because I am going to sit at them. Do you think you can convert a sow's ear into a silk purse?"

"I might find I have a silk purse to start with, and what if I should unwittingly reduce it to a sow's ear?"

"Father, where *did* you find him!"

"Dr. Gerkes will tell you for himself tomorrow evening, if you will join us."

"Have a footstool ready for me every evening, Doctor Gerkes. I'm going to try a new way of showing myself a good time. My present one is a flop. Until tomorrow . . ."

Poor Jennifer. She meant it. But, as a matter of fact, she saw him exactly two subsequent times, that high-exciting and excited winter of her twenty-third year. Once when muffled from her knees to the tip of her nose in an ermine-and-sable wrap, she had rushed downstairs between two young men who were making noises with their teeth like ukuleles, just in time to nod to Gerkes as he came out of her father's library with a stack of books in his hand.

The second time, she had seen him quite crazily, through a keyhole. She was never to be quite clear about that, however. It was six o'clock in the morning, and she had been "on a party" with Berry Rhodes. The door before which she had crouched had lurched about so; and so had the figure of Dr. Gerkes, seen crazily through the keyhole.

J ENNY, standing before a full-length, three-sided mirror, did an uncharacteristic thing. She removed from the front of her peignoir of coffee-colored lace, a small cascade of ruffles, which left her chest bare, daubed powder on to the V, and then stood off to survey. Her bathroom, an enormous one guiltless of tile, cleverly disguised in rugs, taffetas, a sunken bathtub with growing plants on its coping, and porcelain water-birds on little stands against a background of glazed Chinese wall-paper, reflected her figure over and over again. There was no angle from which she could not contemplate herself. Profile. Semi-profile. Full front. Back. She bent into them all, surveying. She was the angular type of woman that wears high neck-ruffs well. She owned dog-collars of jewels; principally pearls with vertical bars of sapphires, emeralds, diamonds, or jade. She need not have feared for her neck and shoulders. It was just that, somehow, the close collar, the narrow cuff, the high ruff of fur at the hands and wrists and neck, gave Jenny what air of distinction she could claim. Tall, narrow, her high coiffure boldly revealing her ears and planes of cheek, there was something studiedly, if remotely, Bernhardtian about Jenny. At least she grasped at the wisp of resemblance and pandered to it for all it was worth.

Yet, standing before the mirror, holding the cascade of coffee-colored lace alternately against her chest and then removing it, she finally decided to leave it off, feeling strangely not herself as she did so.

As a matter of fact, she was not herself. So strangely not herself that once she crossed her arms over her flat chest and hugged her shoulders in an exultant little fashion.

The no-longer-to-be-evaded truth of it was that Jenny, whose impeccable wifehood, extending over a period of twenty-three years, had been an easy virtue, was excited away and beyond her usual and curiously volatile air of composure, by the fact that a young Argentine, named Ramond Lopez, was coming in for a five-o'clock cocktail with her in the conservatory.

It had been arranged in the hurried breaking up of a party at the Ambassadeur the previous afternoon. Abbey Chadwick had asked twenty to tea and dancing, including young Lopez, who was said to be a paid dancer at Florentine's, a gigolo of exalted type who mingled socially by virtue of his connections, but who, nevertheless, was paid by the management. He had sat next to Jennifer at the Ambassadeur and had coaxed her to attempt a tango which she had never before ventured on a public floor. He and a Spanish girl professionally known as Cleo, had danced two Brazilian ballroom numbers at one of Jennifer's dinner dances a few weeks previous, and been paid handsomely for it.

The son of a partially defunct coffee king, whose fortune had been spent in defending his daughter Bianca from the charge of having shot and instantly killed her young *roué* of a millionaire husband as he was leaving his racing-stable, Ramond's anomalous position kept him hovering precariously between two worlds. He had been a mere lad in school, in Switzerland, at the time of the notorious case of Bianca Lopez Dakin, but the swift tides of family fortune, the death of his father, a little later the death of Bianca, and the paltriness of his inheritance, had swept him from Rio Janeiro. He was any young man with a dancing-figure and a personable air.

It was said of him, as it was said of his kind, that women contributed chiefly toward his support. Possibly. It is certain, however, that Jenny, whose social world was a happy hunting-ground for the hired or more subtly rewarded gigolo, had never bartered in the strange coin of that realm except in the out-and-out terms of signing checks to paid entertainers for services rendered and received. The case of Ramond had been different from the case of Nemo, the case of Tom and Dick and Harry, only to the extent that he had occasionally been present in social capacity at functions where she and Jennifer dined or danced.

It had all come about so suddenly that it seemed to Jenny her confused senses must be playing her a prank. As tidy about her emotions as she was about the objects on her dressing-table, and more and more given of late years to going about to all occasions and functions without Rarick, the man beside her at dinner or in an opera box or with whom she danced, catalogued readily according to these tidy emotions.

Whatever Rarick might hold against her, Jenny was given to reminding herself, infidelity by word or action, as wife, or mother to his children, could never be one of his indictments.

The former, on those not infrequent occasions when she brought this subject to the fore, Rarick let rest uncontroversial; but the latter, which was scarcely true to Rarick, was more than he could hear without rebuttal. The very fact that Jenny's children adored her, caused him to contend bitterly that she misused her power by smothering them beneath bracelets and shields.

Be that as it may, here was Jenny now, standing before her mirror, hugging her shoulders and shaken to the very foundation of that temperamental frigidity which had always stood her in such good stead. Ramond Lopez, cross between a gigolo, and somebody or other's tame robin, and who taught the tango for fifteen dollars a lesson at Palm Beach during the season, had suddenly walked devastatingly into her consciousness. She could trace its inchoate beginnings back to the night of Jennifer's dinner dance, when he and the Spanish girl, the fellow Nemo and a beautifully sinuous little Russian, had alternated in exhibition dances. Later Ramond had asked her to sit out a tango with him in Rarick's conservatory, of all places! A brackish retreat, this erstwhile breakfast-room, of hot-smelling soils and difficult pottings in Osmunda leaves and sphagnum moss, and which was devoted almost exclusively to orchid plants imported from Brazil and Japan. In the various processes of their hybridization, they were seldom, as Jenny and Jennifer were constantly complaining, sufficiently presentable to save them florist's expenditures.

Jenny was not the one to invite the highly special attentions of slim young men with Latin eyes. She danced with them, dined, and cocktailed, even flirted in that rather excited brittle manner of hers; but, outside of that, her slate was clean. The security of that state of her mind was unconsciously apparent in the thrust of her clean scimitar-thin features.

A young wag of a society writer for a caustic weekly had described Jenny's face as two profiles pasted together. It was enormously apt. Lopez, at Jennifer's dance, had sat among the unflowering hybrids of Rarick's odontiodes, cypripediums, and other curious orchids of purely botanical interest, and with his immediate eyes covering her face like a mask of sweet ether, had solemnly refuted this delicious indictment, paying her, instead, breathy compliments that somehow failed to arouse her usual sure-fire ability to laugh a bad boy cruelly into his place.

At Ramond's lispings, something starved in Jenny

had lifted its desolate head. Excepting for the months of courtship, when an eager, rather timidly idealistic young clerk had wooed the intelligent-looking Jenny Avery on the "chigger"-infested banks of the Meramac, there had been precious few words, except in platitude, addressed warmly and closely into Jenny's eyes.

Almost immediately after her marriage, the alienating affair of the twenty-five hundred had mattered terribly in their relationship.

Bitter with having given, bitter with having allowed himself to accept, once Rarick had seen her reaction set in, the honey dried out of the brief flower of marriage.

No, it had been many a day since close, fervent things had been said to Jenny. Ramond had made her suddenly and hurtingly aware of it. Something in her had thawed and was aching. Ramond, half her age, had interpreted her with a melancholy kind of wisdom.

"Why do you try to deceive me, as you do the others, with your icy manner?" he said to her, with the slight accent that lifted his lips in a flare off his square white teeth.

"My dear boy," she said, starting to be brittle and annihilating in the cocksure way she had, "you are now in the act of telling me how misunderstood I am."

To her surprise, he was neither annihilated nor subdued. He caught both her slim cool wings of hands, half-buried under wrist-ruffs, in the grip of his own.

"You must not talk like that to me. You do not mean what you say. You are the most interesting woman that I know. One cannot bear to be in the company of the insipid young girls, once he has known you. Do not pretend, Mrs. Rarick, that you need to be told that you are fascinating. Sometimes I think you are as Dante would have been if he had been beautiful and a woman.

Sometimes I think you are most like Bernhardt. Then I think you are like the best of both of them."

"Why, you foolish boy!" she said, the words, from lack of conviction, slow and stiff on her lips. American men simply did not look at one like that. They had not the eyes. . . .

"I want to see more of you, Mrs. Rarick. I want to know you. Am I impertinent ———"

He was.

"—or just one more admirer. After all, I cannot be what you call in America, such a 'total loss,' Mrs. Rarick, or I would not have the good sense to recognize so quickly a brilliant and worth-while woman when I see one. It is easy to dance with your beautiful girls over here—but they are not so nimble with their brains as with their feet and tongues. Am I impertinent?"

He was. Yet how amusing of him! Here was no mere patent-leather-haired gigolo, with a gift for wearing evening clothes and making middle-aged women horrible. Impudent of him to have insinuated his fingers up under the fur cuff of her long, tight sleeve—in flames—she did not withdraw them ———

There was a letter between Jenny's bodice and her flesh, as she maneuvered before the mirror. It was a line from Ramond, confirming what had been the hurried arrangement for this afternoon's cocktail.

Lest you forget what is unforgettably important to me. This afternoon at five, where the orchids dare not bloom for fear of comparison.

RAMON.

The "d" off the "Ramon" had somehow excited her more than the note itself. She was aware, as she sat up that morning in bed and put the square white envelope back on her breakfast tray, that her legs, which were stretched between the sheets, were trembling and would have doubled under her had she attempted to stand. The place at her side, with the covers folded back by Rarick, as he had risen from his night there, was still dented with his body. Through the years, there had been no gesture from either of them to alter these arrangements in any of their town or country homes, with the exception of the camp in the Adirondacks, where the women's quarters of *de luxe* simplicity were in one twenty-four-room log building, and the men's in another of equal size.

A wave of self-pity, not unmixed with anger, drenched Jenny as she sat and dipped strawberries-in-November, into a small brown bowl of sour cream. What a starveling she must be, if just the ordinary homage and admiration from a boy such as Ramon could bring about all this turmoil within her.

Why, in the last few years she and Rarick had left off even pecking each other good-night. She had been aware of it, and, in the spirit of letting the old cat die, had managed to seem asleep first, if they retired together, which was rare.

It was well over twenty years since the days when he had placed kisses against her lips when he came home evenings, or stretched himself out after dinner on a couch, holding her hand while she sat beside him and read aloud. Twenty years, or was it ever? There were limits to the memory of the flesh. The feeling of the print of caresses had long since died from Jenny's. Not that Jenny was a type to whom the end of every road was the arms of the man she loves. Her temperamental frigidity saw to that. And yet, suddenly sitting there in bed, the sense of desiring a great deal and being not desired, stabbed through her consciousness.

Life was passing her by. And for what? For nothing

more than a dumb-animal response to the instinct to abide by her sense of wifely duty. For what? For Rarick, to whom even her fidelity might be a matter of indifference? For her children? Bless them, they were no worse and possibly not much better than the average. Life was going to be bountiful to them. Jennifer would marry brilliantly. Avery, you somehow felt about him, even then, in his adolescence, was sure in some way to be as distinguished as he was rich. She would be crowded out of their lives. And then what? A specter of an old age with Rarick, whose eccentricities and cloistered habits were sure to grow upon him, stalked down a corridor of her imagination—then what? —— Thank God, thank God, it was still left in her to feel that cut of thrill at the left-off "d."

Ramon was coming.

She handed the small cascade of ruffles to the maid in the Breton cap and hurried out as if she dared not glance back at this symbol of the soiled inner workings of the mind of Jenny Avery Rarick, mother of two grown children.

Ramon was in the conservatory, poking about among goldfish which darted about a beautiful wall-fountain of Pulhamite stone that Rarick had brought over, with its lichen still clinging to it, from a rock-garden he had admired in Taormina.

He kissed her hand, lifting back some lace first, and then regarded her in long silence, a slight film of moisture across his eyes making them deeper.

The quick picture of half a dozen men she knew, including Rarick, flashed across her mind's eye. How clumsily they would have paid this same simple tribute. Mark House, an American who had been fabulously rich all his life and lived much abroad, always employed this continental greeting. But how clumsily, creaking where his shirt bent, and leaving the disagreeable feeling of smear across the knuckles. A Count Luckow, whom Jenny suspected of casting amorous eyes at Jennifer, who had only ridicule for him, had this habit gracefully. Rarick, somehow, would not visualize.

She could imagine that, to a young man like Ramon, whose masculinity was not mere maleness, there must be something chapped and a little funny about the unkissed hands of American women.

Twenty and more years of the perfunctory pats of greeting and adieu from Rarick had been Jenny's sole share in a world which she was suddenly aware must be filled with the grand passions between women and men. Not that anything she had not received from Rarick mattered, but the slow anger of resentment flared just the same.

Women who had been less meticulous than she about their marriage-vows were loved women. There were women of Jenny's acquaintance, of great wealth and social security, who had not been meticulous, whose wifehood was far from irreproachable, but who somehow had the gift of demanding full measure of homage from their husbands.

Precious little Jenny had demanded or received. A stab of self-pity, the immemorial self-pity of a woman feeling denied, cut Jenny. Rarick as a husband and lover! It was inconceivable that he could be missing in his turn any of those things he denied her. The lover had died back there in the beginning; and for the twenty and more subsequent years she had been living with a husband. What would even this Latin-eyed youngster, who was paying her pretty, slightly old-fashioned compliments, and letting his eye linger far too long on the spot where the insert of ruffles had been removed, think of her sterile kind of life if he knew? Really, his eyes, black-velvet ones of deepest nap, were naughty, roving as they did, from hers down to the tip of the V-neck which she had calculated before her mirror. A wave of self-disgust made her redden. With a prim reaction, over which she had no control, she suddenly felt stripped, and withdrew her hand, to clap it against her chest.

He regarded her with gentle reproach.

"Why are you like that?"

"Like what?"

"Shy, like a—like one of those beautiful wild pumas that used to live on the edge of one of my father's estates in the interior of Peru."

Puma! She did not know whether to laugh down what she regarded as his absurdity or incinerate him with the rebuff of which she was so capable.

"You don't understand the strange wild beauty of these graceful creatures. You must not think the comparison odious, Mrs. Rarick."

What were you to do with a boy like that, whose sweetness was indomitable?

They sat on the coping of the fountain, against a backrest formed by a Malaga-grape vine the thickness of an arm. Delicate Asia Minor aconite crawled along the coping; and even though not one of Rarick's hundreds of species of orchids was at the moment in bloom, an overheated air of exotic humidity prevailed.

"You're a silly boy for making me indulge your whim for a cocktail in this ridiculous conservatory of my husband's, where nothing ever really blooms, but unpronounceable, unwearable species and expensive botanical things are always about to happen and somehow don't. Except by the time orchids are ridiculously cheap at every corner florist's."

The impersonal portion went sailing over his head.

"I know it is only a little glass house, but it cannot

ever seem quite that to me, since it is where you first let me dare know you a little better."

"I'm afraid, dear boy, there is nothing to know. If I am still water, I am not only the kind that doesn't run deep, but perhaps the kind that doesn't run at all."

"You do not expect me to believe that."

No, she did not, but she said it again.

"You are a liberal education to me."

"How liberal?"

"I am tired of all your pretty girls here in this country who have no faces in particular. You have a face."

"My dear boy, are you given to profound observations like that?"

"You must not make me ridiculous. I mean you have a face that hangs like a cameo in the memory."

She looked at him, and, through the glazed fabric of a skin that did not easily take the flush, blushed with the surprised sweetness of a girl.

"You naughty Latin boy. I am old enough to be your mother."

"I am glad, though, that you are not. Fancy the tragedy of having to be no more than son to Duse or Cleopatra or Bernhardt."

"My boy doesn't feel that way," she said, clambering back to what safety-ledge she could.

"Don't say that."

"What?"

"It hurts me."

"What?"

" 'My boy'—in that tone. I am jealous, Mrs. Rarick —not of him—but of all the life that has claim on you ——"

She had the impulse to rise and rebuke him, and, instead, permitted his hand to wander again toward the thick fur ruffs at her wrists. Then a butler served cocktails, and they were silent and at nice distance while he puttered; but the eyes of young Lopez, above the three cocktails he tossed off, were over her face with the sweetishness of an anæsthetic mask.

"I'm going to send you along home now," she said, and rose. There were no lights, and a thick hush of November snow was falling against the glass walls, closing them in.

"I don't want to go home, Jenny."

Jenny. The plushy way he had of saying that. The impertinence of his saying that. The dearness . . .

"I don't want to go home, Jenny, without something to tide me over until next time." That plushiness in his speech was not from the effect of the three cocktails, but from an excited lisp, adorable to her, that seemed to crowd his speech.

"Impertinent," she said, frightened, in an exultant way beyond anything that had ever happened to her, and putting out a stiff arm to ward him off.

He used the arm as a lever to draw her toward him. To the silence of the big white flakes that were pasting themselves against their glass inclosure, he dipped the back of her neck against his arm and sank his lips down on to hers.

RACING home from a charity bazaar, where she had raffled off character dolls with conspicuous success, to change her clothes for a tea dance at the St. Regence, a surprise awaited Jenny.

Avery was home.

An envelope addressed in his large free hand was handed her by the maid in the Breton cap.

DEAR MOTH:

Hullo! Surprise, eh what? I'll wait in my bedroom until you pop in on me.

Av.

Avery home!

The first thought that flashed through Jenny's mind, as she stood with the note dangling among her purse and gloves, flooded her with such self-disgust that, on the very heels of it, she went hurrying to Avery's room, as if in expiation, the enormous sable coat that wrapped her from eyes to knees still dangling back off her slight shoulders.

If only she had gone straight from the bazaar to the St. Regence, without having bothered to come home and change into a taupe Lanvin gown with a high neck-ruche of chinchilla that Ramon liked. It made Ramon nervous to wait. Actually gave him indigestion, which asserted itself in little splotches of pink across his forehead. High-strung. . . .

A lump of mortification was in Jenny's very soul as she sped to her son. Was Avery ill? Crazy thought, but this was the first time she had seen Avery in the two months since—Ramon. Would he—could he—sense anything different? No. No. No. She need not reproach herself where her children were concerned. She had been plugging harder than ever for Avery's speedboat. Would—Avery—being home—make a difference to Ramon? He had never seen her with her boy. With Jennifer, now, it was different. With that not-to-be-resisted lisp of his when he attempted to employ the idioms of American slang, he called them the "Flip sisters." But Avery—Avery, though only sixteen, had a grave, rather precious quality. His blond straight youth, while boasting a maturity of appearance that matched some of the young fellows who trailed around Jennifer, was shot through with the most knowing perceptions. Would Avery, with those curiously delicate perceptions, sense that in the two months since she had seen him, strange, turbulent, and high emotions had been sluicing through the slim being of his mother?

How annoyed Rarick would be if something only casual were bringing Avery home in the midst of his semester. He had come down so flat-footedly against it. Surely Avery could not be ill. . . .

He was standing in a striped-flannel dressing-gown, tamping tobacco into his short-stemmed pipe, when his mother entered. The contents of a large pigskin bag, good accouterments, littered the room. A portable phonograph was open on the table, with a disk on, and a needle in position.

"Good for you, Mother! I was afraid it might not be you. Peacock tells me father often gets home nowadays around four."

"Avery, you're not ill?"

"Nothing so pleasantly explanatory of my sudden return to the magnificent fold of the family," he said, giving his parent a lift off the floor as he kissed her.

"Avery, you're not in trouble of any sort?"

"Not the kind you think."

"What other kinds are there?"

"Deep psychological fee-fie-fo-fum ones."

"Avery, don't tell me you've started to be foolish about a girl—or anything like that," she cried, flashing a glance, even in the suspense of her sudden suspicion, to her wrist watch.

"No, I'm off women," he said, with elaborate grandeur and innocence of them, that made her take his long, pale cheeks between her hands and kiss him.

"Darling, tell me what has brought you home in this sudden fashion. You know how set your father is against it, since all those supper dances we used to drag you in for. Tell me, son, I've only a moment between appointments."

"Mother, be a brick and cancel. How can I talk to you if you've only a moment? I must see you before father comes in. Please manage."

She stood fluttering between her indecisions. After all, the important thing was that Avery was well. Some schoolboy predicament no doubt, that seemed enormous enough to the schoolboy living it. Ramon hated to wait. Waiting acted as an actual physical depressant upon him, from which he was slow to recover. Jenny had learned that. Their most violent quarrel had resulted from her arrival twenty minutes late at a small tea-room in West Seventy-sixth Street which they were beginning to frequent for its obscurity. Women who took tango lessons of Ramon learned quickly, too, that to keep him waiting was to receive only desultory and sullen attention, instead of the subtle thrills they came for and paid for.

Jenny's virtue as wife and mother had been founded on no principle of life or religion. That she happened to possess it up to now had apparently been a matter of no counter-forces sufficiently strong to imperil it. Raging to see Ramon, who in five minutes would be beginning his wait for her, Jenny regarded this slender choirboy-faced son of hers, while turmoils battered her. He was not an easy son. Never had been. There had been long and frequent sieges of difficult child-illnesses and curious phases of mental reserve. His schooling had not been an easy matter to settle, what with his father's desires, the boy's, and her own. She had won her points, where Avery was concerned, too slowly to have them appear won.

The years at Newberry, and now his freshman year at Eastern, had drawn Avery out of his reticent, inhibited, boyhood precisely as she had predicted they would. Avery was pretty much of a regular fellow now. He had "made" the right fraternity. The son of a former Vice-president of the United States had sponsored him for K. A. K.; and the Avery who used to hide from his riding-master and feel squeamish in a rowboat now rode his own polo mount and did not remonstrate at Jenny's high desire for him to own a speed-boat. As a child he had feared water.

Yes, Avery was pretty much of a fellow now. In fact, she was fond of admitting, a little slyly and with innuendo that was without foundation, that he was too much of a fellow.

"Boys will be boys" flowed in relief off the lips of Jenny, who had spent her quota of time doubting if her boy would. Ah yes, boys nowadays knew how to handle their love-affairs, various tooth-cutting amours and indiscretions, as skilfully as they knew how to handle their cars. That was to presuppose that Avery had always handled his, just that casually.

Avery, always more or less at shy odds with life, with

his father, and even with Jenny herself, had not been the
gay and uncomplex youngster that Jennifer had been.
Even now he was sometimes dark and turgid water to
her. Had she failed him as confidante on those occasions when he had seemed to want to grope his way
into her understanding of this or that plight of his?
Chiefly psychological ones that she had found it hard to
comprehend. She had read books on adolescence. In
a vague way, they accounted.

Once, on one of his Easter vacations from Newberry,
Avery, to whom his mother was by far the happiest
aspect of his holidays, had tried to read her excerpts from
a very private journal which he had kept for three years,
and which locked with a key he kept on a chain with his
fraternity symbol.

She had felt deeply the spirit which prompted the confidence, but was conscious of having failed miserably to
understand what to her had seemed the rather embarrassing vaporings of a young mind floundering to climb
out of some sophomoric morass. It was a phase of
adolescence, she concluded, as she dismissed the sense of
failure that had followed these private disclosures of
some of the mental travail of her son. No one could
quite be expected to be able to comprehend the tortuous
and tortured workings of the adolescing mind. From
the books she had read, it would be rather abnormal to
find Avery normal at this stage. All would work itself
out. As a matter of fact, of course, a boy's father was
the proper confidant at such times. . . . But secretly,
Jenny gloried in her strategic position in the minds and
hearts of both her children. It was a sort of trump card
up her sleeve; it was the writing on the wall of who was
who.

Was she about to fail again of her coveted place in
the eyes of her son? If Avery were impelled to once

more put before her the difficult and even embarrassing torments of his expanding and maturing mind, would it not be better, after all, to evade the issue, than to fail in it?

Let Avery have it out with his father! Let them become acquainted and find a common language. It was not even fair to continue to stand as buffer between them. Great responsibilities, that had to do with his father, were ultimately to descend upon this young boy. Better to try to have him cross the stormy Niagara gorge that divided the two of them.

But, in her heart, Jenny knew that the source of all this hurried disposition of her immediate predicament was the fact that Ramon was waiting. He must be chewing at his lip now, and sliding in and out of the waistcoat pocket that lay against the slim torso of his dancer's body, a platinum-and-diamond watch, the thickness and diameter of a silver dollar. Jenny's first gift to him.

"Mother, I know I'm putting the cart before the horse, to try and make you understand the result first, and then give you the reasons that led up to the decision, but the fact is, I'm done with college."

Then it *was* something schoolboyish! Let him have it out with his father. Eastern was the ideal college for a son of the rich. Important connections. Socially right. Proper setting. Rich men with sons about to inherit vast responsibilities, chose Eastern for their boys. Ramon was waiting ten minutes by now. High time Avery and his father were making each other's acquaintance.

"You talk as if such decisions were a matter of course, Avery. I'm surprised."

"I knew you would be, Mother. That's why I want like the dickens to talk to you before the explaining to father begins. Or maybe you'll talk to him, Mother?"

"I cannot always be taking sides with you against your

father, Avery. After all, he is your father and my husband, and must be respected."

That, ever since the advent of Ramon, was part of
her new psychology of atonement to her husband. She
had applied it directly to Rarick the few weeks just
passed, causing him no surprise in particular, because
he was no longer sensitive to her doings. Her son, however, looked up at her in almost startled surprise.

"Out of whose book of life have you torn a new page,
Mother? Not your own?"

Now he was going to be abstract! That was the difficulty about being able to understand Avery. It made
her proud of what she was pleased to call his depth; but,
just the same, he was at the stage where he was forever
vaporing about life. As such. It was a thoroughly concrete affair to Jenny, life was. Witness the precise situation of Ramon waiting for her. It was hard to treat life
as a generality. You talked about your own life, of the
life of some one in whom you were passionately interested. Just life as a subject was sermon matter, or something you did not discuss except under precious circumstances.

"You've only three more years at Eastern, Avery.
There is something about the idea of a college degree!
It's an asset in after-life. Avery T. Rarick. Century
Club, Racquet Club, Eastern Club. It's fine to hear one
man say of another, 'We finished at Eastern together.
We made the polo teams together at Eastern!'"
(Ramon was capable of going off, after waiting a half-
hour.)

"Mother, I want a couple of years to myself."

"Yourself?"

"Yes. Alone. Mother, I want terribly some time to
myself. In Europe. On my own. I imagine Paris is
as good a place as any for a place to get one's bearings.

Or, better still, some off-the-beat places like Sicily or
Greece. I'm fed up. College is all right for a certain
sort of fellow; I'm wasting my time at it."

"That's ungrateful, Avery. I've almost won your
father over about your boat."

"Mother, I need to tell you a few things about myself.
I'd have told you long ago, you're so sweet. But you
dodged; and I do hate like the dickens to say them . . ."

Then it was to be in the key of the writings in that
locked journal of his. Darling, silly adolescent! Ramon
was waiting.

"Avery, I cannot stand the strain of the rôle of go-
between for you and your father any longer. Isn't it manlier for you to face him yourself? This is too serious
for me. You yourself must ask him for what you
want ———"

"Why, mother, do you know I've never really wanted
anything before? It is you who have always wanted for
me. That's what makes it impossible for me to really
get at father. He thinks I'm the fellow who has wanted
all the things I've never really wanted."

So! It had come home to her. So much sooner than
she could have dreamed. It was for this she had practically alienated her husband, worn down her vitality,
sacrificed her peace of mind. From the very infancy of
her children, Jenny had been fighting for what she wanted
for them; and here was her son interpreting it for her
in a way that robbed her of any of the fruits of sacrifice.

"Avery Rarick," she said, with everything reproach-
ful in her voice that she could muster, "I cannot believe
my ears."

"Mother dear, you mustn't take it that way! Let me
explain."

Ramon was waiting.

"Listen, dear, I must ———"

"Mother, I haven't hopped on to this decision today or yesterday. I'm everybody's total-loss at college, dear."

"That's a pretty disheartening thing to have to hear, after the long wrangle I had with your father, who wanted a state university. Really, Avery ——"

"I'd be no go at any college, Mother. It's hard as the devil to try to explain—even to you."

"Yes, Avery," she said, mashing out a cigarette off which she had taken two puffs, and trying to bite down an impatience that was almost a frenzy within her; "I should think it might be." Ramon was waiting.

"Mother, what do you think?"

"I can't. I don't," she said, and pressed her eyeballs.

"Mother, for the last six months I've been carrying only one course at college. You might as well know and have it over with."

"You've made excellent connections. Donnie Chattenfield told Jennifer that Hal is inviting you to White-castle for the Christmas holidays."

"Mother, doesn't that surprise you?"

"Why should it? The Chattenfields weren't always as socially secure as they are now. I ——"

"I mean, doesn't it surprise you that I've only carried one course, and that a dead-cat one in current events?"

"Of course it does ——"

"It doesn't really, old darling, because you've never thought about it one way or another. But anyway—even my address at college has been a fake one, Mother. I've faked."

"Avery!"

"I haven't lived on the campus for six months. The college canning-factory began to tin my brains, so I moved out of it. I've rooms up on the hill with an artist and his wife."

"Why, Avery Rarick, how could you!"

"It's the only thing I could do, Mother. I'm not cut out for the college-factory. Matter of fact, if I am cut out for much of anything, I haven't found out yet what it is. That's what I want to talk about. You've been such a brick getting Father to put up with me, that it's kind of rotten to bring this home to you after the way you maneuvered for Eastern. But it would have been the same at Penn, or whatever state university it was Father preferred. It isn't that I haven't been working. I have—after a fashion—worked, if you'd call it that!"

"Oh, Avery, don't meander. Talk to the point."

"Right, Mother. I mean, I've been scribbling. Writing a little. Verse and stuff. Pretty rotten. Wouldn't like to see it, would you? Might give you a better idea of why I think a couple of years on my own—knocking about Europe—alone—alone—would put me straight—with things. Mother, you're not listening!"

She lifted her tormented eyes to him, which for the moment she had closed against the milling of her inner frenzy, and made the pretense of having heard.

"That is all stuff and nonsense, Avery. You are to bide your time at college, and next summer take that trip to Norway and Sweden with the Stanley-Blake twins."

"I don't give a damn for those saps, Mother."

" 'Those saps,' as you are pleased to call them, will some day be two of the most powerful men in America."

"I tell you I need to be alone, Mother. To find myself."

"Oh—Avery ——"

"I know! I sound like a letter to a newspaper. Well, I'm capable of writing one like this. 'Editor, *Daily Bunk*. Dear Sir: What should a young man of seventeen years of age do who simply cannot get interested in life as he sees it about him. I cannot find myself. Everything becomes disgustingly monotonous. Not interesting enough to call for any real effort. I'm a perfect failure to date, and unless I pull out, may remain so for the rest of my days on this supposedly glorious earth. Everything about me is as interesting as a morgue, where I am concerned. What's wrong with this picture?'

"Letter from Editor to Morbid Young Man: 'Your symptoms, young man, include indifference to whatever you do and the belief that a congenial task would reveal your hitherto unappreciated values. As you see the world, it is sadly out of joint, and you wonder why others are so indifferent to the pearl of great price hidden in your personality. Young man, behind your inability to connect with life, lurks an egregious self-centeredness and an exaggerated idea of your own consequence.' "

"Avery, I can't bear it. You're too funny to be borne. Stop it, idiot! How can one take you seriously?"

"But I am serious, Mother. I'm clowning Hamlet for you."

How slenderly handsome he was, his father's son around the eyes and brow, but son of his mother in the lean, lithe figure. As he sat there on the edge of the table, dangling one long cleverly-clad leg, and showing, as if to excellent stage-direction, his clean blade of profile, he was like one of those well-made youths in English society-comedies.

"Avery, I simply must go. My advice to you is to pack yourself back to college without even letting your father know about this—brainstorm."

"Mother, I'm in hell!"

"Then you *are* in some trouble, son," she cried out, a sudden terror dilating her eyes.

"I know, Mother, I know, it all sounds like tommyrot," he cried, and struck his breast with a gesture that immediately became sophomoric to her, once he followed it up with words. "But can't you understand? The hell is here inside me. I must get away. Alone. To think— it out —— It's too cluttered up here. I can't stand the clutter. I'm sick of being me. And doing the things a fellow has to do if he is me. Give me a year or two on my own, Mother. Get Father to. I want to think. I want to think my way out. . . ."

"Of what?"

"How do I know? How can I try to tell it, when you sit there thinking of other things. When you won't understand."

How dear he was! How inexpressibly dear. Hurtingly young. Silly, sensitive, sophomoric dreamer. She had never seen him like this. At least not exactly like this. She wanted to take him in her arms. . . . Ramon was waiting.

"Mother dear, be a brick. Put it up to Father before I have to face the music. Make him see that I need a couple of years away—to myself ——"

"I simply must go, son."

"He'll never understand, Mother. Coming from me, the suggestion will only antagonize him. I can't be myself with Father—any more than I sometimes think he can be with me."

"Hush, Avery."

There was one principle of hers which Jenny had never even bent, much less broken. She could not bring herself to discuss her husband's shortcomings with his children.

"I must go!" she cried, wildly. "If you insist upon coming home from college with such ideas, son, it is manlier that you should face your father yourself. Tell him just what you have told me."

"I can't! I can't! You know that."

"Then begin to learn now. I cannot always be buffer between you. Tell him what you've told me."

"Not in a thousand years. He'll want facts. I haven't any."

"Here he comes. Tell him now."

"Mother, for God's sake! You wouldn't do that ———"

For the first time in her life, Jenny would. She was off and gone, down the corridor, frantic with haste, just as Rarick, attracted by his son's voice, paused at his door to peer in.

FOR several years now, Rarick had been cultivating this habit of extricating himself from his office at four o'clock in the afternoon. It was not easy, except that he had found that the closing of his multifarious day, whether at four or six or eight, was sure to leave an overflow of affairs to which he could not get around.

The year that Rarick instructed his chauffeur to enter his office at precisely the stroke of four, and, regardless of who or what might be present, hand him his hat, the force began to refer to him as "the old man."

As a matter of fact, it was Rarick's conclusion that these few precious hours of late afternoon which included the sedative one of twilight, if properly induced, could be made to stack upon the credit side of health and vitality.

His golf consisted of those hours spent in the forest-like silences of his library, where he read little, if at all, but where glyphs and triptychs; helmet and sword of Doge's guard; "Virgin and Child"; Auvergne art of the fifteenth century; pillars of stone decorated in Roman cups; red velvets inlaid wtih heraldic leopards, played effect after effect into his solitude.

He could sit in the dim splendor of this hall, and out would creep the mood to empty his pocket of its strange fires of stones of the earth and place them in smoldering rows along a strip of black velvet which he kept concealed behind the cushion of a divan. Out of his organ, "Father's Folly," there came pouring to his pressing of a button the storied action of "Tosca" or "La Bohème," told in the illuminated stained glass above the triple grin of keyboards. Musical cataracts that leaped in glory over the din of a day that had been lived to the tune of dishpans, hair-nets, lingerie ribbon, and forty thousand small dolls made out of imitation peach-skin from the Vermont factory. Countless and ever-fascinating devices lurked within the Gothic maw of this pretentious instrument. Symphony orchestras, Japanese bells, xylophones, bird-notes, and cymbals. Violin solos, sextettes, octettes, "Chimes of Normandy," Bach, Verdi, Guilmant, Handel, Saint-Saëns, Bonne, Mendelssohn, and a reproduction of the Vatican choir, with the lifted faces of the singing boys rising chastely above their surplices and glowing softly into stained-glass flesh.

To Rarick, who scarcely knew his son, there was something of Avery in these pale soprano boys, a look of spiritual contact, until he invariably jerked himself away from a comparison that, no sooner made, seemed ridiculous.

Avery, indeed! Speed-boats. Plus-fours. Oriental-pearl studs at seventeen. A growing suspicion that all was not open and above board about his college had been Rarick's. Something not quite *bona fide* about what Avery had to say about his life there ——

The suspicion moved up a notch at the sight of his boy, standing in the French-flannel dressing-gown, with the contents of his open bag scattered about the room, and the plane surface of his lean, pale face plastered with a look of panic that was positively grotesque as his father leaned in at the door. The flash of Jenny's sable coat, as she sped down the hall, had not been lost upon him, and now there came to him rather belatedly the consciousness that he had been hearing the dim patter of her and Avery's voices all the way along the corridor.

The thrill that he invariably experienced over this narrow young person he called son, shot through him before his first resentment had time to leap out.

Good youngster! A bit too thin. Needed filling out.

A bothered look to him. What made him gape like a fish that had just been landed, hook and all? The scent and the echo of Jenny still lay on the air. Conniving again, filling Rarick with a roiling sense of outsider in his own home. Heads together, the two of them had been shutting him out. Some scrape had brought him home, no doubt.

"Well, Father, here I am."

The little man stood in the doorway, shoulder-high to his seventeen-year-old son, head up, hand thrust into the groove between his coat buttons. After all, your prisoner was innocent until you proved him guilty. Illness, or whim, or unavoidable difficulty might have brought Avery home. Surely he would not dare to be showing himself in the midst of a school-week, for some of the nonsense frivolities Rarick had come down hard against, such as Jenny's plans for the social divertissement of the youngest set.

"This is a surprise, boy. At least to me," he could not help supplementing.

Hang it! Why had he added that? It threw the boy still further off his ease.

"I guess it is sort of a surprise to me, too Father. Hadn't particularly planned on coming, until I found myself driving down. One of those decisions a fellow kind of makes for a long time without knowing he's doing it. All of a sudden it's made! If you see what I mean."

"I see," said his father, in the polite tones of not seeing at all.

"Will you sit down, Father?"

The boy did have oyster-shells under his eyes. Ill-health? Dissipations? Well? What?

They seated themselves, facing each other, on two straight chairs. It occurred to Avery miserably, as he swept one of them clear of a litter of his belongings, that he and his father were forever facing each other on straight chairs.

With his tongue as thick as a rusk in his mouth, the determination to unbend came flooding over him. A fellow had a right to some kind of a decent break with his father. Old gentleman wasn't God. Regular enough fellow, no doubt, if you once broke through the crust. Crusty with crust, though, no doubt of that. Low-down of mother, to leave him flat—but here goes.

"You see, Father, here's the situation," began the son of Rarick.

They were going to get on! Sometimes a man and his boy just naturally came to a place where they began to get on. Avery was old enough now to understand. . . .

"I'm mighty anxious to hear it, son."

Now that was a handsome enough beginning of the old gentleman! Many a fellow and his 'gov', after starting it off on the wrong foot, had hit a pace. Not a bit improbable but what the old gentleman might be the one to understand more quickly than anyone else, that a fellow needs to somehow—get his balance. God, though, could anyone understand, except the fellow himself who was living through this particular hell?

"The situation is this, Father."

"Yes, son." Patience. Patience. Shouldn't expect a lad to come directly to the point like a business man. What the dickens was the trouble with him? Bothered-looking boy, no doubt of that. Well, it was a good time to get at him. This fine, straight fellow on the chair before him was his son. The pleasurable years were about to begin. The time had come to draw this boy into his life. This boy was no stranger. This boy was his!

"Yes, son?"

"The situation is this, Father." What in the name of Heaven was the situation? Sitting there, facing his

father, frantic for point of contact, now-or-never blazing
in his bright blue eyes, words seemed to log-jam back
in Avery's throat.

You didn't sit opposite one of the titan business men
of the country—of the world, for that matter—and tell
him that your soul was hurting you. You didn't sit opposite the director of a string of banks, a merchandise
king of two continents, the biggest individual dispenser of
pins, Eskimo pies, and ink-erasers in the world, and tell
him of the strange torments, the nervous panic, the de-
spairs, the ecstasies, the strange stirrings of the desire to
love and be loved, or the yearnings for some power to express the wonder and the pain of those first faint stirrings. You didn't sit opposite a small, literal man called
your father, whose ideals were as well hung as his paint-
ings, and tell him that the world was a manhole into which
you felt yourself falling. It was one thing to pour forth
these torments and ecstasies and lonelinesses into your
journal, which locked, or into the trunk of verses that
were your own disembodied nerves, jangling away for
dear life. It was another to sit facing this small remote
man, your father. "The situation is this, Father."
What in God's name was the situation? One did not dare
to say to one's father, "Life is too much for me, Dad."
One did not quite dare bring to the point of discussion
the curiously recurrent thoughts of the lips of women
that were flashing through his torment . . . the desire to
create . . . the desire to live beautifully . . . the need
to be alone to work it all out. The confusion . . .
somewhere there was a father to understand . . . not
this father. And yet—strange little man—he liked his
organ with the horrible stained-glass operas. The fires
in the stones of the earth had witchery for him. The
salty wisdom and humor of the old fossil he kept up in
the yellow suite tickled and delighted him. What the devil

was the truth of this man, his father? What the devil was the truth of himself, Avery, sitting there in torment, idiotically repeating over and over again, "This is the situation, Father."

"Go ahead, son."

"As I had been saying to mother, just before you came in, or rather, it's been running through my mind . . ."

He and his mother had had their heads together as usual. She had been first in his confidence. This was the method cooked-up between them, of approach to the ogre. Damit! Jenny was a good mother, a more successful parent than he was, no getting around that; but a man was entitled to the first-hand confidence of his boy!

Was the old gentleman stiffening already?

Damit! damit! this boy was his. The only thing on earth he could look to train into being closely and intimately his. There were a hundred things he needed to begin to get said to this boy, if ever they were to begin to prepare for the intricate problems that lay ahead for both of them. A good way to begin was to give in. Why not on the speed-boat! That was what he was most probably wanting. Damned dangerous playthings of the rich. Speed-devices for going nowhere. Things. More things to alienate him from the power to be tranquil. The way to get at these youngsters, though—Jenny had the right idea—was to give them things. Things. The way to get at Avery was the way of indulgence. Youth wants indulgence.

"Well, I suppose if there is something you want, son, you're beginning to be of an age now where you've got to depend on your own good judgments."

"That's mighty fine of you to say, Father."

"I sometimes have my own ideas about these things, Avery. Some day, when you don't have to get back to college, we'll take time off and ——"

"But, Father ——"

"—talk some of these things out. We haven't ever had much to say to each other about you and your relationship to this big world you are preparing to grapple with. It's a bigger and more complex world than falls to the lot of most youths. I'd like to talk to you along those lines ——"

"But, Father, that's not what I want to ta ——"

"It's all right, son; I understand this may be a bit premature. No hurry. I think I know what's brought you down from college today. Want you to start back this afternoon."

"But, Father ——"

"Don't like sloppy attendance. Don't like sloppy anything. Wait a minute. Hold your horses. You're going back with what you came down for. I don't like speed-boats, as a general rule. Don't like speed-devices in general, when they've no other purpose than saving time that you don't know what to do with after it's saved. Nerve-racking. Extravagant. Dumb. But I figure you're getting to an age when your own judgments should count. I'm glad to give in. Is that all right with you, son?" said Rarick, and took out his check-book.

They sat there, knee to knee, in their straight chairs, their faces seeming to swim together as twilight came to blur them. Rarick, a sudden sliding blur to his son; Avery, a sliding blur to his father.

"Is it all right, son?"

"It's all right with me, Father—if it is with you—I guess."

"You guess?"

"I mean—it's all right with me, Father—if it is with you ——"

The pen of Rarick began to splutter along his check-book.

THE consciousness had long since begun to dawn upon Jenny, in whom the impulse to climb was an acquired, rather than an inherent characteristic, that she had started off, socially speaking, on the wrong foot.

The advent of the John G. Raricks, from out of the Middle West, had not been a planned campaign, for the reason that the need for strategy had simply not occurred to her until the propitious moment had passed and the house of Rarick had settled. Subsequently her mistakes had been fast and successive. After the dust of the publicity attending the purchase by John G. Rarick of the famous Ficke mansion had been laid, Jenny, appalled by the lull, had snatched, with more nervousness than diplomacy, at old relationships, mostly families of wealth and no particular social position, whose migration from the Middle West had preceded theirs.

Thereafter, the Raricks bobbed about in uneven waters, sometimes riding up to quite a social crest, but in an erratic, unstable way that was precarious, and then, just as likely as not, sliding down again into the valleys between the waves.

No gainsaying the fact that the Raricks were invited to six houses outside the social register for every one within. Jenny's awareness of social-register discriminations did not even begin to dawn upon her until well after the move, when that dawn came up like thunder.

The time was not slow in coming when she was to encounter the difficulty of rounding up a formal dinner composed of the people she came gradually to realize were the right ones, and when she was to scorch under such mortifications as sending out thirty-six invitations to the alleged right ones and have twenty-eight regrets come home to roost heavily upon her heart.

It was not exactly in the spirit of snubbing. The Raricks were not sufficiently in the running for that. It was just that in settings where even great wealth required proper exploitation, the Raricks had somehow not arrived right.

What brought this home with sudden acuteness to Jenny was the fact that the Isaac Slocums, whose wealth and social connections back in the St. Louis days, when they were neighbors in Westmoreland Place, were comparatively negligible, had moved East considerably after the Raricks, and were now moving securely and consistently in social circles which Jenny achieved only sporadically.

Betty Slocum's careful social sense had accomplished that. She had planned ahead. She had surveyed, and ended by employing, at a vast sum, the services of a woman of impeccable social position, whose chief financial resources flowed in bountifully in return for achieving a wedge for the socially ambitious. One of Jenny's sources of undying regret was the fact that at the time such services would have been invaluable to her, she had never even heard of the Slocum method of crashing the social gate.

There was no going back. The best that could be hoped for was less uneven sledding.

The mistake had rebounded most cruelly on Jennifer. Passionately Jenny had wasted heartburn on the futility of wishing that Jennifer and Avery had been born to her in reverse order. An eligible son, somehow, millions in his offing, would have accelerated social matters. As it was, Jennifer, always popular, whirled nevertheless in three worlds. A Bohemian one which her set invaded in "slumming-parties"; an outer-fringe one which represented wealth and perhaps a bit too much gayety; and, far too occasionally, the one within the walls which the Slocums had scaled by careful maneuver and which Jenny had mistakenly planned to hurdle by a running high-jump.

It was not, Jenny felt sure, that Rarick money could not have accomplished anything that Rarick money set out to do; it was that Rarick money had not taken its psychological moment.

These realizations began to marshal themselves into Jennifer's younger and more nimble mind the first year that she was out of Miss Pratt's School for Girls. To begin with, Miss Pratt's School had been a mistake. The daughters of millionaires attended all right, but not the daughters of the socially-right millionaires. Jennifer kept a stiff and even an impudent upper lip about it all, but in the seclusion of talks with her mother those lips of hers could drag at the corners.

"Where do they get off, leaving us out! I wouldn't give a plugged nickel to go to the Monkton-Beck's cotillion. I thought cotillions went out with bustles, anyhow. But what do you bet they don't forget father's name on their Joint-Disease Hospital subscription list?"

"Let them get it!"

"Don't be silly, darling. You know perfectly well Leila Monkton has as good as got you down for five thousand."

Jenny did. "Well, just the same," went on Jenny, whose eyes were heavy from a sleepless night over this same case of omission, "what can you expect? Your father never accepts an invitation of any sort. People don't know quite how to approach us, the women of the family always either asking permission to bring another man, or attending alone."

"Nonsense, Mother! Look at the Slocums. Does

their old man ever show himself? Look at the Tur-pitzes. The face of the husband and father of that family has almost become extinct. Fewer and funnier husbands is the social cry of the hour. Bring your own gigolo. Don't kid yourself along, darling, that's not the reason we're zero."

In the inelegant parlance of her daughter, that was precisely what Jenny was doing, casting about within her troubled spirit for some sort of satisfactory explanation of a position that was hourly becoming more enigmatical to her.

"There's nothing mysterious about it, Mother, we've treated the exact science of social climbing inexactly, that's all."

"But just the same, Jennifer, assuming that we are horrible people, with intellectual harelips and no 'g's,' this is a country where money is supposed to buy everything."

"And so it does, if you know how to go about spending it. Money will buy anything from a plush horse to an Aubusson tapestry. You're out of luck if you go after the plush horse when Aubusson tapestries are the swanky buy. We should have employed a social, interior-decorator to keep us from making mistakes such as cultivating plush horses, like the Ben Wimans or the Maxfield Doons. Not that I would give one blondined Wiman hair in order to crash into the Monkton cotillion. But just the same, you've got to know your onions."

"Do you know, I sometimes think," said Jenny, contemplatively, and with the crinkled look of continuing to break her head for more satisfactory explanation, "that there's such a thing as being too nice? There is nothing more ghastly than the hung-on smile of trying to be too amiable."

"Perhaps, socially speaking, darling, we haven't got 'It.'"

"Nonsense!" said her mother, regarding her with tilted lids of admiration. "You have every kind of 'It.'"

"Oh, I get by in a crowd. That is, if I can manage to care enough. I'm so damned half-baked! Even the desire in me to be something besides the thing I am is half-baked, or I'd go be it. I've got a brain, Mother."

"Use it, Jennifer," said her mother, regarding her through lids that were untilted now. "On Berry Rhodes."

"You're being disgusting, darling," said Jennifer, and rose to her height, stretching as a cat stretches, one arm climbing over the other.

"Don't be an idiot, Jennifer, you're too intelligent."

"In other words, the beautiful and reluctant daughter of wealth must jerk her family into social security by marrying the scion of a great family. What is a scion, anyway?"

"Jennifer, you're being coy. It's horrible."

"Honestly, Mother, you're the one who's being idiotic," cried Jennifer, and began to flush in waves.

"Berry is a person on his own, you've said so yourself. Why not come out and own you like him?"

"Why Mother, you pain and surprise me!"

"You're not clever in the rôle of *ingénue,* darling. A little awful, in fact."

"Well, all right, if you insist. He's a bad boy, but I like him. God knows why, but I do."

"You like him because you have the good sense to believe in my adage that it is as easy to fall in love with the right one as with the wrong."

"That adage gives me shivers down my spine. But then, so does Berry."

"Leslie Edgerton hasn't asked you to her dance to-night because she loves you."

"Mother, you continue to pain and surprise me."

"Berry got you asked there. She must have thought it the better part of wisdom not to refuse."

"It's all off there!"

"Are you sure, Jennifer?"

"That's the devilish part. I'm not."

"Jennifer, there's one thing I must say for your father. He never played for small stakes in his life."

"There was all that talk that Leslie's trip to Europe was a trip to Brooklyn to have a baby—Berry's."

"You know that if that were true, it would have been marry-the-girl at the point of the merciless Edgerton tongue!"

"Berry's a queer, evasive devil of a darling-on-wheels. I don't know where I get off with him."

"Find out."

"Of course he got me asked out to the Edgertons' to-night, but I don't give a damn. I'm going! With him. I like him, Mother. Hang it! I like him," said Jennifer; and, and to add to the horror of the sound of her own voice giggling in a key beyond her control, the laugh petered out suddenly and became a thin cry. "He's a bad boy, but, hang it! I like him."

"You know perfectly well that he is better than the average would be in his position. He has everything, and besides, a clever girl can settle him down. Jennifer, if you would!"

"You mean if I could."

"You can."

"I will."

THE great-grandfather of Leslie Edgerton had once been governor of a Confederate state. It had cost the grandfather of Leslie Edgerton one million and a half dollars to run on a foredoomed ticket for President of the United States.

The father of Leslie Edgerton had married a Miss Henrietta Crosby, of Crosby, Connecticut, and had retrieved the million and many more by subsequently inheriting, by proxy of this wife, the Crosby watch-factories.

The paths of the Crosbys and the Raricks crossed occasionally, chiefly at Bailey's Beach, public charity functions, bridges, bazaars, teas, and occasionally in a purely social way.

Jenny had ventured to include the Crosbys in what had been the largest dinner dance of the season, with which she had magnificently set the winter ball rolling the night after the opening of the opera.

The Crosbys had "regretted."

Jennifer had cried, with her usual irrelevant questionnaire, which she hurled, while smarting, at such situations, "Where do they get off? The Edgertons don't set my hair on fire."

Be that as it may, when the Edgertons regretted, one of the high-water-mark hopes for their dinner had fainted within Jennifer and her mother.

Leslie had sat opposite Jennifer at a Hunt Club subscription-luncheon two days later, and made no reference either to the occasion of the dinner dance itself, which had caused talk because of its elaborateness, or to her regrets.

That had somehow rankled in Jennifer more than the original refusal. It was as if, with a preciosity that was chiseled thinly into her face and lay along the delicate arch of her brows, Leslie had set about wounding a wound.

A Rarick had never set foot on Parmley, where the Edgertons kept open house all winter on their enormous estates skirting Tarrytown.

Jennifer was about to set foot there now. A small, bizarre-looking foot, in a white-fur sandal that was mounted on a four-inch ivory heel.

Parmley ran back into the Pocantico Hills. The house itself rose off a cleared eminence in the heart of four hundred heavily wooded acres. A terrace, tiled in bright blue, shone around it like a lake. Marble stairs, flanked with balustrades and lions, led to the blue-tiled terrace from lower ones of green turf. The building itself was a long low one, of enormous width, no particular depth, and a whiteness to it as if a Mediterranean sun were perpetually beating down. Some wag had tagged it "Carnegie Library" because of this low width and the pairs of Carrara lions that crouched beside the four flights of marble staircases.

The Edgertons had decided to have a sense of humor about this sixty-eight-room white elephant, which five years previous had been rushed to completion in time for Leslie's birthday. Henrietta Edgerton promptly christened it her "white *bête noire*" and had the coping of the superb swimming-pool, which was out of natural rock, elaborately inlaid in black and white symbolic beasts of two heads and four tails.

The white crash of this house into the finest stretch

of forest land within its radius from New York was a
sore point with Tom Edgerton. It had cost easily over
a million and a half, and there it stood, an affront to his
taste, his intelligence, and his dignity. It was the sort
of home a war millionaire might have erected out of an
overnight fortune.

Truth of the matter was, and bitterly he knew it,
Henrietta had been deep in an affair with the architect
who designed it.

Tom's sop to his sense of the ironic was to be unfaith-
ful to his wife, on every possible occasion, in this house
which had turned into a monstrosity because she had insisted upon giving *carte blanche* to her lover, the nincompoop young architect on dancing legs, who had created it.

"We're a pretty lot," Leslie Edgerton had once said
to her father, who, when in his cups, could laugh uproar-
iously at a remark he would slap her clear, heart-shaped
face for when sober. "We're a pretty lot, Dad. The
only thing virgin around here is the soil. If!"

Jennifer and Berry tilted into the three-mile driveway
of that virgin soil on two wheels at a sixty-mile clip.
They had driven out in Berry's underslung, boat-shaped
roadster. Jennifer at first had remonstrated, holding out
against cramming herself, in her slim sheaf of baby-ermine
gown, into a crouched position in the natty sports-car.

"You're a dog, Berry, to even ask it. I'm not dressed
for a football game."

"Come along. Be as boyish as your bob. I'll wrap
you in a raccoon coat, and that little white mitten you're
wearing for a dress won't turn a hair," he said, and
brushed aside a butler who had been holding some more
white ermine for her to slide arms into, during the
twelve minutes of this controversy.

She liked his riding her down this way. Old cave-man

stuff, she told herself. Putrid-old. But she liked it. Wasn't often a fellow with millions, only grandson of a personage like old Rodney Rhodes, and more millions to come on top of it, came in a package like Berry. Personality. Brains. Brawn. At least if Leslie had to have a nervous breakdown, it had been a little worth-while to have it over Berry. Jennifer had heard she had a nervous twitch to her face nowadays, that was part of that nervous breakdown.

"Nervous?" he said, letting out a rip of speed, as they cleared the city line.

"Not to the point of breakdown," she said, and tilted a look at him from the low crouch into which the car forced her.

"You girls give me a pain in the neck," he said. "Innuendo. All lies."

"I'm sorry, Berry," she said, and laid a hand against his driving arm. "And I'm glad it's all lies."

"That's right," he said, "be yourself," and smiled at her with white teeth set in a face that had been polished tan by the sun.

"What self is that?"

"The self I like. You're a darling, Jennifer. I strongly suspect you of having brains, too, and you're brainy enough to keep them carefully concealed under that Joan of Arc bob."

"Give me a light, Berry."

He flecked on his lighter and held it to her while the car sped swift and sure under his lone-hand grip.

"Oh!"

"There, you had it!"

"No, you burnt my lip. Let's stop anyway, Berry. I can't smoke in this open boat. Draw in here."

"You little designing designer," he laughed, and drew

up. "It's darling of you, though, to want our ride to last."

"It's darling of you, Berry, to have got me asked out to the Edgertons' tonight. I'm on."

"Nonsense!"

"I don't give a damn for them or their parties, except for you ——"

"By God! I think you lisp! Let me thee your tongue."

"There!" She darted it at him. Quick. Pink.

The sultry haze of late October twilight, sharp with the smell of burning leaves, twined about them.

"Let's see it again."

His quick close kiss went against the second dart of pink.

"You sweet Sweet," he said, out of its long endurance.

She pushed him back, her face suddenly smeared with the pallor of excitement.

"Berry, let's you and me be low-down honest."

"I choose the first. You be honest."

"If you had half an idea of how honest I'm going to be, you'd climb out and hitch-hike your way back to town."

"Fortify me for that exigency—this way," he said, and kissed her again, his strong lips flaring so that involuntarily she drew the back of her hand across the feeling of the wetness of his teeth against her face.

"Berry, you and I weren't born yesterday."

He made to kiss her again.

"Don't do that."

"You egged me on."

"I know, but ——"

"You are so blamed honest, Jennifer, it makes a fellow want ——"

"But now I'm going to be awful serious."

"Awful is right, as applied to seriousness in all its forms."

"Awful serious, Berry."

"It can't be done, Jen. I'm immune."

"Berry, marry me."

He tightened as if a lock had sprung.

"Certainly. But I haven't my music with me."

"Berry, get this. I'm serious. Marry me. Don't answer. Just listen. You're no angel, Berry. God knows I'm not. I like you. A lot. I want you to respect that. I'm pretty crazy about you. You're a bad boy, Berry, but neither of us is sprouting wings. I think it's a swell plan and I'm sober. I'll marry you, not to reform you, but to reform with you."

"The only way to get me to marry the girl, Jennifer, is at the point of the well-known gun."

"Bing!" she said, and cocked a finger.

He grasped it and locked it between his teeth.

"I don't know whether you're spoofing me or not, but let's not be serious tonight, Jennifer. Isn't it enough—this night—us—this way ——"

She let her head swing back against the crook of his arm.

"Damn you, darling," she said, "you're standing up the girl."

"Jennifer, let me know you tonight—afterwards—my rooms?"

"You go plumb to hell, Berry," she said, pushing him from her with high laughter. "Step on her, we'll be late! And if you don't behave, the girl will leap from the car and her mangled remains will be found on the roadside by an early-morning farmer carting his carrots to market. Daughter of Dime Millionaire leaps from speeding car of son of rubber-heel magnate!"

"Jen! Nee! Fer!"

"Step on her, I said."

It was to her high, fast, and incessant laughter that they tilted into Parmley on two wheels at the sixty-mile clip.

AT THE last moment, and to the rushing of innumerable servants, the Edgertons had turned their dinner dance out-of-doors. The suddenly limpid October, the imminence of moon, the belated perfume of late white honeysuckle, had pressed their way into the ballroom, which was spread with fifty small tables and elaborately laid out across one end with a complete bar, brass rail, polished counter, battalion of bottles and glasses, and the faithful verisimilitude of a sprinkling of sawdust.

The milky light of one of those pale nights that never becomes quite dark poured down on to the blue-tile terrace. Tables had been dragged out there. A hurried platform for musicians was being set up between one pair of the lions, submerging one flight of terrace-stairs. Lanterns were run up in the groves and along the edges of the swimming-pool.

A formal party had suddenly gone violently informal. Tom Edgerton, already convivial, had conceived the idea, along with the change of party-policy, of dragging out a vast iron pot on a crane, to boil corn-on-the-cob in the open. The bar was being set up in a pergola. When the first guests arrived, Leslie Edgerton, in a bouffant white gown with wired panniers and a tumbler in one hand, was still in the act of trying to convey to a gardener her idea of how a small red bulb should dangle from the pointed left ear of a marble faun.

It was true that every few moments her rather pretty heart-shaped face twitched as if her nervousness were a prankish jack-in-the-box. The small red electric bulb refused to dangle from the left ear of the marble faun.

She grasped it from the servant, and, leaping to a stone bench, began to adjust it herself.

She was in that position when Jennifer and Berry and a smattering of early guests appeared on the wide marble staircase. At sight of them, she swung herself by the neck of the faun, legs out in a rigid horizontal, and began kissing him against his chilly lips.

It started out as that kind of party.

The way, Jennifer had long since decided, to feel at ease at what she called these closed-corporation functions, was to pretend to be as intimately a part of them as everyone else was, or pretended to be.

A sense of not belonging; of not knowing these people on the easy informal basis they knew one another, assailed her, and seemed to lock her tonsils and stiffen her heart on those occasions when she penetrated into the social fastness of the gayer, if less conservative, elements of these safely intrenched families. Their intimate talk that took so much for granted. High bandying of Christian names where she was addressed as Miss Rarick. References to past functions to which she had not been bidden, and to future ones to which she would not be bidden.

Not that she was not very much part of these scenes. The Edgertons moved in swift, newspaper-headline sets. But even here, she was consciously Miss Rarick. The way to keep a stiff upper lip when you were ill at ease and inwardly frightened was to see to it that you were conspicuously Miss Rarick. You listened, when the two on either side of you at dinner leaned across you to indulge in familiar discussion of an important social function to which you had mysteriously and damnably not been bidden, with a smile as bright as platinum drawn across your face. You let them make up a party around you to go off cruising in warm waters on the yacht of the father of a boy who had just kissed the back of your neck, and laughed at some sally about the Delaware Gap and the Delaware Yawn, as if you were not stinging at the omission.

The lively Miss Rarick was loud in her laughter. That was part of the stiff upper lip. She was daring in her dress, but impeccably so, never erring beyond the bonds of chic. A good fellow up to a point, and that point, as she was fond of putting it, an exclamation point.

When Jennifer walked down the wide staircase of the Edgertons' famed blue terrace, with Berry at her right and a one-armed chap named Roger Madison, descendant of a President, at her left, her heart was in her mouth; insolence in her smile; and a burning humiliation before Berry, beating about in her.

Perhaps he had never realized she was not spoofing. He had, though! He had. *He had.* He had jumped like a sprung trap when she had come out with it. Perhaps he had thought her a little spifflicated. God, make him think I was tight! No, no, no, he wouldn't. They had not even stopped for cocktails before they drove off. There came that hateful Irene Annescy! How did one address her? Hello, Irene? Or just Miss Annescy?

Miss Annescy solved it. "Hello, Berry! Haven't seen you since three A.M. Good party at the Ruhls', wasn't it? Hello, Roger! Say, you're driving with us over to Edgecombe from here for a sunrise cocktail. Howdo, Miss Rarick!"

Damn them! Damn life! "Berry darling, that's my ankle you're climbing."

With the exception of a center-table which seated twelve, the flocks of surrounding smaller ones were for six. Berry and Jennifer were at one which adjoined the larger one, presided over by Leslie.

Berry's absence from that center-table was one of those

elaborately casual maneuvers which usually fail of their purpose and become merely elaborate maneuvers.

"Berry's been banished," said a Miss Steen der Venter, who was narrow and caustic and something of a town legend because she continued to refuse to sell or build on fifty fabulously valuable feet of vacant lot on Fifth Avenue, but maintained it as a playground for her three black poodles. "I scent a diplomatic move!"

"I'm making him eat at second table, Van Steen; his manners are too atrocious for first," cried Leslie, whom Berry had once accused of overhearing, no matter how large the crowd, any reference to him.

Almost immediately the occasion began to progress. The amusing feature of the bar kept a steady stream of young men skating across blue tiles, imperiling waiters, and returning with assorted tumblers of assorted drinks, which they balanced precariously, to the squeals of women in *décolletée* who feared for their shoulders. A Miss Flavverdale, impoverished, but one of the right Flavverdales, the one, by the way, who had managed things for the St. Louis Slocums, began by insisting upon carting Berry off before the fowl course, with a napkin filled with dinner rolls to be crumpled into the goldfish-pond.

"I want to stay with my field-mouse," bawled Berry, and began to stroke Jennifer's ermine and pull at the fringe of soft black tails which bordered it.

"Don't be an idiot, Berry," said the efficient Miss Flavverdale; "I'll buy you a five-and-ten-cent one."

"Was that a dirty dig?" said Jennifer to a beautiful boy beside her, whom she did not know, but who was in the first throes of getting drunk on champagne, which he kept sipping, while he refused all food.

"A dirty dig," he repeated, rolling his extraordinarily blue and luminous eyes. "A dirty dig." Apparently the octave of his conversation, at least at this stage, consisted in repeating the last three words of what was said to him.

"The Beautiful next to you, Miss Rarick," sang out Leslie Edgerton, on a sudden surge of geniality, when she saw Berry hauled protesting along the Mediterranean of blue tiles, "is Jules Wilke-Barre. He's going to cut a tooth for us later in the evening!"

A Wilke-Barre! A thrill shot through Jennifer. Despise herself for the snobbery of it as she would, it was impossible not to bristle with awareness among names that were whole planetary systems in the social firmament. This naughty-eyed, beautiful-eyed boy, whose knee had to be shoved away again and again as it approached hers, a Wilke-Barre! Here, gathered at these fifty tables, were the youngsters of the mighty ones of the land. Madison. Rhodes. Flavverdale. Wilke-Barre.

She leaned toward Wilke-Barre.

"I thought you were Bobby Shaftoe, who went to sea with silver buckles on his knee."

The youth she thought was Bobby Shaftoe, who went to sea with silver buckles on his knee, was asleep, his chin resting squarely and precariously in the shallow crystal basin of his empty champagne-glass.

Before the crash came that was to gash the Rossetti-looking Wilke-Barre chin with splintered glass, Berry was back, in great and rising spirits.

"Glory! what a night!"

Its glamor was out over Jennifer. Its pollen fell over the scene and in a sheen across her flesh.

"It was on such a night as this ———"

"———that I made the damnedest mistake of my life," said Berry, and jerked the great athletic hulk of his body back to his place at the table.

"Leslie's been looking for you, Berry," said Irene Annescy.

"Finders keepers," said Berry under his breath to Jennifer.

She flashed her face, with the indescribable pallor of moon over it, upon him.

"Mean that?"

"If I ever meant anything, I mean it. Find me, Jennifer."

"You won't let me."

"Try me."

"Don't be darling to me, Berry, unless ———"

Beneath the table his heavy palm clamped down on her knee.

"How can I help it, when you are darling to me."

"How do you mean that?"

"I'll tell you later ———"

"I'll not drive back with you alone unless ———"

"Unless what?"

"Unless I damn please," she said, and swung her smooth bare shoulder from him and turned to talk to Wilke-Barre, who was having his chin nursed by a princess of Greece.

Tom Edgerton began to beat a tom-tom in an effort to drum up trade for his boiling pot of corn on cob. He was voted ridiculous, because, while the party had gone informal, so to speak, the food had remained strictly *de rigueur*. It was difficult, after mushrooms under glass and duck soaked in sherry, to warm up to the impulse to nibble the mealy pearls off the cobs which Edgerton forked up out of the fine hullabaloo of boiling pot.

Most of those who ventured never quite reached the boiling pot. The gardens lay embalmed in a night through which the moonlight poured like spring showers.

Marble curve of benches gleamed in among hedges.
Islands of shadow crawled back into the groves. The
waterfall that fed the natural swimming-pool made silver-
tipped commotion. The dinner broke into dancing almost before the tables could be cleared from the tiles. It
was as dreamy as absinthe to tango out there under the
stars.

Six Hawaiian boys in shellacked hair sang to Argentine music. A jazz-band alternated. A Spanish slip of
a girl, with hips which she managed like a spaniel shaking off water, danced solo with Ramon Lopez. Her
bold, sinuous body-beauty went through you in points of
excitement. The give of the slim jacket of her ribs as
she doubled with a boneless ductility back over his elbow.
Slitted eyes of Ramon, braced for her whirling body to
spin into the close insinuating haven of his arms. Slow
shuffling feet, too sensuous to leave the ground. Faces,
as through a curtain of moonlight, dimly; the Spanish
girl's fore-shortened upper lip hiked back to reveal small
wet teeth; Ramon's face, sliding down like a warm brown
breathing lid—over hers. . . .

"God, Berry, they're wonderful," said Jennifer.

His body, through it all, as they stood in the thick
fringe of onlookers, had been crushing against hers. It
had been her dance with Berry, vicariously.

The pair broke into a tarantella then, as if to gloss
over the thickening moist-lipped faces that had begun to
lean out of the human wall around them.

"Come on, Jennifer, let's get out of here. I need a
drink. I need eleven drinks." They backed off without
much disturbance, moving slidingly and unnoticed along
the tiles; moving hand in hand down the broad reflect-
ing steps; moving slidingly toward the grove above the
grotto of the swimming-pool.

Patches of moonlight covered the floor of the grove

like lily-pads. Water, skedaddling down rocks to feed the pool, was the only sound. . . .

"Life ought to be sweeter to us than it is, Berry. What's rotten with us?"

He stared, with his head in her lap, at a patch of pale sky that reminded him of his star-sapphire studs.

"What say?"

"You're not listening."

"I can feel your voice. It makes darling little vibrations."

"I begged you not to get tight, Berry."

His eyes fluttered heavily and closed as he began fumbling out on to the moss for the frosted quart bottle and two glasses with which he had fortified himself from the buffet table that was now being spread down beside the swimming-pool.

"You can't get tight on champagne, my field mouse. You get divine."

Her fingers were in his hair. Her lips gave off a tiny fume.

"You've stood me up frightfully, Berry. What if I were to go home and blow out that portion of my anatomy called brain, with a mother-of-pearl pistol?"

"I'd embalm you in a block of ice and keep you in a casket of rose quartz."

"You are as slippery as a glass eel."

"You don't know the half of it, my darling, or the half of the half of it," he cried, and rolled over and dug his face into the soft fur moss of her gown. "God! I'm ten kinds of a fool!"

"Sweet ten kinds."

"Rotten ten kinds."

"Tell me one of the kinds."

"Fee, fie, fo, fum. The kind that daren't like little white field mice."

"That daren't?" she said, and lifted her head as if to listen. "Why?"

"Let me alone," he cried into her lap, "with your whys and your whys and your whys. Why are all you girls such why-hounds?"

"Sh-h-h! Berry's tight," she said, smoothing his hair.

"Just go on doing that," he said, still into the thick whiteness of her lap. "Just go on doing that—and talk ——"

"Why should I do all the talking and you all the evading?"

"Is this evading?" he said, and reached up to stroke her cheek.

"Berry, Berry, what is it we want . . . ?"

"I know what I want ——"

"I feel like I belonged in one of those psychological novels they're writing nowadays."

"The darling has read a book and everything."

"Where nothing happens except in the tortured brains of some tortured author's brain-children. The cross-eyed school of literature that looks inward, and does nothing about it but look and look. Life isn't that way. Life moves. Life is motion. Time doesn't pass. We pass. I may be in a mess, but I don't intend to sit in it and stew."

"Stew in my arms, darling."

"I hate you when you're tight. Am I tight, Berry?"

"Not tight. Divine."

"Let's be good, Berry, and sober, and live so that, after it's all over, it will have mattered a damn whether we have lived or not."

"You're good, Jennifer. You're a good gal. That's what ails you."

"You're no good, Berry. That's what ails you."

"You're what ails me."

"Then, for God's sake, Berry, play fair with me! Oh!
Get up, Berry! Look! They're throwing light on the
pool. It may slip up here. How long have we been
away? What will Leslie say?"

A cone of light swung through the grove. He dragged
her swiftly back.

"Don't go, Pussy."

"Berry, we must."

"Don't go."

"Look, the crowd is coming down to bathe. There's
Elsie Risdon in a bathing-suit. She never travels without it. And Ramon. He looks as if he were painted in
gold leaf. It's beautiful. It's terrible. It's like one of
those Stück pictures—horrible loveliness. Look at the
Wilke-Barre infant there in that patch of moonlight.
He's going to dive. It may sober him. Where on
earth did Tom Edgerton get those striped trunks?
Bacchus gone wrong. Vine leaves in his hair, or is it
confetti? This is one of those swimming parties of the
idle and debauched rich that they read about out in
Dubuque and turn Bolsheviki or try to imitate. I've
never seen one happen so true to form. Look, there
comes —— This is awful!"

They crept to the edge of their ledge, which looked
down from an eminence on to the half-natural, half-con-
trived grotto. Slim silhouettes, all fays in the moonlight, sat on the coping, along which crawled Henrietta
Edgerton's little *bêtes noires,* and dangled bare legs into
the moon-reflecting pool. A slope of hillside marched
down to the pool, inclosing it like a crater. Figures were
strewn over the hillside, helping one another down
declivities, in monkey-chains of twos and threes. The
Spanish dancer, clad in a mere dash of suit, the exact

henna of her flesh, leaped down from crag to crag like a bit of lightning, zigzagging off the edges of rock. The Falstaffian figure of the over-stout young Philip Londo swaggered down in an improvised bathing-suit, a sweater tied by the sleeves about his great middle. The Spanish dancer leap-frogged over him, took the tip of the diving-board, and sliced downward like a quick thin blade. Voices in the moonlight had the musical flow to them of water. Over the ledge they peered, secure, arm in arm, their bodies flat to the soft moss, seeing, unseen. It was a scene of a Paul Veronese canvas, set to music by Stravinsky, and directed by the buxom figure of Tom Edgerton, who went stamping among his guests in his striped trunks, dragging shrinking and reluctant maidens, with dry, beautifully powdered legs, to the water's edge, immersing them, leaping back up the hillsides for more of his strange and spectacular prey.

"Berry, there's Leslie! In the black suit."

She felt his head move; but even as she spoke she pressed it down again into her lap.

"She must be looking for us! Why the dickens did we do this, Berry? It's this loony moonlight. We've been gone over an hour. Leslie shouldn't let herself get this tipsy. Thank goodness, she's going to dive. It will sober her. Berry, hadn't we better slide around to the house and get into bathing-suits and ooze quietly into the crowd? Oh, Berry, I hate to!"

He raised his tousled and troubled-looking head.

"Guess we'd better," he said, with a sudden kind of soberness.

It made her wild that what she had just said should have this power over him.

"Berry," she cried, and caught his face in the cup of her hands and drew it to hers closely; "Berry darling—tell me the low-down—let me hear you deny, yourself, the horrid rumor that you and Leslie—oh—oh—no ——"

Due to a loud series of shouts through cupped hands which Tom Edgerton was directing at an electrician, the entire scene below suddenly slipped into the incredible beauty of a moon-silvered darkness, the cone of search-light shooting upward like a great tusk of ivory, drench-ing the hilltop forest in glare, drenching the figures of Jennifer and Berry, lying there so closely face to face on their bed of moss.

To the bathers beneath, it was as if the heavens had opened in the fashion that was supposed to reveal God seated on a throne of mother-of-pearl. Only, there sat Berry and Jennifer instead, bathed in incalculable am-peres of luminosity.

The figure on the tip edge of the diving-board was a figure transfigured.

"Leslie," cried Henrietta Edgerton to her daughter—the only voice to find itself in that blinding shift of scene—"Leslie, don't!"

The spring-board began to jiggle. It made a creak-ing noise. Then came the voice of Leslie, poised on the tip of the spring-board, her arms shooting out as her silhouette became a cross.

"There you are!" screamed Leslie, and danced up and down on the spring-board. "There you are!"

"Leslie!" shouted Henrietta Edgerton.

"There you are!" called Leslie up to the glare on the hilltop. "Pretty ones! I'll tell the world! I'll tell the world!"

"Leslie!"

"World, that's my husband up there! We were mar-ried yesterday. Never mind why. Keep this marriage a secret for him a few weeks, so he can settle his affairs?

The devil I will! What affairs? His five-and-ten-cent affairs. The devil I will!" screamed Leslie, and dived.

At four o'clock of that translucent October morning, with a moon still retreating in a high sky, the only daughter of the thirteenth richest man in the world sat crouched in a huddle no larger than a spaniel, outside the door of Doctor Gerkes.

She did not quite clearly know why she was there, except that inchoately, fragmentarily, her fuddled brain had telegraphed to her fuddled feet the road to Gerkes. She did not know why. Truth of the matter was, she was generally not quite clear, except for her sense of the lump of shame. She was the lump of shame. The world was a wave, tossing a lump of shame.

There was a slit of light beneath Gerkes's door. Behind that door, Jennifer's fuddled sense told her, Gerkes would be sitting in a monotonous gray herring-bone suit, or, worse, the stiff gray-flannel dressing-gown she had seen hanging on the door of his bathroom the day of her exploratory trip. A small gray man, about as exciting as chalk dust. Behind that closed door he was sitting in a limitless world of ideas. The stones of Venice and the stones of Alexandria and the stones of Carthage were not mere stones to him. Like the flint and arrow-heads on his tables, they looked up at him with the wide revealing eyes of immemorial man. Heaps and heaps of these strange lusterless stones covered the fine table-tops of that room. Wisdoms were behind that closed door—and quiet——

It was then that Jennifer scratched faintly at the panel, like a little dog, not so much because she particularly wanted admission into the room, but because she wanted some of the kind solitude she seemed to sense there.

After a while, on limbs that were too wavy to carry

her, the young Miss Rarick, in the white-ermine frock and her coat dragging, began a tortuous and shocking journey down the hallway, on all-fours, knee after knee, the palms of her hands padding softly along the carpet.

Her maid, dozing as she waited, heard the soft noises, ran down the hallway, and horrified, lifted and carried her bodily to bed.

It was about then that consciousness that there had been scratching noises came belatedly to Doctor Gerkes, who had been bending to scrutinize a dated altar-stone, 575, of Maya civilization, said to have been unearthed from the city of Matzap Ceel.

Opening his door to peer out into the now empty hallway, a faint smell that reminded him of the dried-rose-leaf scent in a third-century mummy-chamber he had once helped to excavate near Luxor, came and caused him pleasantly to sniff.

IT PLEASED Rarick to be a patron of the arts. He liked to think that opera committees came to him to make good their deficits. Little-theater groups were appealing to him more and more frequently. Child musical prodigies of piano and violin virtuosity were constantly being brought before him.

It pleased him to sit, a Mæcenas, in his library and make chapels of his fingers and pass judgments in which he was solely assisted by Hellman, who had graduated from a South St. Louis music-school, and Alfredo Ludovici, the violin member of a chamber-music quartette which Rarick had supported for years.

Children, for the most part, were brought by mothers whose agony of nervousness was almost invariably cruelly transmitted to their prodigy offspring. Again, they were sent by music-school teachers, personal friends and some without even benefit of introduction, feverishly seeking the wedge of an audition.

Hellman arranged these auditions. He was high-handed about it, thinking nothing of keeping a mother and an alleged violinistic prodigy waiting for weeks at their hotel for the Rarick summons. It was Hellman who arranged the interviews with little-theater committees, art-foundation groups, endowment-seeking organizations, and scholarship-fund seekers, weeding out at his discretion, but lenient in his judgments, since it seemed perpetually pleasing to Rarick to sit in tribunal.

With the exception of the Firenzi Quartette, which, thanks to Rarick's generous maintenance, had become world-renowned for the perfection of its *ensemble*, the success of most of Rarick's musical *protégés* was still to be achieved. To be sure, there was a thirteen-year-old Milwaukee lad, named Isa Friedberg, studying at Fontainebleau, and for whom great things were predicted; and little Leontine Bachrach of Brooklyn, thirteen and a half, who had played a piano-recital at Town Hall with outstanding success, was making spectacular headway with his teachers in Munich.

But not infrequently, Rarick's fervor to serve the arts outclassed his critical judgments. The little Norwegian lad from Flagler, North Dakota, whom, against the better judgment of both Hellman and Ludovici, he had chosen to endow with his patronage in preference to the small Russian boy from the Boston ghetto, was now playing viola in a theater orchestra, while the small Russian boy from the Boston ghetto was winning honors as a soloist of the first rank. There was also the case of a pretty and enormously promising young soprano whom he had lifted from a stenographer's desk in a broker's office to the conservatory of Milan, and who had returned to America, homesick, after the second Italian month, to marry a runner in the brokerage office where she had formerly been employed.

As Hellman and Ludovici used to remark with a wink between them, the old gentleman took these debit results gamely, apparently more than compensated for failures by the majesty of his rôle of patron of the fine arts and by the first-water success of the Firenzi Quartette.

Of this last there was no question. Taking over, after one hearing, the four friendless Italian youths who had finally succeeded in winning audience, Rarick had supported them, exploited them, and launched them securely into success. It was his bounty that continued to supply them generous budget for travel, study, and leisure, long after their financial need of him had passed.

When not abroad or on American tour, they occupied
a pleasant old house in West Ninth Street, fitted with a
vast music-chamber across the top, and which, except for
their tenancy, Rarick would long since have profitably
converted into a skyscraper apartment-building.

Evening after evening, during these town periods, they
played chamber music to Rarick alone, occasionally
Gerkes present, semi-occasionally one or both of the
Jennys appearing on the scene.

Frequently, the Quartette, which had long outgrown
private-home engagements, played at one of Jenny's functions when she decided to have a "bit of music." But
after the Firenzi Quartette became closely associated
with the name of Rarick, she abandoned that habit, because it smacked of home-made economy, buying instead
the professional services of some stellar vocal or violinistic attraction whose fees were notoriously high.

Besides, there came to be something about the very
faces of the members of the Quartette—as they sat on
the small platform which was rolled in for them to the
organ end of the library—which was repellent to her,
because, by association, they suggested one of Rarick's
quasi-Napoleonic attitudes. He liked to crouch into an
enormous tapestry chair, done after the unicorn at Cluny,
at the far end of the room from their platform, head
thrust forward and downward on his chest, a little forelock, which Jenny sometimes described to herself as his
Della Fox Napoleon, down over his brow, and his curiously intent gaze seeming to hook into the music as it
flowed past.

His imagination, more than his senses, appeared to
come awake to the warm reality of chamber music. The
tumbling figures of a Tiepolo ceiling, garland-wound,
music-wound, became a grove in which lazy fancy could
wander. There was a tragic and a comic mask, divided

by a flaming torch, woven palely into one of the tapestries that faced him. To Bach or Strauss or Massenet, these faces could tilt into laughter or screw to tears. They became his own face in layers of moods that were heart-breaking to him for their pathos or their absurdity. Again, to him, some of these faces were sublime. They were the faces of the Rarick he might have been. Some of those Rarick faces were as beautiful as Avery. Some of those Rarick faces had it in them to create the very music to which he was listening; some, to create the drama of the tragic mask. No Five-and-Ten-Cent Rarick of the Five-and-Ten-Cent thing. No industrial magnate in a tin crown. Here, under the weaving spell of music, he became the Rarick he was, deeply, secretly, and terribly, within himself. No patron of the arts, but a creator! No piler-up of wealth. Dispenser! Four-and-twenty Raricks all in a row. . . .

Projects came to Rarick under the weaving motion of music. New loans. New stores. New policies. It was in this room, for instance, to evening after evening of the peregrinations of the small music of Schubert and Haydn, that the mammoth idea of the Rarick Building was born.

Layer by layer, to its dramatic seventy-three-story splendor, it rose on a scaffolding wrought out of these strange spirals of inspiration that seemed to wind up through him when his imagination responded to a stimulus it comprehended not at all. Story by story, to its eminence as the tallest building in the world, this Taj Mahal of industry took form. It was to take eleven years to realize, thirty million dollars to construct, and it rose out of Schubert and Haydn and Chopin and Brahms. It rose out of the winding of the imagined faces of his children as they appeared warm and sympathetic to him among the garlands of fancy that came to life on the Tiepolo ceiling. It rose out of Rarick's visions of himself, creating the kind of beauty that money could buy.

Mozart, Schubert, Smetana, Schumann, Beethoven. His knowledge of music was negligible, and his choice of selection often secretly amusing and chromoesque to his Quartette, but somehow it was impossible to patronize Rarick musically. In one breath, he might call out, across the long reaches of the room, for "Träumerei," "Narcissus," and the "Scarf Dance," but the Beethoven C-major, op. 59, with its gymnastic and tuneless 'cello-passages in the first movement, was just as apt to be his next choice. He might not remember the name of a composition or a composer; but he could hum a thread of *motif* for them, or demand this or that movement by describing its tempo.

"Play those wild gypsies dancing in the bonfire-light," was his way of requesting the last movement of the Schubert G-major, op. 161. Or, "Play that flowing, running one," for the Andante Cantabile from Tchaikowsky's Quartette, D-major.

He was an interesting, an interested, a solitarily grand audience of one. On those rare occasions when Jenny or Jennifer found time, or found it the better part of wisdom to pause for a snatch of one of these evenings, they did so, usually perched on the arms of chairs like brilliant birds of passage, their evening cloaks trailing, their ears cocked for the summons to depart. When Gerkes dropped in, after a lecture he had either delivered or attended, it was to slide into a straight chair which he kept for himself in the loft of the organ, where he could tilt back and nap to music whose chief function, where he was concerned, was to soothe him. Usually these evenings wound up with beer and talk of the habits of immortals among musicians, chiefly between Gerkes and the members of the Quartette.

"Now, take that countryman Verdi of yours; from

what they tell me, he must have been pretty much of an ordinary fellow, apart from his ability to compose," was Gerkes' way, for instance, of starting Gigli Fortuno, the 'cellist member of the Quartette, who was well informed on the subject of musical personalities, and whose father had personally known Verdi.

Sometimes, throughout these discourses, Gerkes remained up on his balcony, tilted back on his straight chair, while the four members of the little group worked themselves up into musical controversy that rose to the climax of shouts and heated disagreement. Occasionally, Gerkes, who dozed or relaxed, would be reminded of a pun or reference, as some name came floating dimly up to him among the floriated arches, and he would call down his comment:

"Speaking of the Fifth Symphony, Sir Henry Larrimore, the inventor of the Larrimore tuning-fork and the foremost living acoustician, told me a good one about observing an audience in Queens Hall during the first movement of the Fifth Symphony. . . ."

Then Rarick: "Tell the gentlemen, Gerkes, the Eurasian theory of the Music of the Spheres."

Then Gerkes: "You Quartette boys, how much do you really know about the principles of harmony? . . ."

Evenings far removed from the banging reality of days that were crowded with four hundred thousand sets of doll-dishes for children, or a pending order for hair-nets that had an annoying rider in the contract.

A patron of the arts sat among his art-objects and listened to a discussion of the arts. And yet it was this very listening that could rankle. His Quartette, when their musical arguments rose and excluded him, was not the Quartette that made him obsequious and played to his wishes. Their manner, between themselves, was that of artist to artist. Their manner to Rarick was that of men beholden for favors that lay outside their stamina to earn. There was, in their behavior between themselves, the unconscious difference between artist to artist, and artist to financial benefactor.

They respected his riches. But Rarick, Rarick himself, well, Rarick was a rich man. . . .

Equally aggravating to this sense of exclusion were the writers, theater groups, young aspirants in this or that form of art, who came to him for patronage and at the same time gave him that sense of isolation from their cause, except in so far as his hands held the strings to the money-bags.

They spoke to him of their projects in terms of numbers. Rentals of theaters. Price of publishing a slender book of verse. Scholarship money. Endowment money. It was among themselves that the ambitious young poets who smote their dissonant lyres of modern verse, and the young playwrights who gave birth, in travail, to their Hedda Gablers of the experimental theater, had their real beings.

They talked projects to Rarick. Lisped in numbers of box-office receipts, yearly deficit, and the ledger-book which they despised.

He was Crœsus, related only to Thyrsus, Sappho, Terpsichore, and Apollo by the strings of the money-bags.

It was in his rôle of patron that the Committee of Internationalists, Inc., which was one day to be one of the most potent forces in the young theater movement in America, came before Rarick.

They were three. A young fellow named Trigoloff, with a crooked and strangely powerful profile, who had written a two-act play in thirty-one episodes which had been produced in a cellar called the Rhomboid Theater. A Miss Virginia Adelbert, with blond hair, cropped, polished, and parted on the side, like a boy's, in tailored clothes, soft shirt, and who carried her crush felt hat under her arm, and her package of cigarettes protruding from a tailored pocket. The third member of this group, Gratton Davies, was a young professor of dramatic composition at a city university. His comedy, "Herod's Mask," had been a success the season before. Here was a fellow of such abounding and amusing enthusiasm that it was inevitable he should have been elected spokesman for this occasion. He had a thatch of thick tan hair, which jumped and fell from the roots, as he sat on the edge of his chair, his opening sentence accomplishing what it set out to do as concisely as a good headline flare of advertising.

"Mr. Rarick, we have chosen you to sponsor what is without any doubt to be the most significant and far-reaching experiment in the history of the American theater. I used the word 'chosen' advisedly, because the man who is granted the privilege of bringing to life our plan is going to get a ride for his money to the peak of artistic-success-with-a-box-office-value."

"Yes, young man?" said Rarick, with a bitter kind of mockery playing around his lips. This was not the fellow himself speaking. This was the young scholar, suiting his phrase, his manner, and his matter to his man. In other words, "selling his idea" to big business.

The fervor of his presentation was all right, but the manner was the rehearsed one of a traveling salesman.

Young Davies was talking down to Rarick in terms of the one aspect of the enterprise that interested him least of all, and yet which was so essential to the very life and breath of their beautiful baby of an idea. Money. Without it, that beautiful baby must perish aborning. Its soul was in the keeping of such as these three young

committeemen. Its shoes, the farina to feed it, the
fires to warm it, were merchant concerns. Rarick's.

"Money, Mr. Rarick, is what we need of you."

His resentments, he told himself were absurd. What
else had he to offer? Presently these three, and the
confrères who spoke their language, would recede into
the laboratories of their imaginations. They could talk
to one another from these laboratories. Where did he,
Rarick, come in? Why sit stiffly before this young
barker up the Himalayas and bark back a bitter "Yes,
young man," into his enthusiasms.

These three before him were in the heyday of their
walking-trip through the Pyrenees. Their walking-trip
was coming off, too. After all, it was something to sit
there, holding their creative destinies in the same hand
that held the money-bags.

"Don't think, Mr. Rarick, that our ideas are all vision-
ary. We don't propose to drive the commercial theater
out of business. Nothing of the sort."

"Now, don't you?"

"No, sir. We propose to supplant, in time—with
thought, with discrimination, with genius, with money—
the garbage of the present commercial theater, by giving the people pre-digested, intellectual, artistic, and en-
tertaining fodder. But it is not so much a matter of
throwing out the commercial theater, Mr. Rarick, as
cleaning out the Augean dramatic stables. That is why
we dare to approach you with a proposition which will
ultimately grant you full return on your money. Not
that you are interested in exacting any such guaranty as
that from us, but ——"

Young rascal! Young walker in the Pyrenees. Young
three there, who presently, once outside his doors, would
revert to the swift, ruthless well-informed talk of their

own world, and who might even ape and deride the holder of the strings of the money-bags. . . .

". . . Of course, I am not here to bore you with our standards of production, the literary ideals we have set for ourselves. . . ."

"Why not?" barked Rarick. "You can't put your cart before your horse."

"What Mr. Davies means," hastened Miss Adelbert, "is that we have long ago threshed out our literary policies. That has been taken care of. It's money we ——"

"Can't see why the money-concerns of such an organization as you describe are a thing separate and apart from its policies. They overlap. My selling-policies regarding an article can only be determined after I am thoroughly familiar with the article itself."

"In the theater, Mr. Rarick, that scarcely applies. Our production-policies have nothing to do with our financial ones. We need an initial endowment of one hundred thousand dollars to put them into what we firmly believe will be a successful practice. We want you to be the man to have sufficient faith in those production-policies to endow our baby."

Impudent youth! Well, what rebuttal had he? Plays were foreign affairs to him. Occasionally, he sat through one with Jenny. He had not seen "Herod's Mask." Doubtless it would have gone monotonously over his head. Music flowed into him, whereas the drama seemed merely to use his brain as a surface of impact. Jennifer liked the Follies and the rapid revues. Once or twice he had accompanied her and sat in first-row seats or in a box. The box was more to his liking. Jennifer said it was because he could hang a crêpe over the railing. But the fact was, the box was more to his liking because, as at the Greek plays he sometimes sponsored, it was possible to remain out of it an entire act without leaving the hole of an empty seat in a row.

What had he, after all, to offer these youngsters, except money? It would be dignified patronage. Miss Adelbert had already won herself a somewhat esoteric position as one of those clever and respected actresses of the intellectual school. Trigoloff, of the crooked profile, was an author and director of rising fame in both fields. The fellow Davies stood to the fore of a certain group of young rebels. What a pity—what a pity Jennifer or Avery was missing such interests as this.

A thought smote Rarick.

"Young people, take my boy into this enterprise with you!"

If he had said, "Young people, take my howling red monkey into this enterprise with you," he could not have struck a more compelling silence across the faces of these three.

"I've a boy. Youngster. Bright as a new nickel. I'd like him to sharpen his teeth, come vacation, on a few young people like you. I'd like to see him get interested in groups that will get him acquainted with some of the things I think he may be missing."

A glance, imbedded in smile, wound itself from one face to the other of the three.

"Your son is interested in the theater, Mr. Rarick?"

"I wouldn't say that, Miss Adelbert," snapped Rarick. "It is I who am interested in interesting him."

"I see."

Of course she did not see, nor did any of them, sitting there so politely mindful of the hand that held the money-bags. Nor did Rarick himself, for that matter. The need of his boy eventually coming into his affairs was more and more a pressing one, the inevitable contingency of primogeniture hovered closer; yet here he was, trying to foist him off on to a vague art-project. As it was, Avery had barely time to spare for these college years. Rarick was not minded to start him in overalls from the bottom up. Why teach a walking child to crawl? But little as Rarick could visualize his son cast into his future, the time was at hand when he must be tossed, as you would toss a youngster who must learn to swim, out into the monstrous sea of five-and-ten-cent things. High, tormenting tides of big business awaited Avery. A mantle of tin armor was hovering over his young shoulders. He was about to matriculate in that relentless university of highly limited enrollment which was to prepare him to be one of the richest men in the world. What Rarick had just suggested was as fantastic to himself as to the three who sat with masks of respectful attention drawn across their faces.

"How's Avery's second act?" was to explode in hilarity from Miss Adelbert's lips as the committee of three emerged from the house of Rarick after this interview, and mounted a Fifth Avenue omnibus for an Eleventh Street restaurant, where more of their group anxiously awaited them.

And yet, after the palpable absurdity of what he had suggested came flooding over Rarick, the idea persisted. Even a few months of contact with these inquisitive pioneering young minds, might help Avery to feel healthy alienation from the world of Jenny's making, which was already threatening to whirl around him. A few months of gambol in these adventurous fields of ideas before the lamb be shorn to the wind of being son to one of the richest men in the world.

"Let my boy in on the ground-floor of this new-theater idea—agree to take him into your fold when he comes out of college ——"

"Why, of course, Mr. Rarick, if he is interested. We

would want to meet him. See what's on his mind. It
could—er—of course be done. Always a place in a workshop like ours. . . ."

"On that basis, then, and subject to specifications which
Mr. Hellman will arrange at my dictation, you may consider that I will seriously take under advisement the
matter of endowing your group."

The three young people who finally, walking on air,
turned their faces toward the Eleventh Street café, left
Rarick sitting there crouched deeply in the enormous
chair which faced the organ.

An idea had, for the moment, completely captured
his fancy. What if the boy had somewhere imbedded in
him a talent for this sort of creative thing. Not as a
vocation. Naturally. But as an avocation. Something
to keep him tinged at least with the adventurous quality
of mind that flooded that young fellow Davies. Avery
must not be cheated of his walking-trip through the Pyrenees. There was plenty of time later for the two-feet-
on-the-ground business of training him to be the son of
one of the richest men in the world.

Presently, Rarick began a letter to his son. Somehow, with the concrete pen on the concrete paper, the
words began to clog in his brain. There were things that
could not be broached out of a clear sky. Nothing had
ever been said between father and son to prepare Avery
for the popping of this notion into the head of his parent.
The dread of seeming ridiculous in his son's clear eyes
began to matter above everything in Rarick's tired brain,
as he sat there, his pen drying above the paper.

It was difficult, practically impossible, to convey to his
boy that the idea prompted by the three avid young faces,
and most of all by the fellow named Davies, had not to
do with their little enterprise itself, but somewhere be-

hind it all was a symbol . . . a symbol of some kind of release which he wanted for his boy.

One could not get that easily said, at least not without danger of appearing ridiculous to a college boy in his teens, who could want for a speed-boat as desperately as Avery had wanted for his.

The letter was to remain in the limbo of unwritten ones.

THE first time Jenny received Ramon behind the closed door of her boudoir, a thousand misgivings assailed her. The creak of a chair was sufficient to stiffen her in his arms; a footstep on a stair startling her eyes into a listening expression, the pupils widening and full of dreads.

"Jenny, that is not nice! Of what are you afraid? Cannot two people have tea in privacy? Why do you not lock the door, if in your great big house you have no privacy?"

"No. No. There must be nothing like that."

"But you make it like that with your nervousness."

"I want your coming here to be the most natural thing in the world. I am going to begin to make it a habit to have afternoon cocktails always served in here. That will make it seem less strange. It is a nice room, isn't it, Ramon—all these soft yellows ——"

"Any room that contains you is a beautiful room."

She took his face between her hands.

"Sweet."

"You do feel that way, don't you, Jenny?"

"You know that I do."

"Then what are we going to do about it?"

A question like that could send the fears rushing back over her.

"I don't know, Ramon."

"We cannot go on like this, Jenny."

"Why? Of course not, Ramon ——"

"It is not fair to me."

"I know that, Ramon. There must be a way."

"There must be a way—for me to live—if I am to go on neglecting my work this way ——"

Once, when he pressed her thus, she had unwittingly asked him, "what work?" and filled his eyes with reproach that looked near to tears. His stalkings in this fashion around the subject of money, somehow sullied perfection.

"I have given up everything, Jenny. My teaching, my ——"

"I know you have, Ramon."

"I love giving up everything; but it has its practical side, dearest, since we live in a practical world."

"I know that. There is a thousand-dollar-bill in registered mail for you now, dearest."

It was like her to see that these transactions took place easily, in currency. He kissed her.

"That is for the thought," he said; "the money itself is horrible, practical necessity."

"That is for the kiss," she said, kissing him back.

He would have slid easily off this sand-bar of a subject, but the procession of her thoughts matched the fact that she lay in his arms and his smooth olive pallor was hers to lift up a hand and stroke.

"How cruel and wrong and spiteful life can be, Ramon."

"Not if we do something about it, to see that it is not so."

It occurred to her, as she lay there, that everything there was to do about it she would never dare to do. And yet it was sweet to contemplate doing it.

In just such proportion as her sense of disloyalty toward Rarick grew, her efforts to reawaken some sort of a relationship between them began asserting itself. With the immemorial psychology of the guilty wife, she developed an entirely new attitude of solicitude where her husband was concerned.

She began the unprecedented business of leaving notes explaining her whereabouts on those evenings when she was not going to be at home when he arrived. Elaborate, unclever, and superfluous notes of evasion. She no longer pretended to be asleep mornings, while he moved about the bedroom. It was with difficulty that she held herself in leash, in order not to overdo these efforts to placate herself.

As it was, Rarick, always obtuse, only dimly noticed, and was not seriously impressed one way or another. Jenny would think ahead for five or ten minutes how best to casually introduce the name of Ramon into her conversation, so that if rumor by mischance should come wagging, he would cast it off as a distorted version of something she had herself told him. When she finally did trump up a manner to remark casually that Ramon was a dear boy, absolutely invaluable as a last-minute escort, so good-natured and harmless, it was to fall on what amounted to unheeding ears. Jenny's prattle, particularly of late, was so constant. It gave you a headache if you did not let it run over the surface of your mind like so much patter. She was unusually nervous these days—talking more than usual.

The anomaly of her position, as she lay there in Ramon's arms, smote and smote her. A woman could want to remain secure in her marriage and yet be passionately in love with some one not her husband. It was possible to want two things desperately at the same time. Not that Jenny was in love with her husband, but she was in love with wanting to remain secure as his wife.

"I want to arrange my life, Ramon—ours, I should say—so that while we are waiting for our ultimate happiness, everything connected with us shall seem casual."

She did not quite know what she meant by ultimate happiness.

"You are the one to be considered, Jenny. It is heaven to be with you—to drop everything—my work—but a man must live."

She did not again say, "What work, what work?" His boyishness was irresistible to her.

"There must be no gossip about us, Ramon. Even if my children are grown, Ramon, I am an ideal to them."

"So are you to me."

"It would kill me to hurt them."

"You are good."

"Thank God, though, I have reared them with sophisticated heads on their sensible shoulders."

"It is you who are not sophisticated, my love."

"I never want to grow sufficiently sophisticated, my Ramon, not to love our love as the dearest thing in life. Jennifer would be the first to want me to grasp at that part of life which has so nearly passed me by."

"I would like, Jenny, to look up the fellow who has that paragraph about her in this week's *Town Tattle*—about the affair at the Edgertons—and punch his ——"

"Nothing like that, Ramon! Coming from you, it would look obvious. If only her father doesn't see it! It will all be forgotten in a week; but meanwhile it is awful. Town talk. They say Berry had to marry Leslie to save her from a scandal and that Leslie had to announce it to save herself from Jennifer. . . . Ramon, what was that noise?"

"How nervous you are, my Jenny! Only something creaking."

"I must get my household accustomed to taking my tea-hour for granted. It will make it so much easier for us, Ramon. Everything in my life hereafter will revolve around that, Ramon."

"Jenny, how soon will we have a nook somewhere—ours—alone. . . ."

She hid her face in her hands.

"Soon."

"How soon?"

"Soon."

"You remember, Jenny, what you promised?"

"What?"

"I am to fix up our nook—and bring you to it after it is all complete."

"Yes."

"It is hard to say what I must say now, Jenny, except that, between us, everything must be said."

"Yes. Yes."

"I want to do that nook terribly. I would be doing something for—us."

"You darling."

"And yet, you see, my hands are tied. I do not do it."

She knew what was coming and bated her breath for it because she did not want it to come.

"It takes money to fix up that kind of a place, Jenny."

She lay in silence against his coat.

"Does it offend you to have me say that, Jenny?"

"No—only I hate the talk of money between us ——"

"I know, dearest, but it must be said. I have given up my ——"

"There is the thousand in the mail ——"

"But I must live, Jenny. Besides, what is a thousand? You would not want me to build you a nook that was not worthy of our love."

"It isn't that he ever questions what I draw. But a conspicuously large amount is noticeable when I have nothing to show for it, and he is sure to think I am indulging the children against his wishes."

"Surely you have money of your own."

"Just a drawing-account. I've never bothered. He is generous."

"But you say, yourself, you cannot even indulge your children."

"That is his one difficult spot, Ramon."

"It is not right. No woman should be dependent!"

"I've never thought about it in that light before. There has never been occasion."

"You mean to say no properties are in your name!"

"Of course, silly! I'm always signing papers. I'm one of the stockholders in the new Rarick Building. I'm a big stockholder in the Rarick Chain. Don't forget that, dearest."

Jenny had not forgotten it. Neither had she forgotten certain easily accessible holdings which it did not please her to relate just now. She had no intention of permitting Ramon to furnish a place such as he described. Not for the present, at least, she told herself, when desire ate through the better part of caution. Having one's cake and eating it, too, was almost as insanely paradoxical as it sounded. Besides, a mental picture that was repulsive to her, had a habit of leaning into her bliss with this boy.

Was she one of the horrible, wattled, painted women, as in the notorious case of the dowager, Mrs. Emanie Bursilap, who at seventy years, after her own youth had fled from her as if in disgust, still kept young boys in luxury for the sake of maintaining the delusion of that departed youth? Was this thing between her and Ramon no better than that? Sometimes it seemed to her she must find a way to peer into the heart of this youth, whose time of life, whose flexible, godlike body entitled him to the first bloom of a woman. He and Jennifer were of an age to frolic in the same gardens—and yet he seemed not to see Jennifer, for Jenny ——

"Dear Ramon, everything will come out all right."

"I love to hear you say that, Jenny," he said, and crushed kisses against her eyes.

This time, of the volition of a force that was stronger than her fears, she reached out and turned the key in the door.

IN THE phraseology of Jennifer and Avery, between whom existed a gay nonsense-code, any period of time fraught with comings and goings, telephone bells, messenger boys, arrivals, departures, in, out, bang, hasten, bag, baggage, up, down, motor-cars, golf-bags, theater tickets, opera wraps, bridge tables, packages, flowers, caterers, bustle and rush, constituted a "day among the Raricks."

Hurried scrawls of notes or telegrams, interchanged between them, read like this:

DEAREST AVERY: It's been a hell of a day among the Raricks down home here. How cum with brother Rarick up among the Campus Cut Clothes Boys?

DEAR JENNIF: This day among this Rarick has been no go. This Rarick has a new speed-boat. This day among this Rarick has been spent feeling seasick in and about said speed-boat. It's a wamble. To be a wamble means to be built for land and live on water. That's me, too. I am built for where I ain't. . . .

That was about as far as these two ever ventured across the chasm of the six years' difference in their ages.

Jennif. was a peach, but you couldn't let off steam to her, because when you tried to talk she was always listening to some one beyond your shoulder who wasn't there.

You couldn't talk to Avery, whose mind was always on his own young stuff. Hard to make out what his own stuff was. But there was something to Avery, all right. The boy ran deep . . . he already knew the strange heart-aches of seeing illusions tarnish and had

learned his game of compromise.   Life among the Raricks
wasn't the joke he pretended it was. . . .

The "day among the Raricks" that precipitated a galling scene between Jennifer and her father began as any
run-of-the-mill day for Rarick, for Jenny, and for Jennifer might have begun.

JENNY'S DAY

This particular one started with a pain in her side.
An annoying neuralgic one, against which she usually
carried tablets in a beautiful gold-and-enamel snuff-box
(Napoleona) which she had begged from Rarick's collection.

Rarick, who had slept no better and no worse than
usual, and whose night had been a procession of projects
for the Rarick Building, dropped into one of his brief
deep slumbers just as Jenny beside him flew awake, her
lids popping back suddenly.

The flooding memory of the night before, when she
had dared, because the chauffeur was new, to drive home
from the opera with Ramon by way of three circumfer-
ences of the Park, came sparkling over her in goose-
flesh.

It made her shudder.   It made her lift eyes that were
still brilliant from the night before, up to the sound-
eating radiations of shirred brocade that hung in a canopy
over the bed and then dropped in more sound-eating
drapes between her and the vista of six full-length windows that looked out on Fifth Avenue.

There was a small blue-enamel French telephone, a
blue-enamel thermos carafe, a blue-enamel engagement-
pad, and the blue-enamel box of tablets on the night table
beside her.   One of these tablets she presently swallowed.

This habit of her early awaking was still abominable to her. Precious hours of needed rest, even when they were filled with contemplations that were sweet to her, were wasted lying in bed thus, waiting for her day to begin.

How he slept! Deep in the cave of his pillow, with his face upward. "Little man, you! What do you know of me—here—lying by your side—sharing your bed? Nothing!"

A fear smote her. What if he knew more than she realized! That was absurd. He was not astute.

How strange, after all these years of the disillusionment of a love-life that had spluttered out like a feeble match, that a Ramon should find her desirable. It made her lie slim and straight in bed, with arms folded across her breast in the beatific attitude of feeling herself desirable.

The aspirin made one pleasantly at ease.

What if that were not Rarick beside her, but ——

She shuddered with a rousing distaste of self. Horrible, horrible, to lie there imagining. . . . There were certain scavengers of thoughts that must be kept locked in the inner boxes of the mind. It made one feel shameful to have a thought like that pop out. Just the same, the whole meaning of life would be changed and exalted if that were not Rarick lying there, but, yes, but Ramon! How horrible of her. How poisonous.

What if Rarick should die? No. No. No! And yet she could never really see the wickedness of trying to visualize the effect upon herself of the death of another. Death was one of the few certainties of life. Rarick would die some day. Either before or after her. If before? She was not wishing it. She was thinking it.

It was difficult to visualize life free of the strain of simultaneously wanting to remain impeccably married to

Rarick and yet continue to be desired by Ramon. A life free of the strain of daring to ride three times around Central Park with Ramon because the chauffeur was new, and yet all the while dreading, with undercurrent of fear, the indiscretion of it. The strain of obeying that trick in her make-up which demanded that she be thrice as solicitous of Rarick for every disloyal act with Ramon. The strain of keeping herself free from the shadow of a doubt in the minds of her children.

What if Rarick should die and his restraining hand were left off that household? What if she were herself, but free! A woman of terrific wealth, suddenly released from over twenty years of the indefinable depressant of a man who had grown rich with his lips tight. Would Ramon be lying beside her then? . . .

She swung out of bed, shuddering, and, ringing for her maid, hurried toward her boudoir.

Her day began earnestly now, with a nine-o'clock appointment with the executive of a large firm of decorators, who was coming to inspect the ballroom, with an eye to erecting at one end of it a gondola-shaped stage, on which Jenny proposed to give a charity fête called "A Doge for a Day."

At ten o'clock she had a henna-rinse and shampoo, a long-drawn but imperative performance that accelerated the pain in her side and made her nervous. During this subsequent hour and a half in the hands of her hairdressers, maid, masseuse, her head in towels, her face under cream, her fingers and toes in the simultaneous process of mani- and pedi-cure, Jenny went through the performance of an interview with her head housekeeper, Mrs. Dill. She was exacting in her enormous household management, known to be fair enough, but demanding careful and detailed accounting of weekly expenditures, which, even after years of the experience of living at the very peak of American high standards, remained titanic to her.

"Thirty dollars a week for milk, Mrs. Dill? We don't bathe in it!"

"That fruit bill is fantastic, Mrs. Dill. What is that item? Five pounds of grapes, fifteen dollars? Well! Of course, I know you do your part, but isn't that buying grapes by the carat?"

"Surely, Mrs. Dill, there is some mistake. Seven hundred dollars for the florist's this month, and only three large dinners. Well!"

The days of her conservative girlhood in the modest house where she had spent the first twenty years of her life were deeply rooted. The servants' wages of twenty-five hundred dollars a month, and the greengrocer, the caterer, the butcher, and the laundry bills in proportion were to remain unabatedly startling to her.

There was one item on these statements which always smote Jenny with a kind of anger. Generous though she was, after a fashion, the fact that the bill for the servants' meat could mount to hundreds for the month was constantly roiling. Mrs. Dill saw to it that their supplies came from the same shops where the family viands were marketed. Of course, the servants should be well provisioned, and one must close one's own eyes to the fact that Mrs. Dill shopped with an eye to her commissions, but it did seem that the ordinary cuts of meat from the ordinary shops should have sufficed for them. She had never found voice to convey this to any of her housekeepers, but the earlier training of the wife of one of the richest men in the world would persist. It would have angered Rarick to have her question these food expenditures for the servants, and it was not, she told herself, that she really did question them. It was the principle of the thing. It did seem that a good stew of fowl would suffice for the servants' table instead of the boned squabs which were sent from Baltimore in cotton waddings.

Certain traits that had been developed back there in the pressed-brick eight-room house in St. Louis had persisted in the wife of the thirteenth richest man in the world.

At eleven o'clock Jenny emerged from the barrage of cold cream to accompany Jennifer to a loft over an armory, there to enter vigorously into a fencing-lesson with a master from Turin. When Jenny fenced, a curious flame leaped into her eyes. Jenny's "glitt," her daughter called it. With her lower lip caught between her teeth, and her face in the tight vise of a grimace, she danced to the steel on the balls of feet that were surprisingly nimble. Her mother's fencing inspired Jennifer—who was lovely at the thrust herself—to peal after peal of hilarity.

"You're the spirit of war let loose, Moth, only don't bite your tongue. Down with humanity! Long live sin!"

Nevertheless, these hours exhilarated Jenny, not only seeming to help the pain at her side, but endowing her with a new sense of body buoyancy. She took an extra lesson a week now. "Good measure for you," she told Ramon. "I must at least be one-hundredth as lithe as you are."

At twelve o'clock in this day of a Rarick, the executive committee of the Manhattan Hospital for Crippled Children met at the home of Mrs. Bursilap Dobson. This home, a somber brown one that still occupied wide footage in a once highly conservative section of Madison Avenue that was rapidly giving way to business, was one that Jenny had never entered on a social basis. Curious, too, because Mrs. Bursilap Dobson apparently went out of her way to be gracious to Jenny. On these occasions of the weekly committee meetings, they exchanged doctor,

steamship, opera-box and motor-car preferences, as well
as lore concerning their sons who had attended the same
preparatory school. Most of the time, at Mrs. Dobson's
request, Jenny remained after the meeting for a bit of
chat.

It stopped there.

To the exclusive Dobson functions the John Raricks
were not bidden. "Where do they get off?" gritted Jennifer between her teeth. "It's town talk that her mother,
old lady Emanie Bursilap, aged two hundred and forty-
six, keeps flocks of patent-leather-haired tame robins and
feeds them meal tickets. None over twenty-one need
apply."

The time had come when this horrid indictment could
send a special kind of chill down Jenny's spine.

At one o'clock Jenny entertained the members of the
executive and visiting board of the International House
for Defective Children at the Cosmo Club. Again it
was not a social group, but the list pleased her, and she
had a typed copy of it sent to the *Times*: Madame
Marcella Tarafa, Buenos Aires. Mrs. Gregory Cripps.
Lady Annabel Metcalf. Mrs. Hugo Thorner. Mar-
quise de Brassac. Signora Testa Pontavice. Mrs. Beaver
Kellog, Philadelphia. The Countess of Pendleton, St.
John's House. Mrs. Turner Moses. Mrs. Willie Bing-
ham Payne. Miss Henriette Shonnard.

Jenny was not a member of the Cosmo Club, but entertained there by proxy of Miss Shonnard. It was
Jenny's way of signifying to the daughter of Senator
Shonnard her desire for membership in this most socially
representative women's club in town. So far nothing
had come of it.

At three, Jenny took a taxicab from the club-house, and
met Ramon at the tea-room in the West Seventies. She
had decided on this much of a definite policy! From

now on, never to appear with him at a public function. For instance, that evening he was accompanying, at Jenny's stipulation, young Miss Clabby Wall to a large charity dinner-dance at the Plaza, for which Jenny had taken a table in Jennifer's name. There were to be twenty guests at her table, Ramon not among them. Jenny had sent an extra two tickets to him by mail.

Unquestionably the need of the small retreat of Ramon's fitting-up was becoming imperative. There was such a thing as being conspicuous even at the inconspicuous little tea-rooms of the West Seventies.

Ramon, waiting in the tea-room, had a headache. Something repulsive had happened. His dancing partner, the Spanish girl, a volatile, gifted creature, desperately in love with a shiftless husband who was brutal to her, had fallen ill of a skin irritation that manifested itself on her face and disqualified her for the dance. The sight of the blemished girl had been abhorrent to Ramon, who had also been obliged to advance the improvident pair fifty dollars to cover immediate doctor bills.

Jenny loved the complete way in which he surrendered himself into her hands. "Life is confusing, Jennifer's Jenny. I have sympathy, of course, but I cannot help being repulsed by sickness. Of course, perhaps some day I may fall ill myself."

"No, darling!" cried Jenny, eager to be omniscient in his behalf.

"You won't hate me if ever I do fall ill—and splotchy, Jennifer's Jenny?"

"I'll nurse you like an angel."

"I am a dog and you are an angel."

"You will be an angel to me, though, Ramon, always?"

"It gave me the shivers just now to see her. I was glad to give her money. It strapped me to let her have fifty, though, Jennifer's Jenny."

"I know that," she said, slipping a yellow bill, that was already folded into the hole of her glove, from her hand into his.

He placed a kiss along a lean, suède-covered finger.

"It is hard not to feel upset, Jennifer's Jenny, when life is just one frusteration after frusteration."

He mispronounced "frustration," with a lisp that was adorable to her.

"Everything will come out all right, Ramon."

"How can everything come out all right, when I am not even to be with you tonight, but must sit with that tiresome little Clabby person at a table that is far from yours?"

"You are going to drive home with me afterward. Around the Park three times."

"Darling—how ——"

"Never mind how. There is another new chauffeur. I could not bear to live through the day, dear, if it didn't mean that much time alone with you."

"I am looking at you, Jennifer's Jenny, across this ugly table-top, but in reality I am kissing you one thousand times."

"And me you, Ramon." Across the table their glances poured.

"I must be at Fifty-seventh Street at four o'clock."

"Damn four!"

"Perhaps I shall drop in later at Perroquet's; but keep away, as usual, dear."

At four o'clock the unmounted body of a specially designed French car was submitted to Jenny in the Fifty-seventh Street show-rooms of a firm of automobile-importers.

At five o'clock Jenny picked up Madame Tarafa at her apartment-hotel and took her to Perroquet's for tea, where Ramon danced. He did not come over; but again, from across the room, their glances poured.

At six o'clock, by appointment, a chinchilla coat, which had arrived by way of Moscow, was delivered to Jenny. In the beauty of twilit snow, it hung from her narrow shoulders as she stood before triple mirrors in her boudoir. She proposed to wear it that night. Ramon had admired one worn by Mrs. Stanley Grimes. Jenny happened to know that the Grimes garment had cost forty-five thousand dollars in Paris, plus sixty per cent duty. Her own, with the duty, came to seventy-four thousand. Rarick, who was completely easy-going about her expenditures for finery, paid such bills as these with puzzlement. Seventy-four thousand dollars to cover a woman's back. Thoughts came jamming to the fore of his mind, but he choked them back. Well—those were the gratifications for which men beat out their lives in the market-places.

At seven o'clock the maid in the Breton cap helped Jenny into a black-satin gown that rose to a high neck in front and to a bare and daring V at the back. As she was looping herself in graduated ropes of graduated pearls, the door of her dressing-room burst open without the preamble of a knock.

It was Rarick. His face, locked in the horrible immobility of a gargoyle, was the color of granite.

"I want Jennifer." A paper was crushed in his hand, and his lips were hauled back from his teeth, making them protrude as they do in a skull.

RARICK'S DAY

That same day began for Rarick with his usual habit of twisting reluctantly out of the belated sleep that came to him just before dawn. It was so good, this early=morning drifting-down beneath the snows of consciousness. It was more like a little death, he sometimes thought, than the sleep which must come to most people. It was so absolutely dreamless. So disembodied. It was as if Rarick shot off into space for these sleeps. They bathed, they refreshed. They pumped him full of the energy you would expect from an eight-hour instead of a three-hour sleep. They were his air-tight retreats. Jenny was already up when he awoke. Sun beat against the drawn curtains. The muffled sound of the city came roaring softly, and he could hear Jenny moving about in her boudoir, giving the nervous kind of staccato orders to her maid that made her attitude toward her servants seem imperious. His opening thought had to do with an idea that had boomed into his brain during the night. Why not erect a concert-auditorium, vast, aërial, dramatically sky-high, on the roof of the seventy-nine-story Rarick Building? There must still be time to adapt construction plans to that daring scheme. A Gothic auditorium of superb twilights. Three thousand seats, each one a *fauteuil*. A cathedral organ, diapason pipes. If only the roof space would permit. Increase cost by millions—better to call in Yardsley the architect at once. . . .

Rarick Auditorium!

There was a note on Jenny's writing-pad for him:

Am using your Hispano this morning, as mine is up for repair. Have given orders to send around Renault sedan for you. Body of French car is here. Man will call to see Hellman. My O.K. will be on bill for chinchilla coat. Do you care to present Avery with one of those three-room portable camp sets? Nice for week-end camping-trips, in which he should be encouraged.

Plans for Adirondack house annex are in your desk drawer, right.

Jennifer wishes to charter private car, Penn., for forty guests for Navy football game, Nov. 18. Your office can arrange.

Saranac Hospital Committee will ask Hellman for an interview with you. Please give generous check in my name. These people important to me. Mrs. Carleton Murray, president. Do not snub. Not home to dinner. Charity dance at Plaza tonight. Going alone.

He preferred Jenny up and out of the room first, and her memorandum, even though so unusually verbose these days, by pad. He had no intention of seeing Mrs. Murray, whose philanthropies were conspicuous and obnoxious to him, or of presenting his son with some *deluxe* camping paraphernalia, which he thought effete.

But how typical, this procedure! He had feigned sleep when Jenny had come trailing in between two and three. Then she had taken the opportunity of his morning sleep to tiptoe off to her dressing-room, from where he could catch her quick spatter of words to her maid. Do. Don't. Don't. Do. It was at least three days since they had met for more than the briefest of periods. There was one of her letters from Avery twisted and thrown on the night table beside the blue carafe. On his way to his dressing-room, the temptation to smooth it out and read it smote Rarick. The salutation, "Dearest of Mothers," smote his eyes from a corner that had not been caught in the twist.

He did not pause to pry into it.

At eight-thirty, an attorney came to sit beside him while he had his breakfast in a small sun-room of superb walnut walls, inlaid with Rarick's collection of bronze medallions. The discussion was in regard to a pending suit against Rarick Chain for infringement of copyright law on a toy edition of a pocket dictionary they were about to distribute in hundreds of thousands at five cents the copy.

At nine o'clock they rode downtown together in the Renault sedan as far as Times Square, where Rarick dived into the subway.

He had been much headlined for that custom of his.

MAGNATE MINGLES WITH STRAP-HANGING CROWD

It saved him eleven minutes. Sometimes he wondered about those eleven minutes. He fought for them through human underground shambles, drew into his lungs the breath off the lips of strap-hangers who lurched their chins into his eyes. In prospect, those eleven minutes seemed incalculably important to him. In retrospect, somehow, they could never be accounted for.

At nine-thirty Hellman met him at the private door of his private office, took his hat and coat, and handed him a drink of Vichy water.

That was part of being a man of affairs. You paid somebody to see to it that you were properly stoked with the amount of drinking-water prescribed by your doctor. Hellman's concern over that drink of water was perfectly simulated. He watched each gulp of Rarick, who was never thirsty, with an interest that was impeccable.

Everything about Rarick's office was contrived to keep out sound. An artificial quiet resulted. Noises began to grind in your ears from that quiet, as if some of the crash of the subway had accumulated against the drums. Rugs ate in footfalls. The battery of push-buttons made only soft, purring sounds. Two enormous electric fans were noiseless. The vast top of Rarick's mahogany double desk, sheeted in plate glass, carried out the noiseless effect. It was empty of even an inkstand. The windows overlooking New York Harbor were high enough to give the scene below——of moving tugs, weaving elevated trains, specks of people——the effect of silence.

Outside of these carefully insulated four walls, two hundred stenographers crashed out furious and alarmed hurry calls for more hair-pins, more peach-skin-faced dolls, more five-cent dictionaries, more toothpicks, and more lollypops to match the shapes of the tongues of the world. At nine-thirty, an order, just dictated, was being typed out there in those frenzied aisles of the polyphonic typewriters, for the largest single order of boys' caps in the history of the industry, while two men sat in conference with Rarick and concluded this perpetration upon the youthful heads of the world of hundreds of thousands of cotton caps with cotton linings and cotton buttons and cotton eagles stitched against navy-blue cotton backgrounds.

At eleven o'clock there arrived, direct from the railroad station, a president of a Cleveland bank and an executive of a real-estate concern, on an impending deal that had to do with a Rarick Chain property-trade on a Cleveland business block that had not yet been inundated with the shop of petty trade, and against which public opinion ran high. This particular situation was an old story; and Rarick took a certain glory in signing papers that were to make way for a Rarick store on a Cleveland avenue that boasted a museum, a library, and a park.

At noon, while the anteroom filled up with an assortment of charity-committee representatives, department managers, factory executives, automobile agents, and bank messengers, two harried-looking architects with portfolios and long rolls of blue-prints were admitted into Rarick's office by a secret door.

It developed that the roof auditorium, being an afterthought, would involve structural changes of appalling magnitude and expense, to say nothing of possible building violations, steel-beam problems, water installations, and engineering difficulties too technical to bear immediate discussion. Everything was possible, of course, but at cost of millions of dollars ——

But the idea of the auditorium had formed, hardened, and fastened into the mind of Rarick. Hellman hovered, during this exhaustive interview, offering such conservative objections as he dared, and urging deferred decisions. Two executives of the company were called in, also a little Russian named Osonsky, an office manager in whom Rarick had great confidence. While the anteroom jammed itself to capacity, the conference dragged on, two difficulties arising for every one solution. But when the architects finally buckled up their portfolios, and the long interview came to its end, everyone present knew that, in pointed stalagmities toward the heavens, would presently arise the Gothic reality of Rarick's popular-price auditorium, built of the people's dimes and nickels, for them, at admission of dimes and nickels. The greatest musicians available were to pour forth the music of the masters to the knick-knack-ridden public that swarmed the aisles of the Rarick Chain stores. It was to cost three million dollars, house two of the most famous Rembrandts in existence, and the organ-builder was to die in its loft, of heart-stroke induced by unbearable excitement, the day the instrument pealed forth the opening-strain of "Ave Maria" to its first audience.

So much for one of Rarick's sleepless dreams.

At considerably past the lunch hour an office boy brought five Graham wafers in oiled tissue-paper and a glass of "half milk, half Vichy," and placed them silently on the desk beside Rarick, who was now talking long-distance to Denver, a receiver pressed against each ear.

At three o'clock, a woman evangelist whose name was constantly skidding across a coast-to-coast press, and who had traveled eleven hundred miles for this appointment, came to confirm a matter relating to her dream of a world-tabernacle on a mountain-top overlooking the Pacific.

At three-fifteen, a German manufacturer of Christmas-tree ornaments arrived with two Eastern managers, and five hundred and fifty thousand dollars was transacted across the empty desk-top.

At three-thirty, Rarick, five members of the International Theater Foundation Committee, Hellman, and two witnessing clerks, bent over that desk for the signing of the Rarick endowment of one hundred and fifty thousand dollars.

At three-forty, the flower-woman on the corner of Broadway and Pine Street, who sold wire-stemmed carnations there for the lapels of hurrying business men, came up to Rarick's office, by Hellman's arrangement, on the anniversary of her fiftieth year on that corner. Also by Hellman's arrangement, and to Rarick's surprised and angry protest, three cameras clicked the picture of him presenting her with a check commemorating the occasion.

At ten minutes to four, Hellman walked as far as the subway with him, handing him a packet of letters to read upon his arrival home.

At shortly past four, after a cup of tea and two more Graham wafers, Rarick let himself relax into the unicorn-chair in his library. For an hour he lay back there, riding the quiet, as a swimmer floats on his back, finally pressing a button to flood that quiet with an organ overture called "Field of the Cloth of Gold." No matter how chromoesque musically, there was something about it that set Rarick's blood marching. He could see himself mounting—always mounting steps, a cloak streaming off his shoulder—mounting—mounting—peaks off in the distance, snow-capped. A viola slipped into a cadenza that seemed to pour from a bird-throat—somewhere—high—was morning air like ice-water. He could see himself mounting—clouds formed and were faces—the chorister face of Avery—a woman's face, with lips desirable—up—up—Pyrenees of mountain-tops. . . .

Presently Dr. Gerkes came in and drank a glass of

hot Burgundy, which a butler brought without his request. He had just returned from Toronto, where he had lectured before a royal archæological society. There was desultory talk of university endowments, railroads, the Abyssinian researches of a Viennese that promised to shake the theories of the alleged beginnings of Tertiary man, and then Rarick, spilling out a waistcoat pocket of pearls, emeralds, jacinths, girasols, asterias, and diamonds, saw to it that his friend screwed a glass into his eye and appraised until it was time for him to climb into what he called his overalls for an address he was to deliver that evening before a scientific society at the Engineers' Club.

Left alone, Rarick began to rip open letters off the packet that Hellman had handed him at the subway. It was after he had read the third of them that he burst into Jenny's boudoir with it crushed in his hand, and his lips flaring back in the fashion that made a skull of his face.

Standing in the multiplying embrasure of her mirrors, Jenny's hand, emerald-incrusted, flew to her throat. What had happened? Rarick knew something! He always did when he looked like that. Dry teeth bare. Terror flew at her. Terror and a sudden loathing for the whole tottering structure of her affair with Ramon. As a keeper of a gigolo she had risked everything. Why mince matters? Keeper of a gigolo! And at risk of security, prestige, eminence. The neuralgic pain that was lurking in her side seemed to leap into her throat—into her spirit. What had she pulled down about her? What terrible crash was this impending? Out of her recklessness, out of her failure to rest content with the security of her eminence, was she about to reap still more failure?

"Rarick," she cried out to him, ready, as it were, to fight for her life, "don't be a fool!"

How terrifyingly like a skull he was.

"Where is Jennifer?" he said along his dry jowls. "I want her."

Jennifer? Thank God, then it wasn't—Jenny! Jennifer, of course. Some nonsense of Jennifer's. This wretched nervousness of hers! How could Rarick possibly have known what her foresight and skill had arranged that he should not know. The prospect of the drive homeward with Ramon through the Park came flowing back. Her precaution to change chauffeurs every so often was an indication of the skill with which she handled this situation. Who could be clever enough, for instance, to tie up chauffeur trouble with the fact that she and Ramon . . . Jennifer, poor child! What now? One saw the child so comparatively seldom, now that the season was on—surely nothing ——

"Where is Jennifer?"

"She must be dressing."

"Call her."

"What has happened, Rarick?"

"Call her."

"The child is probably in her bath. Is it as imperative as all that?"

"Call her."

"Tell Miss Jennifer," she said in French to the maid in the Breton cap, "to come here at once. Her father wishes her."

What row was this now? Jennifer, poor child— could you blame her?—had been distrait and erratic in her movements ever since that wretched business at the Edgertons'. Hard hit, poor child. But as if there weren't just as good fish in the sea as ever came out of it. Jennifer needed change. The camp, perhaps! **Could** her father have got wind of that messy occasion at the Edgertons'? God! what a bore Rarick could be! No wonder his children shied from him.

"I wouldn't start rowing with Jennifer this time of the evening, Rarick. What's wrong? Won't it keep until ——"

The maid returned.

"Miss Jennifer is dressing and is already late for an appointment. She will come to Mr. Rarick in the library tomorrow morning."

Rarick strode past the words, across the hall, and, without preamble of knocking, into his daughter's suite.

"Rarick," cried Jenny, and strode after, "don't be a fool!"

Jennifer, evidently just risen from bed, was sitting on the edge of it, in a web of a nightgown that fell off her shoulder to the elbow, and pulling on a bit of infinitesimal stocking.

"Why, Father," she cried, and jerked a bit of the web across her, "you mustn't come in here!"

He hated a display of undress even in the formal attire of the women of his family. This Aphrodite rising from the foam of lace and chiffon offended him less than the bare backs they wore tapering into the waist line of evening-gowns.

"Put on some clothes," he said. From the layer of tousled bed-clothing of more pink and more lace, his daughter regarded him throw a scowl at a jungle of hair that had fallen forward over her eyes.

"I think this is pretty thick, Father," she cried.

Her mother picked up a white, tufted, swan's-down robe, and tossed it to her.

"Put this on, Jennifer," she said, in the cold, measured tones of her disapproval of Rarick.

What a bore—what a bore the man was! Joyless.

Still a hardware clerk at heart. Little man, you. No wonder the flame that burned in Ramon was warming to her rigid heart. Thank God for Ramon! What was that paper. . . .

Thrusting the crumpled sheet under his daughter's eyes and slapping it with the back of his hand, Rarick lost no time.

"Explain that."

The letter was from Tom Edgerton:

. . . unless, Mr. Rarick, this situation is to result in tragedy for all concerned, I beg you to call instant halt to matters between your daughter and my son-in-law. To add to an already outrageous situation, Leslie is with child. I regret the imperative need to bring before you what I am sure must be your first knowledge of this dangerous dilemma for all concerned. Unless you force it to an immediate solution . . .

A low cry escaped Jennifer. Pain. Rage. Surprise.

"Damn him! Damn!" she cried and began to sob instantly and wildly into her bare palm, which she clapped against her mouth. "Damn! Damn!"

"It seems to me," cried Jenny, frightened, "that Tom Edgerton had better mind his own eggs in his own basket."

What was this? What was this? As Jennifer had recited it that muddled morning after, both the Jennys had sat in merciless indictment upon the behavior of Berry, and of Leslie, too, for that matter. Jennifer had hurled at him merciless invective, wallop, and relentless appraisal. Surely, in these weeks subsequent, Jennifer had not been seeing Berry? The idea that Jennifer was cruelly hard hit was preposterous. What was this? Had Jennifer, for the first time, violated her mother's confidence? That little fool there, that little fool man, there, what did he know about handling her?

"I want to know," shouted Rarick, seeming to gnaw

on his words with his long dry-looking teeth, and standing directly up before his daughter as she struggled into the sleeve of her robe, "what there is between you and Berry Rhodes?"

"And what if I don't choose to tell you?" she cried, already breathless, as if the interview were of long duration instead of only just having begun.

"Don't rag her, Rarick."

"Shut up!" he said. How his jaw slid around in that circular, grinding movement! Thank God it was Jennifer and not herself on the rack before him. She could defend Jennifer——

"Either you tell me the exact situation," went on her father, brushing the crest off of a wave of small, incredibly sheer pillows, as he began to waggle a finger at her, "or I'll have the Rhodes dog here himself, or go where I can find him."

"If you do," cried Jennifer, wrapping herself in her arms, as if to withdraw from possibility of contact with the threat, "I'll kill myself."

"Jennifer, for God's sake, you must learn to talk quietly to your father."

"How can I talk quietly to him? How can I talk at all to him? How can I talk to anybody? Get out! For God's sake, get out! Give me that letter!" She snatched it from her mother's hands and began to twist it the shape of her own twisted lips. "Leave me alone! Get out!"

Her father caught her by the wrist, jerking her toward him until her teeth gave a click.

"What is this man to you?"

She began to sob, her face naked and dark as she struggled for her hands.

"As if you would understand if I told you."

"What is he to you?"

Suddenly, as if the realization of her trap came flooding over her, she let her wrists relax in her father's grip and dropped her head forward until her brow was almost against his hands, before her incredible words came.

"I love him, Papa," she said. "Help me, Papa, I don't want to love him. I want to hate him and I can't. Help me, Papa. Please, please, Papa."

His heart was in his mouth. His knees trembled. The "papa" had almost unnerved him. The silly revealing child's word. Papa. A primitive phonetic word that must have had its etymology along the toothless gums of babes. He was too racked to make a sound. Papa, help Jennifer. . . .

"Oh, my darling!" cried Jenny, stung to quick, pouring tears. "And Mother never knew. Mother never knew. My baby, what has come over you? This isn't like you!"

"I know it isn't, Mother. It's not me. That's just it. I'm not myself. I want to hate him. I want to keep hating him. And I love him, Mother. Isn't that terrible?"

"My dear! My sweet! It is just an infatuation. He isn't worth your little finger. My dear—my sweet!"

This bare-backed woman, with the little notches up her spine that were repulsive to him, and the narrow head with the pink hair brushed up straight to accentuate it, was wresting the situation from him. She was superb as she drew the head of Jennifer to her narrow breast. Superb with being her mother, while he stood dumb before the emergency of his daughter, even though, at her words, "Help me, Papa," his anger had dissolved into the flood-stream of his heart. Still he remained there, dumb, while Jenny, whose pain flowed in the relief of tears, was wresting from him what had been perilously near being a moment of contact with his girl.

"*You* help me, Mother!"

"Why, darling, Mother never realized———"

"I'll break every bone in his body," Rarick began to repeat, suddenly. "I'll break every bone in his body."

"That *would* be helpful, Rarick," said Jenny, regarding him above the head of her daughter with cool, slitted eyes. "One of your typically diplomatic moves."

"I'll break every bone in his body."

"Mother, Mother, make him understand! There's really been nothing between Berry and me. If he goes to Berry, I swear I'll kill myself——— I tell you I've been the—the aggressor. I am the one———"

"Shh—h-h, my darling! I understand."

"You see, Mother, it hasn't been Berry."

He was out of it now. It was Jennifer and her mother. Jennifer in the cradle of her mother's arms, like a child.

"Yes, yes, Mother knows———"

"Down inside him somewhere, Berry's got a sense of honor. I'm the rotter. I haven't let him be. After that night—even. I've kept wangling him. To meet me. To be with me. Every once in a while I think I'm cured and try not to see him. I've tried to be cured, Mother. I've been in hell. I'm sick, Mother. You try and make Father see that. I'm like a drug fiend. I love him and I don't want to love him. He's snide, he's swine, I keep telling myself. And now that Leslie's going to have a kid, that makes me twice swine. O God, I—I think I am going crazy, Mother."

She was like something wild, crouching beneath the wing of a protecting arm—the bare, gleaming arm of Jenny—her muddled eyes staring through the jungle of hair at Rarick, who, having released her wrists, stood back, flabbergasted.

"Shh-h-h, darling! I see———"

"Make him see———"

"Yes, yes, I'll make Father see. Mother knows.

Mother understands. Jennifer's nervous. Jennifer has had a bad dream and Mother is going to take her away— far—up to the Canadian camp, and get her rested and cured."

Jenny had wrested his moment from him, all right. A cry raged in the silence of his heart. There they crouched from him. The Jennys. "Papa," she had mouthed, like a child. So far as he could remember, she had never, even in her little-girlhood, called him that before. What a curious thing to have happened! This little girl, this sick little girl, this pure, good, smart, terribly alien little girl, calling him "Papa." And Jenny had wrested his chance. God damn her! No. No. No. God bless her! This bare-backed woman, with the ridges up her spine that were repulsive to him, was divine, at the moment, as she babbled sentimental mush to this girl!

"Sh-h-h, Jennifer! You're going to get well."

Her sobs began to subside as she looked out fearfully under the wing of her mother's arm.

"I'll get well if he will leave me alone."

"Sh-h-h! Father will leave you alone. Won't you, Rarick, if I promise to help little Jennifer, who wants to get well, to be rid of the idiotic notion that she is in love. Won't you, Rarick? Won't you?" sang Jenny, in the monotony of singsong, rocking her body in soothing motion over the crouched figure of Jennifer.

"I won't ever see him again. I don't want ever—to see him again ——"

"Sh! That's right. She won't ever see him again, Rarick. Don't cry, sweet! Mother will help you. Nothing has happened between them; and for you to see Berry would not only be absurd, but dangerous. Your answer to Tom will only be the fact that Jennifer won't ever see Berry again. Isn't that right, Baby?"

"Yes, Mother."

"We're going away for a little while. Up to the Canadian camp—to fish—and get well. I'll wire we're arriving." (Ramon could come up for a week.) "Aren't we, Jennifer?"

"Yes, darling."

"You hear, Rarick?" said Jenny, always rocking, always crooning. "We're going up to camp—to rest—to get well."

He sat dumb in the pool of his defeat, glorying, in a curious, crooked way, in the power of this angular, eccentric woman he called wife, to mother his children, yet filled with a crushing, impotent anger that baffled and tortured him because he could not define it.

"You go now, Rarick, while Jenny puts Jennifer to bed and gives her a bromide to make her sleep. Sh-h, my sweet ——"

"Put me to sleep, Mother. Don't let me finish dressing to go out and meet him ——"

"Shh-h! Now go, Rarick, while Jenny puts Jennifer to sleep."

With the sensation of having no sensation at all, Rarick pressed at the hand on his daughter and went stumbling from the room.

Dr. GERKES was coming down the hall toward the small rear staircase he used for his exits. He had just had his dinner. A butler was hurrying with the remains of it hoisted on a tray. Gerkes was in his nondescript top-coat, his collar already turned up against a fine sifting November mist that was falling into the twilight.

Where might he be going? Wherever it was, the desire smote Rarick to join him.

Gerkes was going for one of his walks around the reservoir in the Park. He did a great deal of his work that way, pounding the neat geometry of footpath that inclosed the boxed-in waters for hours on end, formulating in his mind and hurrying back to write.

He was a known figure around that reservoir. Pedestrians, mostly with dogs, nodded to him. Men around the waterworks knew him. Many the blustery trip when he had things all to himself, and the grit of ice hung to his lashes, and the wind, into which he bent the top of his head, caused even his skimpy coat-tails to balloon.

"I'll join you," said Rarick, who was not much of a walker.

"Come along," said Gerkes, practicing a rule never to be surprised. They descended by a grand staircase instead of Gerkes's choice of a rear one, and two butlers swung them solemnly out of the doors that were copied from the Florentine Campanile, into the prickled gray wash of drizzling November.

Rain hung in the air like a curtain. It made of the evening a bead portière. Through it, lights climbed mistily up the new architecture of skyscraping buildings with receding terraces.

Rarick stood on his top step, no higher than a match to his house. Traffic rolled by, filled with the silhouette of lives that he supplied with their five-and-ten-cent needs.

It struck Rarick, in that moment while he paused for Gerkes to light his pipe, that his own house was little more than an omnibus filled with the hurrying figures of those who were also alien to him, except in so far as he supplied their five-and-ten-thousand-dollar needs.

Jennifer, as she had sped past him, in that instant before Jenny had snatched, had called, "Save me, Papa!" What atavism was that? Tucked away in what recesses of her haughty little heart was he papa to her? In the confusion, she had doubtless lost track. And yet the Jennys were not all to blame for the confusion. It was the confusion that had confused them.

Crash, was how his brain felt. The confusion of what seemed to Rarick the falling of huge copper disks through jazz-splintered space that was bottomless. And the space was divided into days. The days of the Raricks.

A battalion of red lights flashed down the Avenue; and in the sudden and, by contrast, deafening quiet halt of the traffic, the two men rushed softly, bodies bent, into the Park.

There were times when the sensation of the falling of the copper disks through the space that was divided into days, seemed to Rarick to go on plunging through the nights. It was as if his body were some kind of infinitude filled with a consciousness of tumult that was almost unbearable.

Even here, in the stretches of a park that held out arms of bare branches of trees to receive them into quiet, the tumult continued to shoot through him in disks.

Ballet Mécanique. The world of the Raricks, still

rent with Jennifer's cry of "Help me, Papa!" operated
on a huge central piston, like a ceiling-high steel wheel
in a power-house. Ballet Mécanique. Where had he
first heard that phrase? Wherever, it stuck. Ballet
Mécanique. His life, his being, his brain were a power-
house for mechanical production. Production. Over-
production. Bing! Bang! Razzle! Dazzle! Ten-
cent hats for ten-cent heads. Five-thousand-dollar speed-
boats for juniors. Production. Bing! Bang! Razzle!
Dazzle! His brain was a switchboard, as high as his
house was high, as square as this Reservoir around which
they were tramping was square. Pip! Pop! Lights
dancing in and out across the switchboard. Power.
Man-power. Horse-power. Candle-power. Water-
power. Brain-power. Ballet Mécanique. Out of the
switchboard of the brain ran a thousand little snaky tub-
ings, to be plunged into plugs. More red lights. Salted
peanuts from Tennessee. Paper snakes from Nürnberg.
Under-arm shields from Trenton. Scalloped doilies from
Brooklyn. Leatherized bags from Oshkosh. Pearl buttons from Seattle. Candied prunes from Santa Clara.
Pasteboard turtles from Tokio.

Production. The world had a hundred billion eyes
that were lights on his switchboard brain. Give me wire
nails out of Pittsburgh. Raw silk out of Shanghai. Size
A-1 cans of peaches out of Sacramento. Washable baby-
ribbon out of Lyons.

Ballet Mécanique. A hot copper disk ripped off the
left plate of Rarick's temple, as he bent into the light
curtain of rain. And another. Disk after disk after disk,
a flying world of them. They clattered, they clamored,
they splintered the rain which spat against their heat.
Ballet Mécanique. The jumping pistons. The coughing
steam. The high cries of steel wheels under trains taking the steel curves of rails. The racing of leather belts

over heads bent to the tricky business of inserting the bit of object into the machine at the instantaneously right instant. Pistons galumphing, steel elbows jerking. Wise old steel jaws yawning for pulp and spewing out products! Red light. White light. Up. Down. Galumph. Give me twenty sheets of tin at a gulp if you would have wire dish-cloths at the Five Cent tables. Galumph! Galumph! Two hundred yards of wire for the ten-cent boxes of assorted nails. Humdinger! Machine-stitched dish-cloths, three for ten. Ga-dash! Ga-dash! Oilcloth books for children. Clunk! Clank! Clink! Kodak-picture albums. Dip! Sizz! Squ! Incandescent bulbs. Spang! Pie-pans. Yeow! The Devil limping over Hell! Chicken-wire at ten cents a yard.

And off the wheel-sized disks that were exploding off the temple of Rarick, began to spin images of the snow-white, copper-banded yachts of the rich. Rows of casinos along white Rivieras, filled with overheated men and women in elbow-deep bracelets, breathing over baccarat. Boys, all with the chorister-faces of Avery, racing close to macadam roads in cigar-shaped speed-monsters that were doomed for collision with the disks. Hordes of Jennys in tight gowns with no backs, climbing up the sides of gold amphitheaters that had been greased, and falling back upon one another in riots of finery. Niagaras of ticker tape and men with kidney circles under their eyes, disappearing beneath the paper snow as it slid between their fingers. Motor-boats; chinchilla coats, a thousand trapped little beasts to the precious garment; four-hun-dred-thousand-dollar ballrooms; carved doors of a Cam-panile; seven town cars; sapphire anklets from Cartier's; thirty-five room Adirondack camps; thirty-four servants; Jenny's crystal bathtub; six thousand dollars' worth of cotillion gewgaws; private cars to football games; eight-thousand-dollar steamship-suites; three-million-dollar life-insurance policies; bracelets, cymbals, shields; and, smothering under the bracelets and shields, the voice of a man's daughter, remote—"Papa—help me ——"

"Do you know," said Gerkes, speaking for the first time as they turned homeward, "that certain anthropological researches seem to be proving conclusively that man owes the dawn of his brain-power to the ice age? When roots and berries, hitherto their principal foods, disappeared, they were obliged to hunt reindeer, and flesh was as easy to chew as raw oysters. That threw the jaw into disuse and gave the brain a chance to become the larger part of the head. . . ."

In THE twenty-three years since her brother's marriage, Hildegarde Rarick, teacher in the primary grades in the public schools of Keokuk, had visited him three times. Two of these highly ceremonious occasions had taken place before the migration east.

Miss Rarick was as full of principles regarding her relationship to her brother's rise to fortune, as a porcupine is full of quills. And, just so, she bristled with them.

From the very start, when rumors of Rarick's engagement to quite a wealthy St. Louis girl had come floating toward her on wings of exaggerated gossip, Miss Rarick had taken her stand.

Nine years his senior, she had never, to use her own phraseology, been beholden to him, and did not intend to begin to be so now. Trained, by the same aunt who had reared Rarick, to become self-sustaining at an early age, she had become that while her young brother was still husking corn for pennies, shaking the uncongenial dust of the farm off her feet, and attending high and normal school in Keokuk by day, while she earned the upkeep nursing small children by night. She had seldom clapped eyes on her brother since. At well past fifty she was teaching the same grade, in the same school, on practically the same basis she had taught at twenty. The check for fifty dolars which had ultimately enabled Rarick to leave the farm for Keokuk, where he had boarded in the same house with his sister for two years, had come from Hildegarde.

He remembered this, and off and on for years had

tried to ram down the resistance she put up against largesse from him; but she not only continued to refuse the slightest boon of any sort, but also vigorously resented any attempt on his part to merge her narrow path with what she was fond of terming "the primrose one" of his family.

It is not improbable that even Miss Rarick's statewide fame as the sister of John G. Rarick was equaled by the peculiar notoriety she enjoyed as the eccentric, socialistically inclined Miss Rarick, who would not accept a penny from her multimillionaire brother, but continued to live in the third-floor front room of the Bustanoby family on K Street and pay for that room (with lighthousekeeping privileges) out of the underpaid earnings of a primary teacher.

It was good copy. Miss Rarick was not. She turned a narrow back on the vicarious distinction that was as sincerely terrifying to her as publicity can be to the obscure, and went her way, not, however, rejoicing.

Before the gyrations of fate, Jenny Avery, and fortune had wrenched the situation crazily away, Miss Rarick had entertained the neat plan of one day joining her brother in St. Louis, and, on a fifty-fifty basis, sharing an apartment with him. They were thus to become really acquainted, after the rather precarious years of their orphaned childhood, and work out one of those pleasant living arrangements that can sometimes be achieved even by relatives.

Rarick's marriage had been a blow from which she had never completely risen back to normal. Everything that had happened subsequently she regarded as part of the huge prohibitive force that had come between her and the ideal of the joint living arrangement on the fifty-fifty basis with her brother.

Besides, from the first instant of her first visit to him, the year after his marriage, she had detested Jenny.

One of those pointed, Chesapeake-retriever women, all peak, had been her immediate and lasting appraisement.

"Do you mean beak?" asked her landlady, Mrs. Bustanoby, when Miss Rarick returned and related her impressions.

"No, peak!"

"Funny," thought Mrs. Bustanoby. "Never thought of it before, but Miss Rarick is sort of all peak herself."

She was, but in the most remote sense from which Jenny was that. She was off her brother's pattern only to the extent of the rather thrust-up manner she had of carrying her head. Otherwise, in a sallow kind of coloring—said by relatives to be after her father, who had died on his sparce Iowa farm the year after John G.'s birth—and in the lean sloping shoulders—said by relatives to be off the pattern of her mother, who had died, lean and racked, bearing John G.—Miss Rarick was any narrow woman, whose thin lips had obviously never been coveted and whose eyes told that story with a thoroughly unconscious bitterness.

It synchronized with Miss Rarick's idea of what she might expect from her sister-in-law, that she should arrive for a long-contemplated visit to her brother, her first trip to New York, by the way, the very evening after the Jennys had departed suddenly for the Canadian camp.

Rarick was on hand to meet her, and that fat Mr. Hellman, who handed her a telegram from Jenny, explaining Jennifer's influenza and imperative need of change, and which Miss Rarick strongly suspected the fat Mr. Hellman of having maneuvered to send himself, by some such device as wiring a friend in Buffalo to wire back in Jenny's name.

As a matter of fact, the telegram had actually come

from Jenny, due to sharp admonitions from Rarick, but nothing could have suited Miss Rarick better than this sudden and allegedly imperative absence of Jenny. As for Jennifer and Avery, Miss Rarick had what amounted to a pathetic desire to know these offspring whom she knew as little as she knew their father. But even their absence was, in a sense, relief. It eased the strain of trying not to appear so completely what she knew she must appear, in their eyes.

It was the first year that Miss Rarick, after thirty-two years of teaching, was enjoying her leisure and her pension at the hands of the public-school department of her small city. For eight years she had planned to use the first two weeks of it becoming better acquainted with her brother.

Well, here she was. At sixty, Miss Rarick looked a nervous, an exacting, and a narrow sixty. She had strong black hair, a face almost the precise shape of an acorn, and penetrating black eyes that partially redeemed her from what might have been sallow ugliness.

She was a strange and rather dread person to Rarick. A cold, remote older sister, whose attitude had always been unspoken grievance, and yet who never would permit him, by deed, the only gesture of which he seemed capable, where she was concerned, to remove some of the cause for that grievance.

The fact that Jenny and Hildegarde were congenitally uncongenial, Rarick's common sense had long since, after those first two harrowing weeks she had visited them when they were bride and groom in St. Louis, led him to accept without hope of retrieval.

But subsequently, Rarick considered that he had done everything possible, so far as his responsibility to this narrow, sloping-shouldered lady was concerned. Even in the first years of his rise to prosperity he had urged her to give up her teaching and live on the income he was beginning to be so well able to afford her.

Later, he had even gone so far as to send the junior partner of his firm of lawyers out to Keokuk, to discuss any arrangement that might be agreeable to Hildegarde, thus sparing her any direct endowment that might prove embarrassing to her.

Her consistency in her refusal to accept a favor from her brother remained flawless.

As Hellman expressed it inelegantly to his wife, "She's a virgin even in her financial relations with her brother."

To Rarick, the entire situation was detestable. Hildegarde's punctiliousness about money matters bespoke an innate reverence for it that her behavior attempted to belie.

Only a woman with a deeply buried respect for the importance of money could have permitted herself so wide and conspicuous a gesture as refusing to accept it from one so well able to give. It was the sort of thing you were expected to respect enormously in a woman like Hildegarde. It was supposed to make her admirable; and did, to the citizenry of Keokuk, who would, for instance, have regarded her money unawareness of Gerkes as meretricious.

Rarick dreaded her. She got on his nerves. She was the antithesis of everything that set him on edge in the behaviorisms of his own family; and yet, he asked himself regarding this admirable woman, was Hildegarde, in the stark rigor of her life, any the better person?

Was he by way of falling into the easy indictment that the rich are all meretricious and the poor admirable?

Hildegarde was close to impeccability. Law, church, and society-abiding. Decent, moderate, principled. Her life was an open moor. It was a moor, all right. Not the moor, either, of heliotropes and mauves, where he had once spent a Christmas. Jenny, in the fashionable name of grouse-hunting, had hankered for a Scottish castle. Rarick had bought one, in Forfarshire, but after two seasons of social struggle that she decided were not worth the candle, Jenny had left it to gather moss and taxes. Rarick had since sold it, at a profit of two hundred thousand dollars, to a Californian with a wife who also hankered for mixed bag of deer, grouse, and social drag.

Hildegarde's figurative moor was the moor of tradition and dictionary definition. A tract of waste land.

The night she arrived, and sat with Rarick in her high-neck black silk, a turquoise four-leaf clover her sole jewel, Rarick, visualizing his glittering Jennys in their places at his dinner table of point-lace and gold plate, felt a surge of bewilderment.

How righteous Hildegarde, in those smug precepts of life which so decorously divided right for her from wrong!

If only, looking at her, listening to her, talking with her, he could have felt that here, in this worthy life, were summed up some of the realizations, mental, moral, and spiritual, that he craved so for himself and his own.

Hildegarde was as hedged in by her grim principles as Jenny was by her lack of them.

She held to the rigid and somewhat obsolete socialism that all men are equal except for the accidental advantages which a capital-ridden country gives the rich one over the day laborer. No rich man could sincerely harbor the hope of a better poor man's world and not choke over the cake that came to his table. Your true economic philosopher reduced himself, by giving away his fortune, to the impotency of poverty, and by virtue of the asinine inconsistency of shearing himself of his power to make his wealth work for his principles, thereby became cleansed.

"I think," she told her brother at the conclusion of a long meal devoted to a discussion of the Kansas coal strikes, closed-shop conditions in Keokuk, the Protestant vote, and a pointed dissertation on lax youth, "that I shall take a 'bus first thing tomorrow and ride down into the congested districts."

"I'll send some one down with you into some of my model tenements."

"I don't suppose Jenny or the girl has much time to devote to study of that sort of thing?"

How smug she was! The mere fact of the omnibus irritated him. Her world operated on a pivot of ready-made principles. She cerebrated about practically nothing, but was quick to practice principle even when meaningless, as exemplified by the 'bus ride when there were idle cars in the garage at her disposal.

She had what Gerkes called a machine-stitched philosophy of the interval called life. All men are equal. Marx or somebody—maybe it was God—said so. No— Plato? Oh no, not Plato! That the scheme of the alleged equality of man did not work out that way, never had, was another matter. Well, anyway, all men were equal. Of course, nobody denied that somebody had to mine coal and somebody had to teach school, and it was important that electric lighting first be invented and then manufactured by somebody, and, of course, there must always be your Goethes and Edisons, your Beethovens, your paupers and your peasants, and, for some reason, the communities of men who must have been wood-choppers contemporaneously with Abraham Lincoln had remained unspecial, while he —— Well, just the same, all men are equal. All men are equal in the eyes of God, anyway, even if He created some of them with low brain-power, low vitality, and a low competency to cope with His great ones of His earth.

How joyless she was! Men digging in subway ditches, women on hospital cots in wards, were jocular in a way she had never been capable of in her life. Life to Hildegarde was a roadbed bordered with spiked principles that shot up like telegraph-poles. She lived as narrowly within her precepts as Jenny and Jennifer lived within theirs. Regarding her across the crystal, this smote Rarick: "It was not what you thought about life. It was not even what you did about it. It was what, underneath all the superimposed structure, you inherently were!"

Take Gerkes, now. Doubting old rogue, the word-magic of phrases such as "the equality of man," left him cool as a cucumber. He accepted their inequality coldly, but was inflamed with the impulse to do something about it on that basis. A better world for bricklayers, biologists, and bankers. He was a hog for truths, Gerkes was; and turning them up now and then with his perennially seeking spade was what kept life the exciting predicament it so apparently was for this lusterless-looking man in herring-bone gray and chalk dust.

God! God! God! Trying to reason out the rightness, the wrongness, the goodness, the badness of life; of the lives around him, of his own, of his narrow sister sitting there in the unconscious attitude of holier-than-thou, munching an almond as if she had not sufficient saliva for its enjoyment, the old panic arising out of his sense of impotency, smote Rarick.

Certain people, he knew, were afflicted with a fear of high places. Their sensations must be akin to this feeling of his. Insane fear of loss of equilibrium. Need to feel his feet grip more closely the earth that spun away from them.

"That is how I shall spend tomorrow, Rarick. No need for you to bother about me. I shall take an omnibus down to the congested districts."

He looked at her and felt that his laughter came like a bray.

"Why not the Second Avenue surface car?" he suggested. And then to himself, "You'll find it much more righteously uncomfortable."

A THOUGHT that he confessed to himself was more amusing than really valid, began to turn in Rarick's head during the following two weeks of his sister's visit. He had urged her, out of what Miss Rarick sniffingly referred to as the politeness of his heart, to prolong her stay indefinitely, or at least specifically until the return of the Jennys.

That was impossible. Miss Rarick was due back in Keokuk for the annual meeting of the executive board of the Keokuk Home for Wayward Girls, of which she was secretary and treasurer.

For seventeen years she had not missed one of these board meetings. It was her boast, Trojan that she was at raising funds *via* the charity bazaar, the church social, and the Christmas drive, that she had never approached her brother for so much as one penny contribution to her favorite philanthropy. Roiled at her principles, which he found so tiresome and conspicuous, Rarick had never volunteered to contribute.

It lurked in Hildegarde, rankled there. She meant, some day, in the course of an unburdening of herself to Rarick which she had rehearsed for years, to confront him with this omission, along with countless other stored-away grievances she harbored. She had even rehearsed the phraseology in which she would throw up to him the fact that the sister of one of the richest men in the world was obliged to see her pet philanthropy actually want for built-in bathtubs! Without ever coming to the point, she was elaborate in her explanations of what was taking her back to Keokuk before the return of the Jennys.

Over and over again she recounted, to his adamant smile, the shortness of budget, the hovering mortgage, the crying need for lavatories with built-in bathtubs, laundries where the girls could do their own washings-out (a good bright laundry would keep many a girl off the street of an evening).

With the same elaborate politeness Rarick listened, as determined that she would ask for what she wanted as Hildegarde was determined not to ask.

"Speak, Fido," said Rarick, with his look of amused silence.

"Why, I've had girls come to me since we've put up the cretonne curtains in the recreation-room at the Home and say to me, 'Miss Rarick, funny thing, but I just don't feel like running around nights any more!' That girl did not realize it, but the simple fact of bright and cozy surroundings was filling a need in her."

It was at that stage that the impulse to throttle, until the prim words fairly bounced off her lips, would overtake Rarick, causing him to smile through his outrageous sense of aggravation. It was at times like this that he could visualize his daughter, her knees crossed, probably revealing their bareness, her mocking eyes pouring their naughty contempt: "Keep the laundry brightly lighted," or "Cretonnes cure the canker in many a lassie's heart."

Nevertheless, it was out of the evenings that he spent with his sister, Dr. Gerkes looking in on many of them, that the thought which was more amusing than really valid began to bestir itself.

Hildegarde and Gerkes got on well. He let her talk. Once or twice they had attended the opera together, two straight, narrow, and dun-colored figures, in the

Rarick box from which the Jennys usually contributed their share of blaze to the tier.

Hildegarde admired Gerkes. Sometimes Rarick suspected her of being more interested in Gerkes himself than in his collections, over which she craned a long, conscientious neck; but the fact remained that she assisted him in various catalogue work, classified some Eskimo needle-cases and Upper Magdalenian harpoons for him, and attended those of his lectures before the Anthropological Institute which were open to the general public.

"It's been a liberal education," Hildegarde told her brother one evening after she had returned from one of these lectures. "A person could live a lifetime and never learn some of the things I have tonight about prehistoric man. And as for Miocene apes—well! And that skull recently discovered at Taunga—in Bechuanaland—yes, that's right. I jotted it down in my notes. Just fancy there being a place called Bechuanaland! Mighty interesting! Live and learn. Have you seen those stereopticon views of human skulls that Dr. Gerkes took in Alaska? Mighty instructive."

Gerkes came in then, tamping down his pipe. "I wish," he said, his mood facetiously biotic, "that the element of the human race which sees fit to attend these so-called popular lectures of mine was as interested in the story of its life as the ladies in my tonight's audience, judging from the flashing of pocket mirrors, were in the angle of light-refraction on their noses. Do you know what Piltdown women are supposed to have used for vanity-cases, Miss Rarick——"

"Dr. Gerkes, I was just remarking to my brother, your lecture tonight has been a liberal education. And to think I never knew there was such a thing as the Mousterian industry . . ."

"Did you ever hear the story, Miss Rarick, of the

Pithecanthropus erectus who got into an argument with a small saurian creature of snake-like stature? . . ."

"Now, Dr. Gerkes, you're going to tease!"

"Perhaps I am," sighed the doctor, "and you've reminded me that I'm too tired for it. Rarick, would you raise your gloating eye from the bloody fire of those balas-rubies, touch the sapphire button with which you summon slaves, and ask the fourteenth eunuch to bring me a large bowl with one inch of *fin* champagne? To swing one inch of *fin* champagne around a rock-crystal basin, Miss Rarick, makes the swinging of the filigree-and-tourmaline censers seem commonplace."

"Explain to my sister, Dr. Gerkes, that reference to the tourmaline censers. That is one of them, hanging up over the Cimabue Madonna there, Hildegarde."

"Don't mind if I turn off the 'Tales of Hoffman,' do you, Rarick? Those doll-babies get me fuddled."

It was out of evenings often as oblique as this one that the idea in Rarick's mind ceased to be quaint and became remotely feasible. Why not? Here were two lone souls playing a solitary game. Hildegarde might react to matrimony as a stiff sponge softens in water. Here might be a new and receptive Hildegarde, who would accept, in the name of their wedding, the financial endowments Rarick could so legitimately bestow.

Gerkes had countless times given voice to the wear and tear upon him of these lectures. Gerkes needed leisure, repose of mind, money, isolation. Hildegarde was past the time when the secluded walks of life would be irksome. Gerkes had constantly spoken about his intention of one day seeking out again, what to him had been the beauty and the fine seclusion of Alaska. Why not? Hildegarde had no youth to shed. Both she and Gerkes, for that matter, were adults about life. If Gerkes was playful about it all, it was partly because his lust for the truth of it revealed to him the unexpected grins, like crevices occurring in terrific masses of granite.

Why not? Given these two people; a dower of a million; facilities; leisure for research. A million for every new truth. Two million! Why not?

Rarick was saved from what might have been an embarrassing hole to have stepped into, in this friendship that was so very special to him, by the soft-footed diplomacy with which he approached the subject the last evening of Hidegarde's visit, after she had bidden good night to the two men still seated over their Cointreau, and ascended to the mauve-and-gold suite of rooms that suited her sparseness so mockingly.

First there had been some talk of a nature that, to his surprise, was so inwardly exciting to Rarick, that it was all he could do to control his voice.

Gerkes had gone off, on the slight impetus of an irrelevant remark about the Rockefeller Foundation, upon the subject of constructive philanthropies, and from that to the more general discussion of vast personal fortunes and their dispensation. It was like him to be able to think aloud on a subject so intimately relevant to Rarick, as impersonally as if he were discussing the map of Great Britain after the Würm glaciation. What he had to say along lines that were fairly hackneyed, for one reason or another, set Rarick to thinking along lines that were new. A slight talk; scarcely more than the thread of a discourse, considering how far-reaching were to be its results.

"I am convinced that the basis of progress, Rarick, is prevention."

"Prevention?"

"Yes. Prevent cancer. It will save the more expensive process of eliminating it. Prevent slums. Prevent wars. Prevent disease. Prevent social abuses. That not only takes terrific moneys, it takes an excess of imagination. A man will give his money to eliminate cancer. It is another matter to make a man living in a cancer-less world visualize the incalculable importance of cancer-prevention. Rockefeller Foundation is a rare and fine example of subtle, far-reaching, and humanitarian expenditure of acquired wealth. A man doing that kind of philanthropy in his lifetime, instead of leaving fortunes to organizations and causes that may outlive their usefulness a few years after his death, displays the power to distribute as well as accumulate. That's what makes this little story of mankind that I putter around with, a full-size job. Finding out the bad places ahead, and then steering around them, preventing."

"That's a pretty big order of a thought, Gerkes."

"Nothing particularly new about it. Preventive philanthropy is here."

"It's new if a fellow hasn't given it any particular thought."

"It's a more thankless job to prevent hookworm than to cure it."

"Doubtless. But the basis of progress, I've always held, in my business, is elimination, Gerkes. Get rid of excess baggage ———"

"I maintain, avoid excess baggage."

"There's a world of practical wisdom behind that idea."

"I'm going to bury myself behind that idea some day —north—where the nights are long and cold and quiet— fit for a man to work in."

Out of a ten-minute silence that continued to be as inwardly exciting as anything that had ever happened to him, filled as it was with the words of Gerkes surging in birth against the brain of Rarick, there came from Rarick something, this laconic:

"Wonder you don't marry, Gerkes, before you dig yourself into those long Arctic nights you're always talking about."

"Extraordinary you should mention that."

What then! The sly fellow had lifted the thought off his mind.

"Fact is, Rarick, I'm about to."

(Sly fellow.)

"Yes?"

(Could it be that Hildegarde had been equally sly? Good!)

"Yes."

"Yes? Have I met the lady?"

"No."

"Oh!"

Silence.

"Who is she?"

"An Eskimo."

"A what?"

"Eskimo. I met Illun twelve years ago on my first expedition to Mackenzie River. Her father is a fur-trader."

"Eskimo!"

"Yes. Then, six years ago, I met her in Nome, where she was stopping with her father's brother, also a trader, and attending high school."

"So . . ."

"She's back in Alaska now, teaching. The Eskimos are close about family ties and the old mother is pretty well along. We've drifted for years. Waiting. But I have about made up my mind that too much is enough. Life is passing us by. I'm going back, Rarick."

"For her?"

"No, to her. Curious thing, from your point of view,

anyhow, but Eskimos, accustomed as they are to rigors of climate, do not thrive in our so-called temperate parts. I do in theirs. I'm going to them."

"I see." Gerkes, Rarick figured, as he sat dumbfounded, would have received news as surprising to him as this was to Rarick, with the non-committal attitude of one who is the complete cosmopolite. Besides, one did not betray anything so personal as surprise to Gerkes.

"The old folks still live out on the edge of the town. But Illun, who is teaching in the next village, lives with an American family of missionaries named Anderson. For solid comfort, Rarick," said Gerkes, taking the crystal bowl of *fin* champagne from a butler, "I recommend a well-built Eskimo house."

"I see."

"I've work to do, Rarick. This scheme of life down here lures me away from singleness of purpose. At my best, Rarick, when I'm surrounded by the world itself, instead of its clatter, I've a single-track mind. One thing matters pretty terribly to me. Facts. Then from there, truth."

"Fine. Fine."

"I need leisure. These lectures—pah! I need simplicity. I need the long white nights for work and my leisure for the contacts with the strange wisdoms of simple people. I need to think. Life with Illun on the Colville River can give me all these. Can you understand this? Down here, everything is going out, precious little coming in. I need leisure, Rarick, damnably, and my finger-nails out of my palms. I've books to write. Collections to assemble. There is knowledge and truth for me to unearth before I bow out in demise. I am one of those scientific-minded hounds with a nose to the truth-scent. Facts are more panoramic, more majestic, more extraordinary than fantasy. I need leisure to run them down."

"And money?"

"God, yes!"

"Would you still go North?"

"More than ever. I tell you, I'm digging in, Rarick, for my long white night. A woman who is attractive to me. Books. Leisure. Simplicity. My big work now lies in assembling knowledge. I need money for men who are still young enough to get out into the fields and feed my mind with their findings. I want to send an expedition to Abyssinia to do some digging there. I want to study certain of the flying-bases between Nome and Shanghai. There are weather observations I want made, over a sustained period, from a Greenland observatory. I want men to follow up the fine excavations that Scotelly started last year before his death in Brindisi. My active years are done. Now I want to assemble and deduce."

"I'm going to give you the money for that, Gerkes."

"That's mighty fine of you, Rarick. I've wondered a bit about you and your plans for making your wealth reap. The root of all evil lies in the root. As I was saying, there is curative and preventive philanthropy. Forestall the root. The great trend of modern humanitarianism, Rarick, lies in preventive measures. The way to prevent fallacy is to know truth. Buy truth with your money, Rarick; it is cheap at any price. Bear that in mind when you decide to put your terrific house in order."

"I'd like to give you a million, Gerkes."

"The world, Rarick, is your debtor for that. Not I."

"I'll assign it as an endowment to you."

"No, don't do that. Organize a fund-committee to finance my expeditions as I need and form them. One that will keep me in bounds, but at the same time give me free enough rein in my choice of actual and intellectual excavation."

"And you?"

"Leave me out, Rarick. I'm headed for my white nights of long leisure."

"Even there, you must live."

"I've saved a bit."

"How much?"

"I think I stack up to somewhere around fifteen hundred in the bank."

"You'll need more."

"Well, you might allow me about fifty a month, Rarick, if you've a mind to. It will cost me around that much to afford the leisure for work."

It occurred to Rarick, sitting there, sharing with his friend their unspoken pangs at the prospect of parting, that it cost his own family about eighteen thousand dollars a week, to afford leisure for play.

FIVE AND TEN

THREE weeks later, the Jennys made the trip down from upper Quebec by motor, a second car, containing two personal maids and the lighter luggage, following.

A premature burst of spring was already on the heels of a languid winter, so that much of the trip was taken on dry roads and to the first freckling of foliage.

Lovely. Lovely. Lovely. Particularly lovely to a pallid Jennifer, who had a habit nowadays of seeing through a glass not so much darkly, as dimly. Low vitality, her doctors easily termed it. There was no form yet to the leaves, or even color. Just the soft pointed promise of them. Lovely. Lovely. Lovely.

Jenny, whose effort all the way down from Canada had been not to seem too constantly excited, was grateful, too, for the loveliness. It helped to account for the exultant something that kept rising and overflowing in her. Ramon was along!

He had spent two of the three weeks with them in camp. Jennifer had been glad for her mother's sake. Her incredible mother, who could while away time, for want of something better, with this boy, pleasant enough timber for an evening's flirtation, provided there was plenty of the slow windings of tango music to sustain illusion, but who had actually sufficed to keep her mother amused during all of what might have been the interminable stretches of their stay at camp.

Could it be that he was smitten with her mother? The slim thought trailed through her tired mind and petered out as she sat looking out at the flashing of spring. . . .

How good her mother had been! How heavenly

good! From that strange and terrifying moment when her father had sat looking at her as if his eyes were conflagrations that would leap out in flame over her body, the dearness of Jenny had poured like sweet oil over the terrible burnings from those eyes.

The indulgent compassion of this woman where her children were concerned! What if she petted them even more than she pitied or understood them? What if to try to explain to Jenny the minute phases of her torture was to bring down upon herself an avalanche of automatic maternalism that sometimes made her wild with frenzy!

"Mother, please, please don't keep on talking. You've said that over and over again. I know you think there are as good fish in the sea as ever came out of it. You've told me. What good does that do me if I don't care what is in the sea? For God's sake, Mother, please ──"

Not even such an outburst could puncture the quality of Jenny's compassion.

"He's not worth the nail of your little finger, much less the mental anguish you are wasting on him."

"I know. I know. I know it all by heart. Only don't keep on saying it, mother, or I'll go screaming mad."

"I know, dear, I know. I know."

"You know!" laughed Jennifer, scornfully, one midnight when clad in pajamas, she had been walking the floor of the long living-room of the main camp, and her mother, hearing her, had tiptoed down with a fur coat thrown over the flimsiness of her nightdress. "You know!" Jennifer had risen from a sleepless bed, and her hair was tousled and angry-looking, and one of her cheeks, too hot, was smeared with crinkles from where it had dug and dug into the pillow. "You know! What do you know of anything that I am going through!"

What did Jenny know? Thank God, Jennifer did not know what she knew; but just the same, sitting wrapped in fur, she hugged herself with knowing. What did Jenny know? She knew the torment and the ecstasy of Jennifer, because they were boiling within her, too— every one of these precious spring-kissed days and nights.

Upstairs, since they had not troubled to open the men's dormitory-camp, in a beautiful old spool-bed, Ramon, who had arrived a few days before, was asleep under sheets that she had personally laid out for him; under thick silk puffs that she had personally chosen. There would be the first two crocuses of spring on his breakfast tray that she would journey down to the edge of the wild blue lake to pick. What did the older Jenny know of the excruciating pangs of love? Impudent Jennifer, to assume she knew little.

"My darling, you are all unnerved ———"

"I know I'm your darling, mother, and that I am unnerved, but, for God's sake, don't keep telling me about it!"

"My darling, do you know what a serious nervous breakdown you are sure to have if ———"

"Pretty question. Oh, no! I don't know. I think, instead, that I am lying in the arms of my lover—his lips are soft ———"

"Jennifer!"

"O God! mother, I'm flighty! I didn't mean that. I loathe his lips."

"Of course you do, darling. He's a dog. My poor darling!"

"I'm a fine darling."

"I'll get you well, my sweet. You're in a trance of infatuation now. You can't help it. Mother understands."

Strange words for one Jenny to be using to another.

Scene after scene Jenny had lived through with Jennifer those weeks, walking her through woods of wild, frozen beauty; through stiff March winds, until their limbs sagged. Tiring Jennifer. Exhausting her. Imbuing her with a sense of nausea for the potion she was craving, until, the last week of their stay, Jennifer was sleeping through entire nights.

Ecstatic nights for Jenny, wakeful even in her tiredness, as she lay there under the same roof with Ramon. . . .

Riding homeward through the woods that were preening themselves for outburst, the something that Jennifer had promised Jenny was dead within her, began to lift its head. Through woods of running sap she was riding back to the city that contained Berry! He would be under a roof that was no farther from hers on Fifth Avenue than the lake had been from the camp. Berry was at the end of this beautiful trail. Would be within easy telephone call. Within messenger call. Berry! Poor boy! How bewildered he must have been these weeks, since that night she had stood him up as he waited for her in his car at a spot which she had appointed at a west-side gate to the Park. The letters she had written him since and never sent! There was one now, tucked on the flesh side of the single little orchid-colored undergarment she wore. The gravitation of the universe was toward Berry ——

Mother had been a brick, all right, content to have burrowed-in up there at camp, while there was some of the season left in town, to say nothing of Florida. Making the best of the unseasonable isolation, content to sit in the back of the car all the hours of riding with Ramon, while she crouched silently beside the chauffeur, where there was relief from the din of talk. Mother had been a brick, all right, but, oh, how damned, damned, damned

futile! As if you could stop Niagara with a handkerchief. As if you could douse a house-afire, with a squirt
of eau-de-Cologne.

Jennifer had learned to sleep in camp. That meant
Jennifer was getting well. That meant Jennifer was
coming out of the trance of the infatuation for Berry,
who wasn't worth her little finger-nail. Jennifer had
promised. Darling dumb-bell Jenny; when the truth of
it was that Jennifer was flying back on purring motors to
the land of Berry. He was in New York. Madness of
her, to have let them put miles between them. He was
in New York—enchanted destination.

It was difficult; it was impossible, sitting up there beside the chauffeur, spinning through spring, to discipline
one's thoughts, when the craving set in to see Berry.
Just to be with him, to watch the squint come out along
his eyelids when he talked; to get the faint cool scent of
him; to tremble to his nearness; to withhold the hands
from making little curved cups of themselves to inclose
his cheeks. His strong hair that was full of a strange
electric life. Berry's life. It was hard to keep down an
insanity of desire through the craving, and to sit silently
beside the chauffeur and say to oneself, as a child repeats
a catechism: "No-good Berry. Cad. Snide. Here is
a man about to be a father. Jennifer, have you no pride?
No decencies? No. No. No. And, damn it, I'm
glad!" The days were fiery furnaces of desire for
Berry. The nights. The weeks. The ride all the way to
New York, hills, dales, mountains, rim-roads, and the
thick slush of thawing mud, was one such fiery furnace.

Thank God, Jenny was content to sit with that beautiful nobody-home of a Ramon there on the back-seat and
let her be.

At Albany she could already begin to feel, in anticipation, that moment of the rounding of her fingers about

the pink-enamel French telephone in her boudoir, that would bring Berry's voice to her. It was wonderful to be able to crave until you suffered like that. Why not? Who was to say where sacred love began and profane love left off? What had Nature's scheme to do with puny, man-made ones? They had sent her scuttling away like any finishing-school girl, to get over a love-affair, as if miles were a panacea. If you could speak of this leaping terrific glory of a thing that was her passion for Berry in the innocuous terms of "love-affair," then the Himalayas were pretty, the Grand Canyon cute, and God a right nice God.

Two hours below Albany, Jenny placed her hand in its white crinkled gauntlet, along her daughter's arm.

"Jennifer dear, we'll go down along the West Side, by way of the river drive, so we can drop Ramon at his apartment before we go home."

Damn! Damn! Damn! That would delay them ten minutes. Her fingers ached for the pink-enamel telephone. . . .

On the other hand, to Jenny, the river drive meant a détour, and ten minutes longer with Ramon.

It was not quite dusk when the car slid up before the doors that had been copied from the Florentine Campanile. A messenger boy was running down the steps. In fact, the doors that had swung open to emit him remained open to admit the mistress of her house and her daughter, chauffeurs, maids, and butlers already scurrying in the service entrance with furs, bags, and what not.

It was strange, in a household where the telegraph-boy was a figure woven carelessly into the pattern of every-day, that the sight of this one running down the steps should have bitten into Jenny's heart with a pang of scare.

"Was that telegram for me?" she asked.

"No, madam, for Mr. Rarick."

"Where is he?"

"In the library. Shall I let him know that you have returned?"

"No."

"If you don't mind, mother, I'll rush on up to my rooms to rest—alone——"

"Yes, Jennifer."

For some reason which she was later never able to analyze, Jenny, instead of following Jennifer to the left, and thereby avoiding the chance of an immediate encounter with Rarick, went up by the right of the broad staircase, and, trailing her heavy motor coat back off her shoulders, hurried to the library.

Its beautiful quality of dusk, as she entered, was being rattled into by the mechanical organ, which was repeating the famous *"Ah! fors e lui"* of Violetta, as if some one had forgotten to turn it off, the stained-glass story of "La Traviata" marching before Rarick, who was seated at the far end of the room in his unicorn chair, a telegram crushed in the hand from which he had just read it.

On one of those flashes out of the blue about which one hears but which one so seldom sees, Jenny looked at her husband calmly and said, "Avery is dead."

He began to nod his head, regarding her all the while with eyes made out of two white chinies.

She started to laugh. She could not stop. She could not stop, because Rarick, sitting there, could not seem to stop nodding. And, nodding, didn't he look for all the world like the bisque bull that used to stand on the mantelpiece in the pressed-brick house of her parents in St. Louis? It had been a black-and-white china bull, with a head that nodded. Every time there were to be guests, her mother used to tiptoe in just before arrivals and start it nodding.

Rarick, replying to her that Avery was dead, kept on nodding like that bisque bull. . . .

FIVE AND TEN

To THINK that out of the innocent dawn of a new day could be minted the phrase, "Avery is dead." That phrase had not existed yesterday.

Twenty-four hours before, Avery had been alive, and, mark you, need not have died. This was not death inevitable and God's will be done. This was not death demanding.

Avery had killed himself.

There had been a small note, written in blue pencil, and stuck into a mirror in his bedroom:

Dears, it was too much . . . A.

They had followed the scent of gas and wrenched the tube from between his teeth.

"They" (a landlady and a negro houseman in a white-duck coat) had been the first to stumble across the strange and almost unendurably precious fact of the death of this life.

"They" had turned in police alarms about it.

And it should have been handled so privately; as privately as the slender spar of a body that had been Avery had suffered. And instead, over this wounded-to-death boy in his casket, the newspapers of the country had become a giant composite ass, braying:

SON OF FIVE-AND-TEN MULTIMILLIONAIRE KILLS SELF NEAR COLLEGE CAMPUS

FAMILY UNABLE TO ATTRIBUTE MOTIVE FOR THE SUICIDE
NOTE FROM HIS FATHER, JOHN G. RARICK, FORBIDDING HIM THE PURCHASE OF A SEVERAL-THOUSAND-DOLLAR CAMP-EQUIPMENT FOUND AMONG HIS EFFECTS

ANOTHER COLLEGE SUICIDE

ONLY SON OF JOHN G. RARICK, AMERICAN CHAIN-STORE MIL-
LIONAIRE, DISCOVERED BY LANDLADY DEAD FROM ASPHYXIATION
DEATH ATTRIBUTED TO DEMAND FOR LUXURIES WHICH WERE DENIED
HIM BY SELF-MADE FATHER

SOCIETY SHOCKED BY SUICIDE DEATH OF ONLY SON
OF JOHN G. RARICK. COMES AS SHOCK TO FAMILY.
MRS. RARICK PROSTRATED. FAMILY IN SECLUSION.

Let them bray. Let them bray. It was better so. It
covered up the private, timid truth. The truth lay scattered in documents, some of them torn across the page;
in composition-books filled with boyish scrawls; in half-
written letters; in hand-written and hand-bound volumes
of verse that lay in a heap on the table on which John
Rarick leaned his face into his hands.

It was as if the contents of the heart of Avery, the soul
and the mind of Avery, unlocked from the vault of his
nineteen years, had been spilled there in broken utter-
ances of torment.

This was his boy out there, in strange autopsy before
him, the history of his defeat, his pain, his lightnings of
ecstasy that had apparently been as unbearable as the
pain, like chipped bits of cornice of the now cold marble
of his being.

There, spread over the table, in writings, were the
truths that for nineteen years had lain hidden from his
father by the mere wall of boy-flesh.

God! God! God! That wall had been flesh of
Rarick's and yet it had shut him out. The door through
that wall, not forty-eight hours before, had been a living, breathing heart with a key to it—nobody to blame—
nobody to blame—least of all Avery—except—unbear-

able loneliness of the thought—not even his mother
had ever found the key to it. Certainly Rarick had not.

He beat with his fists upon the table; he scorched his
eyes upon the revealing lines of the documents that had
been brought him from his dead son's effects. He read
and reread:

This boy, then, written there on the scraps of paper,
whose torment had been the strange inchoate torment of
poet, adolescent, dreamer and diviner, potential lover,
and adventurer in Hellenic islands around which flowed
the blue Mediterranean of imagination, had been the
Avery of the flesh. The fledgling who had smoked the
strange little hooked pipes, that looked insolent and
smelled badly. The Avery who had piled up card debts.
The Avery whose wants, at least as interpreted by his
mother, God forgive her, had been the speed motor-
boats, the special-body roadsters, the dressing-cases,
gold-fitted, the five-thousand-dollar camping outfits, the
monstrous checking accounts, polo ponies. . . .

Some lispings of what Avery had really wanted rose
in faint perfume off the pages of the book of sophomoric
verse which he had written in a fine, painstaking, private
kind of chirography that bore no resemblance to the mod-
ish scrawl he had shown the world.

Even his very handwriting had seemed to curl inward
—away——

He had tried, in those notebooks, for the perfection of
the sonnet. In fourteen lines, had begged the right to
"walk the untessellated grandeur of simplicity." The
boy who at seventeen had appeared in Sunday rotogra-
vure sections for the perfection of his riding-accouter-
ments, wrote in plaintive, if obviously Shelleyan mood of
that "brighter freedom," and of "peace, cerulean-blue."
Sang in whispered numbers among the ruled pages of the
composition-books of "the pain that lies under the heart

and is canker there." Rarick followed these lines with the stub of his finger, and went back again and again. "The pain that lies under the heart and is canker there . . ."

"Avery, was that your only heritage from me . . . that hurting canker there . . . ?"

Dears, it was too much . . . A.

What was too much? Jenny, you, up there, can you answer that? What had been too much for him? What had?

His bewilderment had been too much. His frailty, his hunger, glimpsed through darting, wing-swift beauties. His desire for some one to share those moments when "pain broke like surf into starry ecstasy." Page after page of Avery, in treble, sophomoric mood, crying for a hand in his, through the aisles that were tormentingly black. . . .

Avery, boy, why not my hand? I would have given . . .

Life had been too much for him.

Pages and pages of saying it in treble iambic and slenderly lyric sonneteering.

There was free verse too, waddling thinly down the white sheets. "My heart is a grail of many-colored glass. It contains me—and yet—want out—translucent whiteness ——"

Not bathos to Rarick, nor mewling of a spirit in the throes of trying to cast off its swaddlings. But Avery, whose heart had died wanting the Pyrenees.

And this was the boy whom his father had not dared to approach on even the matter of an experimental theater. . . .

This was the boy . . .

There were pages of the journal that broke the heart,

when it was endurable to read them through . . . "My dear mother, who is everything to me and absolutely nothing. . . ."

"When I look at my own mother and father, I realize that I have never seen anything so beautiful as their marriage is dreadful . . . there are worse lonelinesses than mine . . . whom I admire so much more than I like . . . Would like to go up to him and say. . . . Look here, Father—— Why—why—cannot even write it ——"

Say it to me now, son. It may seem too late, but not for everything. Say it to me now ——

". . . .Mother, now, has nothing to fall back upon but the excitements that take the place of imagination. What I cannot understand is Jennifer, who is so much more than clever, and yet to whom cleverness matters above everything—nice Jennifer who cares so terribly—about the things that are not worth caring about . . . if only father would . . . if only father would ——"

That, too, was unfinished. If only father would what? Call it back to me, Avery—if only father would what? ——

There was a fragment of a letter that had apparently been crushed and torn in three pieces. A third of it was left. It had been written to his father on the subject of a year he wished to spend in Paris.

". . . months of hesitation lie behind this request—feel the need of getting my bearings—think we could understand each other if only—my great admiration for you—hesitate to say—too much for me—time to think—alone—hesitate—unable to say to you face to face—what I—alone to think and work and dream—please don't think—beauty of ideals—please don't think—young man must believe first and—hesitate to say—Father please ——"

Upstairs, Jenny lay on her bed, chill after chill of crushed heart, crushed pride, crushed hope, racking her thin body. Rarick had tried his part in comforting, but everyone who appeared in the room seemed to stalk at her out of this catastrophe, so finally the doctor forbade even Rarick, or Jennifer, who sat for the most part in her bedroom, close to its pale walls, and huddled there.

Down in the library, which seemed to wrap itself grandly about this occasion, was stretched the boy out of whose incredible act had sprung the new-coined phrase, "Avery is dead," lying straight and beautiful as ivory in his casket.

"God! God! God!" cried Rarick from his clenched lips, through his clenched eyelids, down into his clenched heart. "Teach me through my failure! Avery, call back to me! . . ."

No way to turn. . . .

Yet, out of all the deluge of mail and telegrams and cablegrams that came pouring through the defeated silence of that house, was one for Rarick, a Western Union message that he kept folded in his pocket and took out to reread occasionally.

At first he had not recognized the signature:

I think I understand the thing you did not get said to Avery.
                                        GRATTON DAVIES.

Gratton Davies? Ah, ah, yes! That likable young fellow on the committee, who had written *Herod's Mask.*

Somehow it was the only message out of hundreds that was to open the way for tears to work their thin, tortuous way from his clenched heart to his clenched eyelids.

JENNY

What, what, in God's name, had prompted this death act of Avery's? How could this darling of her indulgence, her adoration, have snipped the cord that bound his heart to hers, as casually as you would snip the cord on a candy-box?

How could an offshoot of her own body-fiber have committed an act so outside the dimensions of her own comprehensions?

One did things like this for concrete reasons. There had been no love-affair. Avery's adolescence had been almost too timid. There had been no debts. Notwithstanding the ugly and humiliating innuendos of the headlines, Jenny had always seen to it that Avery's pockets were well stocked, even when his bank account was exhausted and his father questioning and stern.

Slow, smoldering conviction became Jenny's that Rarick had been the stone wall before which Avery had found life meaningless.

Rarick had crossed him so constantly. Passively, rather more than by deed or stricture. That was what made it maddening to her and subtle. You could not quite put your finger on—anything. And yet, it was impossible not to know how dumbly and how gropingly he had failed to understand his boy. Rarick was not vicious. He was just part of the failure . . . Her heart even bled for him, as he sat alone, looking at the glow in his stones for hours on end now, or with Gerkes, in those weeks preceding his departure, while the organ plowed up the more melodious of the operas. Sometimes, particularly after the departure of Gerkes for absurd points north, Rarick was just sitting. Pity of a sort lay in her heart for him. Pity of sorts lay in her heart for herself.

She had been a good mother, neither Avery nor Jennifer nor even Rarick himself had denied her that. Wherein had she failed? Or had Avery failed? Her dear. Her beautiful. She had seen to it that his hands were crammed unto bursting with all her love and indulgence could give him. Nor had she stopped there, which would have made indictment of her easy. She had crept into his spiritual life as far as she dared. She had once discharged one of his tutors whom she suspected of being agnostic. When Avery was twelve, she had attended a series of morning lectures, at the Plaza, on "You and Your Child," and had taken him for a drive one morning before he left for Newberry, and told him " plain little facts," to which he had politely listened, without surprise or embarrassment, or even, she suspected, enlightenment. The one, "Babies, dear, do not just grow under the heart; it is not quite so simple as that," had not quite come off as the lecturer had anticipated. Avery had sniggered.

But he had sent her roses that afternoon. When he was only fourteen, there had been grace to Avery! Tears were at the edges of her lids these months after the death, ever quick ones, ready to flow.

To go back and back and back, could there, after all, have been a hopeless passion for a girl? Or a woman? Or was there something secret and terrible that a mother could not understand? Ah no! Avery was innocent. There was the case of young Tremoil, the college-senior son of Augustin Tremoil, president of the Civic Bank, who had been a college suicide over his hopeless infatuation for the happily married wife, eleven years his senior, of a French viscount. No, no, there had been no such attachment in the life of this boy of hers. Nothing in his papers indicated it. Or, for that matter, indicated anything. Just bits of verse—so sweet—and the journals of any growing lad. She had not read them through. Rarick had sort of hogged them greedily for himself, as if for what comfort he could squeeze out of them. Jenny had for herself the sweet, personal mementoes.

Things. Avery's beautiful platinum watch, the flatness of a dollar, that had ticked near to the dear tick of his heart. Avery's beautiful books. This superb edition of Shelley. His collection of portraits of Shelley. His beautiful pearl studs that had lain to the beat of his dear heart. She had thought of the pearly quality of his pallor as she had purchased the set. Avery's signed photograph of Tagore. Out of it all, Jennifer had only asked for his mauled copy of Marie Bashkirtseff.

Yes, Jenny had the dear things. Over them she cried and she cried. His own portrait, in a soft shirt open at the neck, and his fair hair seeming to fly backward to some breeze.

Dears, it was too much . . . A.

What was too much, my darling? Avery, my darling, what, oh, what? Avery, am I in a dream? Are you dead?

It was to Ramon she turned.

"Oh, my darling," she told him over the small table of a smaller-than-ever tea-room in West Ninety-seventh Street, where they were venturing to meet, "you must be everything to me now."

"You will not let me be."

She knew what he meant. Ramon was more and more restive. This furtive meeting here and there was degrading. To both. Sure as fate, it would begin to attract notice. Cannot get away with this kind of thing indefinitely.

"Yes, yes, darling, but———"

"But why procrastination? This eternal procrastination. Two years of it now . . ."

"Darling, you are killing me. If ever I needed to mark time, it is now. Lightning has struck my life . . ."

His beautiful black eyes could fill with tears for her.

The death of Avery, whom he had never seen, had affected him in a manner strange to him. He, to whom sickness was an ugly misdemeanor, felt a strange beauty in Avery's kind of death. He thought of this boy nights, as he lay trying to sleep. He had died with the flower of his body in full bloom. No decay. No organs withering of disease. Avery had reminded him of some one who had looked through the door of life, found what he saw not pretty, and bowed out. The superb insolence of that gesture cast a strange luster over the mother of such a boy.

She had given life, and the power of death, to that slim blond fellow whose photograph, in a soft shirt with the neck open, was smeared now with her tears. The glow of vicarious mystery was out over Jenny these days. How damnable life was! Ramon, who wanted desperately to live, yet found it so hard to be allowed to live. Struggle. Struggle. That most precarious of struggles for existence off the whimsical bounty of women. That strange boy in the photograph, with the open collar and the hair flying backward like a woman's in the wind, had willed not to live, because the bursting cornucopia of life's good things for him had overflowed and suffocated him.

What a strange, a terrible, a revealing, a shameful note, "It was too much."

Too much, when Ramon, who loved life, was starving. Well, anyway, starving for the good things of life. Perhaps this tragedy was writing on the wall. Good times ahead. Out of the machine-stitched infatuation which he allowed himself for this enormously rich woman, must come security. Yes, "allowed oneself the infatuation" was what it amounted to. One must live. It made it pleasantly decent that in his relationship with this woman, who could do much for him, he had been able to steam up a certain modicum of fascination. It gave him ethical standing with himself.

Curious, slim, greenish woman, sitting opposite him in the glamorless little tea-shop. Mother of a beautiful boy who had done a strange, wild thing. Her grief made her sweet.

"Sweetheart, when you cry, your eyes are like deep pools filled with sea water that cannot break into surf."

"What would I do without you, Ramon? I need things like that said to me. I'm frightened, Ramon. Life has showed a fang at me. Ramon, I was a good mother to him. You know that!"

"You were too good, Jenny."

"You mean I spoiled ———"

"God has no use for protection. It leaves Him idle ———"

"You are perfection, Ramon."

"I am kissing you," he said, letting his eyes, that were velvet to her, lie along her narrow fretted face.

"Ramon," she said, giving words to a thought that had smitten and smitten her, "do you think it—possible—that some way—somehow—my boy—could have known —about us ———"

That thought, too, had flashed through his brain.

"That, Jenny, you know is impossible."

In a way she did, only the thought would wedge in.

"He idealized me. He was sensitive. That could kill . . ."

"He was too much of a poet. He would have idealized our love."

"You dear! You would see it that way."

He laid hands over her small cold ones.

"Strange you," he said, confusing her with the strange aura of the strange death that hung over her.

"Am I strange to you, Ramon?"

"Only in the sense that the strange is beautiful and full of mystery, like a little sea-flower captured in a bottle."

"In that sense, Ramon, I think I was strange to my boy."

"Strange . . ."

"He must have found life too—too ——"

"Too exquisite."

"Too exquisite."

Too exquisite. They bandied words, prettily minted ones, across the table, their glances jeweled with points of excitement.

"Too exquisite on one hand, Jenny—too putrid on the other."

He meant Rarick. The strange, locked sense of her second-rate loyalty kept her silent. With his capacity for reticence at the right moment, he let the conversation end abruptly, as at a precipice, folding her once more into the cloak of his dark-velvet glance.

"It is easy to imagine a death for love of you, Jenny."

"You are all the strength I have, Ramon."

He put out his hand again, stroking hers, insinuating his palm beneath her palm.

"Ramon, dear, please! Those people at that table are glancing at us."

He drew back stiff, taut, flushing down into his collar; and suddenly she too flushed riotously.

"Dearest—of course. I have not forgotten what you asked in your note. Here—forgive ——"

She felt out timidly for his offended hand, pressing it, leaving a small, folded five-hundred-dollar bill in it.

JENNIFER

"The death of Jennifer Rarick's brother has played the dickens with her," people were saying in one way or another.

It had played this kind of a dickens with her, sobering her in a way that made her dull, most of all to herself.

"I've gone dry rot," she said one night to her mirror, propping her cheeks in her palms and gazing at herself through a sudden attack of inertia that had swooped down upon her in the midst of dressing for an early-dinner appointment that had kept her knees feeling like sand under her all day.

The dinner appointment was a clandestine one with Berry. They were to meet and dine at a business men's chop-house near Wall Street. Afterward, Berry was to join his mother-in-law for another dinner and a benefit performance of "The Port of Salute." Jennifer was also to dine with Hartley Slocum at the Ambassadeur Club and go on to that same occasion. It was not the first time that their respective appetites, blunted by the six-o'clock clandestine meal near Wall Street, were later to be commented upon in the course of a second and more formal meal.

It made it easier to eat as they met. Berry had discovered that it kept down Jennifer's late tendency to hysteria. Jennifer no longer made terms, but complied.

There had been only four such occasions. The death of Avery had been a crash into the apple-cart. Why couldn't life jell neatly the way it did in the copy-books? According to rhyme and reason, if there were such, this hit between the eyes, this barge into the solar plexus, this death of a boy, should have jerked her to the sanity for which she had prayed those weeks at the camp. This should have made an end of that monstrosity of her state of mind and soul and heart toward Berry. She should have come through the fire of that ordeal of the death of a life that had been sweet to her, cleansed. And here she was, with the feeling of running sand through her knees, dressing to meet Berry. Waiting to meet Berry, as she had been waiting since last they met.

"I can't go," she said, and began to cry weakly to herself in the mirror. "I'm too tired to go. I'm too sick to go and I can't not go."

"Damn it!" as her eyes dried. "Berry was so much tripe." Many happy returns to him on the birth of a son, and may the next be twins! Well, it would be worth the trip down to the Wall Street restaurant to see him in this new rôle of father. Comedy lay ahead. . . . You didn't go sober over life just because of death—you certainly didn't go sober over death.

Avery had been in on the know, that was all, and had seen fit to pop off. Thank God, one Rarick had dared to be honest about the waste of time so solemnly called life. An Indian philosopher had said it! Time passes. We don't. Avery had turned into Time.

Fool nonsense called grief. One hurt, yes, like the devil. He had been such a regular kid to be on to life that way, secretly down inside of him.

He had written her a letter only a few weeks before. It was soggy now with her secret tears:

DEAR JENNIF: Come on up to college over next week-end and let's talk. I'm for cultivating more of that indoor sport among the Raricks.

She had sent him, by telegraph, what she called one of their nuttyisms.

Darling, can't. I'm doppling with a darling doppus to a chic shindig on Saturday.

The darling doppus had been Berry and the chic shindig a furtive rendezvous with him at a road-house where the tables offered the doubtful seclusion of little three sided booths.

"Oh, darling," she cried into her palms, sitting there half dressed before her mirror, her maid dismissed, and lacking herself the impulse to lift brush to her hair, "how in on the know you looked in your beautiful coffin. Were you just afraid, Avery, or was it something too terrible and adolescent to understand—or, I wonder, Avery, were you just low-down frightened and a quitter? . . ."

"I'm frightened," said Jennifer to herself, and lifted her face out of her hands to regard it in the mirror. "You've knocked what few props I had left right out from under me, Avery. I don't want it all, any more than you wanted it, only I don't know what to do about it. I haven't got the guts, or I've got too many, to do it your way. Which is it, darling? I don't want to get dressed. I don't want to go on. There's no place to go. All dressed up and no place to go, Avery. That's me. Why the devil did you, darling? It's a mess. Was it on account of the Rarick? God! but you did for him, Av! He looks as if somebody had put him wise, five minutes after they had been sold to the McCreey chain, to five million toy balloons that went cheap at enforced sale. He isn't a bad party. He deserved a better break. So did you, darling. Damned little I did to see that you got it. That's wisdom after the event, like the Raricks. Why did you do it, Av? You've been on to the Jenny ever since you were born. We both know that her square is crooked, but it looks square to her. I'm for her, Av. So were you. Why did you do it? I know—I know— only I can't say it, any more than I can describe the taste of tripe. Damn it, Avery, life's got a core to it somewhere! Look how many have nibbled through to it. The Rarick suspects the core, only he hasn't nibbled through. Gerkes has nibbled through, but on a cotton apple. The world you thumbed your nose at, and quit cold, is the Rarick-world. There are better ones. That's why the copy-books say riches can't buy happiness. That's why Indians, who sit and look all day at their navels, are happy. Damn it, darling! I don't want to sit all day and look at mine. But I want to be happy, sweet Avery, and be something decent to atone for the way life didn't come off for you. Damn it, I do!" sobbed Jennifer into her sobs.

A clock struck then, and Jennifer began climbing into what she would have called her "dud." A lace frock, the beautiful color of coffee, well creamed. It weighed less than half a pound, cost three hundred and sixty-five dollars, and its trade name in the fashion-show of the French *couturière* who had created it, had been "Irresistible."

Berry kept her waiting twenty minutes, so that she sat alone in the business men's restaurant, trying, behind her flaming discomfort, to look interested in the large menu proclaiming its specialties of grilled dishes. Fool to have come! Berry at last was probably going to stand her up. He had begged her to leave off writing, not meaning it, of course. Perhaps his new dignity as father of his son! Strange, how curious that made her to see him, although to visualize him, even vicariously, in the rôle that was almost unbearable to her, was pain. Berry was the father of Leslie's child, and here was Jennifer waiting for him, the week after the birth, in a downtown restaurant, as she sat trying to hide her face behind the huge menu of grilled chops and planked steaks. Sickness of spirit smote her. She was on the point of pushing back her chair and leaving the waiter an apologetic tip, when the revolving-door spun Berry into the room, and with his usual capacity to make any place he entered look busy, a hat girl, two waiters, and a *maître d'hôtel* bowed him to his place.

He ordered abruptly, without consulting her. She liked that. There was a great straight seam horizontally across Berry's brow. She tried to remember if it had ever been there in unbroken line before.

"Well," he said, and rubbed it, "this hasn't been what you would call a nice getaway. Too many lies."

How matter-of-fact he was, and hot-looking, as if he had perspired. Business men looked that way after a hard day. It made him appear like a big rumpled boy. That softened her.

"You might have spared me this waiting around beneath a grilled mutton chop, Berry."

"Good lord, Jennifer!" he said, and looked at her with incredulity in his big chiseled face. "Do you realize that I had a kid born a few days ago? Nine pounds, all to the good."

There was nothing to say to that, and so she stared with her palm up against where she felt her throat beating.

"It's a hell of a job, getting born, Jennifer."

"Well, what do you expect me to do about it?"

"What do you expect me to do about it?"

They stared and stared across the catsup-bottle and the A-1 sauce and the jar of chutney. Stared as if they could never have done with staring.

"Look here, Jennif, make allowances."

"For what?"

"Good God! for the birth of a man's son."

"Berry dear ——"

"Jennifer dear ——"

"I'm dense."

"I—I'm—I guess I'm confused, Jennif."

She wanted to feel, and she was not feeling; so she spoke words that she felt she would have spoken had she been feeling.

"Dearest Berry, we've passed that milestone."

"Whew, yes!"

"We've never exactly discussed what then—but doesn't

it seem to you like release, Berry? Like a release for us, now that it's over?"

"Where do you get that, Jennif?"

"She'll be back in normal health now—Leslie ——"

"I see."

"There's no question of money. You've both so much. . . ."

"What the devil . . ."

"What the devil?"

"Yes? What? I say, Jennifer, it *is* a hell of a job getting born."

"Well, as I seem to have remarked before, what do you expect me to do about it?"

They were staring again, across the chutney, staring and staring in incredulity at each other. Simultaneously, the impulse to laugh smote them. A side-twisting, strangulating gust of it shook Jennifer, not hysterical, but what Berry later designated as an eleven-dollar, orchestra-seat, below-the-belt laugh. He swept in on it. Waiters turned away to hide their smiles behind palms, as, gasping, they regarded each other across the table through the thick lenses of laughter-induced tears; and no sooner were their faces untwisted of their simply inexorable mirth, off they were again. It buckled them around the waists. It strained at the chest. It jammed in their windpipes and made them purple and full of exhausted little "oh's" and "ah's."

"Oh! oh! oh!" gasped Jennifer, and clasped herself at the right side of her waist line.

"Good lord!" panted Berry, and kept wiping at his tears, and poking his handkerchief back into his breast pocket, and wiping his tears again and poking it back. "I've paid eleven dollars an orchestra seat for a laugh that didn't come through like that. Whew! Now how do you think we got that way, Jennifer?"

"I don't know, Berry," she said, still laughing in a soft exhausted way.

"Give you my word, Jennif. I think we were laughing at us."

"I hope so, Berry. It will help me to seem funny to me."

"What about me?"

"I—I'm afraid all of a sudden you are funny to me, Berry—and that's fatal."

"To what?"

"Us."

"Us is a nice word, Jennifer, when applied to us."

"You don't mean that. You wish to God I'd let you be."

"Then what?"

"So you could settle down to being what you are at heart. A husband. A fast, rich, gay stockbroker on the side, who thinks girls were made to pinch and wives were made to have nine-pound sons. A father whose son is a miracle, chiefly because he resembles his daddy."

"Pretty picture."

"I hate it more than you do."

"Hang it, Jennif! I'll say it, even at the risk of bringing down that well-known scorn of yours—that kid, getting himself born as mine, gave me the kick of a lifetime."

"So it should, Berry."

"Hang it, Jennif! I'll say it again, even if I afford you the laugh of your life, that kid getting himself born as mine gave me the kick of a lifetime."

"I hope it's the only one he'll ever give you."

"Not nice."

"Sorry, Berry."

"Dear girl . . ."

"Don't say that, Berry."

"Now what?"

"Because it's as if—as if I lifted the words off this table and put them on your lips."

"You should have been a writer of fantasies."

"I'm a liver of them."

"Nothing fantastic about this mutton chop," he said, and slid a black-handled steel knife into the "specialty of the house."

"And I am expected to nibble boned breast of chicken with Hartley Slocum at seven," she said, slicing down, too, into mutton that flowed red.

"And me, breast-of-something-or-other with my mother-in-law, who will have many a bone to pick with me besides, if I'm late. Jennifer, ever see a new kid?"

"Yes. They cause strong men to falter and bad girls to trek across the snow ——"

"Damn it, I like my kid! Now what are you going to do about it?"

"I'm afraid, Berry, I'm going to be noble."

"God forbid!"

"I'm going to give you back to your wife and your chee-ild."

"But I don't want to be guv."

"You do. Only, this surreptitious thing on the side with me satisfies the bounder instinct in you. I satisfy your instinct for show-girls. I'm one to you now, being pinched."

"God, you can say the low-down to a man, Jennifer!"

"Funny, Berry, that I can say it to you so quietly. I'm all helped. Look, I can throw away my crutches. Note the way in which she carves her mutton chop until the bloody juices run, scoops up some baked potato and says, 'Pass the A-1 sauce.' I'm awfully afraid something has happened over this mutton chop, Berry. I'm out of love. I see you now in your true light. Perforce, villain, you're a family-man at heart. You're a Babbit in sheik's clothing. I'm for you, but not after you."

"If a man did the square thing by you and himself, he'd turn you over his knee and spank you for making a continual fool of him, going and coming."

"That's all that is needed to give this occasion the truly heroic ending it deserves. I'm renouncing you, Berry, not—denouncing."

"Why the devil . . ."

"Is your kid all beety and underdone? Do his fingers twine around yours? . . ."

"Gad! a woman has got to be sure of herself to get away with that. . . ."

"Does the sight of his crib warm the cockles of your heart? Why is it cockles are always warmed? . . ."

"Damn it, yes!"

"Berry, there are little spangles all across your forehead. You're perspiring. Not nice. Hanky."

"God! I wouldn't treat a dog the way you're treating me."

"Neither would I. The husband-and-father technique applies to this case better than canine technique would."

"I'll go!"

"Berry, I'm *for* your kid ——"

"I know you are. You're so damned for him that I strongly suspect you of being noble ——"

"Maybe I am. But if that's true—it's such easy, incidental nobility—it's easy for me to want to play square by your youngster and your wife, Berry—chiefly because I've come to the conclusion that one good husband and father is worth more than a bounder."

"But, Jennifer ——"

"But, Berry ——"

"Damn it, Jennif! now that this has happened— maybe it is for the best."

"Maybe, nothing. Surely, you mean. Here, Berry, my hanky. Wipe your forehead—it's damp—and pay our check. You'll be late for Mother-in-law."

"That's my business."

"No, Berry. Thank God, now it's my business to see that you're not late for Mother-in-law."

They drove uptown in his car, their fingers interlaced after an old fashion between them, his knee ingratiated against hers, but in a silence that began to embarrass.

"I say, Jennifer," he said, as they approached the Plaza. "I say——"

"Don't say, Berry," she said. "It would spoil the perfect thing that has happened between us. Wait until I've gone, and then say 'Amen. Fini. Curtain.'"

She alighted, leaving him standing bareheaded and perspiring, as she ran up the hotel steps.

That was the night, after dinner and the benefit performance with Hartley Slocum, that Jennifer met, for the first time, the author of *Port of Salute*—a young man named Gratton Davies.

An IDEA began slowly, surely, and roundly to form itself in Rarick's brain. With the characteristically slow metabolism of a mind that thinks its way cautiously to destination, even the consummation took place so gradually that up to a certain point it was scarcely perceptible to Rarick himself.

It was his way, nerve-racking, sometimes, to those dependent upon his decision, to wake up one morning with clear-cut plan of action seeming to spring full-grown out of long periods of what appeared to be a languid series of procrastinations.

For instance, over a period of four and one-half years, Rarick had held up certain final building decisions that had delayed the breaking of ground for the Rarick Building almost beyond the endurance of those intimately connected with the gigantic project.

At the conclusion of the fifty-fourth month of procrastination, certain franchise developments and new subway constructions gave the delays a most providential significance, although it had been impossible to get out of Rarick whether he had foreseen, maneuvered, or been just characteristically slow, careful, and lucky. There were those who maintained that both the franchise developments and the subway constructions had been the outgrowth of only the last six months of the four and one-half years, and that it must have been foresight, not insight. Hellman, who possibly was closest of all to this particular situation, maintained a face carved out of cherry-stone, insinuating with his manner, that circumstances similar to this happened too frequently to leave doubt, in any except the most obtuse, of the enormous quality of generalship behind such slow-moving maneuver.

On the other hand, there was Jenny, wife, to whom all things were still flowing from the accident of her initial twenty-five hundred dollars. This success of his, engendered by her, was merely going on succeeding and succeeding. . . .

The ideas, which, it seemed to Rarick now, must have been slowly congealing in his subconscious mind for years and years before a chance dissertation from Gerkes had jelled them, so to speak, had reached, these months since the death of Avery, a sudden consistency.

Half-thoughts, semi-intentions, parts of ideas, seemed to come awake. It was to be expected that Rarick, in his upper fifties, should already have expended much thought upon the growing problem of the ultimate dispositions of his ever-accruing fortunes. A man pondered over his riches. Pondered and vexed himself over apportionments, contemplated, wondered, and faltered. Rarick had done his share of all of these, and, from time to time, always with ultimate revision in mind, had made temporary wills to cover the exigency of sudden death, adding codicil by codicil, as occasions arose.

It was when Avery had been dead a six-month that the slowly congealing major idea became determination.

Day after day, in the maelstrom of his affairs, in conference, in trips of coast-to-coast inspection, on tours through the raw scaffolding of the partially erected Rarick Building; night after night, sitting in his library in discussion with Gerkes, poring over his amulets or his orchids, the idea, gathering specks from all corners of his mind, was slowly swimming into pattern.

"The wealth which man draws from his fellow creatures as clouds draw moisture from poisonous and sweet waters alike, must be made to descend again in productive rains, or what availeth it?"

Or what availeth it? Avery had answered that. His death had simultaneously seemed to promulgate and answer that question. Without progeny of son, Rarick sat in his Gothic aisle, pondering his responsibilities of disposing of a wealth that up to now had chiefly accrued interest and objects.

According to the charts of the companies that carried his enormous insurances, his span of life was two-thirds spent. Even with long-life expectancy, and somehow in Rarick that expectancy had never run high, the time had come when a man whose share in the wealth of the world, if you figured it per capita, was several millions of human heads, must prepare to put his house in order.

"The wealth which man draws from his fellow creatures as clouds draw rain from poisonous and sweet waters alike, must be made to descend again in productive rains, or what availeth it?"

There were books on Rarick's night-table, Adam Smith's *Wealth of Nations,* Shaw's *Socialism for Millionaires,* Karl Marx's *Capital,* Stuart Chase's *The Tragedy of Waste,* Veblen's *Theory of the Leisure Class,* Weston's *Economics for the Business Man,* William Morris's *Letters on Socialism,* John Stuart Mill's *Principles of Political Economy,* many of which he found out-of-date, confusing, un- or mis-informing, and coldly technical.

Disposition of wealth, life being what it was, human ties being what they were, was not a matter that springs so completely, as the theorists seemed to reckon, out of the tenets of mathematics, sociology, and geometric, economic patterns. Human equations of greed, ego, blood-ties, preferences, hates, loves, sentiment, emotions, irrationalities, devotion and lack of it, leaned into the situation.

The disposition of over one hundred million dollars according to a man's temperament, family, dependents, hobbies, preferences, philanthropies, altruisms, wisdoms, principles, and conscientious convictions, was a highly personal and complex matter, to say nothing of the responsibilities, ethical and sentimental, for which there was no proviso in the erudite volumes of economics, sociology, philanthropy, or wealth in relation to peoples, land, cities, industry, and countries.

The time had come, it seemed to Rarick, to formulate into words of legal document, the groping convictions of years, which, aided and abetted by what he regarded as certain brilliant thinking of Gerkes, the death of his son had solidified in his mind.

Disposition of wealth. This much beyond a doubt: The members of his family who survived him must be made safe from his millions. These millions must be made to accumulate something besides interest and objects. Bracelets and shields, as he had read it storied of the Greeks, had also bewildered his son out of life. Smothered him to death. This much beyond a doubt: The members of his family who survived him must be made safe from those millions.

Wealth need not be in itself the arbitrary symbol of man's ability to exploit man, as it was painted in stiff chromo against the minds of people like Hildegarde. Capital, yes, might be interpreted as that which you in your strength continued to draw from the weak. Wealth, if you were worthy of it, was what you turned back to them, wisely minted. . . .

The time had come when Rarick contemplated with obsession the turning of his capital into wealth, wisely minted, into the largest crusade of preventive scientific and sociological research ever launched as either group or individual enterprise.

The wealth which man draws from his fellow creatures was not to descend in a crushing, golden mantle
upon such shoulders as Jenny's, to whom those fellow
creatures by now had become so many millions of mag-
gots eating away the impedimenta of life for her, that
she might walk in glory.

It was thus out of the freighted solitudes of the long
evenings of the long months following the death of
Avery, that Rarick began writing the document that was
to be his last will and testament.

THE day the last steel beam was laid across the seventy-ninth story of the skeleton of the Rarick Building, Hellman arranged a ceremonial; a luncheon to take place under gay awnings on an improvised platform erected among the mortar and bricks of the parapet that surrounded the Gothic auditorium that topped the tallest building in the world.

It was a motion designed chiefly to catch the eye and headline of the press. Tables were set up exclusively for reporters and feature-writers at the most spectacular end of the platform, overlooking more span of bridge, rush of skyscraper, and bird's-eye panorama than had yet been achieved from roof-top.

There were about seventy guests. Mayor. Aldermen. Health Commissioner. Lieutenant-Governor. Borough Presidents. Superintendent of Schools. Chief of Police. An ex-mayor of St. Louis and old personal friend of Rarick's. A half-dozen leading St. Louis citizens. The eight most important executives of Rarick Chain, Inc. President of the Gray Department Store Chain, in which Rarick was reputed to hold large interests. Vice-president of Chicago Transit Company. Owner of the San Francisco *Commercial Journal*. Attorney-General of the State of Pennsylvania. Max Lindsey, internationally-renowned corporation lawyer. Doctors, lawyers, merchants, yes, and even a fire-chief. Myron Stahl, District Attorney. Ramon Lopez.

Wives had been invited. The publicity value of women present was incalculable. Editors would give photographs of a mixed assembly twice the space. Jenny had realized the indiscretion of asking Ramon; and yet the explanation of his presence had seemed so obvious, almost too trivial to require comment. She had motored down for the ceremony from Roslyn, where she had been superintending the doing-over of the brace of six beautiful bedrooms that overlooked a rose-garden, and had picked up Ramon, who had been week-ending at the Breckenridge Scotes', at Scotes Manor, where she had stopped for luncheon. She had given him and Eulalie Lett a lift to town, dropping Eulalie at Charvet's for a facial, and bringing Ramon along to the ceremonies. Nice boy—so obliging——

Indeed, so trivial was the circumstance, that when she explained it to Rarick, he scarcely heard; his nervous attention focused instead, on the arrival of guests, as they stepped out of the narrow, improvised elevator that they were obliged to take in three shifts, changing from one at the twentieth floor to another, and then out again at the sixtieth into a third, which completed the ascent.

Public ceremonial occasions were such painful and excoriating anathema to Rarick that his consistent failure to accept civic and honorary rôles could be traced to what amounted to an insurmountable disability to occupy a president's or chairman's position. Even board and directors' meetings at which he must preside filled him with apprehension. Usually he evaded parliamentary procedure by calling conference in his office and seating the group about his desk, this colossal shyness also accounting for the almost total lack of social life in his scheme of things.

Hellman, who was always averring, averred that this inability to glean the best from his fellow men, coupled with a certain humorlessness, was what kept Rarick from his place among the truly great. Gerkes, in his totally different way, practically said the same thing, when, one day, apropos of Woodrow Wilson, whom he had known personally, he deplored Rarick's policy of going it alone.

On those rare occasions when his appearance at formal functions—such as the Rarick Chain Twentieth Anniversary Banquet, the annual Rarick Chain conventions, the laying of the cornerstone of the Rarick Building, the dedication of the Rarick Stadium at a Missouri university —was imperative, it took more hours of steeling his will to make these appearances than even Hellman would ever realize.

It was rumored that Rarick paid Hellman, who was supposed to write his speeches, stage such necessary formalities as these, and appear as his proxy wherever opportunity presented, the sum of twenty thousand dollars a year.

As a matter of fact, he paid him thirty.

This was one of the occasions when not even the machinations of Hellman could prevent the affair from falling mercilessly on the shoulders of Rarick, whose place of honor at the head of the T-shaped table, even before the guests were assembled, had become dreadful to him at the sight of the small ivory gavel there.

The page of typewritten address, of decorous phrases, mock humility, and suave platitude, lay folded in the pocket of his stiff-feeling cutaway; steep sills of language to be crossed by his faltering lips. Presently, at whispered word from Hellman, he would push back the fluted-paper cup of untasted pistachio ice-cream, rest his cigar on the edge of the saucer of his demitasse, place the neat circle of his watch in very precise position, clear his throat, strike his gavel, and curtsy to the Mayor.

Your Honor the Mayor, ladies and gentlemen, friends —guests ——

It was going to be blowy up on the roof. Gusts of

wind snapped the bunting. The sheet of paper containing Rarick's speech would be sure to wave and rattle. Sometimes, in spite of having memorized, it became necessary for Rarick, because of the numb nervousness, to read his address.

Greeting his guests as they stepped out of the makeshift elevator, the tongue of Rarick lay like chamois in his mouth. The great little magnate swallowed his tongue. The great little magnate was heavy with dread.

The panorama from the highest roof in the world unrolled before his glazed eyes. Dime by dime, brick by brick, he had built his pinnacle. It was of steel and it seemed to him it swayed a little in the high wind that was going to be sure to flutter his sheet of speech in his nerve-tortured fingers.

The Rarick Auditorium tilted its Gothic-shaped eyebrows out over the vastest expanse upon which windows had ever gazed. It seemed to Rarick that too many forces were meeting here for his endurance to bear up under. The agony of the nervousness. Altitude. That insistent, that terrible sense of the swaying of steel. The harbor moving out to sea. The crawling, remote island below, the streets as negligible-looking as slots. The dipping heavens. . . .

Congratulatory phrases and the shrill extravagances of the women cluttered the high, clean altitude.

Marvelous. Breath-taking. Oh! Oh! Oh! Dramatic! Stupendous! Incredible. Finest—biggest—highest —tallest—most terrific—most expensive—gigantic—Oh! —Oh!—Look!—See!—What?—Where? Finest—tallest—highest—so—American!

One shook hands. One accompanied this one and that one to this ledge and that. That down there? Oh, of course, the Equitable Building. Over there? I say, Hellman, is that Metropolitan Tower? No-o—think

that's the Municipal Building down there. Telephone
Building. Oh no, forty stories higher—wonderful—panorama—finest—biggest—tallest—highest—so American——

As Hellman confided to his wife, a large overweight
woman, who was in turn suspected of writing Hellman's
speeches for Rarick, the old gentleman was a ton of coal
on top of the occasion. In all of the scene of anima-
tion on the half-completed roof, Rarick's was the one
hesitant figure, requiring, on the part of Hellman, constant watching and steering, or inevitably he gravitated
to a corner, there to stand unanimated, his twitching
hands under his coat tails, making inaudible replies to
the high falsettos of the women, meeting, but never making overtures of conversation to the men.

As a host, Hellman again confided to his wife, as he
rushed past her to pilot Rarick to the Commissioner of
Police, the old gentleman would make a first-rate funeral-
director.

Motion-picture machines ground. Cameras clicked.
Groups leaned against parapets and were photographed.
The wife of the Mayor, in a feather boa that was well
known to rotogravures, was snapped with the wife of
Rarick, who posed tall and lean, with sables high about
her neck and wrists. The entire group of sixty was
photographed. Then twenty. Then ten. Finally Rarick
and the Mayor.

Luncheon itself, served by a bankers' club in Wall
Street, was a cold and tasteless affair by the time it was
relayed up the seventy-nine stories. The wind was a nag-
ging one that became bothersome to the women and
forced Senator Grimes to dine with his high hat clamped
tightly down against neuralgia.

There were souvenirs. Snow-storm paper-weights of
the Rarick Building enclosed in crystal.

At the escarole-salad course, Miss Jennifer Rarick, slender in black tailored things and high white fox, apologetically late and becomingly breathless, arrived with a young man named Davies, for whom an extra chair had to be crammed beside Jennifer's.

The occasion marched to the address by Rarick, who, by the time the pistachio ice-cream arrived, knew that this was to be one of the excessively nervous times he would be obliged to read his few remarks.

He did so after coffee, the decorous phrases, the mock humilities that had been written for him either by his secretary or by the wife of his secretary, dropping heavily on to the assemblage.

On occasions when Rarick made address, Jenny invariably rolled bread balls and kept her eyes down. Zigzags of disagreeable sensation ran up and down her spine. From his place beside her, the knee of Ramon pressed up sympathetically against hers. "Awful!" she whispered, and pressed back; "he simply should not attempt it."

The voice of Rarick went over its rutted road:

". . . share with you—proudest moment of my life—generous public—lifetime ambition—service of the people—humble servant—owe everything to generosity of those who have encouraged [applause]—temple of music dedicated to people [applause]—from the people back to the people—your generous coöperation—my humble efforts—fine spirit of coöperation in my organization [applause]—thanks due to officials—employees [applause]—I wish I had ability to express—dedicated to people—dedicated to people ——"

"Awful! Awful! He said coöperation eleven times."

Ramon's knee so gently pressing hers! It made it easier, after the polite applause had died down, to look up from her plate.

Thank God, chairs were scraping back. Another horror of an occasion over. Curious, that the figure of Rarick could be so consistently a depressant. Never knew it to fail.

"You mustn't mind it, Jenny."

"I do mind, terribly. Why does he attempt it? Oh, Jennifer, there you are! Wasn't it ghastly?"

"Not at all, Mother. Father is my idea of a bat in the pulpit, or is it belfry? I love the bat, if only I didn't have such a horror of getting him caught in my hair. Gratton, you're supposed to be a word-prestidigitator. Pull me a phrase out of the blue that can do justice to that view down there."

They leaned over the parapet, young and exultant, stricken with the wonder of what they were, even more than with the wonder of what they beheld.

"It's the book of life written on a postage-stamp," he said.

"Putrid! I can do better than that. It's the story of the circulation of the blood being told by those crawling caterpillars down there."

"Zero. It's Lucifer being hurled, and splitting, as he strikes bottom, into land and water, skyscrapers and taxi-cabs."

Elegant, but dumb.

The wind in their faces could not budge her in the tight black helmet that covered her head like close hair. It lifted the light tan thatch of Gratton's, though, as if it were a wig. It was difficult to indulge in any but a breathless sort of discourse, and yet, they did discourse, these two, smartly at first, young, exultant, and high-keyed each to the other's presence.

"The roof of the world isn't so cozy as the low little old thatched ones of Devonshire and English poetry."

"After spending a summer in a picturesque, damp, uncomfortable and gloomy thatched cottage in Sussex, I am convinced that love in a cottage may lead to lumbago."

"Love! Must all conversational roads lead to love?"

"Pretty many, I suppose, between the delightfully un-attached like ourselves. Daring to assume that you are as unattached as I yearn to believe."

"Your way, I suppose, of asking how, or if, I have recovered from my last devastating love-affair?"

"Many a true word. . . ."

"Many and many a true word . . ." she said, fastening her hard, hurt eyes upon him. "Well, to whom it may concern, the dead past has buried its Berry. I'm so unattached it hurts! I think I'm in love now, with the idea of being in love with you, Gratton."

"I wish you could manage to get all the way through to being in love with me, Jennifer. I need to be rich. I've a low kind of Indiana background that I don't seem able to live down. I can't feel the swank in evading my creditors. An unpaid dry-cleaner's bill will insist upon keeping me too worried to tackle a second act."

"An admirable but low instinct, my lad, not acknowledged in circles of the highest creative impulse."

"I know it! But hang it all, my highest creative impulses, whatever that means, get all obscured by fear that the dry-cleaner's thirteenth child may be dying of rickets, for need of pure, fresh milk. Of course, dry-cleaner can probably buy and sell me ten times over, but that doesn't seem to lessen my obligation."

"Go on."

"Where?"

"Not being all the wise-crack things we seem to pretend to be, whenever we are together."

"It's you who sets that pace, Jennifer."

"I need the wise-crack, to divert the eye of the beholder from seeing through how I do my poor little mental tricks. You don't."

"Jennifer, are you being humble?"

"I want to be."

"That's terrible! It somehow . . . hurts. I prefer you naughty."

"I think you do."

"I think I don't—really——"

"Gratton, guess why my face aches."

"Too loaded with the seductiveness of youth and beauty."

"Don't rag. I am being profound and introspective. Altitude does that to me. My face aches, Gratton, from pretending to look like what it isn't."

"Perhaps it is your heart that aches, Jennifer."

Their bright young eyes poured against each other and she did something that was adorable to him. She placed her hand up against the region of the heart in question, and her lips came lightly apart like a small, thirsty bird's.

"That's it! The ache is down there and my face hurts from pretending that it isn't."

"It's too dear a face to ache."

"Meaning expensive?"

"Not kind, Jennifer."

"If I were to start in allowing myself to be kind to you, Gratton, I might not know where to stop."

"Wonderful of you to say that."

"Wonderful to be able to say that."

"It's nice, our being this way," he said, on a blurt of words.

"Yes. It rests the face."

"What on earth do you mean, Jennifer?"

"Being this way. Just simple. To hell with persiflage."

"I hope it isn't all due to altitude that you're so nice today. Perhaps attitude has a bit to do with it?"

She grasped his arm. "Look down there, Gratton! See that steamer. Looks like a fruit-boat, nosing into slip."

"Where?"

"No, darling, we're not docking boats this season on top of the Woolworth Building. Look to the left. See, there's the Aquitania, beyond her are two ferries passing one another, and just beyond them there's a steamer sliding alongside her pier."

"Yes! Two red funnels."

"Right. I want a port, Gratton. I want to slip alongside a pier. That's what Father always says about you. You've destination."

"What kind of port do you want, Jennifer?"

"A snug harbor into which I can bring useful wares— such as they are."

"Yours would be first-rate."

"Are you thinking, or saying, that?"

"Both?"

She hooked into his arm.

"Aren't I grotesque to you, Gratton, up here on this peak of dimes. Don't I appall you?"

"In a way, yes."

"Look at Father over there. Bewildered, frustrated, with dimes. Sometimes he seems to me like a little man whose eyes have turned to dimes and whose spirit cannot shine through them. Dimes have flowed over his life, making of it a metal prairie. My mother stands in the middle of such a prairie. I do. My brother lies buried in it. This building is a monument of dimes to the futility of dimes . . . and in a way, a monument to the curious, groping genius of my father. I am part of his great frustration—Gratton—never for a moment doubt but what I know that."

He laid his gloved hand against her mouth as if to crush back the words and the wind tugged at them, and beyond, where both their gazes focused, the harbor looked like a tarpaulin being dragged.

"There are times when I come perilously near liking you perilously, Jennifer."

"Like me enough to understand me, Gratton."

"Then you understand him," he said, and nodded to the form of Rarick, who seemed perpetually to be hovering on the edge of groups to which he did not quite belong.

"I try," she said, on a small click of teeth. "I try. I try. I try. Believe that."

"Curious how simple he seems to me. A man who is too stern an idealist to compromise. A man who asked for bread and got a gold nugget."

"A gold brick, if you mean me."

"I don't."

"I'm crazy to help him. I'm crazy to—love him."

"I should think his pathos would help you to that; the pathos of his terrible, heart-breaking grandeur."

"It does."

"Jennifer, you are sweeter today than I have ever known you. Please don't ever again let your face ache from looking like what it isn't."

"Yes, but what about my heart?"

"It's a dear heart. In the right place."

"Gratton, if you prove that to Father, some day, when I do things for him that he won't believe I had it in me to do, will I be proving it to you at the same time?"

"If you haven't already."

"I need more money than anybody in the world, Gratton. The chances are that I'm apt to always have money.

I wouldn't want ever not to have money, and yet, I suppose that the only real chance I'd ever have to show what I think I'm made of, is to wake up some morning broke —God forbid!"

"I'm beginning to strangely suspect you of being made of what you think you are."

"Don't make this strong man weep, Gratt. She might proceed to tell you how ghastly lonesome and misunderstood she is. Than which . . ."

"Don't take advantage of my youthful susceptibility. I am on the verge of thinking you more of a person than is good for my peace of mind."

". . . and so, snapping out of the mood of better-self which had crossed her fair and petulant face, the fêted and ill-fated heiress to the Rarick millions hurled her champagne tumbler from her hand and—ate the glass . . ."

"Idjut!"

He stooped to pick up her glove which had fallen crumpled to her feet.

"Give me your hand," he said. "I'll draw this on for you."

"Are you suing for my hand?"

"No."

"Well, then, keep my gauntlet until you are ready to come suing."

"Idjut," he said again.

This was the conversation between those two, as they stood at the parapet, overlooking the world, high wind in their faces, and their words jerked off their lips and swallowed up by gusts. Once or twice Rarick hovered. The very atmosphere about them was built up of the kind of particles that kept him gingerly on edge. Their sureness and brightness and youngness oppressed him with a sense of his own unsureness. He felt ill at ease, just as much so, in a very different way, as he did when he bobbed about helplessly among the dancing young men with no faces in particular, that Jenny dangled around with her as you would bangles on a bracelet. That was pretty generally his feeling about the narrow young dancing-men, who looked as if they might be slid back into their shoe-boxes at night, and put in place along the shelf.

This Davies, now, was another matter. This fellow had a sure, uncompromising look to him. He knew what races were worth entering—for him. He knew his track —he knew his goal. . . .

Even as he stood there, keyed by the slim Jennifer beside him, to his facetious worst, Rarick, abominating what was sure to be the flying foam of their conversation, was ready to like him. He had written that message, "I think I understand what you failed to get said to Avery. . . ."

"Well, young man," said Rarick, greeting him a little later, "how is the enterprise coming along?"

"Not for the moment, so surely as this one of yours, sir. This building has been headed for its roof ever since you laid the cornerstone. We are not certain yet where we are heading."

"We've just come from a reading rehearsal of one of Gratton's plays, Father. Talk about not seeing the woods for the trees! We couldn't hear the lines for the adenoids."

"That remark, I shall explain to your daughter when I have her alone, Mr. Rarick, was both unæsthetic and untrue. The fact is, the cast at the moment doesn't measure up."

"Gratton's polite way of saying, Father, that the first thing the committee did after feeling money in its pocket was to go out and buy the most expensive Broadway cast-ing-director they could find, thus launching the experimental idea safely and smugly toward the commercial theater from which it was so passionately revolting when you came across. You should have endowed Gratton, Father. Not a half-baked idea."

"Jennifer!"

"Modesty ill becomes you, my young man. You may leave something to be desired as a playwright, but you are as bona-fide an idealist as ever let himself in for a bumping. But anyway, I'm for Gratton's play, Father. Louder and funnier—more situations and less psychology —is all anyone could have asked of the first rehearsal. Also a new and not quite so comic hat for the leading lady."

"I'd like to come around sometime, Mr. Rarick, and talk to you about this baby of yours . . . that is what it is, in a way . . . your money made it possible."

"Are you speaking of me, sir? Father, I think the young man is about to sue for my hand."

"Jennifer, idiot, if your comedy cannot be funnier, let it at least be deferred. I've a notion you'll be interested in seeing first hand, sir, what we are doing with your money. Jennifer isn't entirely correct in what she says; but it does seem that with money in our cash-box the committee is about to commit the understandable error of becoming pretentious. I'm for adhering to our pre-affluent *répertoire*. I would like to talk over our production end with you, sir."

A broad, slow smile moved across the sallow features of Rarick, seeming to widen them, his lips lifted, revealing seldom-revealed white oblongs of teeth, then drew back as slowly as portières.

"My hours, young man, for conferring advice for the furtherance of our native and esoteric drama are for the present overcrowded, but if you will consult with my Mr. Hellman, he will arrange an appointment."

"Darling," said Jennifer as they turned away, "I wish to commemorate this occasion by sliding down seventy-nine stories and rushing to the first corner orangeadery for an ade—or a ginfizz. You may not realize it, but you succeeded in eliciting a smile and a witticism from my father."

"I'm for him."

"I'm of him."

"That makes me vicariously for you."

"Viciously, did you say?"

And so on and so on and so on, as, stepping into the elevator they began descent through the stories of steel that were rising to the tunes of the jingling of the dimes.

By unexplainable oversight that offhand would seem almost impossible, Rarick, what with Hellman rushing off with the newspaper men and the guests paying their departing platitudes, was left on the roof alone after the elevator man had made his last descent and apparently gone from the building. There were no bells. It meant a walk down thousands of stairs that were little more than ladders. For an hour now, the sun had been in behind banking clouds, the wind stiffening. Meanwhile Rarick waited, hoping for a return of some of the waiters to clear away the few remaining camp-chairs, or for a watchman on his rounds.

It was not unpleasant up there on the rim of his skyscraper, except that with the rising wind he could have wished for a warmer coat. Clouds scurried low, and the heavens seemed to scamper. Vessels with slanting funnels were riding out on their first lap eastward. There were a few coming in. You could tell by the direction of the slant of the funnels and the way the waves fawned at the cutting prows.

With the instinct of man to ponder from high places,

Rarick, looking out, looking down, stood with his elbows on a parapet and his cheeks crushed between his palms.

The leaping bridges rushing to jerk land to land. Ships that not improbably were majestically putting to sea or making harbor on some such petty mission as dolls with peach-skin faces or pressed-tin ash-trays. Belching funnels of fruit-steamers that were packed with enormous cargoes of green-skinned bananas to sell by the puny penny-piece off East Side pushcarts. Vertically below, the winding of the crisscross streets, slots into which to drop your dime; the winding play of elevated railroad; the animated dartings of the specks of little humans rushing about with hearts buttoned up underneath their coats. The moving clouds, the moving streets, the moving waters, the ever-moving specks of heartbeat. The little Rarick, elevated on his parapet of the nickels and the dimes. The little Rarick—contemplating. . . .

What Rarick was actually contemplating at the moment, as he stood there in the midst of space, in the midst of a Saturday afternoon—his last guest gone, Jenny with her narrow youth, Jennifer with her heckled and heckling companion—was, that here he stood with miles of steps to walk down and no place in particular to go after he had walked them.

One of those hiatuses which, because they occur so seldom in the map of a busy man's affairs, flabbergast.

Well, here goes!

It was almost dusk when he reached the street, after the fifty and more flights of stairs, mortar streaks along his coat, the dizzying descent and the Saturday-afternoon bedlam of shoppers, ferry-boat commuters, trucksters, newsboys, clerks, stenographers, brokers, causing the scene to seem to sway by the time he reached sidewalk-level.

Women with oilcloth bags, that had been stocked at a Rarick Five-and-Ten across the way, jostled him.

There was a small triangle of park opposite, set out sparsely with the geometry of two dusty maple-trees, two scrofulaed benches, a refuse-can, and an inset of gray grass. There was a vacant place on one of the benches, between a bulging woman with one of the oilcloth shopping-bags and a sandwich man who had unhooked his boards and had sat down to rest from them. There Rarick slid in.

The red front of the Five-and-Ten was ground into the pallid scene. Its windows glittered. There was a handkerchief display this week, of pink and blue and striped cotton squares. Rarick had sat in conference on this buy of the two million run-of-the-mill output of a New England concern. The vista that faced him was plastered with the small cotton squares edged in a horrible kind of cotton lace that presently, after a washing or two, would fray into so much string. Cotton handkerchiefs, destined to dry against mirrors and windowpanes; cotton handkerchiefs for the customers with the cotton-looking faces who poured in and out. They brought their ten-cent pieces to this fount of abominable things with an acquiescence that had pathos in it. Kitchenware, celluloid fine-combs, under-arm shields, glass jewelry, were the mission of these men and women who, from the heights only a few moments before, seen as specks, had seemed sublime. Ten-cent trailers after ten-cent things!

He watched them come. He watched them go. The woman on the bench beside him began to open a package and count hair-pins. Rarick pins. Children emerged from the red front opposite, jamming Rarick lollypops along tongues. Women lugged Rarick mops and Rarick clothes-hangers. Men came out with Rarick celluloid collars and Rarick ten-cent socks tucked into their coat pockets, and more Rarick lollypops, for more babies, turning gummy in their Rarick paper bags.

The feet that turned in at the fount of Rarick were for the most part tired, crooked feet. The splayed feet of women who have borne too many children under too many handicaps. The side-tilting feet of men who are on them too many hours a day. The pitiful feet of girls in short vamps and tall heels. Tawdry feet, filled with a mysterious eagerness.

Contemplating them for at least two hours, Rarick finally dove down into the subway, and home, to write throughout the evening at the document that was slowly becoming his will.

THE third day that Jenny's meals, every nine of them, had consistently disagreed, she rather angrily decided to see a specialist.

Deep down within herself she sensed the trouble. As a child she had been subject to fits of nervous indigestion following punishment or spells of rage. She had subsequently outgrown all this, and, for the years since, had enjoyed the singular hardihood that is so often the lot of the wiry and apparently nervous temperament.

Jenny could and did truthfully boast that she had never spent a day in bed. Small ailments, such as the sciatic twinge that had come of late, yes. But in the main she was entitled to regard herself as a creature well thewed.

The old nervous unease, asserting itself in this physical fashion, was, as Jenny frenziedly diagnosed it to herself, due to a sense of panic that went to the very roots of her being. It smote her with terror, with a sense of aloneness, with a growing despair of years, such as nothing in her experience had prepared her to meet.

Ramon was growing tired. The symptoms were out in him. The guarded manner. The wary voice. The evaded appointment. The placating manner. The roving eye. Slowly, surely, unrelentingly, the realization was closing in on Jenny.

His telephone no longer responded to her call when too well she knew he was lying within reach of it. The old punctiliousness about appointments was a thing of the past. Almost invariably now it was a matter of waiting for him; and on one or two occasions he had failed to appear at all, sending a telephone message, explaining unavoidable delay, by way of the cashier of the tea-room where already Jenny awaited him.

His tendency to be irritable was growing. He disliked the pink, Chinese polish to her finger nails; hated the manner in which she shrouded her throat in furs and tulles, and told her so.

"It makes you look so blamed manufacturedly exotic."

"But, Ramon, you once told me that Dusé and Bernhardt——"

"Never mind what I once told you. This is now."

"Why, Ramon!" she gasped, tears spurting. "Why—Ramon!"

He had leaned over the table of the tea-room to pat her hand, as you would the hand of some one who innocently irritates you beyond endurance.

"Never mind, dear."

Never mind! Jenny was minding to such a degree that when she laid herself in bed at night, after a day filled with a tormenting attempt to drown out with activities the rising fears about Ramon, the blood kept whirring in her veins and flooding her with flushes.

The boy was tiring, no doubt of that. More-frequent exchange of handclasps that left notes of larger and larger denomination in his palm did not seem to matter, except for the moment.

The pallor of terror was high in the face of Jenny these days; so high that Jennifer, marveling at such a lapse in her mother, reproved her for rouging badly.

"A bit thick, darling."

What was Ramon wanting? The apartment? The retreat to which he used to refer? Her discretion continued to shrink from that. The present suited her so well. Careful. Satisfying. Cautious. Having your cake and, as Ramon repeatedly added these days, eating it, too. But, curiously, even that mooted subject was laid now. Ramon no longer talked in terms of their jewel-box of a rendezvous which was to be of his designing.

Was Ramon's eye straying? The younger girls, including Jennifer, interested him strangely little. Significantly little, the men would have put it. He had appeared at the opera in Mrs. Emanie Bursilap's box of late. But that was unthinkable. Emanie Bursilap was a great-grandmother, and sixty-eight if a day. Rich beyond the count, it is true, but a rather horrible great-grandmother, with a wattled, wrinkled face that had been lifted into a mask, and a neck with grooves for the pearls to nest in. A naughty old gray bat of a woman, jealous of her own daughters and haunted by terrors of becoming what she already was.

Had the time come when Jenny must face her issues? What issues? It was unthinkable that this outward scheme of things, this scheme of having her cake and eating it, too, could ever be any different until—until what? Until something happened! Well, things did happen. Death changed the maps of families. Women had been left widows before—free —O God, forgive me for that thought ——

Ramon must be placated. There had never as yet been a time when Jenny, in Ramon's behalf, had drawn against her account for sums that would be noticeably unusual. But, in a pinch, that could be managed. There were ways of arranging with jewelers and furriers for bills to be presented for goods never delivered. That was a common device employed by women who, unbeknown to husbands, lost large sums at gambling. You arranged with your furrier, for instance, to send in a statement for a five-thousand-dollar mink coat. You returned the wrap, but paid the check, which in good time was returned to you in currency by your tradesman. . . .

When one was desperate . . . and yet, somehow, terribly, relentlessly, Ramon did not seem to want to be placated. What—what in God's name did one, who felt the universe slipping, do to reclaim it? . . .

It was then that digestion seemed to go nervously back on her and that Jenny decided to visit the specialist. Actually, Ramon's antipathy for illness was something reprehensible, of course, but at the same time, adorable and fascinating and fastidious in him. His sympathies poured out, you felt sure of that; but the little sense of aversion would creep in, wounding his æsthetic sense. Illness to the young blade Ramon was decay, antithetical to his sleek beauty. No wonder that he shrank.

Illness was something from which you protected Ramon.

As a matter of fact, be it said for Jenny, illness, hers, was something from which she, in general, protected those about her.

It was an acutely wretched week of physical distress that preceded this visit to the specialist, about which neither Jennifer nor Rarick had inkling. Not even the maid in the Breton cap, a stanch south-of-France woman, who had served Jenny well and long, knew to what extent she had been in torment.

The physician, a social-register one in East, slightly East, Sixty-third Street, to whom she finally presented herself, directed her, after discovering that the seat of her difficulties lay in an anatomical area two and three-quarter inches removed from the region on which his skill focused, to an eminent man in East Seventy-second Street, who, after a more or less cursory examination, awaited Jenny in his office, while she climbed back into her clothes in the examination-room.

A trying moment, this interval between physical examination and doctor's verdict, and one that added to Jenny's state of general nervousness and made her sharp with the attendant nurse.

It was not that she feared. It was more the idea that in the handsome adjoining office was sitting a professional figure endowed with the power of certain vital verdicts.

If there were anything serious the matter with her—well, that was life—and death.

If there was something only superficially wrong—dear Ramon. . . .

The verdict was neither so good as she had hoped nor so bad as she had feared.

Some digestive complication. His manner was casual and reassuring. Thank God for that. Life was good. But the best method of diagnosis and determination would mean a short period of observation at a hospital. Few days. A little troublesome but nothing to worry about. X-rays. Fluoroscope. Test meals. A chill rattled itself against Jenny. Hospital!

"Nothing to be alarmed about. Most efficient method. Merely a checking-up process."

"Yes, yes, of course."

Then and there the matter was arranged by telephone.

"A large suite, doctor?"

He placed his hand across the mouthpiece.

"The hospital is too crowded to allow for suites, Mrs. Rarick. You are fortunate to be able to obtain a single and bath. Is Friday all right?"

"Yes."

The suite did not matter, except for Ramon. Flowers to the ceiling of a sitting-room. Chaise-longue. None of the onus of illness. One simply could not be ill in a hard white hospital fashion, for Ramon's sake. . . .

". . . besides, Mrs. Rarick, I have no intention of confining you to the hospital those few days. You may leave every afternoon after we have tinkered at you for a few hours, but you must have all your meals at the hospital and return six o'clock evenings for your dinner and early bed."

Perhaps, then, Ramon need never know! There could be nothing seriously amiss with one who was allowed such leniency. Come to think about it, Bettina Slocum had been obliged to undergo such observation last month, only to discover that her trouble all the while had been due to nothing more than tooth infection.

Ramon need not know. Friday, Saturday, and Sunday would pass quickly. She could disappear under pretext of week-end. Nuisance, having to tell Jennifer and Rarick. And, oh dear, Friday was the Gluxom dinner (not that the Gluxoms really counted) and Saturday the automobile contest at the Garden, a society competitive gala contest for the most beautiful car. Jenny's new special-body Twin Hercules had just arrived from Italy —oh dear. . . .

What a disgusting nuisance! They rode you down formaldehyde-smelling corridors on something that resembled the hand-trucks on which porters rumble trunks at railroad-stations. They stood you up against walls and unwound you of your last decent shred of sheet, and forced you to drink lead-heavy liquids that made you transparent, so that they could watch the tiresome processes of your alimentary canal or whatever it was. They stretched you on a table and covered you with metal plates and took pictures of your liver or whatever it was on the side where the sciatic pain made you feel like a persimmon. They punctured your perfectly good arm and drew thimblefuls of blood that felt like bucketfuls. They counted your pulse and they counted your blood and they took your metabolism, whatever that was. Internes, such unhandsome ones, laid dingy ears to your heart. . . .

So Jenny took the overhauling, for the most part in good nature, rushing back to the hospital apologetically late, and creating in her wake a confusion, a specialness, and a lavishness that were as outwardly annoying as they were secretly impressive to the nurses.

The rich Mrs. Rarick was a patient not soon to be forgotten even in a hospital designed to meet the needs of the rich. Jenny lay in her narrow bed that was fluffed up as if it were a shell to hold the pearl of her magnificence. The young internes related among themselves, in hilarity, the amount of clawing it took to part the sheets and the laces and the billows that confined the patient. Placing an ear to the breast of Jenny was not just that. Laces crept up around the stethoscope like saucy surf. The slim ridge of Mrs. Rarick was the least of all in that bed. Silks, laces, scents, puffs, made it riotous. Jenny, packed in splendor.

Rarick sat stiffly in the room the evenings he came to visit her. Strangely, his comings created almost as much stir as the arrival of a motion-picture star, two weeks before, for a major operation. Nurses and internes remained on duty, past hours, to catch glimpses of him as he arrived and departed. The head chef lurked behind a doorway. But for the most part, except for Jennifer, who darted in and out, and the maid in the Breton cap —who occupied a room adjoining—secrecy prevailed.

At the end of the three days, Jenny, her maid, her pillows, her special bedding, her framed photograph of Avery, her bottles of scents, her thermos flasks, her silver flower-vases, her special breakfast china, her frilled bed-jackets, her character dolls and stuffed dogs, departed from the hospital for home.

Three days after that, the reports on her tests were completed.

SOMETHING that had not happened to Rarick in years occurred one morning. At least it had not happened to him since his clerkship days in Schwebbe's hardware store.

A peremptory command, in the form of a hand-delivered message, lay on his desk. Hellman had laid it face-up on the top of his sorted mail.

It is imperative that you come to my office alone at four o'clock this afternoon. Regard this as confidential.

JOHN NOON.

Noon was the man under whose care Jenny had been during this recent little disturbance. An illustrious figure in medicine, who had recently operated on an ex-President of the United States, and who was almost certain to be called in first or named as consultant in the illnesses of the great.

Could this little upset of Jenny's have a graver significance than he, Rarick, had realized? She had made so light of it. He had scarcely regarded it as more than a faddistic bit of rest-cure. His trips to the hospital had impressed him chiefly for the air of festivity in the sick-room. Jenny lying in her frills and going through what she called rigmarole. Even Dr. Noon himself, whom Rarick had encountered there on one of those occasions, had held her pulse lightly and joked at her joking.

Women got out of gear like that. Not Jenny, it is true, but the expensive hospitals fairly yawned for the run of them.

There was something about this wiry woman, Jenny,

that had seemed to him, immediately after his marriage to her, to be highly cutaneous, as if she were incased in an armor of brittle, but resistant skin. Pain did not get at her. She never perspired. Her hands had the cool, polished feel to them of having been dipped in tallow. It struck Rarick that he had never seen her blood. If she had ever pricked her finger, it had not yielded a drop.

That was why, without his being able to analyze it concretely, the idea of Jenny in any kind of physical predicament was difficult to conjure. She was part of a surface, just as she had lain lightly on the ridiculous ruffled bed in the hospital, making no physical dent. It again smote Rarick, funnily, that in her place beside him, Jenny never left dent. Or warmth. Her side of the bed, when she rose from it, was as cool and untouched-looking as if human form had not rested there. And now this from the doctor under whose observation she had been, suggesting that, after all, Jenny might be more than just a corporeal surface. . . .

It is imperative that you come to my office alone at four o'clock this afternoon. . . .

He did what was rather unusual for him. He thought up a pretext for telephoning Jenny. She was not at home. Her secretary, the pale Miss Dang, offered to locate her at one of three places. André Trianon's for a facial and wave. The Children's Charity Show, in the Leslie van Blarcoms' ballroom, or in the Oval Room at the Ritz.

"No, never mind."

There was something reassuringly normal about Jenny immersed in her usual kind of morning, which was crammed to capacity with the piffle of such minutiæ as facials, marionettes, Oval Room.

Probably it was on the score of just this frenzied

futility that her doctor wanted to see him. A woman as high-strung and curiously nervous as Jenny might go on indefinitely and then snap. At least that was what you heard was constantly happening to women in society, and perhaps more especially to those so frantically on the rim of it. Well, you could not expect even so astute a man as this Noon appeared to be, to understand. No need to acquaint him with unnecessary facts, of course; but precious little Rarick could do about it. Jenny wanted—well, Jenny wanted what she wanted.

Nevertheless, at four o'clock, Rarick stepped out of his car and into the tall, narrow building that contained the four stories of offices, laboratories, consultation-and-observation rooms of Dr. John Noon.

The trip from the first step into the lower hall up to a fourth-floor waiting-room was past five women in the starched uniforms of nurses. One verified his appointment, and as he gave his name, mysteriously the news was transmitted, and portières began to stir and eye-gleams to appear between slits of door and curtain.

"The Five-and-Ten Rarick! Sh-h-h-h!"

Another nurse for his hat. Another to admit him into the two-passenger elevator. Another to operate it. Another to meet him as he stepped out. And still another to turn him over to still another, who rose from a desk in the waiting-room and advised him that his wait would be brief.

It was. His summons into an inner office came almost immediately. It struck Rarick with surprise that he was trembling. Here was a firm that dealt in human destinies. He was doing business with it. What if Jenny had a deep-seated illness of the blood and bone? All this was nonsense about her corporeal specialness. She was frailty. Women somehow, soft, complicated creatures that they were, were subject to mysterious maladjustments. There were special hospitals for the diseases of women. What if Jenny . . .

An old man sat at an old desk in an old room. At least, the Dr. Noon of this room looked older than the Dr. Noon of the hospital. His desk was as uncluttered as Rarick's own. Again it was the uncluttered desk of a busy man. There were two sheets of white paper spread on it.

Jenny's destiny, thought Rarick, as he seated himself on the leather edge of the chair proffered him.

"I have sent for you, Mr. Rarick, before communicating with your wife. In cases like this it seems best."

So then, Jenny did not know . . . "In cases like this." The great man was meeting just another case. Jenny's, perhaps a little special by virtue of the impact of the name of Rarick, but to a man like Noon, who ministered to the powerful ones of the earth, not sufficiently differentiated to remove it from the category of "cases like this."

"Yes."

"Mrs. Rarick's tests are in. I am going to explain our findings to you."

"Yes."

"You are not, I take it, the man to want beating around the bush."

"No."

"There is a possibility that Mrs. Rarick's trouble may be a major one. I say possibility advisedly, because an operation may reveal it to be an unmalignant complaint that will respond to surgery. Miss Bart, bring in Mrs. Rarick's X-ray plates."

What a devilish formula for saying everything there was to be said, without saying anything. Surgery. Malignant. Operation. Major. So! This was the whither of all the frenzied, struggling, ambitious years of the

Jenny Avery whose eyes, way back there in the St. Louis beginnings, had turned with his toward the dream of the Pyrenees. This was the whither? That he might sit in a doctor's office, twenty-five years later, without ever having walked those Pyrenees with her in the flesh or the spirit, and listen to what sounded cryptically like her doom.

Jenny, who had seemed so frenziedly to be going some place through all the years, must at last pause and heed. . . .

"Here are our findings, Mr. Rarick. See this negative." There was a wall-frame ready to receive it, with an electric bulb behind, that made transparent the story of the flesh of Jenny, told in bits of waving lines and clumps of shadow. So there was the bit that was Jenny —on glass—in light—in shadow ——

"Those heavy spots in there, Mr. Rarick, are what concern us. The X-ray cannot reveal their depth. But these shadows indicate er—a—an obstruction—alimentary canal—may merely be ulcerous—if inoperable—close up wound—but better to explore—in other words—imperative that the attempt at surgery be made . . ."

God knows that was plain enough. All this elaborate preamble boiled itself down to the fact that Jenny must go under the knife. Either her complaint was operable or not. The exploratory knife would tell, and, if operable—well, then, science, skill, turn of the knife, destiny —what—Jenny was sitting squarely in the lap of the gods. . . .

"The exploratory knife will tell?"

"You have about summed it up, Mr. Rarick. It is not improbable that Mrs. Rarick's complaint may prove itself to be of a nature that will respond to surgery."

"Of course."

"I am sorry to have been obliged to call you here on

such a mission, Mr. Rarick. There is, of course, reason to feel concern. On the other hand, there is reason to feel optimism. Strong constitution, excellent health-history . . . hope . . ."

"Of course. Of course. . . ."

". . . In case you feel the need of more opinions—stand ready to call in consultants—but nothing puzzling in the situation—no emergency, but advise haste—immediate operation—every day may count. . . ."

"Of course. Of course. Of course."

"I—shall discreetly advise your wife—do not acquaint any other members of your family—keep atmosphere free of anxiety—spare her any undue nervous shock—I will be the one to advise her—make all arrangements—within week—exceedingly regret—better to look situation squarely in face—keep sanguine—extremely glad to have met you, Mr. Rarick—long been an admirer. Rarick Building fitting monument—uncertain weather for this time of year—Miss Scow will show you to the elevator—Have Mrs. McCormack come in—Good afternoon, Mr. Rarick ——"

Late sunlight lay on the stoop of the house as he left it.

"Where, sir?" said his chauffeur, after he had stood at attention for several minutes after Rarick had seated himself in the car.

"Where? Just drive."

SACRED COW," a three-act comedy by Gratton Davies, produced by the Internationalists, Inc., failed.

It was one of those failures *d'estime* that closed its doors to a large audience of repeaters and deadheads and received obituaries and epitaphs from a minority not mighty enough to sustain it.

It was a galling failure to Gratton. "Sacred Cow" had been purposely written in the out-and-out key of high comedy. A burlesque in sheep's clothing, the bray to sound behind the straight-faced baa. Nothing of the sort happened. Gradually, but surely, during rehearsals, it seemed to Gratton that his play became broadly the thing he had wanted it to be only inferentially.

"Sacred Cow" as a social satire wore its burlesque on its sleeve, and, failing, carried down with it three years of the work and high hope of its author.

As Gratton, in the scant words he had to say about the *débâcle*, remarked, it was not the failure that hurt. A good legitimate failure that was a fellow's own, was one matter. But, hang it! "Sacred Cow" had not been his failure. It had been a failure of interpretation, direction, and production. His own version of "Sacred Cow" still remained to be seen.

Gratton's tongue had been so neatly in his cheek when he wrote that play; and yet, all the loud braying had gone over the footlights in his name. In his young, passionately ambitious, rebellious name.

In the eyes of certain of the groups about whose opinions he youthfully still cared most, he had written a rather obvious and old-fashioned slap-stick satire.

To Gratton, at that stage, the most damning of all possible indictments was "old-fashioned."

In the eyes of certain critics who, even while they admitted his intent, scored him for precisely the indiscretions of which he had been guiltless, he had sprained a wrist trying to be clever, but a wrist that very conceivably might some day write the significant comedy of manners that this one seemed to forecast.

In the eyes of the box-office, he had committed the fatal sin of failing to entertain.

And so Gratton wore his failure ruefully, if silently. It hurt.

Strangely enough, and bothersome to her because she thought it despicable, a sense of relief welled in Jennifer when Gratton's failure came.

But she had not until then realized with what submerged sense of dread she had read the brilliant manuscript, lingered through many of the rehearsals, attended tryouts, and for long hours sat opposite Gratton across a restaurant table after a siege in the theater had been particularly trying or discouraging to him.

Dispassionately, Jennifer desired success for Gratton. But passionately, greedily, almost enviously, she was jealous of it. He was somehow more closely hers while he only skirted achievement. Not that he ever permitted her to cross certain ice-barriers of aloofness in him that baffled and wounded her terribly; but while he was hungry and hankered, she was sort of a self-constituted wailing-wall. He needed her to come to when he was tired and discouraged almost beyond endurance, as they began in rehearsal to bray his play. He sought her out over their favorite restaurant table in the bow-window of a small restaurant opposite the theater, or they journeyed down for a kitchenette-brewed luncheon in the quiet of his three small rooms over a bookstore in West Fourth Street, or just walked around the milling block of the theater, or sometimes had tea out of beautiful little white jade Ch'ieni-Lung cups in Jennifer's small sitting-room, which had been redone in Chinese lacquer.

There was no outside world to lean into the quiet of these little retreats. Neither Gratton's world, which was one you wedged into and which would not come to you, nor Jennifer's, which seldom, if ever, played up that kind of street. Gratton came mighty near needing Jennifer, those days of rehearsals, and Jennifer was jealous of her rôle.

His success might snatch it from her; and about Gratton, to Jennifer at least, was something of the foreordained kind of success of a single-track mind. There was about him, even before he achieved, the aroma of a man who cannot be deterred. He had given up a place in the throne-room of a magazine that was rapidly becoming the most significant publication of the sort ever accomplished in America, without a backward glance, because the time had come, due to a scanty inheritance, when he could afford to fasten his level eye upon the goal of his choice.

Gratton wanted to say it in dramatic form. You knew inevitably that sooner or later he would. Without compromise. He had started to do that with his magazine.

Jennifer, in inchoate fashion, sensed this. Elusive, self-sufficient by nature to a degree that she found terrifying, his success, when it came, would hedge him in more securely into a world which he loved a little more than he despised, and which he was one day to rebuke brilliantly in two plays, "Marsdon and Son" and "The Tragedy of Laughter."

Gratton wanted one thing, really. To get said this brilliant foment. Jennifer knew that and found it frightening.

She told him so one evening, about a month after "Sacred Cow" had gone down to its by no means ignominious failure. They were at dinner in his rooms, a Japanese student, who came in by the hour, serving them at a table drawn up before the fire.

It was Jennifer who had first suggested these excursions to Gratton's rooms. Their booky, firelit shabbiness rested her. Fascinated her a little. They were intimate, lived-in, purposeful sort of rooms. They pretended no period. They catered to the needs of their owner. The need of a good couch, with a head-lamp for reading. The need of an extra-built table with a spacious top for spreading papers. The need of book-shelves, that had overflowed into stacks of volumes standing in rows on the floor.

The smell of these rooms was tobacco and wood fire, leather and wire-haired spaniel.

When Jennifer had first suggested their going there, Gratton had acquiesced at once. As a matter of fact, she had only said it out of an indefinite desire to arouse in him some spark of the personal or protective. Gratton should have demurred at subjecting her to what might so easily be interpreted as a compromising act. Instead, he casually agreed, in the impersonal manner so characteristic of him.

In all her subsequent visits to his rooms—for meals, for afternoon cocktails, for brief interludes in between the exigencies of rehearsal—Gratton never so much as lingered at the business of helping her remove her wraps.

Her coming was too impersonal to matter much one way or another. He fell in with her suggestion to dine at a restaurant just as casually. It was as it should be. It was as Jennifer, bruised, would have told you she desired it to be; and yet . . .

"Are you as self-centered as you seem, Gratton?" she asked him one evening, after the Japanese student had washed his last dish and departed, leaving them seated over coffee.

"I reckon I are, Jennifer. I think an awful lot of me."

"You do nothing of the sort. You are interested in everything from better Chinese babies to the decadence of our decade; from the decline of philosophy to 'Kilts, why plaid'? Things and movements and causes and literatures and new schools and, to use a grand old smear of a phrase of my father's famous fossil, Dr. Gerkes, who eloped with a Lapp or something off-color, things ideational are your major interests. I want you to be interested in me, Gratt. I may not be ideational, but I'm mighty nice, if I do say it as shouldn't."

"Hang it, Jennifer! I'm not even sure you're nice!"

She raised her eyes at him across the small litter of after-dinner dishes between them, bit off a third of a lump of sugar, and drank her coffee through it slowly.

"You mean that, Gratt?"

"I think I do, Jennifer."

"I'm not so sure, either, that I'm nice," she said, slowly.

"Wonder if we both mean the same thing by nice."

"Don't qualify."

"Haven't the slightest intention of it. I don't know whether money has harmed you, Jennifer, but it hasn't made you a nicer person."

"Money-conscious!"

"One has to be, where you are concerned. Every bit of assurance you have is, consciously or unconsciously, founded on your recognition of the authority that goes with great wealth. Any stock dramatist could write you, Jennifer. You are fundamentally, I think, sound and fine, but . . ."

"Don't qualify."

"Damn it, Jennifer, I'm not! That's just it. You cannot imagine that I would dare not to qualify. That's part of your assurance. But let me go on. Fundamentally sound and fine, but cocksure with a sense of power. Spoiled, chiefly because you are spoilable material. Grown simply big and not big, simply. Chaser after false gods. Wise-cracker. More self-ful than selfish, but a little of both. Clever. Good mind and nothing to do with it. A giver, but considerably more of a taker. Vain, but not without reason. Good intentions. Feeble execution. A non-producer. A personality. A faker. A darling Jennifer, that's you."

"Yes, Mr. God, but why, since you say that I am fundamentally f. and s., don't you make me over?"

"I haven't the right."

"What if I give it to you?"

"What if I can't?"

"I see. You mean you haven't the right that goes with caring enough to do a big job like that?"

"If you will be personal, I wouldn't be it that cruelly, if I were you."

"I'm lonely as hell, Gratton."

"Are you, really, Jennifer, or is it just a dramatic state of mind that for the moment, seems desirable to you?"

"Lord, you're cold!"

"What are you lonely for, Jennifer?"

"For the kind of thing you are not saying to me now."

"Well put, my lamb! May you never know more of

the reaches of profound loneliness! I know a lonely man, Jennifer. Your father."

"Well," she cried, high and angrily; "well, well, what if he is? So is everybody connected with him. Shut-outs from one another. And Father, don't you forget it, has done his share of shutting out. All of us have, in our family, I'm afraid. My brother—between us—we—we —somehow managed to shut Avery out of life. Mother is a shut-out if ever there was one. God knows Father is. I am. The rich Raricks, if anybody should ask you, are a bunch of bankrupts. You talk about Father being lonely, damn it, as if I didn't know! Well, just the same, you can't do anything about somebody who lives on Mars, can you? Neither can I do anything about Father. He is simply where I can't get at him, wherever that is. Damn it, always has been! I've tried. Father is a man who ordered a ham sandwich and a cup of coffee from life, and got stung when the waiter brought him caviar and diamond-back terrapin instead. I'm part of the banquet he found himself served up with, along with the terrapin and caviar. He can't digest me. Lonely—as if I don't know how lonely he is . . . !"

"You don't really, Jennifer. You perceive it with that clever brain of yours. You don't know it, though, as one who is really lonely can know it in another."

"I suppose you mean as you can know it."

"Yes, Jennifer."

She blew him a ring of smoke; and across the table, in the mellow light of an old-fashioned oil-burning student-lamp, with a parchment map of Eastern Europe for a shade, they regarded each other slowly.

"Have we the newfangled complaint called sex-antagonism, Gratton?"

"I don't think the discussion important here."

"You never do, when it concerns us. Are you open to

a discussion about dialectic writing, or how about the use of pleonasm in Irish drama, Gratton?"

"Jennifer, that isn't kind."

"You're not."

"You're so blamed brittle, Jennifer. You break to pieces under a fellow's touch."

"How do you know? You've never touched me."

"That isn't worthy of you."

Tears sprang across her eyes.

"Just like me to blurt that out to you, of all people, whom I most want to impress. Don't think I'm in love with you because I said that."

"I don't."

"I want—oh, I don't know how to say what I want out of life, Gratton—but I want—passionately——"

"That's it, Jennifer. You're a wanter. You want and you won't pay."

"Do you know the nicest thing about me, Gratton?"

"I think you are the nicest thing about you, Jennifer."

"No, the nicest thing about me is the fact that I like you, Gratt."

"Don't say that. It hurts. First, because it is not true, and secondly because I hate your arrogance; but your meekness would just about kill me. Humble, you would break my heart, Jennifer."

"I am humble, Gratt, before the things you stand for."

"Good Lord! don't say that, Jennifer!" he said, and kicked back his chair and began to plow into a rubber pouch for pipe tobacco. "I'm jolly well what you said I am. A self-centered, would-be egomaniac, trying to get on, by crawling away from that center known as self. . . ."

"Your saying that I am fundamentally f. and s. means a lot to me, Gratt."

"You are, Jennifer, and some day somebody is going

to sink the proper kind of shaft and mine the f. and s. out of you."

"Who and how?"

"A husband with the sense to understand you."

"I think I prefer to remain fundamentally unsafe and unsound."

"The devil you do!"

"Your way of rubbing in the fact that there is a serious possibility that I may be in love with you."

"Scarlet-fever symptoms may only mean measles."

"You mean because of what I was idiot enough to tell you about Berry?"

"No; but now that you remind me . . ."

"Be careful, Gratt . . . because if there is any sure test for me to determine whether or not I am in love with you, it is to compare what I am feeling now to what I did not feel then. The most counterfeit part of that entire situation was me. Not Berry."

"Out of the frying-pan and into the divine fire," he said, and tilted her face with the tip of three fingers.

It was the first time he had ever touched her.

Reliving the scene to herself later, at home, in bed, under covers, it seemed to her that she had felt illuminated, like a switchboard. Lights had popped out all over her, in goose-flesh, each prickle a bulb. He had done it with the light touch of three fingers, tilting her chin slightly backward.

She remembered with a flaying flush that she had sat down on the couch and crammed a pillow into the small of her back, and, trying to command a level voice, had said, "Sit down, Gratt, here, beside me, and let's talk things over." Knocking out his pipe, he had said, with a casualness that made her ridiculous:

"No. Come along. There's a mystery-play over at

the National, and I feel in the mood for who-killed-cock-robin."

He had felt in the mood for who-killed-cock-robin when, at the touch of the three finger tips that had tilted back her chin, Jennifer had been brought to realize how phony had been everything that preceded this. . . .

IT WAS after midnight when Jennifer arrived home after the mystery-play. The lift, if you used it in the dead of night, made a soughing noise that could be disturbingly heard throughout the house; and, after her habit, she wound up the great curlicue of staircase instead. A rose-window, bits of its floral design said to date from a twelfth-century cloister at Tours, shone down into the majestic forest of stone pillars of the hallway. Under it, Jennifer paused for a moment. She loved its bath of color. Like an enormous flower it bloomed over the tiredness of her spirit that transmitted itself in fatigue to her body and made the walk upstairs a drag. There were rings under the eyes of Jennifer, and her cheeks were narrow planes of pallor. The tiredness that had clamped down upon her after she left Gratton, made her shoulders droop and her feet creep. She wound on slowly. . . .

There were routine signals along the way, to tell her certain trifles that registered languidly along her brain. Her father was in bed. She could tell by the closed bedroom door and the color of the rim of night light. Her mother was not yet in. The figure of the maid in the Breton cap nodding in a chair with her mouth open, as she passed Jenny's boudoir, testified to that.

Ever since she had been old enough to take cognizance of it, there had been something horrible to Jennifer in the idea of the bed and bedroom which her parents had so submissively shared throughout the years. It was one of the few subjects Jennifer had never dared broach to her mother. But it was horrid to her. There was some-

thing of a tomb about that chamber. In it lay dead love.
About it were strewn wilted passions. Two husks lay
side by side in it, desire long since dead. Florentine
chamber-of-horror. . . .

Jennifer's maid was waiting for her, and there was a
glass of chilled orange-juice on a table beside her bed;
and on the bed itself, her night things of rosy satin and
pale lace. She fell out of her clothes, and into them,
gratefully eager to have her lights out before the arrival
of her mother. So long as a lamp burned in one or the
other of their boudoirs, they never went to bed without
exchange of tiptoe visits. Youngish visits, curled up on
the chaise-longue in Jennifer's dressing-room, or Jenny's.
A curious quality of girlishness had persisted in Jenny.
There had never been a time when to Jennifer, who
adored her, there had not been something of sister in
their relationship.

Just the same, it was with a sense of relief that Jennifer found herself deeply in bed, lights clicked out, and
still no Jenny.

The sense of hurt that was out all over her had not
necessarily direct bearing on the evening she had just
spent with Gratton. It was rather the sense that had
risen to its culmination with this evening, that nothing
she could hope to be or do was to have bearing upon the
life of Gratton. He was constantly flipping her off, as he
would ash off his cigarette. She merely had flavor for
him. He sometimes said of her that she gave him
appetite for work.

"By sense of contrast?"

"Probably."

And probably it was. Not because she exhilarated him.
Not because she was some one who was restless for his
achievement. His plane of life was one that excluded
her. And suddenly, lying there in a little knot of pain

in bed, Jennifer, as she had never desired in her life, wanted access to that plane. Everything that heretofore had been of prime importance to Jennifer was secondary, if not second-rate, to Gratton. Always had been. Unconsciously, in what he revealed to her about his past life, was he constantly showing himself up to her. The things that mattered most to her were the things that Gratton had never even had time to despise.

For instance, the two years that Gratton had lived in Oxford, England, doing graduate work there on money he had earned waiting on table at a summer hotel, Jennifer had been making notoriety for herself at the baccarat tables of Cannes. The summer he had spent living on seventy-five cents a day in a room in Assisi that overlooked the upper and lower chapel of St. Francis, and writing one of the plays that helped make his trunk excess baggage, Jennifer had been lying most of her days on Lido sands in a bathing-suit that looked painted on, her head lounging against the lap of a well-oiled young Italian count to whom she was reported engaged. . . .

How far the Raricks had missed fire! Two of them, Jennifer and her father, lying there now, with elaborate walls between them, in a pile of grandeur that rose above them in the elegance of this Rennaisance tomb, one of them lying out there in a slim boy's grave, into which the worms must be finding way by now.

What sense of defeat was there perching now in the heart of her father, lying, himself, not forty of the appallingly expensive feet from her own bed. What bankruptcy there? What had Gratton meant by the really lonely person of her father? What indictment against her had lurked in his eyes? No. No. Rarick's loneliness was of his own making. He had built it up massively about himself. Jennifer had not been cast out, because she had never been let in. Presently her mother would come home, carrying on her narrow shoulders enough in chinchilla and square diamonds to support a family of ten through a lifetime. She would go to that room—to that tomb—to that bed—to that sleepless little heart-twisting bankrupt there—Father ——

After a while there was the sound of Jenny in the hallway. Jennifer, lying there, could hear the tinkling noise her sequined gown made as she came along. Like the welt that her body left on a bed, the footfall of Jenny was light. It fell past Jennifer's door softly. It turned into snow, falling into a dream of Jennifer's, that she was walking ankle-deep in it toward a student-lamp that burned in the window of a small mellow house, and that smelled of leather and a wire-haired terrier and a pipe that hung from an amused-looking lip. . . .

Jenny had been to the closing function of what had been a series of elaborate entertainments in connection with a Street Fair which had been held down the center of Park Avenue, where junior members of social-register families pinned fifty-dollar carnations on the senior lapels of telephone-directory families.

Socially and financially, it had been a success. The Street Fair charity-week had concluded with a supper dance held at the residence of the chairman of the executive committee, Mrs. Grant Fillimore Speigel, Sr., who had contributed her enormous ballroom for the purpose.

Entrance was by one-thousand-dollar check, and then only if you were bidden. It was one of those occasions when the Raricks were sure not to be overlooked. It was the first time Jenny had ever set foot in the old-fashioned Murray Hill home of the Grant Speigels. The evening had been sufficiently dull to keep its social inviolability to the fore in Jenny's mind. She had apparently made a personal dent upon the consciousness of Mrs. Grant

Speigel, and there was an engagement between them for luncheon three weeks hence. The evening had been more than justified. But her shoulders ached from fatigue; and once or twice during the supper, which you ate off of knees, the old sense of sickness had overtaken Jenny.

Ramon had not been there. She had taken Tom Lamentier, widowed brother-in-law of a Wilke-Barre, on the thousand-dollar check that should have admitted Rarick himself. Ramon, on one of the absences that was becoming more and more intolerably mysterious to her, was off on a week-end at the shooting-lodge of one of the sons-in-law of Mrs. Emanie Bursilap, an inclusion that was fantastic, so far as the burly Harrington Powers, who had married Edith Bursilap was concerned, and which must have been manipulated at no small discretion by his mother-in-law.

But at any rate, Ramon was returning tomorrow, and Jenny was lunching with him, quite openly, as they did upon rare occasion, at the Ritz. They must talk things out. Oh, how imperative it was that they talk things out! Something corrosive and frightening was at the heart of Jenny.

There was a list of memoranda under the lamp of her dressing-table that had been left there by her secretary, Miss Dang, and holding it down, as paper-weight, a small jeweler's package, with a red seal splashed over it. It contained four dreaming, perfect little pearls, which she had ordered clipped off the end of one of her necklaces and mounted as studs. Ramon's. The time had come when Jenny, no one the wiser, was resorting thus to the device of clipping such gifts off the edge of her magnificence. She had already presented Ramon with star-sapphire cuff-links off the rear end of another necklace; and the large canary-diamond center to another cigarette-case had been pried out by a jeweler and replaced with a blue diamond from a ring which Jenny no longer fancied. The canary had been worth thousands, and it was like Ramon, lover of beauty, to defer selling it, even in the face of needs that clamored.

One memorandum reminded her of an exceptionally early morning-fitting at Valli Sœurs before her eleven-o'clock contract-bridge lesson. Propped up conspicuously against a Lalique perfume-urn was an isolated item: "Dr. Noon telephoned that he will expect you without fail at his office at one o'clock tomorrow (Thursday)."

A stab of concern smote Jenny. For the first time since her period at the hospital, a sense of the old discomfort had been over her at dinner. Tiresome old body. Well, Dr. Noon would have to wait. Apparently his findings were not bothersome. There was something casual about the message. As it was, the bridge lesson would have to go overboard. Ramon was meeting her early.

The maid slid her out of the sequined gown and laid the string of square diamonds in a satin-lined box with a groove for each stone, and placed it and the chinchilla wrap in a steel vault at one end of the bathroom.

In her underthings, Jenny looked like a paper doll. Most fastidious in her personal habits, there was about her one specific carelessness that her maid swapped below-stairs with servants who are hawklike in such appraisals. Invariably Jenny went to bed with her make-up on. It was as if her frail flesh, tested by function after function to the limit of endurance, could not hold up under the smearing process of having it removed. Jenny slept in her painted lips, her mask of white enamel, and her high and narrow coiffure.

It was this Jenny, in a black-chiffon nightdress through which her body shone like a narrow candle, who finally made her way to the room where already lay her husband.

Lightly, in the painted mask off which her lips stared so redly, she placed herself beside him, drawing over her half of the sheets and coverlets. Lightly, silently, she lay wakeful beside him.

Lightly, silently, he lay wakeful beside her.

DUE no doubt to subtleties of presentation, the news that she was to be let in for a surgical operation did not at first come as shock to Jenny.

Lying face downward on her chaise-longue, with her arms flung to a peak over her head in an attitude of relaxation taught her by a masseuse she had brought home from Stockholm one summer, Jenny's predicament, phase after phase of it, began procession across her awareness.

Good Lord! What was the matter with her? Sitting there in his office, himself seeming so invulnerable to body ill, perhaps Noon had told her everything except the truth. What if I have cancer? Millions of women have had before me. Was Noon holding off facts that might terrify —— Nonsense! A man like Noon had no time for subtle psychological evasions. Besides, no man could simulate his kind of casualness. . . .

Good Lord! acting like an old-wife poring over a medical book and reading her own symptoms into every page. Not every woman with a pain in her side had cancer. . . . Good Lord! . . . Fool—fool—fool ——

Take the case of Mrs. de Witte Yonge, wife of the Austrian ambassador, with whom she had recently had the honor to dine. Mary Yonge had just successfully undergone a major operation. You belonged to a negligible minority if you still boasted an appendix. Dr. Noon seemed of the opinion that much of her own difficulty might hover around that superfluous organ. So interesting to hear Dr. Noon explain the history of the atrophy of that organ. . . . Dr. Noon so graphic. . . .

Come to think of it, Jenny's florist-bills alone—to say nothing of inroads into Rarick's conservatories—to friends who were constantly convalescing from operations in hospitals, were enormous. Naturally you got things the matter with you in the course of a lifetime. Didn't expect your motor-car to run without overhauling, did you? Well, same principle applied to the human body. . . .

Of course, the serious side to the story might be in the cards, too. Didn't cross that bridge, however, until you came to it. Particularly if that bridge happened to be across the Styx. Nifty of herself to indulge in grim humor at a time like this, Jenny decided. Don't cross the bridge across the Styx until you come to it. If Fifi Putnam, with her tubercular history, had survived three major operations, why not Jenny? Dr. Noon had been by no means certain hers would be major. Lydia Mason, to be sure, had died on the table, but Lydia had been awfully wrong on the inside ever since the birth of her third child. Besides, the—the sort of thing that did for Lydia, ran in her family. Look how Georgie Prescott had gone to his operating-table weighing one hundred and twelve pounds, and now tipped into the heavy-weight amateur class at all the private boxing-bouts at the Beaverbrook Club. An operation was something to be casual about these days. In the main, Jenny truly was. There were little scare-spots in her. As a matter of fact, the day she saw Noon, she had returned home from his office instead of going on to meet Roxy Gravure at the Dog Show, where Roxy was showing a pair of the finest Kerry Blues ever registered.

The very smell of Dr. Noon's offices, she told herself, had been unnerving. They invented everything else, why must doctors' offices and hospitals continue to reek to heaven of the suggestion of antiseptic. . . .

Then, too, this season of seasons, just when Jenny had made what she considered her most important social wedge! Mrs. Grant Speigel had undoubtedly taken a fancy to Jenny. Herself one of the founders of the Cosmos Club, she had all but volunteered to put Jenny up for membership. They had lunched together. Jenny was already harboring the plan of arranging an elaborate function around the dowager figure of Mrs. Grant Speigel. The surgical operation would put a serious kink in that important plan. In countless plans.

Then, of course, there was that wave of recurring fear about Ramon. In the scare-specked hours which followed her knowledge that in a week she must go on the operating-table, her thoughts and fears, trepidations and concerns, had floated about without anchorage.

It was difficult to imagine Ramon coming to her through the etheric smell of hospital corridors. Prying nurses! She had successfully kept the period of her observation in the hospital from him. But this time he must know. How curious to be confronted with the need of telling Ramon that she must go to a hospital for an operation.

There were situations in which you simply could not imagine certain people. Perhaps, though, thought Jenny, on the anxious drive home from Dr. Noon's, it is just the providential circumstance to tide us over this bad place. Jenny, in laces, on her bed of pain, wan to him, esoteric, might conceivably, by way of temporary and delicious lassitude, fascinate more than in health.

He had been distrait at lunch at the Ritz the day before. Terribly so, the lurking pain in her side seemed to collide with the fear that kept knocking about in the region of her heart.

There was a card crushed into the hand that was flung high over her head as she lay on the chaise-longue. It was part of the damnable wrongness. It had added to her impending state of high nervousness to receive this invitation from Mrs. Grant-Speigel to week-end at her place in Lenox beginning the very day that she had arranged with Dr. Noon to enter the hospital. The night she would probably be plowing her way out of ether, a wound in her side, was to be a gala one at the opera, when a visiting queen was to sit in the Gerinald box, which adjoined the Raricks', to say nothing of the minutiæ of plans that clotted the lines of her engagement-book and which suddenly had become part of a daily routine that was precious.

Then there was this business of telling Rarick and Jennifer—to Jenny, a shamefaced procedure of trying to get said to your intimates the intimate things that had to do with the plights of the flesh. Jennifer must not be frightened. Rarick would be kind. . . .

Lying there, crushed into a silence that moved in a procession of her incipient terrors, there crept slowly into Jenny a desire that had to do with Rarick. Even if her illness turned out to be as responsive to the knife as it promised (Noon had been so casual!), there persisted in Jenny a sense of need of Rarick. To be sure, he would in all probability do little more than sit humbly beside her or at best say lusterless things, but just the same he would be there!

An impulse to cancel her four-o'clock engagement with Ramon at the tea-room the next afternoon flooded over Jenny. But even as she considered, she knew that, punctiliously, dragging herself up from the chaise-longue, she would be at the appointed place at the appointed time.

It was in the intervals between seeing Ramon that revulsions like this could sometimes overtake her. Revulsion of self. A commiserate desire to creep back somehow into the old unevil life with Rarick that dated back to the days when she had first set up housekeeping and had presented a first child to the serious young man who, with his feet on the clay banks of the Meramac and his eyes on the Pyrenees, had wooed her.

Time and time again, these periods of revulsion had ridden her, and time and time again receded, leaving her marooned on the strange shores of her infatuation for this boy with the eyes that nowadays were more insolent than amorous, and whose half-baked æsthetics, even as she succumbed to them, she realized were spurious.

For the moment, in her fright, Jenny turned to Rarick. Ramon, who hated illness, might find her ugly to him. Rarick, on the other hand, was not the man to waste impatience or rebellion upon the inevitable. His sympathies, always susceptible, were not hard to muster. He was a kindly light on a landscape that to Jenny had suddenly become threatening and sinister.

Jenny, who had no God in particular, except one she resurrected for herself in times of great stress, felt suddenly and terribly the need of God and Rarick. Her emergency God had last been on her lips in her paroxysms of grief and pity over Avery. She was about to have need of Him again. His name bubbled along her lips in tears. God, get me out of this. God, pull me through. God, make a better person of me. God, I need you. God, spare Jennifer any shock. God, forgive me all—everything. And, strangely, paradoxically, even as she lay there, chastened of mood and supplicating: God, keep me well and desirable to Ramon.

AND, of course, she did see him that following afternoon at four. As a matter of fact, she sent a chauffeur to her milliner's so that she should have to wear a new tall and narrow Russian turban of black krimmer that glittered down the front with a long dagger of diamonds. Ramon might find it effective and amusing. Her white face, long and narrow as the hat itself, not a rim of hair showing, was almost like a transparent face, on to which had been hung a deep-crimson butterfly made of two painted lips. Strange, glittering Jenny, at whom people stared without admiring.

As usual, on the edge of one more experience of seeing Ramon, her revulsion fell away from her and became anticipation that tingled.

There were picked words with which to tell Ramon this thing; words that would not offend or frighten or hurt him. Ramon was a sensualist by extraordinary virtue of the fact that he shrank so from wounding the senses. His senses. She would wound them ever so much less than she would charm them. . . .

Riding along in a snide taxicab toward the place of their appointment, the ordeal ahead of her began to set itself like a stage.

She saw herself, tilted on her hospital bed, surrounded by tall Lalique jars of lilies and a jade bowl of green orchids with flecks on them, at her side. She would bind her hair in a tight fillet, so that her face shone out like a sly, sophisticated nun's. Ramon had once jerked the hair back from her face, held the bandeau of his handkerchief tight above her brow, and called her that.

Sly, sophisticated nun. She liked being called that. Sly, sophisticated nun. He had not meant it really, had said it to her in the key of endearment and had kissed her throat through the barrier of high, scented ruche that closed it in like a wimple. Well, well, no matter how hard had been the sledding; the wretchedness of the deception; the dreadful sense that somehow Avery, Jennifer, and Rarick had been smirched, and decencies that sprang from the very magnesia of the soil of the years in St. Louis, defiled . . . it had been worth it.

To have never had this, toward which she was riding in the abominable yellow taxicab with cigar-butts on its floor, lean into her life and redeem some of its vanished luster was unthinkable. It had been worth it . . . was worth struggling to hold. . . .

Contrary to his habit of late, Ramon was in the tea-room first, seated at the small table toward the rear, under a wall-bracket of one incandescent bulb with a pink-paper tissue shade. They could count on this place to be fairly empty at this hour. She could smell his cigarette smoke and see the black shellacked armor of his hair as she entered. Their public habit was to shake hands formally. It struck her with chill that the hand which had used to cling to prolong that instant was something inanimate that had to be propped around her own, like a dead one.

What subsequently happened, although she was not to realize it, amounted, considering the facts of Ramon, to a display of courage on his part. With what secret misgivings, fear of scene, and perhaps terror of slaying with pain, Ramon must have prepared what he was about to launch without giving her opportunity to preamble, Jenny was never to know. He came at her in short hammer-blows that left her stunned and unable to resuscitate in time to stave them off.

"I want good hot tea quick," she said, and drew off the long, beautiful gloves which she always wore in heavy, loose crinkles along her forearm.

"I cannot stay to tea," he said, shortly.

The pain in her heart and the pain in her side began to thump simultaneously.

"Why not, dear?" she said, evenly.

"I am going away."

"Where?" she said, evenly again, as if her words were to be quiet oil on so much troubled water.

"You have seen it coming. You have made it hard."

"What, Ramon?" she said, trying to quiet herself, and the jumping of the pains, with the thought that always there had been women who had been forced to face just such stark misery as this one of losing love. There might be women, at this very moment, in this very city, who were being crucified as she was being crucified. . . .

"I am sailing straight for Seville tomorrow with Mrs. Bursilap. We will be gone—indefinitely."

"You mean Mrs. Emanie ———"

"You know whom I mean, Jenny. It is your way of always making it so hard for me."

"But, Ramon—Emanie Bursilap—seventy, if a day—grandchildren. . . ."

"Beggars cannot be choosers. You know what I am by temperament. I cannot struggle. One must live."

"Is that why ———"

"No, Jenny. You wanted, as you say it so well in your language, to have your cake and eat it, too. You were too afraid for yourself. You were not generous. I mean in the spirit. You would not risk. I go with Mrs. Bursilap, and her granddaughter Ellen, to Seville, as secretary and interpreter. Ellen does not know it, but there her grandmother and I are to be married."

"I see," she said, her lips feeling so dry and gritty against her teeth that they felt to her as if they must make a scraping sound as she lifted them to smile. "I see."

"I am glad you do. I have never pretended to you that I am what I am not. One must live."

"I see."

If only she could stop mouthing "I see!" She wanted to cry out into the cheap, tawdry stuffiness of that tea-room. She wanted to see his face darken because her fingers were at his throat. She wanted to hurl arms about his knees and anchor there to this lean, narrow pillar of her happiness. And there she kept sitting, smoothing her long, sinuous gloves which were the color and scent of gardenia, and mouthing, "I see."

And suddenly it smote her that in her hour of need, there she sat in a specked, third-rate tea-room, being dismissed across a dingy tablecloth by a narrow young man who was trying to keep his furtive eyes pretentious. Jenny, who had borne Avery, who had been too precious for life, and Jennifer, in whom leaped flame; Jenny Avery who, twenty-six years before, had been wooed by a serious young man whose mind was tipped with beauty, sitting there being dismissed by a gigolo who had found her fare too meager.

"I see."

"The—Mrs. Bursilap does not know about—this. She is not so broad about some things. You must never ———"

"I see."

She looked at him from under the high, narrow turban; and his eyes, as if hooked on to the dagger of diamonds, would not travel down to meet hers.

"I wish you happiness, Ramon," she said, politely.

"I will have to be going," he said. "Packing." And

placed a dollar-bill under the glass of orangeade he had pretended to be drinking before she arrived.

"I see."

It dawned upon her, as they neared the door, that the aluminum-colored limousine which she had noticed at the curb as she stepped out of the taxicab, must be waiting for him.

"I will take you home, Jenny," he said, flushing.

"No, please, a taxicab," she said, and shuddered along her teeth.

He hailed one, and, assisting her into it, stood bareheaded at the curb, replacing his hat, as she drove away, with a swinging gesture that had given her many a thrill.

Even as her misery blurred her last glimpse of him, the fantastic and devastating thought smote her that his young, slim body-beauty had gone back into the sea, as a fish floundering off its hook dives back, only to be baited again.

NOW that the bolt had come straight and sure at her feet, there was only a deathly kind of fatigue of the spirit, hard to endure, but far from being the active torment against which she had been steeling herself.

Ramon going over into the fold of Mrs. Bursilap suggested the wattled and ugly thought to her of a bright bird of flight being folded into, along with little insects of prey, the webbed wings of a bat, and fast becoming part and color of that horrible under-arm débris.

There were folds of old flesh down the face of Mrs. Bursilap that must be down her body too, and pleats of loose skin along her upper arms, and a cave of shadow on either side of her lean old nose that made her bat-like. And as if to bear out the unconscious cousinship, she wore gray mostly, fine chiffons that floated and formed web between her body and arms.

Ramon folded into that, was something to shudder over, rather than to shed the salt tears one locked in the keg of one's heart. She had shuddered her share, hurt pride, shocked vanity, loneliness, and a modicum of grief for a fantasy that had perished, going down before horror of Ramon and horror of self.

It was as if suddenly she had walked out of some foul lethal garden into gray but open day. Rarick was in the day, precisely as if she had been off in some long, embroidered faint, from which she had just emerged to find him precisely where she had left him. A little grayer, a little graver, without eagerness, certainly without gayety, and, consistently as ever, remote from her. And yet so substantially there; for which, and without shame, she showed her gratefulness.

She woke him up one night, as she thought, out of a sound sleep, when her growing panic of the operation was heavy upon her.

"Rarick," she said, softly, filled, there in the dead hours of the night, with a lonely fear that if she did not speak she would cry out.

He stirred lightly as he lay motionless in his insomnia, not quite sure that she had spoken.

"Rarick, could you wake up for a moment?"

"Yes. What is it, Jenny?"

"I am all right. I want to talk, though."

She thought, a little bitterly, that she need not trouble to reassure him, who had no anxiety for her.

He was relieved that it had come. He had been lying there, pitying her in her sleep. A week had passed; and since she had not spoken, he had resolved to see Noon again the following day. But now it had come. . . .

"I've been meaning to tell you something of a nuisance, Rarick. You never asked about what they found at the hospital—so there seemed no hurry."

"I knew if there had been anything serious . . ."

"There isn't. But I'm in for an operation."

He tried to lift his words carefully into the casual.

"That *is* a nuisance," he said after a pause. "I thought perhaps there might be a little ulcerous condition there."

"That is exactly what it is."

"It is wise to operate, then, and clear up the difficulty once and for all."

She could not help but reach out her hand and touch his lightly at the surge of relief that flowed over her at his calm, inferential way of regarding her recovery.

"I think so, too, Rarick."

"We had better have it over at once, then, Jenny."

We! Nothing he could have said would so have snatched away her terrifying sense of aloneness. She found herself wanting to reach out and touch his hand lightly again, and refrained.

"Any time you say, Rarick."

"Suppose you let me take the matter in hand. I will arrange with Noon."

"Yes, Rarick." She felt so small, lying there beside him, so in need, so oppressed by sudden awareness of how solitary to be born——how solitary to die!

"I guess I'm a little frightened, Rarick. There is something about the knife—like cutting the rope to a moored boat——"

This time his hand felt for hers.

The very texture of her flesh, it occurred to her, scorchingly, had been softened, since last he had touched it, by a lover's touch. If flesh, except by way of act of lips, could speak. . . .

"The inevitable is frightening, Jenny, but chiefly because we usually have to sit on the rear seat and watch some one else at the wheel."

She thought he was going to moralize, and stiffened.

"Let's be honest, Rarick. Ulcers may be another name for—for anything. O God! Rarick, I don't want to have anything terrible happen to me. I've so much to do, Rarick. So much that must be straightened . . ."

The mother of Avery was lying beside him, frightened. The feeling of chronic open wound somewhere around his heart began to move.

"We are going to come through this, Jenny."

"We are, aren't we, Rarick? It isn't that I am afraid to die——"

It was!

". . . it is just that I'm not ready, Rarick. So much to be straightened."

Was the matter of this tawdry affair with the Spanish dancer with whom she was fiddling away time lying heavily upon her, he wondered, some of his dull and passive anger against her riding him for the moment.

"I don't want to die, Rarick. I need you to bolster me over that silly fear. I mustn't leave Jennifer. I mustn't leave life. Funny; all of a sudden, it's so sweet. We haven't made much of a go of our lives together, have we, Rarick? Why?"

"Yes, yes, why?" How was it that the business of living had so cruelly deterred them from life itself? Jenny, here in her blazing tent that was hung in bracelets and shields and all the barbaric splendor of old, of which he had read in the histories, trembling empty-handed before a God she had never before found time to contemplate. She had paid God. Pew-rent. An occasional Sunday-morning obsequy. Ready-made reverences. He had approached with a new closeness when He had taken Avery. But now—now ——

"Rarick, strange that we who have had so few joys together must always share the sorrows—first Avery—now this ——"

Avery. Avery. Avery. His lips, from hurting, could not bear to say the word.

"I give myself the pollywoggles, Rarick, talking about death."

"Then don't, Jenny."

"You must help me through, Rarick."

"I will, Jenny."

"I mean the courage part. 'Spiritually,' is the way the pious pulpiteers would say it. I do dread death, Rarick. Tomorrow I'll laugh at tonight's pollywoggles. It's the nights—they get bad—you can help ——"

"Yes, Jenny." How? He wanted to. The mother of Avery must have it in her to rise on spiritual wings out of that fear.

"If I die ——"

"You are talking morbid fancies. . . ."

"If I should die, Rarick."

"But why ——"

"I want a beautiful casket. You can give it me. I want the most beautiful. One that will hold them for many a long while."

"Why dwell on such non ——"

"You can do that for me."

That was what he could do for her.

"Somewhere back, Rarick, when I was a girl in Central High School in St. Louis, I remember we used to read in class, wasn't it Héloïse or Annabel Lee or somebody slim and white in a poem, who dreamed of a casket lined in ailanthus leaves out of beaten silver. . . ."

He supposed so, but why plan for death when there was life to be thought of? . . .

"Life, of course. Perhaps a better life than we have been pulling off together, Rarick. Death does terrify. . . ."

What an Imperial Highness even the shadow of death could be, forcing to their knees those who approached. . . . "I shall never live to be an old man," Rarick had once said to Gerkes, "therefore I want to make a friend of the idea of death early." Jenny had neglected to make a friend of the idea. Poor Jenny. He would have given much not to have been too shy to reach over and fold the startled whiteness of her body against what comfort he had to offer. Fear was pecking at her. . . .

"You know that beautiful ivory panel that you use for a chest door to your collection of jades? The one with the Virgin Mary seated, with a crown of pearls on her head?"

"Byzantium of the ninth century," he said, mechanically.

"Isn't it catalogued as the lower side of a casket?"

"Perhaps."

"Rarick, I want that panel for the lower side of my casket."

"Yes, yes; but that, we hope, will be many a long day away."

"And those beautiful Episcopal croziers in gold and ivory, from the Walton Collection, that stand beside the organ, I want them for head-pieces. You can afford to build me the most beautiful casket in the world, Rarick, starting with those priceless antiques of old ivory and old gold. Don't line it in satin, Rarick. I shall hate to lie in shiny white satin like a Catholic cook who has saved up for her funeral. I want to lie in leaves— ailanthus leaves of beaten silver . . . you can do that for me. . . ."

Of all the things he ached to do for her, now that the open wound of his heart was bleeding in pity for her fear, this was what she wanted of him. There was a pair of lines from Chaucer, engraved on an ivory oliphant of his collection:

> A pair of tables all of ivory,
> And a Poyntal polish'd fetishly.

That was all he could do for Jenny. Send her "polished fetishly" out of the tent that was hung in the splendor of bracelets and shields.

"Of course, Rarick, I'm pretty apt to turn around on you and not die," she said, pertly and mockingly out of the darkness, on a rattle of the brittle, malicious kind of humor she practiced. "You may not be rid of me, after all."

"I don't want to be, Jenny."

"Do you believe, Rarick, in a beyond?"

He did passionately, now that it held his son. He dared not, however, because of the shyness, tell her that his belief in that ultimate reunion was chiefly what made the strings of days, laden with their job-lots of rubberized table mats and gilded curtain rods, bearable. You could not exactly tell a woman like Jenny, who, even while she quailed, might suddenly rattle off into one of her brittle moods, that somewhere across the chasm of death, a story that had never been spoken was waiting to be told by you to your boy.

"I believe in something, Jenny, beyond myself."

"Do you ever pray?"

"Yes; but, like you, chiefly when I despair. I don't suppose you would call that worship, so much as fear. . . ."

"When Avery died, I didn't fear. I blasphemed."

He could not talk about him—to her——

"I fear now, but I don't pray, Rarick."

He wanted her to pray. Deep in his heart he knew that her need of prayer had come.

"Do you think it unbearably silly of me to keep wanting a casket made of ivory and old gold?" (Perhaps Ramon, passing around it, would see her lying there, the lovely color of the old ivory itself. Croziers at her head and feet. Priceless ones, the beautiful shape of a shepherd's staff, one showing the Virgin and Infant, the other the Crucifixion. . . .)

"I think it silly of you to be dwelling on death, although it sometimes seems to me, Jenny, that life is a means to death."

He had not meant to say that.

"What?"

"Try to sleep."

"Rarick, I—want to say to you—it sounds so silly—it will seem sillier in the morning—but now—tonight—I feel as if I want to say to you ———"

"Get your sleep, tonight."

"Perhaps ———"

He wanted to hear and yet could not bear it. She wanted to get said what she could not bear to say. She had no real faith, herself, that once more in health, she might not ridicule this craven hour of her low-ebb. Nor had he.

Jenny, God willing, what with that wiry nervous vitality of hers, was in all probability going to recover. Why subject her, who, with her eyes on death, had cried only for ivory and old gold to contain the dust of her body, to any more self-revelations?

"Get back to sleep, Jenny."

"Yes."

Dozing off, she hated Ramon, pimp, who had tucked himself securely under the arm of a bat. And yet—in case—there was always the septic danger of an operation—in case—she wanted him to have to pass around the ivory bier, time and time again, and look upon the strange ivory beauty of her, lying in ivory. . . .

At ELEVEN o'clock the following morning, Jennifer, without appointment, presented herself at her father's office, to be met by Hellman, whom she disliked and who in turn considered her a snip.

"Your father's morning is filled with important conferences, Miss Jennifer."

She looked what she always felt toward him. Spitfire.

"Save that, Mr. Hellman, to tell to some one who wants to sell him spool-cotton or teething-rings." She looked pert and as natty as a little sailing-vessel in rig. Her hats were always such right affairs; this one, a warrior's tight helmet of cocoa-colored felt, fitted her head like a wig. She was cocoa-colored from head to foot, in simple, unrelieved lines, a triple necklace of faceted amber beads lying in golden rope along her flat chest.

She was a thrill to the enormous office force on those rare occasions when she appeared, eyes slanting at her from all sides.

Almost too chic, slim, svelt, right, there was an air of artificial cocksureness about her that in some way must have accounted for Hellman's sense of animosity.

"Tell my father I am waiting, Mr. Hellman."

"The Des Moines manufacturer with whom he is in conference, Miss Rarick, has waited in New York two weeks for this interview. Your father is not even taking telephone interruptions."

"I'll wait," she said, and flung one silk knee over the other as she sat herself down in the desk-chair Hellman had been occupying.

He took up a pad, scrutinizing.

"His next appointment is with Mr. Harold Bolt, president of the Banking Trust Company. Mr. Bolt is already here. Your father is lunching with Mr. Hiram Biltman and Mr. James Biltman. Most important."

"Is it true," said Jennifer, helping herself to one of Hellman's cigarette-sized cigars, "that there is some prospect of Rarick Chain being incorporated with the Bilt Chain? As usual, my information comes from outside patter, but I do think that the old gentleman would be wise as hell to get out from under."

"I am scarcely in a position to say, Miss Rarick," said Hellman, who was.

"Suppose I'd better tip off my friends to buy Rarick—common or preferred?"

"I'm scarcely in a position to say, Miss Rarick," said Hellman, who was.

"Do cigars make you feel sickish?"

"No," he said, and thought: But you do.

"I'll finish it if you have to carry me out on a litter. Is that father buzzing for you?"

"Yes."

"Tell him I am here."

"Mr. Bolt will . . ."

"Tell him I am here."

When Jennifer was announced, the immediate thought smote Rarick that Jenny must have told her of what was impending. Yet that could scarcely be the case, since he had not yet conveyed the information to her that he had arranged with Noon during the morning that she was to enter the hospital that day week. Jenny was not the one to burden her daughter with such family-freight before it became necessary.

Now what?

The sight of her father in the settings of his offices was always impressive to Jennifer. Then, if ever, he was in the faint Napoleonic cast that she, too, suspected him of sometimes trying to achieve. The short, rather thickening body that he seemed to press to the ground with twice the weight that was actually his. The look in his eyes of seeming to see beyond some Elba. The way the thinning, center peninsula of his graying hair dipped into forelock. The "R" embossed on a wooden seal over the mantelpiece and on to his stationery that stood in a Florentine "R" embossed leather box.

What elements of greatness had gone afoul in her father? What elements of greatness had gone afoul in him in the same fashion that elements of cleverness in herself had likewise gone afoul? What little there was to her had gone afoul . . . dear knows, dear knows. . . .

Her father faced her, with the light from the window over his shoulder and full on her face. An old sense of unreality, where this girl was concerned, smote him. This urban, highly-polished, unillusioned, sure-eyed adult was his. He had begot one whom he scarcely knew.

"Well?"

"Guess this is the last time I'll ever visit you in these old offices, Father. This time next year you'll be in the Rarick Building."

"I think so," he said, and leaned over the vast smooth surface of his desk, to move a crystal paper-weight half an inch. His way of dismissing preamble and asking her to come to the point.

"It's about Cataract Lodge, Father."

He paused in the act of withdrawing his hand from the paper-weight, his attitude listening.

What had she heard, and how?

"It's a large order I am about to ask, if anything can be in the nature of a large order for you."

What had she heard? . . .

"As I have figured it out to the day, Father, we have occupied the Cataract exactly six and one-half months in four years."

"All part of the larger waste," he said, dryly.

"I knew I could count on you for that agreement," she said, too brightly.

Smart girl. Pretty girl. His. It would be easy to be proud of Jennifer. He thought of a sales-manager's slogan that hung over the desk of one of his department managers. "Be Yourself." Jennifer was not. Least of all, when she was with him. Something must be wrong with him—Rarick——

"Father, I've talked over a plan I have in mind with Mother, and it is all right with her, if it is with you."

Whatever it was, rest assured she had talked it over with her mother first. The old jealousy stirred miserably in Rarick.

"I have lately had occasion, Father, mostly through Gratton Davies, to mix up with some of the girls and boys who write, or are trying to write. You know, the beginning crowd that is trying to get it said in plays and verse and articles and such. Novelists. Fellows who hold up the mirror, mostly crookedly. Dramatists, meaning the set that is still writing plays for the trunk or bottom drawer. After seeing these struggling writers knocking about the bedlam of this town, an idea has begun to knock about my so-called brain, Father. Most of them need a decent place to work. The notion that a nation's epics and not-so-epics must necessarily be composed in garrets, went out of style with whipping-posts."

Her brand of pretentious cleverness was always anathema to him. Be Yourself.

"Father, let us hand over Cataract Lodge as a sort of all-year workshop to this crowd from here and everywhere, who haven't got the where or the withal. Let's rescue 'literachure' from the jaws of the hall bedroom, the sound of the steel rivet, the smell of the lodging-house, and the sight of city swill. I've always had such a yen myself for writing, Father, without being able to do much more than make a cross-sign for my signature, that after meeting a few of these youngsters—I kind of thought—well—give me Cataract Lodge to turn over to them, Father. There are forty-eight rooms, not counting eight big airy ones over the boat-house and eight over the garages. Create a foundation committee, Father, deed over the Cataract and the three hundred acres, and maybe some day you will have given lodging to the birth of the great American novel, or the near-great."

What was she up to? Was it possible that she and this young Gratton Davies ——

"Think it over, Father. It's a grand idea, and our chance to have about the only kind of finger we can ever hope to have in making the world safe for genius. It's a concrete, definable world, Father, if you make its hair-pins, its jig-saws and its salt-cellars. There isn't such a well-defined law of supply and demand for soul-commodities. It pays better to manufacture mirrors than to hold them up to nature. That line sounds like Gratton!"

Gratton again!

"Father, am I a daughter denied or indulged? I know the appraisal on the place. One hundred and ninety thousand, without the buildings. You would think nothing of that for a factory site, Father. Regard this as an intellectual factory."

Her way of capturing his understanding. Regard this

as a factory site. His way of being important to letters—factory site—manufacture of ideas. . . .

"Father?"

Pretty Jennifer. It was part of his consistent faculty for error, where his family life was concerned, that she should come to him with such a request at a time like this. For a moment he played with the idea of a recapitulation of his plans. He wanted to capture her, pretty thing, so shy of him, with sugar on his finger tips; but his plans were too deeply laid; so deeply laid that what he finally said was twice too portentous.

"It is unfortunate that you should come to me at this time on such a mission, Jennifer. I have had on my mind for some time to discuss a certain matter with your Mother; but now that her illness has come up, I do not want her bothered. Cataract Lodge is sold."

"Sold?"

"Possession does not go into effect so long as I exercise my annual option-privilege of renting it from the new owners."

"You sold Cataract over our heads!"

"I suppose it amounts to that."

"Why?"

"For reasons too intricate to enter into here."

"You mean to tell me ——"

"Are you catechizing me?"

"Father, you are not in any possible money difficul ——"

"No, I am not."

"If I thought it were that, then of course I would under ——"

"You would be a misled young woman."

"Then why?" she cried, and stamped her foot, a quick sheet of tears forming in her eyes. "Why?"

"So far as you are concerned, Cataract Lodge is still

yours, to do everything you want with except give away. I like your impulse, daughter, but it is out of the question."

"But why?" she cried, ising and stamping the desk three times with her gloved hand. "Why? Why? Don't treat me like a half-wit, Father. Why did you sell Cataract Lodge?"

"For the same reason that I have sold Thousand Island Camp and Beaupré and the Nice property."

"Father!"

"For reasons of greatest importance to me, but with the leaseholds which I have retained in each case, of no great importance to you or your Mother, since you are left free as ever to use them as you have heretofore."

"I think it is abominable," she said, frankly crying now. "Mother and I have every right to feel rottenly treated. Of course, it is all yours to do with as you will; but it might have been decenter, Father; it might have been kinder, it might have been treating us more like human beings and less like chattels, to have told us."

"I meant in good time to tell your Mother. This illness changed that."

"Mother isn't as ill as all that. . . ."

"Never forget this, Jennifer. I have deeply-founded reasons for every move I make. You have never taken the time to be logical. . . ."

"I—I simply don't know what to say to you, Father. You have me flabbergasted, as usual. I came here full of a desire to do something that had a wallop in it for someone besides myself. I came here because, God knows why, I still harbored the shred of a delusion that there was some way to get through to you. Somehow, this seemed to me the kind of thing, if I put it up to you—even if the idea did come from me—might help not only others, but—but us. I came here with the de-

sire to give a leg to the kind of people who are going
to do in life what I haven't the guts or the brains or the
character to do.   But I don't want Cataract Lodge now.
Even if it were yours to give—the desire has died.

"What I came most of all wanting out of you, I should
have known I wasn't going to get!" cried Jennifer, "I
should have known!" and stalked out of the office, with
the bright tears standing in her eyes, and leaving him
seated there, smeared with pain and pallor, the look of
hunchback out in his face.

JENNY'S secret apprehensions grew. She was afraid for her flesh. Rapiers of hot steel were beginning by now to jump through the pain in her side. She did not betray by word, the rising tide of fear; but as her mind began to take on the cruel habit of visualizing that moment when the ether-cone would descend and consciousness plop over into lethal torpor, the skin began to stretch across her face like hauled tarpaulin. No one must be allowed to see her in that horrible aftermath when a vagrant mind led one to say dangerous, revealing, etheric things. What was that slide of steel into the perfect mesh of her flesh to reveal? . . .

In a way, these thoroughly mundane terrors, reasoned Jenny to herself, were blessed antidote to that whipping of the spirit to which she had so cruelly been subjected by Ramon. Literal stabs of pain kept her mind to the literalness of the flesh. . . .

And yet, to Jennifer, even though her father had said to her once in a voice that had for the moment given her pause, "Your mother may be a sicker woman than we realize," there was something of a game in this going of Jenny to the hospital again.

Jenny had seen to it that it was like that.

"They think I've an appendix," she told her daughter, "and I'm going to have it out for all it's worth. I don't see why I should spare my friends. Look at Irene Dinehardt. Freddie figured out for me the other night on the back of an opera-program, that she was in the hospital three weeks and cost her friends thousands in gifts and flowers. I've sent my share. Now let them send theirs."

True to her word, she began to spend her mornings, torn as she was with frenzied desire not to be alone and yet not to exert herself, looped around, in the angular way she had of sitting, the blue-enamel French telephone in her boudoir, notifying friends.

By hook and crook, mostly crook, her daughter laughingly assured her, Jenny had managed to prevail upon Dr. Noon to stretch hospital routine sufficiently to obtain for her a three-room suite, which was accomplished by the simple device of opening doors between the ordinary type of room.

There hung over the Rarick household the air of some one about to be married or about to set out on a voyage of exploration. Boxes and packages began to arrive at the house three days before Jenny left it. Books. Bed jackets. A tiny tickless clock with a radium-and-ruby face. One of the first of the packages was a bulky one that sent Jenny and Jennifer into hilarity, including a chuckle from Rarick. A large cactus-plant arrived, well boxed, and with its tough, hand-shaped leaves sprouting needles. Hildegarde had sent her sister-in-law a token of her concern, a card with this angular message attached: "With the hope that your pain will be no greater than a prick from this cactus."

"One prick from Aunt Machiavelli's floral offering and your convalescence will terminate suddenly, all right," cried Jennifer, between gusts of laughter.

"She meant well," said Jenny, and sat down suddenly with darkening eyes fixed on the ridiculous sprawling object.

A flash of the first real concern she had felt or expressed, darted over Jennifer. "You're not turning forbearing and last-will-and-testament, are you, darling, just because you're going in for an appendix? You know perfectly well that your austere and well-meaning sister-in-law is a turkey-gobbler with a wattled neck."

"God forbid!" said Jenny, and contemplated the frenzied-looking cactus with all the absurd wryness she could muster.

"Jenny Avery," cried Jennifer, huddling up beside her mother on to the chaise-longue, where she was resting between telephone calls, "I couldn't bear to have you turn forbearing and turn-the-other-cheeky. It would frighten me into a half-belief that you are really sick. Please be cheeky, darling, instead of turn-the-other-cheeky."

"Jennifer, if anything unforeseen should happen . . ."

"Mother, I can't bear it! Why are you talking like that? You mustn't frighten me, darling. It's disgusting."

"Jennifer-idiot, stop being a cry-baby all over my new water-wave. I haven't the slightest intention of terminating my earthly engagement at this time. I am speaking of the unforeseen . . ."

"Oh, I know. Of course."

"If I should die, Jennifer ———"

"Mother, I can't bear it. You'll make me hysterical."

"If I should die, Jennifer, of which I haven't the slightest damnedest intention ———"

"Then cut out the requiem mass."

"I want you to be a good girl . . ."

"And not smear my pinafores . . ."

"And not smear your pinafores, and be good—and happy, Jennifer. I haven't been either. I'm rotten at moralizing, darling; I've never done much for you except love you and . . ."

"If you say that, I'll drown myself under eighty of

these pink-satin pillows. If I'm a mess, I've myself to blame. Myself, my own self, nobody but myself."

"As a mess, Jennifer, you are clever, beautiful, rich, and desirable. I want you to be good and happy. I haven't been good and happy, Jennifer."

"If you don't stop it," cried Jennifer, taking a long strand of her mother's red-sun-colored hair between her fingers, "I'll yank." She did, and as they fell together among the heaps of pillows the telephone, for the dozenth time that hour, began to crow.

STRANGE days for the Raricks. Family dinner three nights in succession, no guests, but Jenny at table in the kind of tea-gowns she affected, high at the neck, low laces or furs crowding about her wrists, the rather mediæval effect blending with the sonorous splendor of the dining-room.

It was all as strange to Rarick as it was to his women. Butlers moved through the vaulted gloom outside the circle of the dozens of burning candles that hung over the table, and swapped comments behind pantry doors at the spectacle of the Raricks dining *en famille*. To be sure, three out of the three evenings Jennifer slid off quickly to engagements, even before dessert, leaving Jenny and Rarick to contemplate, with self-consciousness, an evening over coffee in the library, to the marching colored-glass stories of the operas.

One of these evenings, the Quartette came in.

It was strange to be sitting with Jenny, listening, while the room filled up softly with the selections Rarick liked best. Mozart B-Major, No. 8, with its beautiful 'cello interlude. Beethoven A-Major, op. 18, No. 5, in its rilling variations of tone and color. There came Schubert, D-Minor! "Death and the Maiden." Fortunately, Jenny neither knew it nor asked about it, but sat with her arms laid out along the sides of her chair, and her head back against the eunuch tapestry, vagrant thoughts drifting on the rhythm-tides.

Ramon was on the high seas by now. On an ocean that sometime, somehow, she had hoped to sail with him. One swallowed the pain, grinding finger-nails into tapestry.

To have had a lover who could endure to be coveted by Emanie Bursilap! Shame of that! To sit there quietly, lapped with the low surf of this small and lovely music, and only the wall of her sick flesh to conceal from Rarick what her heart knew. Little man, you. Rarick, with his head slightly forward and his fingers forming a chapel. We are stranger to each other, even now, than if one of us had never been born. How like you, to touch your finger-tips that way! Lightly. Shyly. Without intensity. Little man, you.

He had changed so little in the amazing years. The same little man she had used to contemplate across the covers of the bed in the house in Westmoreland Place in St. Louis. A hunchback face. A hunchback without the hunch, but with the hurt, lean face of one. A little bitter. Frustration. Well, well, well, what about her frustrations? Avery's? Jennifer's? God spare Jennifer. What was out over Jennifer? She was soft these days, in a lovely way, and subdued, in the way the fellow at the 'cello sometimes placed a lulling hand against strings that had been struck. Was Jennifer in love with Gratton? Soon get that nonsense out of her head. Strange that the brilliant match she was sure to make was so slow in coming. "I am too needed by her," thought Jenny, "to be snatched out of life." Best to sit tight with Jennifer. Let her have her head with this Gratton fellow. Up to a point. Strange that a youth like Rodney Martens, thirty millions, a Brownlee Martens, direct descent, clever, brisk, up-and-coming, literary after a fashion, had never, somehow, troubled to follow up his casual acquaintanceship with Jennifer. Something could be done about that. Best to go slowly with Jennifer. Let this present absorption in the playwright fellow wear itself down. . . . I am too needed here.

So this was how he, Rarick, largely lived his evenings. His colored-glass operas. This Quartette. His unpronounceable gems, that, when mounted, were ineffective and looked only semi-precious. Even Gerkes, fossil, had gone. Found himself a squaw bride off somewhere in a blubber-eating country. That, too, was Rarick for you! How like him to pick for his close friend a man to whom an Eskimo bride was satisfaction! What was there about him, Rarick, that created the little area of isolation around him? Even Jennifer, when she spoke to her father, rarely looked him in the eyes, but between, as if staving off his glance. That was not right. Her period of convalescence would be a good time to soften things up somehow between these two. After all, he was entitled to his daughter. Since the death of Avery, it had always seemed to Jenny, fantastically, that the furrow between Rarick's eyes was the shape of a cross. He was entitled to Jennifer. Naughty Jennifer, so alien to this man, her father. A kind father, in so far as his understanding went. It was time to see that he got some kindness in return. He was being kind now. Trying to please. Trying to help her cast out fear. And yet, there was nothing she could do for that little man there, or that he could do for her. It was terrible, it was vacant, it was loathsome to sit there beside this man—this husband who was being kind to her—parched, as with a thirst, for the kind of kisses that Ramon, pimp, on the high seas with Emanie Bursilap, had to bestow. God, I need to be forgiven. . . .

IT COULD be said that Jenny, narrow, frilled, as elaborate as Bernhardt, and her pallor quite beautiful, went to her ordeal with something of the fanfare of Marie Antoinette riding her tumbrel through the populace. The motor-car that bore her was followed by a smaller one bearing outfittings that were part of the pomp and circumstance of her arrival. A bed-cover of ermine, with a heavy double fringe of black tails. An almost-life-size photograph of a head of Avery, framed in jade, his young throat bare, his eyes unsmiling. The cactus, for a laugh. Flowers, anticipating her arrival, were stacked in hospital vases of painted tin, only to be rearranged when Jenny arrived, with her urns and her vases and her graduated silver bowls.

The hospital—one accustomed to the vagaries of the celebrated and important—grinned, the impersonal patter of the most highly personal environment in the world passing around from nurse to interne to doctor.

"The Five-and-Ten Mrs. Rarick! New-rich, but, oh, how rich!"

"Hope she takes a fancy to the fine hand behind the ether," said the anæsthetist, "and endows my children's ward at Island Hospital."

"Hope she hears of the beautiful, Titian-haired, and virtuous girl in the supply department and decides to make her an heiress," said the red-haired miss in charge of the linen-room.

"Do your best, girls," admonished the head nurse; "she may come through and endow our joint-disease wing."

"She can have her millions," said a girl in the training

department, "but, oh, how I could do with a ninety-five-dollar civet coat in Macy's window. If only she would take ninety-five dollars' worth of fancy to me."

And so on, as Jenny, who came in like thunder, was put to bed in a bower that later, an interne said, made him feel as if he were wading through a meadow to reach her pulse. A meadow of the elaborate magnificence of Jenny. There were present, at her installation, the maid in the Breton cap, who, after seven years, knew practically no word of English, but understood Jenny's execrable French to the syllable, and the English girl named Daphne Dang, whose rôle was not exactly definable, but who had been at Jenny's elbow in rôles of every capacity from seamstress to masseuse to secretary for the last ten years. Peacock, the first butler, whom Jenny had hired for his name, carried in cushions and a screen of Aubusson panels to protect the opening door from revealing sight of hospital corridor.

It struck Rarick, as he entered, that not a friend had felt close enough to intrude upon this arrival. There were already telegrams and notes that Jenny opened and pinned against the screen. They were the personal touches toward which she seemed to be stretching her long, cold, clear-looking fingers as toward a live grate.

He wondered, without bitterness, how she had managed with the Spanish dancing-boy about whom she was always being so elaborately casual. Poor Jenny! There were the records of the social struggle of the years pinned along that Aubusson screen. A poor, insecure record. It would never do to express some of the surge of tender sympathy for her futilities which he felt sweep over and hurt him for her. This was the time to be quick and concise and clear and sure. That was the manner which seemed most successfully to keep her in a state of feeling reassured. Treat it all as a matter of

course. Give directions as you would for the arrangement of one of her ballroom functions, or charity bazaars.
Jenny caught gratefully at that spirit of casualness. It
hypnotized fear.

But a last-minute dread had reappeared. If only she
did not prattle as she came out of the ether. At best,
there had always been something terrifying to Jenny
at the idea of losing consciousness. There were imperative reasons why Jenny must not prattle. Steadfastly
she ground into her mind the intention to go down into
unconsciousness with her mind a blank, no loose fears,
memories, thoughts, desires, or regrets floating around
in it. Yet, what furtive bits of seaweed of unspoken
thoughts might drift to the surface of a mind unanchored
by consciousness! A new fear smote Jenny. Suppose,
with Rarick standing beside her bed, she should unconsciously reveal to him the tortuous secret windings of
those underground rivers of her mind that carried so
much along them that was traitorous to him. Then, too,
how could she endure the thought that her daughter be
smirched with some of that flotsam and jetsam, as it
floated to the surface and revealed itself in words?

A terror of delirium began to settle on Jenny.

"Rarick," she said to him, as he stood beside her bed
the evening before her operation, "I want you to promise me something."

She had been so free of this mood of last-minute prom-
ises. It astonished him that never once had she spoken in
terms of her will. She had one, made the tenth year
of their marriage. A simple, hand-written document,
duly legalized. As a matter of fact, she had never been
acquisitive in that sense. For purpose of tax distribu-
tion, huge holdings were in her name. These papers she
had signed without even troubling to read them.

Now Rarick began to chide her, in the playful mood she seemed to demand of the occasion.

"What solemn promise? That I will not break the will?"

"Seriously, it will be terrible to me, Rarick, if you or Jennifer come into the room to visit me until a day after the ether has worn off and I am once more my presentable self. I don't want you or Jennifer to know how green I can look. Promise me that."

"Of course," he said.

What lay in the troubled hinterlands of her mind? What was she afraid of revealing? As if there were anything much that Jenny could reveal to him that he did not already know or suspect. Poor, frightened Jenny! For the first time her affairs were in danger of slipping a bit out of her hands. He wanted her to keep them there as desperately as she felt that need. No more than she, did he desire the revelation of those fetid places that had gathered scum in the years of swampy silence between them. Ugh!

"Jennifer, see to it that they don't come near me with one of those hideous Mother Hubbard hospital nightgowns. If the pain in my side doesn't kill me, the touch of canton flannel will."

"I'll dike you out in silk, mi-darling, and a fol-de-rol of lace."

"Don't let them be efficient and hygienic and sheety about my bed, either, Jennifer. No matter what kind of damaged goods they bring back to it, I want to be tucked back into this—make them stack it up for me while I am attending my own op., darling. It will occupy your mind."

"If you aren't careful, I'll make the bed myself."

"Then I hope to heaven you have to lie on it."

"Isn't she beautiful, Father, lying propped up there in her well-known magnificence?"

"You look very well, Jenny."

She slitted her olive-colored eyes and turned her head away. One was supposed to feel chastened in hours such as this. She did, of course. But what if her secret distastes of the inadequacies of this man, persisting even now, should leap through and spatter him with words of contempt?

"I want you to go now, Rarick. You, too, Jennifer. Promise me that you will both remain out until they have me all out of the ether."

"We promise."

"Of course."

They were a constrained lot, the three of them, and finally, all bent to keeping casual, there were good-nights; and the final departure went something like this:

"Don't forget to have Miss Dang telephone my regrets to the Planets. Rarick, hadn't you better keep this emerald ring of mine in your waistcoat pocket along with your other glitts? I forgot to put it in the safe."

"Let me slide a packet of this Mirabel sachet under your pillow before I go, Mother. It's the latest squak. There are some novels and a copy of *Vanity Fair* and *Town Topics* in that lower drawer, Nurse, in case my Mother wants to read. I'll bring around the new *Spur* tomorrow."

"Good night, Jennifer."

" 'Night, Jenny Avery."

"Good night, Rarick."

"Sleep well, Jenny."

"Sure to. Good night. . . ."

The bed that Jenny left the following morning for the operating-room was built up during her absence, by her daughter, the maid in the Breton cap, two nurses, and

Miss Dang, into its pyramid of finery. Tilted, there was a look of cornucopia to it, the way the avalanches of little laces and the fine pink mists of sheets seemed to spill.

All morning, it stood waiting in its elaborate sort of trance for the return of its occupant.

Jenny was not to come back to it.

It was one of those operations that after the first few moments, become hopeless.

IT CAME as shock to Rarick, that the suggestion to unload himself of the great property of his town house should come from his daughter.

They had been sitting over after-dinner coffee, on one of those evenings which, during the months since the death of Jenny, his daughter had dutifully apportioned off, as if allowing him just so much time out of the more-than-ever crowded budget of her days.

In a sense this was true. Since the death of her mother a rigid, self-made rule, which she had not allowed to lapse in the fifteen months, except during the periods of absence from the city, had been to set apart two evenings of the week, either to accompany her father to a concert or opera, or remain with him in his library.

The concussion of her mother's death, coming, as it should not have been permitted, out of an ignorance and innocence of the facts, had been an irritant that sent her skyrocketing into a state half noisy, half hysterical.

"I don't give a damn for anything now!" she had cried, the morning they had begun to pluck the finery from the waiting hospital bed of Jenny, as you would pluck the feathers from a swan. She had gone rather consistently about not giving it.

"I'd be a fine one to go into mourning, wouldn't I?"— when she troubled at all to explain. "She would be the first to hoot laughter at it. She despised long faces and emotional side-shows."

That was probably true. There had been no ostensible period of mourning for Avery, even in the days when Jenny's face had resembled a wax mask that was melting downward from the corners. To Rarick, the formal period of mourning did not even occur.

The affairs of household went on pretty much as usual, except that after the first blank weeks of shock, Jennifer began to cram the evenings with occasions. The formal dinner, never too frequent a function with Jenny, because of the strain of Rarick, who never attended, became the rule. The house glittered, that winter, with the clusters of lights at its portal going full blast, and the curb lined with motors. When the solemn doors swung backward, loiterers, who sometimes stood in line formation on both sides of the stoop, could glimpse the molten glow of Hispano Moresque art: the grand staircase that wound upward with the curving gesture of a lovely woman's two arms; the liveried figures of butlers in knee-buckles and claret-reds; the round burning pool of the rose-window, with its dominant purple of crushed grape.

They were mixed parties Jennifer held that year, frantically-assembled parties, without social rhyme or reason; social-fringe assemblages that Jenny would have tried to avert; sometimes parties with the servants mopping up small pools of wine from the dining-room floor the morning afterward, and scraping the marred surface for fresh waxings.

In the main, Rarick did not protest, except on the occasion when young Rodney Martens, finding one of the butlers' bicycles propped in a rear hall—where he must have been groping, between dances, for air to clear his fuddled brain—had ridden it into the ballroom about three o'clock in the morning, plunging into a great crystal-and-lapis-lazuli candelabrum of fifty bulbs, toppling it over, blowing the fuse, and crashing the evening into darkness, as he landed in a ringing mess that stirred the household and reached Rarick as he lay abed, sleepless.

"I dislike to have to mention it to you, Jennifer; you are no longer a child, but either you pick your friends with more discrimination or don't have them here."

That was the evening, seated over coffee, in the library, her eyes level and burning under her straight bang, that Jennifer burst forth:

"Let's chuck it, Father. Sell the house!"

Sell the house! He could have told her, almost as far back as her mission to him in behalf of Cataract Lodge, that he had already sold it.

"That is," she added, grinding out her cigarette with a sort of fierce enjoyment at the timeliness of her thrust, "unless you have already."

He had.

"It's a morgue. It's a tomb. It's a mausoleum. I hate it."

"Then what?" he said, with his chin touching his shirt-front and his eyes up at her.

"Then what? Anything. Take me to—to Korea— Abyssinia—at least they are destinations."

He regarded her slowly, as if he could not have done marveling that she had no wisdom. She had been away twice that winter. First to Paris, scuttling home after a month, full of what she called the French heebie-jeebies. Later on, there was a yachting cruise out of Florida waters, for which she must have stood sponsor for all expense. Rarick's impulse, when Hellman presented him with bills amounting to twenty-one thousand dollars for this week's divertissement, had been to discipline her by radical way of refusal, under threat of public declaration, to meet any such future expenditures! But when the time came for him to take up with her the matter of what he regarded as wanton and cruel waste, she took her place across the table-desk from him with a child-like obedience that made her suddenly seem very small to him and tortured, and something failed him. There was a wild kind of distress about Jennifer, these days. She had the look of a person who wants to rip open his collar for more air. She had the rolling look to her eye of someone frightened. The disagreeable thought smote Rarick that almost anything might happen to a girl that taut. What hurts you, Jennifer? he wanted to say to her. Tell me where the trouble lies?

She could not have told. He realized that. It is possible that he himself could have analyzed it before Jennifer. In those bruised and somehow resentful months after her mother's death, self-analysis in Jennifer had given way before a sort of dull pride in her capacity for pain. You were wretched. You blazed away with a chronic kind of grief for the slender slab of Jenny lying out there beside Avery in her ivory casket lined in silver ailanthus leaves, that the Sunday papers had got wind of. Hers not to appraise. Hers only to clasp hands to a throat that was always thickening with tears, and hanker for the strange kind of maternity that had gone with Jenny.

"Jenny Rarick has left me in a hell-hole," she once told Gratton, whom she was seeing on fitful occasions. "I can't seem to get out of it, chiefly because I can't seem to want to get out. Isn't it strange, Gratt? I know I'm in hell, but I can't want sufficiently to climb out. How do you make that out?"

"Stop trying to make yourself out, Jennifer," he had replied. "That's your trouble, perhaps."

"I hate you," she had replied to that, and walked out of his room. He did not follow. Waiting on the threshold outside his door for a moment, it had seemed to her that nothing ever in the world could matter so much as his following her, to unlock her clenched hand and tuck his into it. He, too, stood waiting on the room side of that door, waiting to do just that, his body rigid, though, against the move.

Rarick, trying as he had done all of her life, to clamber on to some basis of intimacy with this girl who was so shy of him, and again watching these months of her misbehavior, began, a little grimly, to understand.

The futility of waiting further was borne in upon him. If the death of Jenny, leaving them stranded in this wilderness of Gothic aisles, had not hurled them into quick and sympathetic understanding, then it was not to happen the way it did in the benign world of people in books.

There was too much in him that still wanted to spank her for the things that still made her wayward and full of self and pretense. She, in turn, could flare at him with the old antagonisms before even he voiced rebuke. And yet, withal, she was an older, sweeter Jennifer, subdued in a way that was even more painful to him than what he considered her atrociousness. It was that new quality in her that saved her the drastic rebuke of the twenty-one-thousand-dollar yachting-week, which had angered Rarick as nothing since her gambling exploits at Cannes. Even her high kind of despair had a subdued quality that made him feel more nearly able to cope with this strange girl who was his. No, the blow of death could scarcely be said to have flung them together, but sometimes it did seem to Rarick that through the long, vertical mists of the Gothic twilights in which they sometimes sat together, they were approaching. . . .

What he said to her this night, over coffee, could not have come off this way a twelve- or even a six-month before, when a high-handed and evasive scene would have been precipitated.

"Are you in love with young Gratton?"

"Damn it, yes!"

There was no surprise in her voice, possibly because her mind was flooded with nothing else but the hypothetical reply to such a hypothetical question. "Damn it, yes! Lots of good it does me."

Constantly he was rebuking her for the coarse, free profanity he despised in general, and particularly in a woman. He let it pass now.

"That is unfortunate."

"You would put it that way."

What did she expect him to do? Reveal how her hurt hurt him?

"Father, do you like him?"

That was scarcely the way to express the curiously hankering eye Rarick sometimes cast on this young man, on those now rare occasions when he came to dine or call for Jennifer. Their talk had been desultory, withal curiously exciting to the older man. Gratton would go walking in the Pyrenees. He had a stubborn, tenacious mouth that already looked pulled as if from veering his own way. It was not that Rarick liked him, so much as the conviction was high within him that this fellow, who wanted what he wanted and would relentlessly go after it, was to be envied. . . .

"Do you like him, Father?"

"Why shouldn't I?"

"You have been known not to approve my friends."

"You've never brought home much worth approving."

"You mean Berry? That was only a yen, Father."

"A what?"

"A low-down infatuation of low-down me seeking a way out of a torment by walking further in. The only reason I have for knowing that there is a shred of decent person in me, Father, is because I like a boy called Gratton, who doesn't give a tinker's dam for me."

"How do you know?"

"He has told me so. It's not the tried-and-true sex-situation that he would scorn to do in a play—bringing two people together after three acts and two hours and forty minutes of sex-antagonism, in order to achieve a clutch-embrace at the final curtain. It won't end that way between us. Gratton hasn't any use for my guts. Pardon anatomical references."

"Have you any use for your own?"

"I'm not so bad as painted, Father. The trouble with me, say I, naïvely, is that I am not any worse than any girl in my position, only I was slightly better to start with, making the total loss more total."

She was uncanny to him in her quick perspicacities, always trembling, as it were, on the border line between her legitimate kind of smartness and her tawdry smartiness.

"How many a true word, Jennifer . . ."

"Yes, Father, spoken in the grimmest jest that can ever befall me. I like him, and the devil of it is, the more hopelessly I like him, the more I like myself for being the kind of person to like Gratton, and the more I like him for being the kind of person not to like me. Do I make myself clear?"

There was torment for you. . . .

"Liking him is the nicest thing about me. The neat and respectable verb, 'to like,' is used here out of deference to your sense of decent restraint. I love Gratton, Father," she said, and smiled at him, and kept it lifted there with the determination of a child standing on one foot.

"Funny thing about Gratton. He's not money-conscious about us. He is not cowed, or infuriated, or impressed—I mean, the way you learn to expect pretty nearly everybody to be except the few-if-anys, who have more money than we have. Gratt doesn't despise money as such. He does think capital swinish. Well, so does everybody, until they get it. I mean, in a healthy way, he wants money for himself, because God gave him a great birthday present. A single-track mind. He wants to write; and legend to the contrary notwithstanding, he does not want to write in a garret. He doesn't think garrets are intellectual and creative clearing-houses, any more than gardens and bright clean rooms are. And Gratton is out for the gardens and the bright clean rooms. Funny thing about Gratt. I think he'd rather marry a rich girl than a poor one, but I won't do."

If, Rarick told himself, his face wry with disgust, this was modern frankness about and with life, then he gave up. The quality of the picture of Jennifer, seated there with her knees flung so that the bare pink of her flesh above the stockings was revealed, exhaling two steady streams of cigarette smoke from her nostrils, and dangling one cockatoo-green slipper from her toes, depended upon the particular retina of the eye and mind of the beholder. The eye and mind of Rarick turned away offended. After all, frankness was a virtue, except when it became indecent exposure. There were parts of one's mind one kept covered, as one kept the body clothed.

"Isn't that terrible, Father, I won't do?" she repeated, and looked at him and smiled with her palms lying open in her lap, loosely, in a way that was pathetic to him.

"Come here."

"Yes, Father."

"Let us talk this thing out. Just you—and me ———"

"I can't. Not now. I—can't ———"

"Then later."

"Father, be good to me."

"How, Jennifer, how?"

"By letting me be good to you."

Trying not to tremble and be silent, he sat and trembled and was silent.

"Child! Poor child!"

"Oh, don't pity me, Father. That way. Don't. Don't. It's you who need that. Don't worry about me. I'm not going in for martyrdom. I'm not going to withdraw from the turgid world and spend the rest of my life spreading sweetness and light through orphan asylums. . . ."

No use, no use, was in his brain.

God, God, why am I being like this all over again, was in hers.

". . . and you won't have to take me on a trip around the world to help me to 'forget.' Also, I decline the Victorian alternative of going into a decline. It isn't done any more. But, Father, Father, what kind of a hit-below-the-belt world is this, anyway? I love him. And I want the right kind of decent constructive life that I cannot work out with anybody in the world but him. And the dumb-bell," cried Jennifer, sobbing out and dashing for the door—"the dumb-bell hasn't got the sense to know it. I won't do!"

Once up in the security of her bedroom, which she made more secure by locking the door, she turned out the lights and plunged face downward on her bed.

THERE came the time, in one of those tall, somber twilights, the kind that Rarick loved as they came stalking as if on stilts into the vaultings of his library, when the pile of his writings, which he had kept stacked in a high and shaggy manuscript on a side-table, was replaced by a single piece of typewritten paper, held in place by a paper-weight of alleged B. C. limestone, in cursive Egyptian writing.

It was a twilight that smelled of snow. There had been flurries of it throughout the day, and by now it clung in small triangles to the corners of windows, and seeped its intangible odor of white, which assailed the nostrils like the feel of camphor, into the room.

There had been a high blaze along the logs, which Rarick, seated before the embrasure of a fireplace in which he could have stood without stooping, had let die to embers. Late light from the high, leaded window above him came pouring down on his back and rested along the stooped ridge of him.

In that posture, the hint of hunch was quite marked. It was a womanish back, narrow, tired, and with a little peak to it, as if he had been hung up and a peg had left its imprint.

There was an agate in his hand, which he twiddled without seeing; an eccentric sapphire cat's-eye, said to be one of two of its kind in existence. After a while he slid it into his waistcoat pocket and drew out a glyptograf cut in old red dreamy amber. Presently the arm of his chair was strewn with stones, Egyptian, Greek, Roman, Etruscan, Renaissance, a ruby from the famous collection of Signor Medina, an Italian Jew of the eighteenth century. Two opals from Lord Arundel's collection. A black pearl from the first Duke of Marlborough. Another that had belonged to Prince Miravisky.

At five o'clock, Gratton Davies, who had walked his wire-haired terrier up a twilit Fifth Avenue, vaulted the snowless stoop of the house with the Campanile doors, gave over his dog to the keeping of Peacock, and was promptly admitted to the presence of Rarick.

It was the first time they had met subsequent to that evening when Jennifer had damned a hit-below-the-belt world to her father.

"I am glad you sent for me, sir," said Gratton, who was easy in all personal contacts. "I've been meaning for a long while to have a visit with you."

"Sit there."

"Shall I remove this array of lapidarian loot of yours?" he said, as, seating himself, his arm brushed a ring of Pectunculus shell and sent it scurrying toward the hearth. "Say, that's an aquamarine there, isn't it? My birthstone." He scooped the stones into his hand, pouring them into Rarick's. "I once had a pretty fine pair of aquamarine cuff-links. Traded them for an Oxford Dictionary. I'm a great trader, Mr. Rarick. Belong back in the days when men bartered merchandise for merchandise. Must seem strange to a man like you, who has built his fortune on the modern rudiments of big business, but I'm like the old Thracians, who couldn't get accustomed to the idea of just a small coin in exchange for a whole flask of wine. I'll trade my aquamarine cuff-links for an Oxford Dictionary much more quickly than for cold cash. That disqualifies me, doesn't it, as too unimaginative for business?"

"Perhaps you do yourself an injustice. One of the most

outstanding business dickers of all time was that of a soul in exchange for a mess of pottage."

"That is the one kind of trade I don't expect to fall for, Mr. Rarick."

"I believe that."

"You may well believe it."

"What is it you want most out of life, anyway, Gratton?"

"That's a large order. You mean it in specific relation to what you've sent for me about, or ——"

"Rather."

"Good! But before we get to it, there is something I have wanted to say to you ever since it happened. I tried to put it into a message at the time. No one could understand better, Mr. Rarick, what the death of your son means to you than I. It's because, of course, I realize the workings of that boy so well. I fought his same kind of losing fight back in those years; only, where he went through the door, I managed to jump back. I— won't bore you; but I could have been that boy of yours, Mr. Rarick—I think I know what his kind of aloneness meant, and the kind of black waters it can put between even those who need most desperately to clutch to one another—well, I know what it means—I know Avery ——"

A row of little cords popped out in Rarick's neck, and it was a moment before his throat would unflex enough to swallow.

"Yi." He had wanted to say "Yes."

"Avery wasn't able to swim across to you, and you didn't see his hands go up for the third time. I made my swim to an island of sanity. I've clung to it ever since. Avery couldn't—make it —— You would have been his island . . ."

"A thought like that helps one to keep on living."

His voice sounded to him like a Lilliputian's. High and narrow. What the devil. . . .

"Well, anyway, Mr. Rarick, that's out of my system. I've spilled it like a ton of coal. But I've always felt strangely entitled to say it to you. Now, to get back to what I want out of life. Don't know as I've ever thought of it that concretely, but I suppose I'm rank enough hedonist to ask nothing more than a certain ability to create within myself, and in turn endow, a certain amount of happiness. Why do you ask?"

"I have always thought of you as a young man who knows precisely where he is going."

"I haven't always known that. I do now. As I tried to tell you a moment ago, my feet haven't always been on the ground. They are now. I may not reach my destination, but I am hell-bent for it."

"I like that. Chiefly because most of my life I have always been hell-bent for a destination that I've never cared whether I reached or not."

"Strange, to hear you, who would seem to have reached a high peak of destination that few men achieve, say that."

"We won't discuss that. The point of this interview is a strange one, Gratton. I am informed by my daughter, that you, to use her own picturesque phrasing, do not care a tinker's dam for her. That interests me. I want to know why."

"Now, look here," said Gratton, without surprise, but unfolding a knee and sitting forward, "aren't you accepting evidence without hearing both sides?"

"That is what I intend to do now."

"I don't know just what your daughter may have told you, but it is just possible, considering the amount of adulation that has been Jennifer's since you brought her into an ornate world, that the slightly tempered qualities I bring to bear upon our friendship may, by token of comparison, appear frigid to your high-handed young daughter."

"Just possible, yes."

"I don't know by what metric system you weigh up tinkers' dams, but I do know that my regard for your daughter is quite unrelated to a tinker's approbrium."

"You might find it difficult to convince her of that."

"Am I to understand, Mr. Rarick, that the young man is being asked his intentions?"

"It is embarrassing and astute for you to put it that way. As a matter of fact, however, you are being asked just that. Your intentions."

"To remain, I hope, in so far as it is going to be possible, one of your daughter's well-wishing friends."

"I see. I suppose you are aware, Gratton, that my daughter entertains a disturbing set of feelings toward you."

"On those occasions when that fact does seem more or less apparent, it is embarrassing to one who is so keenly on to himself as I am."

"It would interest me, as her father, to know just wherein my daughter fails."

"Oh, come now, Mr. Rarick, you are too keen a man to attempt to place me in an utterly equivocal position like that."

"There is nothing equivocal in honesty, Gratton."

"I like your daughter, Mr. Rarick. I don't feel called upon, however, to qualify, even to you."

"You are entirely right not to feel called upon. I was appealing to you."

"I see. I'm sorry. Jennifer likes me, Mr. Rarick. I'd be a fool not to see it. She may be in love for the first time in her life, if you will permit me to say so, both of us knowing Jennifer as we do, with some one besides herself."

"No doubt of it. That is my justification for opening this subject with you."

"That being the case, her being in love is no special tribute to me, but rather to herself. Jennifer, of course, thinks otherwise. She has told me, bless her funniness, that her self-esteem is being enormously bolstered by the fact that she likes me. That is poppycock. A big sweeping energy like Jennifer, intelligent, gregarious creature that she is, must have outlet."

"But?"

"I hate like the devil to say it to you, particularly since it does not convey to you what extent I am in danger of being in love with your daughter, but Jennifer does not quite come through, Mr. Rarick."

"It's fine of you to be this honest."

"It's fine of you not to kick me out for a presumptuous, if well-meaning idiot."

"To get back to Jennifer . . ."

"One of the reasons I have tried not to see much of Jennifer since her return from her cruise, Mr. Rarick, is practically an admission of my own weakness. She fascinates and amuses and delights me more than any other woman I have ever known. She is full of the power to be pretty nearly everything she is not. . . ."

"Right."

"Mark my word, Mr. Rarick, your chance for a bunch of fine realizations lies buried somewhere in that girl."

"Right."

"On the other hand, she is arrogant and without a certain type of pity. She is sophisticated without taking the time to use her fine brain to be wise. She is super-critical without being profound. She is without great accomplishment and intolerant of others. She has a genuine intellectual curiosity, but pretends to despise what she and the rest of her set term "highbrow."

"You are despising the setting of the ring, rather than the stone."

"Perhaps. I do despise the picture of Jennifer and her set. It has always been a facetious credo of mind, Mr. Rarick, that great personal wealth, even fabulous wealth like yours, is a maligned institution and that in private fortunes there lurks great power for good. In my heart, though, I am coming not to believe it. The very things I despise in Jennifer are the things great wealth should have corrected in her and somehow didn't. Look at this room. Kings, artists, dreamers, contrived its magnificence for her. This home. Beauty, prodigality, dignity, peace, and out of this conspiracy of the so-called better things of life has come a flimsy Jennifer caring passionately about few of the things that make life so passionately worth living. Hang it! if I were not so afraid that it would mean that I am dangerously near loving her, I would hate her."

"I think I see clearly everything you have said."

"You can't. Diametrically different as you are in some things, you and Jennifer are fundamentally alike in others. She's yours."

"I want to say some things to you, Gratton, that I don't believe I have ever formulated even to myself, much less put into words before."

"I feel like the devil. The things I've let out aren't usually said, and then, hang it all, I've said just about half, and the less important half of what I feel."

"This seems to be the time and the place for saying. I don't mind telling you that much of what you have just admitted, while not new to me, is bitter. I'm not so resilient any more. I'm near to sixty, young fellow."

"Not ——"

"Oh, not so old, but, as the span goes, time to put the house in order."

"It's a big house."

"An appallingly big one. I'm going to tell you about that house. The house that Jennifer lives in."

"The house-that-Jennifer-lives-in. That should be the nicest house there is!"

"Perhaps, in view of all you have told me, there isn't much point, but I'm going to say it anyway. I want Jennifer settled, young man. She is twenty-eight now. Motherless. Her brother is gone. I am not going to live to be an old man. There are certain things we know irrevocably. That is one of them. I have always known it. I will not get old."

"I hate to hear you say that."

"I would give a great deal if you could like my girl."

"That's what I meant just now when I said, I've said just half of what I feel, and that half the less important half. . . ."

"You probably know, without my dwelling upon it, the failure of a parent I've been to her."

"It's been a mutual failure."

"She's got brains and sweetness ——"

"God knows she has. Too much of both for my peace of mind. You're going to reap from them, too—mark you ——"

"I want to tell you a little about myself, Gratton."

"Yes."

"Young man, I am worth one hundred and eighty million dollars. And yet, personally, I have never succeeded. My success succeeded."

"I see what you mean."

"In my youth, Gratton, I wanted one thing out of life as hard-headedly as you seem to want one thing. My success snatched it away."

"I think I summed it up when I said once of you that you asked for bread and got a gold nugget."

"Excellent. I would have a hard time getting a jury to vote me sympathy, but I am as short of success, today, Gratton, as you see me sitting here, as I was in the days when I used to figure my plans on the backs of envelopes behind a counter in a hardware store."

"I know that."

"That is why there is something about a young fellow like you, so sure not to be deterred; something that to an old fellow like me, is just about sublime. I want you to look at me, seated here as you say, in a home contrived by kings, and try to understand some of the things that I am going to tell you. Follow?"

"Yes."

"First, as to family. You see me practically bankrupt. My wife gone. That I cannot discuss, even here. Need I say to you," he went on, and began to twist his face—"need I say to you that my life was finished the day Avery took his? We never got to each other. But I—no fool like an old fool, that boy was my reason for having the endurance to fight through the black and colossal years of my success. He made the nights, filled with my wakefulness, endurable. He was the hope of my loneliness. He was my real success waiting to be accomplished and in my dumbness, I crossed him in everything that did not point toward that success. I saw the paraphernalia of wealth crushing him. The steam-roller flattening him into a pattern just as you see it threatening Jennifer. I saw his success in picking out a rich man for his father, threatening to succeed. I have

no graces, Gratton.   If ever a man was lacking in manner, that man is me.   I had no way to ingratiate the boy,
no talent for parenthood.   I didn't deserve him.   I let
him starve for the very things I would have given my
life to feed him.   He got lost, you see, in the maze of the
things and the things.   I don't intend to have that happen
to my girl. . . ."

"It needn't."

"I am not a man to take life lightly, Gratton.   My
wife used to say of me that I lacked a cardinal sense of
humor.   I have never believed she was right.   That is
the last thing a man wants to believe of himself, but
it is true that I do not take this matter of my colossal
wealth lightly.   I have given it more profound thought,
its relationship to the world from which I derived it, the
economic scheme which made it possible and my responsibilities toward those sources, than even you might think.
I am not an educated man, Gratton, like you.   But I
have thought my share and pondered . . ."

"I once heard it said of you, Mr. Rarick, or perhaps
read it in some magazine, that you never reached a conclusion that was not based upon at least several of the
best opinions you could muster and that those several
opinions were almost invariably all yours."

"I've gone my road alone.   Open the third drawer of
that table."

"Here?"

"Yes."

"Take out that pile of manuscript."

"This?"

"Yes."

"Whew!"

"Yes, five hundred and forty-eight pages longhand."

"Yes and what fine, steel-point longhand.   **Yours?**"

"Yes. Brevity being the soul of wit, that would just about be the bulk of my story."

"Your life?"

"Everything but, and yet nothing else. It is the story of the house and man my wealth built. Of the walls it reared for me and the hearth it kindled. It is filled with moralizing, the kind nobody will take the time to read. It is the result of my study, my thoughts, my experience. It is my last will and testament. But more of that presently. I wonder if you happen to have heard, Gratton, rumors that Rarick Chain is about to be absorbed by Bilt Chain?"

"Yes."

"They are founded on fact."

"You have completed that job."

"Yes. And now I have a new one. A stiff one. The job of dying a poor man. The entire philosophy behind that determination is in this stack of papers. The years I have left are few in which to give back intelligently the one hundred and eighty million dollars to the people from whom I have earned it. Earned it, mind you. If there is anything miraculous about the vastness of my wealth, it lies in the fact that corruption has passed me by. The average man—and woman—Gratton, is beholden to the object, the inanimate thing for his comfort and much of his happiness. I have filled the hands of the masses with objects and cluttered their minds with the easy happinesses of which they are so capable. I have stuck more atrocious paper flowers into more atrocious glass vases than probably any man in the history of the world. I have anointed the tongues of the masses of children whose humdrum lives stand ready to snatch them out of youth, with the red of the sticky lollypop, and they tell me that the sin of ugliness and cheapness is upon me. That may all be true, Gratton, but I know to

what extent I have made living easier to the masses whose
days are chained to the trivialities of things. My daughter Jennifer owns a six-carat pigeon-blood ruby ring.
The craving for that ring is deep in the hearts of
millions of women like her. I partially satisfy that
craving in red-glass ten-cent rings. Women with scalded,
horny hands can now cope with their dishwater in ten-
cent rubber gloves—there is a side to my colossal, absurd,
undignified bartering in snide objects that is labor of
mercy. Don't you forget it."

"One isn't apt to, after hearing you."

"The wisest man I ever knew showed me the way to
give back what I have earned. He never, even in his
great wisdom, knew to what extent his mind was endowing mine. I refer to my friend Felix Gerkes."

"Yes."

"It was he who first set my mind working along lines
toward which I had previously had only a sort of subconscious predisposition. My friend is at once a simple
and profound man."

"I see where Mengelberg intimated in Berlin the other
day, after commenting on Gerkes's last book on the
theory of life, that the Nobel prize is once more about to
come to America."

"That will mean little to Gerkes."

"It should mean a great deal to you, who have made
so much of his contribution to knowledge possible."

"Probably it does, Gratton. That's a snapshot of
Gerkes there on the table. It came this morning."

"I'd never recognize him in his beard and all those
fur togs. Is that his wife and—papoose?"

"Yes."

"Curious."

"Not nearly so curious as we must seem to him. Gerkes
has learned a peculiar secret. That is why he is, I think,

the only happy person I know. He is never impatient for his tomorrow. That enables him to completely live his present. The present and the future are inseparable to him. The one is constantly in the act of being enveloped by the other. Tomorrow is something he does not have to hurry toward. There is going on for him the perpetual phenomenon of his present turning into past, as the future encroaches and becomes the present."

"He has the face of a happy person. So has the woman!"

"He took his wife from the Eskimos, whom he considers the happiest people he has ever encountered. I was about to tell you, not meaning to digress to the subject of my hobby Gerkes, that it was he who unconsciously sent my subconsciousness to the surface. Before he left us down here, for his new life in the North, he used to sit around with me evenings, and more or less idly, let fall out of the vast storehouses of his mind, some of his philosophies on preventive philanthropy."

"Yes."

"Oh, I know most of it might have seemed obvious to a man like you, Gratton, but it was strangely new to me at the time. I realize now that much of what he said had been smoldering in my subconsciousness for years, but just the same, it was he who started me on the concrete thinking-out and writing of this shaggy monstrosity of a manuscript. Three years it has been in the writing. One of its by no means most important results is, that you see me sitting here, Gratton, in a house that, pending my death, is only a loan to me. I no longer own one stone in it, but lease it from those who do, and with the sale of some vast lumber properties in Maine and Canada last month, I now own not one acre of God's territory with the exception of certain colossal and indirect mortgage holdings which in their turn will be converted. I am, of course, still a man heavily encumbered with wealth of practically every sort of valuable human possession, but already forty million of my dollars are committed to preventive philanthropies."

"It isn't easy for a man whose bank balance has never been larger than nine hundred dollars, to have much of a conception of forty million dollars."

"I have endowed no cancer hospitals, but have given, with what I hope is the cumulative wisdom that is coming to men who have come into the phenomenal kind of wealth that is possible only in this country, great fortunes toward the prevention of the disease. Nothing new in all this, you say. No, but look more deeply into it and see how prolonged has been the infancy of this idea. And there is but little time left for me. My money must pour back to the people in a fresh blood transfusion. I want to wrap no rags around social sores. To accomplish, I must personally administer my moneys while I live. I must die a poor man. You see that?"

"Yes."

"My sole heir is my daughter Jennifer. For that reason and another equally important one, she comes into no properties at my death except a life income of eight thousand dollars a year. You live on less, don't you?"

"Yes."

"Comfortably?"

"Fairly."

"She will be stripped pretty bare of the paraphernalia that has made of her some of the things we have just been discussing, Gratton."

"I can't imagine her."

"I can."

"She will plunge like a roped steer."

"At first."

"I wonder if you are wise, stripping her so bare of the paraphernalia which has become part of her."

"There is the girl under it. The one who eludes you."

"I don't believe, Mr. Rarick, that wealth is necessarily destructive to the individ——"

"Nor do I. On the contrary, I am convinced, for instance, that it is the business men of different civilizations, the gatherers of material wealth, who have built the foundations for art. Civilization has advanced on their gold bonds. Many of the patron saints of the creative life of Greece were the business men."

"Think of the gigantic power for good you are about to release out of the nickels and dimes of the people."

"I have thought—and thought—and out of it has come my philosophy of why I must die a poor man and why this wealth that I have drawn out of the coin purses of American people must be released back now."

"Tremendous idea. . . ."

"My power to forecast the nature and needs of the future is limited. Vast accumulations like mine must cope with the contemporary problems of the people who helped to create the wealth. What is the use of leaving five million dollars to build tubercular hospitals when two years after my death, it is not impossible that a cure or a preventive may be found for the white plague. Let future generations wrestle freshly with their fresh issues. I want to leave no moneys that a few years after my death must be expended upon dead issues because of a will made during the period when those issues were alive. My death, Gratton, is a much more important matter to the world than my life."

"In a special sense, yes."

"So you see, my surplus fortune is not mine to leave Jennifer, even if I would. And I would not. It is difficult for me to talk to you any further than I have, young man, about my feeling of what the effect of stupendous personal wealth has been on the little group of my family. But just the same, Gratton, therein lies the tragedy of my life. A tragedy I do not intend to see perpetuated through the sole surviving member after me, my daughter, who will live to thank the dead hand that at first may seem so cruelly disciplinarian to her. . . ."

"I simply cannot imagine Jennifer on eight thousand a year."

"I can. Hand me that paper on my desk."

"Here?"

"This single typewritten sheet is the boiled-down version of the five hundred and forty-eight pages of that manuscript. This simple sheet, Gratton, is my last will and testament, duly sworn and witnessed. My philosophy of life, and of death. My bow to the world, my tribute to it, my hope for its betterment, my bow out of it. My sighs for its defects, my hope for its future. My hope in my child. My faith in her. Listen," he said, and began to read.

When Gratton was moved by a scene he was writing, especially in those earlier years before his "Tragedy of Laughter" had been written, he always complained of the physical discomfort he experienced while at work. His ears rang. A curious little elevator of hunger seemed to ride up and down the pit of his stomach. His tonsils wanted to burst and his ears became bright, polished pink. Jennifer once wrote of him in a monograph: "I could tell how the work on 'Tragedy of Laughter' was coming by the color of his ears."

In addition now, to those roaring symptoms, Gratton, after Rarick had completed his reading, had a horrible fear he was going to cry. Not tears, but some brute noises. The sound of an emotion scraping bottom, as the soul of the man who had just read had scraped bottom.

"There, in a nutshell, is some of the wisdom I have tried to squeeze out of my defeat, Gratton. Not much of a job to a literary man like you—but it's my legacy. . . ."

"Well—guess I'll be getting along now. Don't suppose you know it. I may be wrong. But seems to me, that's the stuff immortal literature is made of—that page you just read me. It's the thing Lincoln poured into his address at Gettysburg. It's as close to God as Senator Vest's plea for a dog. It's Shelley and Goethe crying for justice in prose. Its wisdom will live after you. I may be crazy, but that is the kind of stuff that achieves immortality. That last will and testament of yours is literature. . . ."

"I don't want immortality. At the moment I want milk and Graham crackers. Have them with me."

"There's Jennifer!"

"Where?"

"I heard her step."

"No."

"Yes."

"Ah yes, I do hear now. Strange that you should have known her step at the great distance of the lower hall. Shall I call her?"

"No—no. I must be going."

"Strange that you should have heard her."

"I've a glove of hers. She dropped it one day. I'll ask to see her on my way out—to give it back."

"Will you ring as you go? I want milk and crackers. Share some?"

"No—no. The glove . . ."

"These evenings chill . . . good warm milk . . . crackers . . . Graham ones."

"Good night, sir."

The wind had risen, hardening the triangles of snow against the leaded windows into crust, and blowing the cold, beautiful smell of snow in through the weather-strippings.

Waiting for his milk and crackers, Rarick, alone, poked up the embers and pressed one of the battalion of buttons alongside the organ.

Seated, small, the look of hunchback in his face, the tall, Gothic twilight climbing into vaulted shadows, the yarn of Pagliacci began to stalk across stained glass, the organ ballooning into the dusk.

Waiting, as he loved to, for the bursting sob that concluded the "Laugh, Clown, Laugh," the chin of Rarick fell forward a little tiredly.

Clouds of music came up like thunder. . . .

THE END